HOME TO STAY
Asian American Women's Fiction

HOME TO STAY

Asian American Women's Fiction

Edited by
Sylvia Watanabe
and
Carol Bruchac

THE GREENFIELD REVIEW PRESS
2 Middle Grove Road
Greenfield Center, NY 12833

Publication of this anthology has been made possible, in part, through Literary Publishing Grants from the Literature Program of the New York State Council on the Arts and the National Endowment for the Arts, a federal agency.

ISBN 0-912678-76-3

Library of Congress # 89-84368

FIRST EDITION

Typesetting by Sans Serif, 2378 East Stadium Blvd., Ann Arbor, Mi 48104.
Printed in the United States of America by McNaughton & Gunn, Ann Arbor, Mi.

COVER ART by Carli Oliver

ACKNOWLEDGEMENTS

In all cases, unless otherwise noted, permission to reprint previously published work has been granted by the individual authors. We are grateful to the magazines and publishers listed below for their commitment to the writing of Asian American women.

Meena Alexander: "Grandmother's Letters" from HOUSE OF A THOUSAND DOORS, Three Continents Press, Inc.

Rosanna Yamagiwa Alfaro: "Professor Nakashima and Tomiko The Cat" from Footworks.

Cecilia Manguerra Brainard: "Waiting For Papa's Return" and "The Blue Green Chiffon Dress" from WOMAN WITH HORNS AND OTHER STORIES, New Day Publishers.

Diana Davenport: "House of Skin" from Yellow Silk magazine.

Jessica Hagedorn: "The Blossoming Of Bongbong" from DANGEROUS MUSIC, Momo's Press.

Marie Hara: "1895: The Honeymoon Hotel" from Bamboo Ridge.

Mavis Hara: "Like An Offering Of Rice" from Bamboo Ridge.

Gish Jen: "The White Umbrella" from The Yale Review.

Maxine Hong Kingston: excerpt from pages 83-88 of CHINA MEN, Random House, Inc., Alfred A. Knopf, Inc.

Shirley Geok-lin Lim: "A Pot Of Rice" from ANOTHER COUNTRY, Times Book International.

Marnie Mueller: "Changes" published in a different form in Voice Literary Supplement of The Village Voice.

Bharati Mukherjee: "The Management Of Grief" from THE MIDDLEMAN AND OTHER STORIES, Grove Press, Inc.

Fae Myenne Ng: "A Red Sweater" from The American Voice and THE PUSHCART PRIZE XII: BEST OF THE SMALL PRESS.

We would like to thank the following people for their help: Stan Yogi, Bill Osborn, Gail Harada, Jill Widner, Russell Leong, Sau-ling Wong, King-kok Cheung, Sara McAulay, Joseph Bruchac, and the members of the Bamboo Ridge Writers Group.

CONTENTS

Introductions   Sylvia Watanabe   xi
     Carol Bruchac   xiii

Maxine Hong Kingston   excerpt from *China Men*   2

Marie Hara   *1895: The Honeymoon Hotel*   8

Meena Alexander   *Grandmother's Letters*   20

Marnie Mueller   *Changes*   36

Elizabeth Gordon   *On The Other Side of the War*   48

Gish Jen   *The White Umbrella*   52

Cecilia Manguerra Brainard   *The Blue Green Chiffon Dress*   62

Tahira Naqvi   *Brave We Are*   72

Tina Koyama   *Family Dinner*   80

Sarah Lau   *Long Way Home*   86

Wen-Wen Wang   *Bacon and Coffee*   96

Fae Myenne Ng   *A Red Sweater*   106

Susan Nunes   *A Moving Day*   118

Amy Tan   *Double Face*   126

Deborah Fass   *The Japanese Mountains*   140

Chitra Divakaruni   *Doors*   146

Sussy Chako   *The Fourth Copy*   154

Wakako Yamauchi   *And the Soul Shall Dance*   166

Jessica Hagedorn   *The Blossoming of Bong Bong*   176

Rosanna Yamagiwa Alfaro   *Professor Nakashima and
     Tomiko the Cat*   194

Arun Mukherjee   *Visiting Places*   204

Hisaye Yamamoto   *Wilshire Bus*   216

Linda Ty-Casper   *Hills, Sky, Longing*   222

Diana Davenport   *House of Skin*   232

Mavis Hara   *An Offering of Rice*   242

Wakako Yamauchi   *Maybe*   252

Hisaye Yamamoto   *The High-heeled Shoes, a Memoir*   262
Cecilia Manguerra Brainard   *Waiting for Papa's Return*   272
Sharon Hashimoto   *The Mushroom Man*   280
Shirley Geok-lin Lim   *A Pot of Rice*   286
Bharati Mukherjee   *The Management of Grief*   292
Sylvia Watanabe   *Talking to the Dead*   310

INTRODUCTIONS

Carol must have known there was something in the air when she first got the idea for this book. There has been such a burgeoning of literary activity by Asian American women writers since she first approached me to work with her on this project two years ago. Maxine Hong Kingston and Amy Tan have come out with novels. Bharati Mukherjee has won the National Book Critics Circle Award. Hisaye Yamamoto's stories have at last appeared in collected form. And these are only a few of the more prominent examples.

As Carol and I read through the couple of hundred submissions we received, we were awakened to the extraordinary variety and range of this literary blossoming. Stories came to us from both coasts, the Midwest, the South, and Hawaii. We heard from women of Malaysian, Chinese, Vietnamese, Korean, Filipino, Indian, Japanese, and Pakistani descent, as well as from non-Asian women who have experienced close contact with Asian cultures.

The body of work we have collected here not only illustrates the diversity of what is often grouped together under the rubric of "Asian American" experience, but, even more strongly, it insists on the normalcy of such diversity in a multicultural society. In his essay, "America the Multicultural Society" (*The Graywolf Annual Five: Multicultural Literacy*, ed. by Simonson and Walker, Graywolf, 1988), Ishmael Reed writes, " . . . the United States is unique in the world: The world is here." Within this context, it can reasonably be argued that the stories in this book have arisen smack-dab out of the mainstream of American tradition. Their cross-cultural perspectives address what is increasingly becoming common American experience. In new ways, in their many voices, these stories tell and re-tell the old American story of coming home to stay.

Sylvia Watanabe

In 1984 I began work on the first collection of fiction ever done by The Greenfield Review Press. Co-edited by Linda Hogan, Judith McDaniel, and myself, the two-year project culminated in late 1986 with the publication of *The Stories We Hold Secret, Tales of Women's Spiritual Development*. In the process of collecting those stories, we received many submissions from Asian American women. I was struck by the strength and diversity of those stories and how each woman wrote from her own ethnic perspective, often in a very American setting. The idea for *Home To Stay* was born in those months of reading and compiling *The Stories We Hold Secret*.

My belief was that Asian American women writers had something uniquely their own to share, something that might teach us what it is like to live in a country which always views one as an "outsider," oftentimes as an "exotic" outsider. At the same time, I believed that those writers were women who shared so many issues with their sisters of all colors, that common threads would be found which would weave us together.

I first met my co-editor for *Home To Stay* through her inclusion in *The Stories We Hold Secret*. Her story, "The Prayer Lady," was included in the fourth section of the anthology, a section we called "Shaking The Mess Out of Misery." (That section was, to quote Linda Hogan's introduction, "full of women who are working at full strength and in full being, full motion, full life. They are whole women. They are healers. They are prayer ladies.") From the moment I made the decision to bring this book of Asian American women's fiction into being, I knew that I wanted to work with Sylvia Watanabe. I have never regretted that choice. Sylvia brought to the book so many ideas—including its title. She also brought boundless energy, enthusiasm, and (most importantly) a wonderful sense of humor throughout. That energy and sense of humor was especially needed considering the fact that all of our work together was done long distance, with Sylvia moving from California to Hawaii and finally to Michigan over the ensuing two years.

Submissions for *Home to Stay* came from all over the world. We received a great deal of excellent work by women who did not find their way to the final selection but certainly deserve to have their voices heard in other publications. As we accepted work the book began to take on an organic quality. It was alive and growing. There seemed to be certain themes which ran through our final choices and Sylvia and I have attempted to group those themes in such a way that the book becomes a journey. It takes the reader from stories with an historical perspective (as in the opening excerpt from Maxine Hong Kingston's *China Men*) to the voices of girls and young women, through family and relationship stories, stories of madness, aging and racism, ending with stories of death and celebration.

I am also excited about the cover art by Carli Oliver. Sylvia discovered this artist's work in Hawaii and it seems to fit the book perfectly, bringing the moods and feelings of *Home To Stay* together in a gentle yet vibrant way.

I feel privileged to have been able to play a role in bringing this special book to publication. I only hope it is just the first of more such collections by other publishers of the yet untold stories of Asian American women writers.

Carol Bruchac
Fall 1989

Maxine Hong Kingston

Maxine Hong Kingston is the author of The Woman Warrior, China Men and, most recently, Tripmaster Monkey. In a June 18, 1989 interview with D.C. Denison, published in The Boston Globe Ms. Kingston said: " 'Fresh off the boat' is a common Chinese-American expression, and I think it is very derogatory. It's part of a Mayflower complex, where you think just because you came earlier, you're more American. Many Chinese-Americans don't want to be lumped in with the immigrants because there is too much of a perception that we don't belong here. We don't want to identify with them because then we might be taken for one of them.

"Chinese-Americans, or any minority people, can't just disappear into the mainstream. You can't change your psyche and personality so that it's indistinguishable from most Americans'. The only healthy thing for Americans to do is to just realize that we are multicultural people living in a multicultural country and that you just have to take all these complex, disparate customs and languages and try to become a healthy, integrated society."

From CHINA MEN

A physicist wrote me a letter about his trip to China; he visited his ancestral village, which, it so happens, is also my ancestral village. He had been born there but emigrated to America as a child. After lecturing at Beijing University, he was given a Volkswagen. Dressed like one of the people and speaking both Mandarin and Cantonese, he traveled about freely. When he arrived at the village, he saw houses from his childhood; the ones that had belonged to families that had sent men to the United States had been decorated with expensive tiles. He met a woman whom he recognized from his childhood as an aunt and went home with her. An automobile and some electrical kitchen appliances were rusting in the yard, stuff brought back from the Gold Mountain; there was no gasoline or electricity in the village. A young man was sitting idle by the door; he was some kind of a cousin. "Stay for dinner," the aunt invited the physicist, but the young man said rudely, "He's too busy to have dinner." The physicist ate at the communal dining room; the commune people also showed him around. Though the land in this area was more fertile than in most other parts of China, he found the farmers less eager to meet production quotas. In the middle of the work day, young men sat talking about how someday soon they would move to the Gold Mountain, where their ancestors, American pioneers, had gone for hundreds of years. The physicist felt that indeed there was something different about the people in our village.

I'd like to go to China if I can get a visa and—more difficult—permission from my family, who are afraid that applying for a visa would call attention to us: the relatives in China would get in trouble for having American capitalist connections, and we Americans would be put in relocation camps during the next witch hunt for Communists. Should I be able to convince my family about the good will of normalization, it's not the Great Wall I want to see but my ancestral village. I want to talk to Cantonese, who have always been revolutionaries, nonconformists, people with fabulous imaginations, people who invented the

Gold Mountain. I want to discern what it is that makes people go West and turn into Americans. I want to compare China, a country I made up, with what country is really out there.

I have gone east, that is, west, as far as Hawai'i, where I have stood alongside the highway at the edge of the sugarcane and listened for the voices of the great grandfathers. But the cane is merely green in the sunlight; the tassels waving in the wind make no blurry fuzzy outlines that I can construe as a message from them. The dirt and sun are red and not aglitter with gold motes like in California. Red and green do not readily blend, nothing lurking in the overlaps to bend the eyes. The winds blowing in the long leaves do not whisper words I hear. Yet the rows and fields, organized like conveyor belts, hide murdered and raped bodies; this is a dumping ground. Old Filipino men die in abandoned sheds. Mushrooms and marijuana grow amidst the cane, irrigated by the arches of vaulting water. People with friends on the mainland steal long-distance calls on the field telephones.

Driving along O'ahu's windward side, where sugarcane grew in my great grandfathers' day, I like looking out at the ocean and seeing the pointed island offshore, not much bigger than a couple of houses, nothing else out in that ocean to catch the eye—Mokoli'i Island, but nobody calls it that. I had a shock when I heard it's also named Chinaman's Hat. I had only encountered that slurred-together word in taunts when walking past racists. (They would be the ones loafing on a fence, and they said the chinaman was sitting on a fence ". . . trying to make a dollar out of fifty cents.") But Hawai'i people call us Paké, which is their way of pronouncing Bak-ah, Uncle. They even call Chinese women Paké.

When driving south, clockwise, there is an interesting optical illusion. At a certain point in the road, the sky is covered with Chinaman's Hat, which bulges huge, near. The closer you drive toward what seems like a mountain, the farther it shrinks away until there it is, quite far off, an island, a brim and crown on the water.

At first, I did not say Chinaman's Hat; I didn't call the island

4

anything. "You see the island that looks like a Chinaman's hat?" locals ask, and visitors know right away which one they mean.

I swam out to Chinaman's Hat. We walked partway in low tide, then put on face masks. Once you open your eyes in the water, you become a flying creature. Schools of fish—zebra fish, rainbow fish, red fish—curve with the currents, swim alongside and away; balloon fish puff out their porcupine quills. How unlike a dead fish a live fish is. We swam through spangles of silver-white fish, their scales like sequins. Sometimes we entered cold spots, deserts, darkness under clouds, where the sand churned like gray fog, and sometimes we entered golden chambers. There are summer forests and winter forests down there. Sea cucumbers, holothurians, rocked side to side. A sea turtle glided by and that big shell is no encumbrance in the water. We saw no sharks, though they spawn in that area, and pilot fish swam ahead in front of our faces. The shores behind and ahead kept me unafraid.

Approaching Chinaman's Hat, we flew around and between a group of tall black stones like Stonehenge underwater, and through there, came up onto the land, where we rested with arms out holding on to the island. We walked among the palm trees and bushes that we had seen from the other shore. Large white birds were nesting on the ground under these bushes. We hurried to the unseen side of the island. Even such a tiny island has its windward and leeward. On the ocean side, we found a cave, a miniature pirate's cove with a finger of ocean for its river, a beach of fine yellow sand, a blowhole, brown and lavender cowry shells, not broken, black live crabs side-stepping and red dead crabs dying in the red sun, a lava rock shelf with tide pools as warm as baths and each one with its ecology. A brown fish with a face like a cartoon cow's mugged at me. A white globule quivered, swelled, flipped over or inside out, stretched and turned like a human being getting out of bed, opened and opened; two arms and two legs flexed, and feathery wings, webbing the arms and the legs to the body, unfolded and flared; its thighs tapered to a graceful tail, and its ankles had tiny wings on them—like Mercury; its back was muscled like a comic book superhero's—blue and silver metallic leotards outlined with black racing stripes. It's a spaceman, I thought. A tiny spaceman in a spacesuit. Scooping these critters into another tide pool, I got into theirs, and lying in it, saw nothing but sky and black rock, the ocean occasionally flicking cold spit.

At sunset we built a campfire and sat around it inside a cleft in the hillside. We cooked and ate a fish we caught. We were climbing along a ledge down to the shore, holding on to the face of the island in the twilight, when a howling like wolves, like singing, came rising out of the island. "Birds," somebody said. "The wind," said someone else. But the air was still, and the high, clear sound wound through the trees. It continued until we departed. It was, I know it, the island, the voice of the island singing, the sirens Odysseus heard.

The Navy continues to bomb Kaho'olawe and the Army blasts the green skin off the red mountains of O'ahu. But the land sings. We heard something.

It's a tribute to the pioneers to have a living island named after their work hat.

I have heard the land sing. I have seen the bright blue streaks of spirits whisking through the air. I again search for my American ancestors by listening in the cane.

Ocean people are different from land people. The ocean never stops saying and asking into ears, which don't sleep like eyes. Those who live by the sea examine the driftwood and glass balls that float from foreign ships. They let scores of invisible imps loose out of found bottles. In a scoop of salt water, they revive the dead blobs that have been beached in storms and tides: fins, whiskers, and gills unfold; mouths, eyes, and colors bloom and spread. Sometimes ocean people are given to understand the newness and oldness of the world; then all morning they try to keep that boundless joy like a little sun inside their chests. The ocean also makes its people know immensity.

They wonder what continents contain the ocean on its other side, what people live there. Hong Kong off the coast tugged like a moon at the Cantonese; curiosity had a land mass to fasten upon, and beyond Hong Kong, Taiwan, step by step a leading out. Cantonese travel and gamble.

But China has a long round coastline, and the northern people enclosed Peiping, only one hundred miles from the sea, with walls and made roads westward across the loess. The Gulf of Chihli has arms, and beyond, Korea, and beyond that, Japan. So the ocean and hunger and some other urge made Cantonese people explorers and Americans.

Marie M. Hara

One of the organizers of Talk Story, Inc. (1978), Hawaii's first ethnic writers' conference, Marie Hara has been a teacher, journalist, and freelance writer. She works for the Honolulu Academy of Arts as a grants coordinator and is involved in Bamboo Ridge and Hawaii Literary Arts Council activities. As a person whose parentage is Asian and Caucasian and who rejects all the labels and stereotypes which connect to words such as Eurasian, hapa, half breed, Amerasian, and mixed blood, Marie Hara is looking at literature and history for new directions.

1895 THE HONEYMOON HOTEL

Surely it was disappointment. A simple matter of being disappointed, certainly. That was the problem. It was clear and not unexpected by any means. Rearranging her kimono properly around her legs, she sat on a western-style chair near a window which looked out across the street to a bustling park. Vendors sold food and newspapers. People in all manner of dress crossed the grass and the dirt road. She noticed Hawaiian women in long, loose dresses. In the distance spread the bare brown and green hills which she had seen from the deck of the ship; from here the mountaintops appeared to be misty in the mid-morning sunlight. Today as they traveled along the harbor in the open wagon, she had taken in the busy-ness of this town called Honolulu. Wagons, it seemed, hauled goods everywhere in an entertaining fashion. She had wanted to say, "It's not much like country living, is it?" Still she couldn't allow herself to comment so forwardly to Yamamotosan. She kept her observations private. She missed being able to talk to Chika.

Except for Chika-san, the other women, her fellow travelers, had all been called for. Chika alone had been left to wait for her new husband. Was her fate to be preferred? Maybe Chika would have to return to Japan if she had been forgotten.

The Immigration Station was a formidable building with intricate wooden decorations all over its multi-leveled roofs and windows. It could be mistaken for a temple, except that it was hardly Japanese in feeling. After the long ship voyage every detail of life on shore took her eager interest. Life here was such a novelty, just as people promised it would be. To think of it, within a season's time she had seen both the city of Hiroshima and now, Honolulu. Remarkable. And here there were no seasons. Curious. She had thought about the persistent heat while they passed long hours in quarantine.

They had to wait endlessly. Sectioned off separately for more medical questions, then lined up all together, and finally seated in a row on a polished bench, each of the women clung to the arm of a shipboard friend. Chika and she sat tensely that way for two hours of fretful anticipation.

Her name was called. When Yamamoto-san stepped out of the group of men to claim her as his wife, Sono saw his face from the vantage of her lowered head through half-closed eyes. She had to compose herself. He looked too old! The photograph she kept in her kimono depicted a smooth-shaven young man. The Yamamoto person who stood at the desk appeared to be at least forty years old and bearded heavily. Sono felt her lower lip quiver and Chika's reassuring clutch growing tighter on her now tingling arm.

So that was how he had managed to trick the family. Certainly people had forewarned them in Hiroshima that the Hawaii men were desperate in their desire to establish families. But Yamamoto-san was known to her uncle. Shouldn't he have prevented such an awkward match, knowing the man's true age? Sono was so obliged to Uncle, indeed, everyone was, for his support through the difficult years. But not to have guided her, when he must have known the true circumstances, his elderly friend's trickery. Yamamoto-san looked even older than her uncle when he moved about so cautiously, talking to the foreigners.

Her mind raced through scattered images, connecting her confusion with memories of her seated family, noisily discussing Sono's marriage, and her life faraway in Hawaii. Unconcerned by the bustle of activity around the bench, she brooded in turmoil. It was Chika who timed the little push forward when the stranger turned to face her.

Sono managed, somehow, to bow and maintain a calm demeanor, while she mentally totalled his positive attributes. He did seem to be clean, prosperous and kindly. He was polite. He smiled. Truly as hard as leaving with him was saying goodbye to Chika when all the papers had been signed, all the questions answered, and all the officials signaled them outward.

For some reason the man called Miura, Seinosuke, who was Chika's husband, was not present. There must have been a delay in his traveling from another island. Without her having to ask, Yamamoto-san promised to check on Chika's situation tomorrow. She looked very unhappy, but she smiled graciously as she bid them farewell, the humiliated Chika, a lonely kimono-clad figure left waiting on the long bench. The other girls hurried off or looked away, not wanting to injure her further with their obvious pity.

When Sono walked out of the building, following Yamamoto-san to the wagon, she had no idea where they would be going. The horse-drawn vehicle, more an open air cart, carried a number of the couples past the waterfront to a three-story brick and wood building. She could not read the English name on the sign in front of the hotel. She had stayed in an inn only once before and this could not be the same. Once in, she noticed with relief that the clerks and maids were Japanese. A tiny lobby with large chairs and sofas quickly filled up with a dozen couples and the women's large willow trunks and cloth bundles. She saw that the other girls, like herself, seemed self-conscious and subdued. Only Kono-san and her sister, Kumi-san, continued to whisper and chatter as usual. Very rudely they discussed someone whose face, it seemed, took on the appearance of "a dog when it laughs out loud." In the silence around them, smiles materialized on the faces of silent listeners. Sono did not appreciate the joke; for all she knew, they were discussing one of their own husbands.

When the manager of the hotel appeared in the main doorway, however, it became obvious that he was the one. Beaming at the company, his lip curled upward in a cock-eyed manner. No one looked more like a smiling dog, Sono considered, than this slightly balding man. Suppose he had been Yamamoto-san. Sono inhaled deeply. There was a new mood of jocularity in the room; the group grew noisy.

Slowly they were being taken upstairs to their rooms. While Yamamoto-san talked with the manager at the desk, Sono gently adjusted the obi around her waist and pressed her perspiring face with a handkerchief which she had tucked away in her sleeve. A slowly growing numbness seemed to spread into her shoulders, causing her to sit up straighter and compose her features into a stern expressionlessness.

Looking surreptitiously at the other couples, she noted with fleeting envy that Tome-san was matched with a vigorous farmer. Sleepy-eyed Tome was no beauty, even as Sono assumed she herself was ordinary in looks. On ship the other women found themselves in idle agreement that Chika was the most attractive, a "born beauty." What an unlucky fate she had found in this place.

In an instant Yamamoto was leading Sono up to the little room over the street. He seemed to prance eagerly up the flights of steps.

"Leave the luggage," he counseled. "They will bring it up later."

But all of her possessions were in the *kori*. What would she have to change into, if delivery were delayed? What if someone was a thief? Frowning, Sono said nothing.

In silence they sat on the zabuton pillows set out on the grass-mat flooring. No table, no tea service, nothing but a tall chair, a lamp and a small window which drew a hazy light into the opposite end of the room, gave the space its details.

Presently her husband spoke, looking directly at her face with an appraising curiosity that embarrassed her. He asked questions about their families in Hiroshima, the crops, and the voyage across the Pacific. She answered each evenly.

"It is to be hoped, Sono-san, that you will be at home here in Hawaii." He cleared his throat and watched her face. Yamamoto-san seemed uneasy and did not continue. He must have practiced, it was such a formal tone.

She was not able to respond and kept her head lowered. She noticed his hands were sunburnt and calloused. Did this mean he was not truly a wealthy farmer? Or was it evidence of a hard-working man?

Directing his comments to her bowed head, he stared at her thick black hair, knotted expertly at the nape of her slender neck.

"Excuse me. While we are in Honolulu, I must go for a few hours' business and will return punctually within the afternoon. Please relax here. Is there anything you would like me to purchase in the shops?"

Sono shook her head. His voice filled her ears. She would have enjoyed walking around with him, but she felt empty and wearied by his strained attempt to communicate with her.

When she was sure that he was gone, she moved to the window to look out at the activity on the ground. She could see a stream leading down from the hills to the ocean. Glittering water. How

12

she would have enjoyed following it up and up into the misty forest. No houses were built on the mountain slopes. One could get lost in the woodsy areas. They looked quite near. And yet, of course, there was no way of knowing for sure.

Standing, she pushed the edge of the thick drapery away. From the side of the open window frame she caught a glimpse of the town. The road crossed a small bridge over flat green river water and led the way past many small shops and saloons. In the distance she saw the roof tops of stone buildings. They had passed behind that area on their way along the docks. Sono backtracked through the memory of the past few hours and the time of quarantine until she reached the weeks aboard the ship. She saw herself standing at the deck of the S.S. Intrepid, looking at the distant shore of Oahu with the tight eagerness only someone seasick too long could muster.

At her side Chika calmly observed, "So we are here after all."

Sono replied, "If only our parents could know that we have arrived safely. All their prayers. They would be gratified."

"Then for our families' sake, we must write letters to send back with the ship." Chika, so practical, comforted Sono, because she understood above all the loneliness as well as the obligation of leaving the family circle. She had been the first friend Sono had made outside of village people. In long conversations they had promised to be lifelong companions since they would be sure to see each other daily on such a small island.

So many plans had to be reconsidered. The island. The husbands. Their friendship. Everything changed as soon as they docked. What would become of Chika-san now? She wondered when she would see her friend again. For that matter, what would her own life be like with this unexpected Yamamoto?

Resigning herself to the situation, Sono tasted her disappointment without self-pity. She had learned from her earliest years that she was not going to be the child favored. That distinction went to her eldest brother. Luck was not to be Sono's domain, and untested expectations were always a mistake. She knew happiness to be a condition where simple needs were met. If there was enough food to eat, enough clothing to wear, enough fuel for warmth and enough family to gather around in enjoyment of a pleasant evening, that was enough for her lot in life. She could be content with those ingredients. She was a poor farmer's daughter who had been schooled in sacrifice. She could hear the voices of the women in her clan reminding her to be thankful that her widowed mother had one less mouth to feed.

Now here was Yamamoto-san who was happy to take care of her needs. She felt ashamed to have found him lacking. Sono knew a little about him. Everyone heard that he had been apprenticed as a carpenter. They said he was a capable man, but he loved to drink and had lost much of his parents' respect through his loose ways. City life in Hiroshima had hardened him. As soon as a friend decided to leave for California, Yamamoto took the chance of joining him to earn enough to send his family his savings. A model son, the villagers declared. He had settled in Hawaii and money regularly arrived in the village. Sono had been impressed by the tale. But in Hiroshima she was impressed by the first three-story building she had ever seen. She had been so impressed by the sight of the steamer that she trembled as she crossed the gangplank. No wonder her mother prayed continually for her well-being. "Is she praying now?" Sono wondered. The marriage had been officially recorded. There was no turning back. "Mother, pray for me now."

Two streaks of tears formed silver pathways on the face of the young girl in the third floor window of the honeymoon hotel. She made no sound in crying and after a while turned away, her attention taken by the arrival of the willow basket the maids had carried up to the room.

The two aproned women, not much older than Sono, transferred a look which referred to the crying girl. They were sorry for her, but what could they say or do? Many of them suffered, the maids saw it all the time.

As they left, politely bowing, they called out, "Thank you, Honorable Mrs. Housewife," as might ordinarily be said, but this time they chorused their words in a childish teasing meant to bring laughter up to every listener's lips. They repeated the absurd inflection and emphasized the dignity of the word honorable with comic expressions. When they succeeded in making Sono giggle to hear their strange manner of speech, the maids thumped each

14

other on the shoulder and disappeared down the corridor with boisterous laughter. Sono's surprise settled into restored spirits and she began to examine the clothes and goods in her basket as if she hadn't done so dozens of times already. Each item represented the spirit of someone dear to her, and their gifts anchored her with their presence.

When Yamamoto-san returned, he knocked cautiously before he tried the door. Sono opened it carefully. To her surprise her husband handed her a large bouquet of lilies, gingers and daisies, as well as a package fashioned out of his handkerchief, tied up *furoshiki* style.

She rushed both to the window, propping the newspaper-wrapped flowers against the chairback and opening the white muslin to find two pinkish guavas, a tiny mottled banana and two small Kona oranges. Sono exclaimed, and Yamamoto beamed as if to say, this is just the beginning, there will be more for you.

For the first time she spoke to him openly.

"Well, how nice of you to consider my feelings." She gazed shyly at his eyes. He coughed. Confident now that she was appreciative of his efforts and would be a responsive wife, he mumbled, "It's the least I could do to welcome you to Hawaii." When her pale skin was flushed, Sono seemed to convey a sweet delicacy beyond the proper wifely qualities he imagined before.

Yamamoto would have enjoyed embracing her then and there as was his husbandly right. Instead, hearing a great clattering noise from the road below, he asked Sono if she had ever ridden in a mule-tram.

In confusion Sono shook her head. "A mule-tram?"

He pointed out a curious open-sided conveyance passing directly below them. It was dragged by a team of rattling collared mules. Both laughed at the same time when they caught sight of a barefooted ragamuffin sneaking a ride on the rear of the crowded tram. A small dog marked with a dark ring around one eye tried jumping up several times to join the boy on the edge of the bouncing bumper. Finally he was caught in mid-leap by his master who smiled triumphantly, showing all of his teeth to the delighted onlookers.

"Things are different here, you see."

"Yes, people can be very merry." Her head dropped again as she studied the floor.

Realizing that she had not been entirely happy waiting for him, Yamamoto decided to take Sono out for a ride to a beach area called Waikiki, past the town of Honolulu.

"Let me show you what is here. You will be amused. The ride is fast and bumpy."

The couple boarded the tram at the turn-around point adjacent to the park across the street from their hotel. Yamamoto pointed out the beauty spots and major buildings along the way. They sat stiffly in their best clothes, holding on to the seats and surveying all the assorted activities of the heart of the capitol of the islands. Fifty-seven years later she would remind him about the miles of duck ponds and rice fields they passed before the end of the dusty road.

Through a small ironwood thicket which reminded her of certain Japanese seaside pines, they walked right next to the ever present ocean which surged and crackled at their bare feet. They carried their footwear and ate their fruit standing on the blazing beach. She became fascinated by the recurrent waves which washed fiercely against a half moon of rocky sand and stretched up to a grove of struggling coconut trees. She said, "This is not at all what I expected; it's so different."

He nodded curtly in acknowledgment without understanding her emotion. He said, "This very ocean touches our home shores. Someday we are sure to return. The gods willing, we won't be disappointed."

She turned her head and wiped away secret tears, because he was so totally convincing. He had been raised, after all, to be a chosen son. With her back to him she accepted his unwavering self confidence and never questioned his lack of worldly success in the more than half century allotted to their marriage.

From a distance the kimono-clad girl and the black-suited man seemed to be locked into a flirtatious battle of wills, a typical seaside lovers' tiff on a lazy afternoon, which resulted in his taking her hand to lead her back to the tram terminal. In truth they had merely decided to return home to their room.

All the way back, the words "we won't be disappointed"

bounced through Sono's thoughts as the tram jostled them up and down from stop to stop.

Surely it was the best thing to do. Chika had accepted her fate. She could do no more. Since there was no way to be sure of anything at all at any time, Sono reminded herself, why not rest with this choice? In the matter of how to feel about things, she would remain in charge. Then it was settled; there was no problem.

The tram passed a field where a Chinese farmer guided an ox through a swampy rice paddy.

To Yamamoto-san she said, "It certainly isn't anything like the farming life we knew, is it?"

Surprised by her comment, he looked at Sono with attention to her observations. He began to tell her all the things he found unlikely or thought-provoking in the ten years since he had left home. Still in conversation when the tram pulled into the terminal, they didn't notice they had arrived home.

At dinner that evening by the doorway to the hotel's Japanese dining room, a bespectacled, portly Miura-san and his new bride Chika greeted Mr. and Mrs. Yamamoto with grateful formality. Startled, Sono grasped Chika's hand in joy.

"Chika-san!" Sono's voice tightened in escalating pleasure over the turn of events. Her friend stood surrounded by a surprising calm. As Sono studied Chika's delicate face, she thought she could see a deep relief that Miura had come to get her after all. At the table Sono decided not to say anything which might lead to further questions. They would have enough time later to discuss this day in detail, she felt certain of it.

Self-consciously dignified, Sono began to serve Yamamoto. Naturally Chika followed, and soon both women poured tea and served rice for the first time to their husbands. Acknowledging a good start and mirroring each other's pleasure, the Yamamotos and the Miuras ate their food with hearty appetites. They maintained a good-natured and respectful silence which graced their table as they ate the meal.

With sincerity the couples toasted each other, wishing themselves good luck. Others in the room looked in their direction and recognized them as fortunate.

Tomorrow they would leave for the port of Hilo and two outlying towns where they would begin the cane-growing work as family units. Tonight they would enjoy the honeymoon hotel.

A man and woman appeared at one of the third floor windows. For a moment they looked at the moonlight on the surface of the glittering river.

Meena Alexander

Meena Alexander was born in India in 1951 and received her Ph.D. in English from Nottingham University in 1973. After returning to India for a number of years and publishing four volumes of poetry, the latest of which was Stone Roots (New Delhi: Arnold-Heinemann, 1980), she came to live in the United States.

"This piece was written one summer in Minneapolis. My father who was working for the UN had fallen very sick in Africa. I went back in my thoughts to my grandfather's death, something I had witnessed as a child.

"There is something of Indian history here. My mother's mother was a political activist, a Gandhian. I never knew her; she died before I was born. One summer I found some letters she had written to grandfather. They were in the attic, tied up with a bit of pink ribbon. I read them carefully, I was haunted by her clear beautiful hand. They lived in stirring times, quite bound up with the struggle for independence in India. When I returned a year later, the letters had vanished. The letters here are fictive, made up again.

"My family belongs to the Syrian Orthodox community in Kerala, on the southwest coast of India. Hence the references to the church. Kerala has a strong tradition of women's activism and grandmother was part of that.

"I had only been in America a short time when I wrote this. I lived with my husband and newborn son. I felt I did not have any place, really, in this new world. In any case it was a struggle; the sense of dislocation was very strong in me. Writing, looking back in that sense made a reparation."

GRANDMOTHER'S LETTERS

(This is a fictive piece struck off, as it were, from the actual.)

My grandmother was imprisoned in the mountains. I think she understood the loneliness of a woman's body as she sat there, looking out at the elichi tree, brown now in the bitter season. She was just twenty-seven when the British imprisoned her. She sat on the floor by the window and a wild light fell upon her.

She touched her thin belly, dark, utterly unscarred. She wondered if she would ever be let out of prison. If she would ever bear children. She saw the grey rocks of the Deccani mountains. She smelt the bitter grasses burnt by the goatherds on the slopes outside her barred window.

She stoops in the light. She picks up her pen and her paper. Her hair is tied back with a red ribbon. It is the very same ribbon that grandfather used to tie up the letters she wrote him when he was imprisoned. Many years after his death I discovered the letters in an old biscuit box, in the attic of the Tiruvana house.

The black syllables flash in my mind's eye. I hold them for an instant. Her pen is dry. She shakes it. The ink spurts. I repeat her letters as I write. I sound them out. I will not slip into the black flood of time. I will save myself.

How carefully grandmother uses her pen. And paper is scarce. She writes:

"Let the rice grow"

"Let the children play in the sunlight"

"There is mud on your cheek, beloved"

The last is addressed to grandfather, who is underground. She does not know if he will ever receive her letters. Barely knowing what she writes, she adds:

"The koil sings in its own light. Those who listen will never forget."

Did she really hear the dun coloured bird cry? Or is she like myself, inventing a great deal? How I wish I had known grandmother. She was dead fourteen years by the time I was born. By the time I was born in 1951, India was already independent, a republic already for three and a half years.

I see grandmother stand on a small wooden crate at the Pakeezah steps. It is early in the morning, the day before Gandhi's Salt March. Her sari tucked into her waist, she addresses the fisherfolk. The crate wobbles a little as she speaks but she does not falter.

"Collect salt water in your palms" I hear her say

"Let the great heat of the sun make salt for you"

"Let the Britishers see how against nature it is to prevent us."

The crowd claps. She steps off the crate holding her pallu in her hand. She is nervous. She tugs at the red and white threads with her thumb and forefinger. Her hair blows in the sunlight.

A tall, thin figure in white rushes out of the crowd. He embraces her, then overcome by shyness stands utterly still at her side, head bent. I cannot see his face.

It's grandfather! What is she saying to him? I wish I could hear. A child runs up with a garland. Grandmother stoops and the golden ring falls over her neck. Her mouth is in the shadow. Grandfather still stands there. Behind them, in the distance, I can see the dark waters of the Arabian sea.

Grandfather stands there and stares at her. It's the very first time he has set eyes on her. For years he has heard of her, her marches, her speeches, her non-violent demonstrations. He has even published some of her little texts in the journal he runs. Now he stands by her side, in the blazing light, drinking in her presence. Side by side they stand, each looking forward, too nervous, too shy to look into the other's eyes.

Someone tugs at grandfather's arm. He has a meeting to attend in the next town. Grandmother stands there, for an instant, in utter solitude, bereft of this stranger she already loves. A pigeon casts its shadow on her head. She touches her own cheek, her eyes shut, as if feeling her flesh for the first time. Then the crowd engulfs her.

Three months after this first meeting with grandfather, grandmother was in prison, charged by the British with disturbing the peace. When they let her out after two and a half years in the mountain cell, she was twenty-nine years old, thinner than ever, thankful at last for the ordinary light. There were blue rings under her eyes, dark smudges under her pupils. Though no one knew it, it was the start of her blindness.

The day of her release, she returned to the Pakeezah steps. Overcome by emotion, she wept a little as she stood there. Her hands trembled in the air. Her crimson pallu flashed in the slight wind. There was salt in her eyes. Grandfather stood right in front of her, next to the leaders of the movement, listening intently. A few weeks later they were married. It took him three years to nurse her back to health. In prison she had refused most of the food set before her and had lived off wild rice and water.

2.

Seven years ago I discovered some of grandmother's letters crammed into a biscuit tin in my mother's house. My mother was her only child. This grandmother Kanda, unlike my grandmother, Mariamma, had died long before my birth. I put the letters together dreaming a little. Most of the letters were written after her release from prison.

I remember the first letter I read. It was addressed directly to grandfather. She was at home now and it was he who was imprisoned.

Kuruchiethu
Tiruvana
January 16, 1929

. . . You have a small window Kuruvilla that looks out on the hills. Unlock the bars with your gaze, deceive the distances till they come swarming off the purple hills hung now with jacaranda bloom. Let the distances uphold you. A stream, a bright blade of grass. Even if the stream is dried and puffs dust rather than water, even if the blade is rusty with death. I am sure from your descriptions that the room they keep you in is close, very close to where I was. Perhaps the bars are identical. Perhaps we look out and see the very same bird, dust coloured, a speckle of blood on its beak, turning in the sunlight at the rim of the hill.

As time passed things became harder for her. She kept going to political meetings. Her friend Balamaniamma the writer was her mainstay in those years.

Kuruchiethu
Tiruvana
April 21, 1930

K. I am not even sure anymore what I say. There is some desolation in me, I cannot touch, with my own fingers. I need you.

At the meeting Dinesh said: "Gandhi wants him to come to Wardah, as soon as he's out."

Your press is running. Each night the pamphlets, still wet with ink, pass from hand to hand. A long line of text, piercing the alien world. The police haven't found out the source, though they've been nosing around.

Balamani and I worked on the last one together. "Liberated India and Free women," we called it. She had a dream: as day breaks, all the women in the new world clasp hands, rise from sullen earth like sun-birds. "Our flesh is light," she told me that night as she worked, inky, covered in sweat. "You are the morning star," she wrote. "All stars since the birth of this universe! Your chains lie useless. They drop through the waters."

There is something more to the dream: in the distance, through the waters, speed English ships, mere tin vessels, their flags limp, speeding to the damp cold little island.

I teased Balamani later: "So many stars! You'll empty out the night sky!" But she takes her dreams quite seriously and sat gazing out of the window, at the stubble, the barbed wire Bhaskar had strung to keep the milk cows away from the strawberry patch. I could not tell what she was looking at. You know that far away gaze of hers . . . one barely knows if she's listening.

I do love her very much, but she has been a little strange of late. She seems obsessed by the Kutubshahi emperor, the last one. "I'm convinced" she said to me the other night "that his madness (crawling up the stairs and all that) was a response to British

24

invasion. Remember his quest took a form. A vanished bird. A dot of blood on its beak."

I left it at that. In any case she did not really want a reply. It was dark and the mango trees made huge black umbrellas that kept the moon out. I thought the foundations of our house shook a little. The water rats were playing in the strawberry patch. I could tell by the silver glint in their tails. So we just sat there, in silence . . .

3.

Grandmother kept going, by herself, though, to all the family gatherings. One of her letters tells of an elaborate christening her cousin had arranged for her three-month old daughter. It is hardly surprising that grandmother found the displays of wealth unsuitable. She wrote grandfather about it in some detail.

Kuruchiethu
Tiruvana
September 29, 1930

Accamma's daughter's naming ceremony was done with such splendour, you might have thought us in Babylon or some such pagan city. Silver, a huge city, mound on mound, from candlesticks to pepper pots. Porcelain, glittering in the sunlight. Lace table cloths! And on the floor, for guests to eat off, piles of banana leaves. A whole forest wasted to name a child!

They are terribly rich and hold onto their estates with an iron hand. I hear the father of the child wields a gun. They carry out floggings on the land. Five elephants in the procession from the church, all from the personal herd, the grandmother took great care to point out to me.

The father's brother was in Western dress. Can you imagine, the ignominy of wearing that dress in times like ours! I couldn't bear to look at his polished shoes. He came straight to me.

"There you are, Kanda!" I've no idea how he found me out. "So you don't believe in British rule? hah?" I should have slapped him then and there in front of all the guests. But he moved away smartly, to the other side of the great copper urn they were serving tea from. I think it's all imported from Belgium or some such place. Then, as I was helping myself to some papaya, he leant over the sugar bowl, grinning from ear to ear: "Your husband's in jail, isn't he?!"

I almost dropped my plate. I sat myself in a corner after that and did not move. It was a kind of rage that would not let me breathe. Through the window, I could see the servants' children, mouths covered with flies, shoving and pushing to get at the heap of banana leaves that were tossed out. Kuru, I felt sick at heart. Thank god Mara didn't come with me.

When I got home, the house was all peaceful, the curtains drawn. Mara was asleep under her little white sheet; I sat down at your desk and signed over the rice fields we had decided on. The Bhoodhan movement will make good use of them. There's such a terrible hunger for land now. Sometimes, I feel that this house we live in, and all the ancestral property are like a great millstone, a granite ring about my neck. I know one day I shall perish because of it: the rooms I inhabit will be mist. My womb full of black berries, fit for the birds of paradise.

"You and I will live in a field," I was going to say, then realized that in that world, we will not need our bodies either. Our flesh and blood is a mere contingency, bound to this earth.

I hear Mara cry. Where will she be, I wonder, in that world? And suddenly I am full of fear. Is the sheet over her mouth? Is she on a cliff, hanging by her nails, in a nightmare? A puff of black wind?

I found her wandering through the fig patch one morning drawn by the wet sticky smell of the frangipani. She was there, almost before I could get to her, poking her fist into a snake hole. I slapped her hard. I was so scared. She burst into tears. "The big rats make the hole. Then the cobra goes in. It'll bite Mara!" I picked her up and ran away with her, feeling the wind on my heels. Then slowed down, out of breath, by the jacaranda tree. I set her in the swing and pushed her high in the air. Through her eyes I saw the great blue sky. There were bees in the honeysuckle that twines around the tree trunks and golden dragon flies in the lilies. Even the dry brown leaves were buzzing with life. "More,

more," she cried out and I pushed her higher and higher, till I too seemed to be flying through the brilliant blue air, into paradise.

It's all there, Kuru, I want to say to you. It's all already there. Paradise I mean. And this terrible oppression of mind and body that we struggle against, is a passage, a birth. I must stop now, my love, I shall write again, very soon. Much much love.

Kanda.

P.S. Yacub says that Gandhi is planning a visit to Tiruthankur. I must make sure he has somewhere to stay. Perhaps even here? He asked about you, Yacub says. They are busy now, with the work in Gujarat. K.

4.

Six months later, the day before her birthday, she felt herself slip into her own eyes, fall through her face in loneliness. Or so I thought, reading her lines. But her humour held her up and that fat Chinamma who haunted her, dropping in and out of grandmother's days. I could hear grandmother's voice so clearly, perhaps with the slight distortion my own voice has as I listen to it.

Kuruchiethu
Tiruvana
February 17, 1931

Yesterday I stood in front of the oval mirror and looked at my eyes. They were so huge, so formless. So black. I picked up the stick of kajal Chinna had given me. Frivolity in hard times my love! Rimming around the sad flesh. Making boundaries. But I stood there and did nothing but bite my lips. "No, I won't do up my eyes," I said. "Let them be. When I'm dead, let the photographers do it!" What a stupid thing to say, my darling.

But I'm funny these days. I wash my face only in well water. And hardly use soap. And wear white, for days on end till Chinamma says I look like a widow! Tomorrow, I turn thirty.

Kuruchiethu
Tiruvana
March 19, 1931

Chinamma was wearing those wooden clogs she always wears and made a terrible clatter on the marble floor. I embraced her. She smelt of fresh soap. She is like an older sister to me, Kuru. She scolded me, for my hair hung in shreds and had not been oiled, because my lips were bitten. She insisted I come with her the next evening to address the college women in Kozhencheri. She forced me to accept. Even mother was glad I was getting out of the house. Chinamma stayed, ate some fried bitter gourd. She is curing her blood she says, though only the lord knows what might be up with her blood and what the bitter gourd will do for it. But she has a vaidyan she sees in Kottayam. She follows all his instructions most faithfully.

The college is up on a hill. You've been there, a small white-washed building overhung with jasmine. I was very eager to meet the women again. Many of them were satyagrahis. I still remember fifty of us, lying on that very road, in the dust, our red and white saris tied end to end, the knots bursting through the dust. Our bodies warm and alive, laid in the dust. "The British truck will not pass! Oppression will not last!" we chanted. It seems funny now, in a strange way. Not the passion, but the utter dispossession of self needed to lie in the road. Our passive resistance. I remember how hot my mouth felt. And how pale the white butterfly above me seemed to be, melting into the sunlight. The British were shouting something in the distance. The road trembled with their boots.

After a while Chinamma said she had to get herself a drink of toddy before the meeting and that I should walk up alone. They would be waiting for me. It was a long stretch of road. Soon the houses were all left behind. Even the small red brick schools. There was just the dusty field, purple now, in the darkness. I could hear my own footsteps. It was unnerving. Like hearing one's own heartbeat. On and on I walked. My tongue felt so dry. Then I started to run. I saw thorn bushes that I did not remember seeing before. They had tiny berries, like drops of blood. I felt like pluck-

28

ing one, to cool my tongue as I ran, but it was dark, and I could not tell if there was poison in that fruit or not. When I finally got to the college, I felt as if I had run an eternity. My ankles were scratched and swollen. I could not stop panting.

5.

There was nothing exaggerated about the next letter. Nothing dream-like. It was as precise as grandmother could make it. It was hardly her fault that she was struggling to spell out feelings that lay outside the ordinary territory of her days. A nothingness within . . . perhaps it had something to do with her father's imminent death.

Tiruvana
May 7, 1931

I watch the grass turn yellow in the rock crevices. People move about me Kuruvilla, but I have no body of my own. Nothing to grasp. A hollowness at the heart of me. Like the passion fruit we saw together in the hills the year before we married. The vine clawing the air, perfectly tooled; the skin golden, the freckles so smooth on its green globe one wanted to lick it. But through a hole near the stalk all the stuff had dribbled out: seeds, flesh, juice. And it hung on the vine, by the blue mountains, a bell, utterly hollow, not fruit, not skin of fruit, deceiving all the world.

It's a weariness my darling. But where does it come from? I can hardly tell any more. I am ashamed of speaking like this of myself, and you in your straitened condition, bound in a small dusty room. But you have asked me to speak, and so I do.

Tiruvana
No date

Yacub must have told you. Father is growing steadily worse. He breathes with great difficulty. His lips turn dry and he chokes; cries out as if iron were crushing his ribs. Mara doesn't go near him anymore. She's afraid. Or perhaps even wants him to die. Last night, I could tell he was listening to the bats in the jamun tree. But when mother came with her Bible, he refused to hear. I think he needs to see you. I tell him, as he lies there, his eyes clamped tight, all about your doings. How you are eating a little now; what you read and write, who else is in prison with you, how Gandhi speaks of you.

Sometimes, when the black seeds drop in the air or the jamun splatters its fruit, father seems to breathe more easily. His nails are growing dry and yellow. Mother, with her nose in the Bible, like a huge warthog, hardly moving yet shouting constantly to one servant or another: bring the fried cucumbers, hot compress, prayer book, bell, bowl. And poor father, laid out rigid in that bed, groaning. There's very little the doctors can do for him. It's as if mother must constantly shout out these petty commands to stop her soul up. She cannot conceive of life without father. I fear for her.

It would be like lacking a foot or an arm. Or losing her silken garb and suddenly finding her body in rags. She cannot face herself, nor herself in the world without his presence. So she shouts and fills up the time, or oils poor Mara's hair without stopping. "It'll all fall off, Mother. For pity. For Christ's sake," I cried at her the other day.

The lamps are lit in the dining room. The curtains have blown open. Mother has roused herself and is setting out the silver dishes. I can smell the starched white cloth from where I sit. I think it's because the bishop has promised to come. He wants to see father. I can see mother open her mouth. She is wiping her mouth with her handkerchief. I am so scared she will call out for me. Mara's asleep my darling. Sometimes at night she cries out. Then I put my cheek by hers and she tucks her arm around my neck. It hardly goes all the way around so she squeezes herself against me. She smells of straw and honey as she sleeps, her mouth wet with milk.

I didn't tell you that as I ran, panting up that dusty road to the college, a song came into my mind. Nothing whatsoever to do with my talk, as far as I can tell. I think mother used to sing it, ages ago. Or it might have been aunt Sara; poor mad Sara found drowned in a well.

Glistening silk
the colour of milk
decking the bride!
Who'll bind up the shroud?
Mama, mama, I'll
come for a ride!

The song has a lovely lilt to it. But it's terrifying. You know that mother keeps her wedding sari in the teak chest. That she will be wrapped in it when she's borne out of the house? "There are many rooms in my father's house." Kuru, forgive me. Forgive me darling. She's calling out for me. And I hear the bishop's walking stick on the granite steps.

September 2, 1931

Already, his death is here, living with us. It knows us. And because it's father's death, we welcome it, a kinsman, a twin, known only at the rare moment of passage. I realize now, Kuruvilla, that I have absolutely no religious faith, but I acknowledge my father's death. It troubles the air. It teases the light. The leaves blacken around it. Last night father sipped a little wine and seemed almost happy.

Father is more peaceful now and sleeps at night.

His death has settled into the house. The huge iron pots of boiling water we keep at his bedside to help him breathe, seem immovable yet part of the ordinary world. Kutan stands by him all afternoon, fanning him.

Now and then, father opens his eyes. In some strange way, he seems to be filled with love. As if his dark blood had fled the wound and light from another shore were pouring in. Bathed in that light, everything is unfamiliar. His bed, the books, spitting bowl, even mother's hand.

Yesterday he raised his fingers and touched her wedding ring. That tiny gold millstone at her knuckle. Tried to say something. But mother fled. I heard her weep from afar. Now she has taken to walking through the pepper vines, ivory cane in hand. Mara follows her, tugging at her hems. It's as if mother does not want to re-enter the house. Yesterday she pointed out a swallow to me. It clung to a pepper vine. "It's come from the other side of death, Kanda," she said to me, pointing with the stick. I barely know what she thinks. Yet she's more lucid than before, and all my anger has vanished.

His death leaps with him. They swing from bough to bough. Little boys who would steal gooseberries. Crying out as the air rushes to their skins.

My father dancing with death, Kuru.

Now, nothing but the stench of the old body.

I hid in the bathroom. I heard the hearse clatter down the gravel path. I walked gravely, as befitting a fatherless child. I buried my head in a hole the gardener had dug. I bit the dust beneath the gooseberry roots.

Tonight, I enter another hole. No sounds come out of my mouth. It's all a great wind, whirling, unfixing the elements. Father's clothes, juba, dhoti, even his skin, unwrapped and whirling as if all the air in the hole were sucked out with a giant breath. His skin rolls off. It stops at his toe bones: five delicate flowers, blue-petalled, perfect, out of which a great scent rises.

Leaves fall on my head. In that darkness, his flesh vanishes wholly. I bend to protect my mouth from the wind. I touch a blue flower and find a tiny foot. I tug and tug, feeling my own skin soldered there, breathing so hard I think I will die. My mouth is horribly open, yet I hear nothing but the gasping wind.

Suddenly, the whirlwind ceases. I find I can pull my flesh away. It does not burn as if cut by a red-hot iron. I lie on my back, breathing ever so gently. In my arms, a little child, Mara. Holding her by the waist, I clamber out of the silent hole, lie down on the damp grass, utterly spent.

There are wild bees about us, in her wet tangled hair, in my armpits. Red ants crawl over us. Grasshoppers, their wings drenched with light, all over our eyelids.

She sucks and sucks at my breast. Milk flows out, over the tiny grassblades, the pebbles, and will not stop. Enough for the whole world. Her tiny heart beats hard.

32

The British are planning large scale repressions, flogging, death in the Northern Provinces. They cannot bear our birth struggle.

So I'm fatherless now, my darling, and he, out of whose seed I am come (though all these are mere words now, no substance left to touch) is gone. Neither wind nor water touch him. It is our love that is left, utterly bereft, whirling. A dry wind of anguish. Knowing the last threads are loosed and father, he who was father, has no need of us any more.

Mother is confined to her bed and will see no one. I do not even know where Mara is. Tomorrow, the feast of the dead. I hear the pots clatter. Axes bite into the flesh of the banana tree.

Mariette Pathy Allen

Marnie Mueller

I was the first Caucasian born in the Tule Lake Japanese Relocation Center. After Pearl Harbor, my father had declared himself a conscientious objector and had volunteered to work in the camps. His aim, he said, was "to do something to make an intolerable situation tolerable." But after two years' work organizing co-op stores at Tule Lake, he withdrew his request for C.O. status; the virulent racism he perceived among many camp administrators and guards persuaded him that there were certain circumstances in which he would take up arms.

As I was growing up, whenever friends or teachers asked me where I was born, I simply said, "In California." I rarely mentioned Tule Lake, and when I did no one knew what I was talking about. In sixteen years of formal schooling, I never saw in a book or heard in a classroom any reference to Tule Lake or the other ten camps to which Japanese-Americans were consigned. I came to feel that if I talked about the camp, I'd be telling a tale about a place that existed only in my imagination. In my thirties, when I began writing fiction, I thought of setting some stories in the camps. But I knew only my mother's accounts of me as a baby at Tule Lake, and my parents were now living in South America, too far away for me to question them in detail. When I went to the New York Public Library to look up Japanese-American Relocation Camps, I found only four entries in the entire catalog—a novel by Jerome Charyn and three nonfiction works.

The only book available was Michi Weglyn's Years of Infamy, which had just been published in 1976. I opened the book to photographs of Tule Lake — windswept black expanses, barbed-wire fences, watchtowers. The captions said Tule Lake had been a high-security segregation center. In the distance, beyond the fences, was a mountain with distinctive jagged peaks. The same mountain beyond the same fences appeared in my baby pictures.

Sitting at the long table in the library's main room, I began to weep — perhaps for the tragedy of the camps and the suffering people had experienced. I give myself that much. But closer to the truth, I suspect, is that I wept for relief that my own history had been confirmed at last.

Marnie Mueller is a widely published poet and short story writer. She is currently working on a novel, Divided Loyalties, set in Tule Lake Camp.

CHANGES

Toru Horokawa sat this morning in May on the steps of his tar-papered barracks, remembering and trying to understand.

What had started him thinking about returning to Japan a couple of years before today was not his son Sam. No, then things had been fine with Sam. As they had been with Huroko. No, what had turned him to thinking of going back to Japan were the Hakujin saying his farm could no longer be his, that his house did not belong to him. His dreams of return began when these white men said his community could no longer be a place that he was a part of.

Toru Horokawa sat now, two years later, looking down onto his wife Huroko's tiny garden, her pathetic garden, he thought, set in the black sand of this wasteland. Across the way were other rows of barracks, black tarpaper against black sand and more gardens that the women and a few of the men had made, trying to put beauty into this place. How stupid of them. Ugly should be left ugly. No sense pretending. He would never pretend again. Not after last night. And this morning.

He thought of himself as a proud man. He always had been so.

What happened last night with his only son Sam and with Huroko could not change that. If even the Hakujin had not been able to shame him, his wife and son could not.

When the Hakujin had said he no longer belonged on his land, he had not been fooled. Huroko said, "No, Toru-san, they didn't say we don't belong. They say it is for our protection and for loyalty to the country that we must move inland."

"Ah, what stupid foolishness. More inland! How much more inland is the place they plan to send us? If I wished to, I could rig up a radio in the middle of this country and signal the Japanese. I am not the stupid man they like to make believe I am. And I am not the sly man they wish me to be. I am only a farmer who doesn't want to be ruined by them."

It was of these things that Toru Horokawa thought as he sat on the steps of his tarpapered barracks on this spring day.

He had not been taken in by the Hakujin when he'd had to sell everything off, not the way his neighbors had been. His neighbors who were so afraid that they wouldn't sell all in time, who were so afraid they wouldn't have enough money to pay off their debts to the banks and the seed and grain stores.

He had told them, "Don't worry, what can they do to you, throw you into prison?" He laughed. He laughed harder when a neighbor looked frightened.

"Don't say that Horokawa-san," they said to him. "Don't put bad luck on us."

"Ha," he said. "They're going to throw us in prison anyway. That's what I mean. What does it matter?"

"We know that," his neighbors said, trying to look proud. "But it is the honor of things. We mustn't have them thinking we are robbers or shirkers."

The honor! He knew he was an honorable man. He was true to his wife. He supported his child. He worked his farm, didn't cut corners the way the Hakujin did. These white men who didn't understand why the Issei's vegetables grew to three times the size of theirs. And he would be an honorable man, too, in his selling off of all his possessions on earth. He would just take his time. He would just demand the price they were worth and if the Hakujin didn't want it at that price, he wouldn't buckle under.

36

"Please, Toru-san," Huroko said to him as the people came and went from their house not buying anything. "Please bring the prices down. I want this over. I don't want these people in my house gloating over our misfortune."

"Let them gloat," he answered her. "Let them think I am a stupid, arrogant man. You will see. They will be back."

"Please," she continued to implore him. "Don't make me have to leave my house seeing all my belongings sitting in sadness."

"I know what I do," he said, cutting off the pleading. "I know I am right."

She gave into him. She always did in those days, he recalled. He only had to say something twice, at the extreme, and she would relent. She had returned in silence to what was their kitchen, though was barely their kitchen on that day with all her things out of the shelves on the counter, on the table, all of her china, her glassware, her tableclothes and pots and pans. This kitchen where she had been a devoted wife and mother was where she now went obediently to wait for the Hakujin. He heard no sound from her so he peeked in. She sat at the enamel red table, staring out the window, out toward their fields. He looked in admiration at her straight back, her strong jaw, at her long hair pulled into a bun, not a strand out of place, her starched blue apron that covered her yellow dress. Here was a worthy wife, a wife to always have by your side. He left the room without speaking to her. She would be fine. They would all get through this. They were too strong to be destroyed.

His son Sam came to him a few minutes later. Sam, who was then sixteen. His only son. His only child. He and Huroko were almost too old when they'd had him. Sam who had always honored him. Even that day he had addressed his father in honorable terms.

And so it was that Toru Horokawa sat on the steps of his tarpapered barracks in the camp they were sent to, and remembered.

"Please, Papa-san, do something to make it not so hard for Ma. Just sell the stuff at lower prices. What does it matter? We have enough money."

The Sam who stood before him that day was still a boy, narrow-chested, soft-faced, Toru remembered. Not like last night, when

Sam's new manhood had been like a mockery of himself. But Toru forced the recent memory from his mind and returned to two years before when he had answered his son that Sam was right, it was not a question of money, he was glad he understood that. It was a question of pride. Of honor.

"And wait and see," Toru said. "The Hakujin will be back. They will carry a picture of our fine possessions in their heads when they go to the other farms. Your mother's china and my farm tools will grow more beautiful the farther they go from our farm. They will see how little our friends value their possessions as they offer them for nothing and beg at the feet of the Hakujin to take their poor items. The Hakujin will return to our farm where the finer things are sold, at lower prices still than they can find first-hand in a store. 'Ah,' they will say. 'These things are cared for by Japs. And you know, if nothing else, the Japs are good at caring for their things. That is what Japs are good for.'"

Without waiting for a response from his son, Toru Horokawa bowed to Sam and turned to walk out to the front porch of his house. He sat on his favorite chair, a wooden upright, and looked out across the road at his acreage as his wife did from her kitchen window. The fields had been plowed. The furrows of rich, brown dirt were all there, rough and broken fertile earth stretching toward the horizon, waiting under the blue, May sky for the seeds that had not been put in this year. Did they cry, he wondered, like a woman who wants the man's sex in her? Did they cry and moan in the night from longing? Well, the earth would have to wait. It would have to wait just as the Hakujin would wait and wait forever, before he would bring the prices down. "Give us your things," they would cry. "Give them to us, please, we need these things." They could cry until the cows come home, as they like to say. He would not give it to those bastards until the price was what he asked for. But the earth. The fallow earth. That was another matter. Perhaps he could go out tonight and with a handful of seeds, ease its longing.

And in this manner, Toru Horokawa sat on the steps of his black tarpapered barracks remembering that last day.

It had been there and then—sitting on the old familiar porch of his farm waiting for the buyers to return to take all his earthly possessions, waiting for the two days to pass after which they would pack up what was left, in the two bags they were allowed to carry on their journey to the congregating center where they were to be processed and sent, who knew where—that he began to imagine returning to Japan. When he thought of his tiny village in the north of the country, he flew as though on the back of a bird to a place of safety, of loveliness. It wasn't of concern to him that the choice had been to either go to America or go to the city and work in a factory, which would have been death to the spirit of the country boy that he was. Death to his love of the earth and growing things. It was never a choice. He got on the boat and floated to America.

As he imagined returning to his village, the pictures that formed in his mind were not of the poverty he had endured in this family shack, but instead the simple beauty of the village with its line of shacks against the clear sky, the smell of wood burning in the charcoal stoves, the sound of rain on his thin roof, and the smell of jasmine flowering in summer. He decided as he sat on his porch overlooking his soon-to-be-lost farm that he would find a way to return to his village a rich man to live out his last days.

These thoughts of return didn't come from any regret of what had passed, no regret that he had come to America or the hardship he'd found here. He had never complained about doing manual labor on other men's farms until he could gather the money to buy his own. He never complained that he couldn't become a citizen and that he had almost had to marry too late to have a child because of the exclusionary laws. He was never even angry at the prejudice of the white Americans. What did they know of him? What they hated about him was not him. In the end he found his way around all their laws. As soon as his son was born, he bought land in his son's name. His son who was a citizen by birth. Where there was a will there was a way, as the Americans said. He laughed and said that to Huroko after they had returned from the land office, the new baby still in her arms, still suckling. "My little citizen, our little American land owner," they had laughed, Toru raising his glass of Sake. Huroko not drinking, but laughing and crying in joy and the tremendous emotion of women when they have recently given birth.

And thus Toru Horokawa sat on the steps of his tarpapered barracks, remembering.

No, he had never regretted the trials he had been put through in this country, because in the end he had what he wanted. A house, a wife, a son, a farm and with it soil he could sink his hands and feet into. A good living. He was a man. It was only with the order to evacuate, to give up his land and house and living, that he had finally had to struggle to find a way to keep his dignity, to remain a man in his own vision. So he imagined returning to his first home, to the place of his ancestors, to Japan.

Though even on that day of the sale of their household, he remained a man, he now reminded himself. In the end he was proven right. The Hakujin came scurrying back like mice to the field and bought everything at his asking price.

"Oh how lovely your things, Mrs. Horokawa," the women said to his wife. "So much finer than the others down the road. So worth the price, we have decided. And we will be careful of them. We'll keep them every bit as fine as you have, we promise you that."

Toru was proud of his Huroko that day. She kept her self. She smiled and nodded politely but no more than that. As she stood in her kitchen he could see the tears building behind her eyes, but only because he knew his own wife of twenty years. They never knew, those Hakujin. They never could know the sorrow they carried in them on that day and the days that followed.

Though that night, he stopped her sorrow for a time. As they lay on the bare floor of their empty bedroom. But not until he had fought with his son Sam and said to him, "You sleep on the floor. You are lucky to still have a floor."

"Aw but, Pa."

"Papa-san still to you."

Aw but, Papa-san, I can't sleep on the floor."

"In Japan I slept my whole boyhood and young manhood on the floor. You, my son, can sleep one night."

That was the end of it. Sam returned to his room. A boy who is obedient at sixteen is a blessing to a man, he thought at the time.

And then he tended to Huroko. She began to cry that May night as the moonlight came into their room. He knew how to

40

make her stop crying. He knew his wife so well. Instead of comforting her, he touched her thing down there, and touched it, and touched it, until she had no place for crying, only the ecstasy of her womanhood. The ecstasy of being with such a man.

Toru Horokawa sat on the wooden steps of his tarpapered barracks and remembered that on that night in May, he had gotten up off the floor after loving his Huroko and sneaked out into the field only in his pants, barefooted, barechested. He had reached into the pockets of his pants, those he wore when planting, and with each handful of seeds he had spun in the moonlight, the soil turning and flying under his feet, the soft brown soil under and on top of his brown feet, and he had flung the seeds as far as they would carry and he whirled and danced and laughed, spinning and spitting out seed onto the land. He had been loyal to the land. He could be proud of that.

But his son Sam had now taken all pride away. Toru's dreams of returning to Japan, of escape, had been destroyed by Sam. He could never return. Japan was no longer a possibility for him. Everything had changed. His world was standing on its head. Even Huroko was different. Since she had come to the camp and not had the house to care for daily, she had begun to make her art, she called it. Little sculptures made from the white shells the women found in the black sand. They were all over the room. Towers. Animals. Frames on mirrors. He had to admit they were beautiful, but again, what was beauty in this ugliness? When she wasn't working on her sculptures, she served in the mess hall. She was lively on the days she went there, so much so, once he had accused her of having a lover.

"No lover, Toru-san, only pleasure at being myself. For the first time I have time to myself and the hours I give to others is paid for."

"Pay, you call that pay," he scoffed. "That's slave wages."

She had bowed to him, but said in her quiet voice, "Slave wages are better than no wages."

The women had changed here at the camp, and not for the good. He should have taken charge before this came to pass, he told himself.

As Toru sat on his steps in the midst of his thoughts, he saw

Toki Honda, the old man, walking toward him, scuffing his feet through the black sand. Toki came to a stop at the bottom of the stairs.

"You coming to the community room today, Horokawa? You going to try to beat me today?" Toki waited for a response from his friend.

Toru Horokawa shook his head. "Not today," he said. Never again, he thought, not with this disgrace.

"Get your mind off things," Toki tried again. "Things don't seem so bad after a good game of Goh."

Toru shook his head, not replying in words this time. So, the whole block knew of his shame. But you, Toki Honda, he thought, you're a bachelor. You can't know a father's pain. A husband's sorrow.

"No, not today," he said to Toki. "Maybe tomorrow."

Toki grinned and said goodbye, he'd see him tomorrow.

Oh, no you won't, Toru thought.

Toru heard the door of their room open behind him. It was Huroko. It was time for her to go to work. Her silly job in the mess hall. He would put a stop to it. With this thought of taking command again, he filled with a surge of hope which disappeared the moment Huroko came and stood by his side and let the back of her hand brush against his cheek. "Toru Horokawa," was all she said, but those two actions, speaking his name and her touch, caused the memories of the night before, the memories he'd kept just outside his thoughts, to break like a powerful waterfall, cascading all the accumulated pain and anger over and into his heart.

He saw Sam standing in the middle of their room. Sam, now a young man, with a few whiskers over his lip. Sam who was no taller than Toru, but grown stockier, stood there in the same room that had been nothing when they'd arrived, a shit hole until he and Huroko had fixed it and made it into a kind of a home with a little linoleum and a wall of sheet rock to give privacy for them in bed. And with curtains they bought at the co-op store and an icebox so they didn't always have to eat in the mess hall.

"Pa, I've got something to say to you. Pa, I'm going to enlist." Sam said. "Pa, do you hear me?"

Toru Horokawa's body had trembled so he couldn't speak for moments. He bit down to stop his jaw from shaking. All he could see in his mind was their first sight of the camp as a family when they arrived at the front gate in the train. He newly saw the high double fence and the barbed wire on top, and the men with the machine guns in the towers. He had thought at the time, I will never co-operate. Then he recalled how just weeks before he'd fought angrily in meetings against the army recruiters coming through that front gate into the camp where they were imprisoned to take their sons to do intelligence work against the Japanese. And now he was hearing his son Sam say he'd chosen to go.

"You don't even speak decent Japanese," were the first words that came through his trembling lips. "You never learned a decent Japanese in all the years I tried to teach you. "Toru Horokawa began to laugh. "How will you fool the Japanese? Huh? How will they think you are one of them? How will you be able to do intelligence work against them, son of mine?" He rose from his chair. "No! No, son of mine." He slapped the boy, his son Sam. Never had he slapped him before.

Sam backed away from him, moving over toward the coal stove in the middle of the room. His face became a blubbering face. "Pa, I'm doing it. Be proud of me. I believe in what I'm doing."

"Toru-san, you stop that. That's our son." Huroko stood up from the table where she, too, had been sitting. They were having a happy supper before Sam entered with his news. She held tightly to the side of the table.

"What? You going to fall over?" Toru taunted her. "You have to hold onto the table not to fall over?"

"You are sour. You are a sour old man," Huroko said to him in a whispered voice that made him realize he was yelling. "I hold onto this table not to hit you for hitting our son."

"No, Ma, don't say that to him." Sam cried.

"I can take care of myself," Toru said to his son, still yelling. "It's you who bring this to our family. You who learned to eat ice cream in this shit hole of a prison. You've turned Hakujin and now you want to fight for them. You kill my ancestors." He hit his fist against the bedroom wall. The room shook.

"Pa, I don't kill your ancestors. I want to fight for my country."

"Your country! What of my country? The U.S. of A., that's your country. Japan, that's mine."

"Shhhh," Huroko said. She held her finger to her lips and waved her other hand.

"I don't care who hears. I have nothing to lose. I had only this life. And my ancestors. And my land. Now I have no place to go. Nothing to show. These hands make nothing, no crop, not nothing. What am I worth?"

In the silence that followed, the two of them, his son whose tears had dried and whose face was calm, and his wife whose anger had left, stared at him. He saw pity for the man he had become enter their eyes. That look almost did away with what was left of him.

"You cannot go," Toru said, trying to gather strength once again. "I won't allow it."

Sam looked from Toru to his mother and back.

"Pa, I'm eighteen. I make my own decisions." He spoke softly, as though to a child.

"Until I die, you are always my son." A huge blackness, as black as the lava sand the camp sat on, entered him, made him move across the room toward Sam. He didn't know what he was going to do, but he knew he wanted to hurt his son.

"Sam, get out." Huroko screamed and ran toward Toru and grabbed onto him. "Get out of here."

Toru tried to yank himself from his wife' grasp, but she had her full weight on him. She was a strong woman. He had never known how strong. He yanked again as he saw that Sam was backing toward the door. That Sam had opened the door. That Sam's frightened face was disappearing into the darkness of the night. The door closed. Toru pulled again, but his wife held fast.

"You are not going after him," Huroko said. "You stay here and talk to me, you sour man."

Toru ceased trying to escape from his wife. He just stood staring into the room that now looked dimmer to him, as though the lights had been turned down, without his son. Without his country.

After a while Huroko guided Toru toward the bedroom.

44

"No, Mama-san, I don't want to sleep," he said when he saw where she was taking him.

"You ready to talk?" she said.

He looked at her. She didn't suffer as he did. Her face was smooth and her cheeks still had high color. She looked to him as young as when they'd met, except for some white in her hair. He knew, of course, if he looked at old pictures, she'd be different, thinner, softer. But in his present sadness, through his old, discouraged man's eyes, she looked like a girl, young enough for Sam, even.

"I will talk to you, Mama-san."

"Sit then," she said.

He sat at the table and watched her spoon the tea into the pot and slowly pour the water in. She made him sleepy, almost, with her tender movements. He'd always loved her hands on things, the dishes, folding clothes, touching his body. Tender hands that had turned so strong tonight protecting their son from his fury. How much worse could things get?

She brought the cups and teapot to the table on a lacquered tray. She stood as she poured the tea and then she sat next to him. They sipped the tea, not talking. The light slowly returned and the room became brighter for him.

"Toru-san," Huroko said. "You must understand that Japan does not mean the same to me anymore. I can't go back with who I am now. My father would kill the woman I have become if he was still alive. I like who I am. Funny to learn it in a prison."

"This prison is death for us." Toru glanced at her. She was betraying him yet more.

"Yes, Toru-san, this prison is death for us. In many ways. We will never be the same again, but. . . ." She stopped.

"But what?" He demanded.

"I had less to lose here. It surprised me how little I had to lose." She looked at him and then away.

"What do you mean?" He became frightened inside. It was as though she was saying goodbye to him. Maybe she *had* found a lover in the mess hall. But he was too afraid to ask. The time before he was certain she hadn't, so he could accuse, be his usual angry, proud self. Now he wasn't certain. Now he worried. He felt like promising her he would become more like the Hakujin, that he would eat hot dogs, anything, drink pop. He couldn't lose his Huroko. Oh, this was worse than losing a son. Everyone lost sons. Sons grow up. But his Huroko!

"All I mean, dear Toru-san, is that it hasn't been so hard for me here as for you." She put her hands out and held his face in them. "Oh, my dear Toru Harakawa," was what she said. "My only, only Toru Horokawa."

"He kills our ancestors." Toru shook his face loose from his wife's hold.

"I know that," she said in a quiet voice. Her eyes looked at the table.

"Doesn't it bother you?"

His wife shrugged, then nodded, but didn't look him in the eyes.

"Maybe tomorrow I can talk sense into him," Toru said.

His Huroko shrugged again, but this time she shook her head.

And thus it was that Toru Horokawa sat on the steps of his tarpapered barracks remembering the changes in his life that turned his heart raw in their newness.

Very early the next morning there was a knock on the door. Toru hadn't slept, but had sat all night at the table. He got up to answer the door and found the round-faced Community Analyst standing there. Mr. Seymour Topol was his name.

"Hi, Toru, can I come in?" This Topol with his Hakujin ways.

"My wife is not fully clothed," Toru said. He didn't want this man in his room. "We can talk on the steps."

Toru closed the door behind him and went out into the day that was to be clear and sunny as any spring day. They sat on the top step.

"Say what it is," he said to Topol.

"I wanted to get to you before there was trouble. I've heard there was an argument here last night. I've heard you were fighting with Sam."

Who was the *Inu?* Toru Horokawa thought. Who was the informer in their block? His mind raced through the possibilities.

"I'm sorry, Toru. But if it gets back to the army that you're

46

telling him not to go. . . . Well." he stopped. He cleared his throat. "I'm afraid they might say you were committing treason."

Toru stared at this Topol who had the look white people's faces get when they want you to know they sympathize with some horrible thing that has happened to you. As though they are hurting as much as you when they say such things as a father who wants his son not to fight against his own homeland is committing treason.

"I'm afraid, Toru, that it's treasonous to interfere with a U.S. Citizen's execution of his military duty. You're going to have to stop."

So ever since Topol had left, Toru Horokawa had sat on his steps, remembering and trying to understand.

But now Huroko, whose hand had passed over his cheek moments before, leaving a spot made cooler by the morning air, continued down the stairs without saying a word. At the bottom she stood looking over her tiny garden with its shell sculpture of a pine tree in the center. She reached in and pulled up a few weeds. She stood rolling them in her hand as she absently looked yet longer into her small plot.

As he watched her, he recalled the May night when he'd gotten up from their bed on the floor and gone into his field in the moonlight. He could feel the moist, heavy soil under his feet. He could remember his laughter. He saw himself in the moonlight spinning and flinging his last seed onto the ground. Remembering, Toru Horokawa knew if he were other than a man, he would now weep.

Elizabeth Gordon

I was born in Southeast Asia (Saigon, specifically) and raised in the southeastern U.S. (Tennessee). In my own experience, I've found there's a certain built-in tension in having a mixed heritage. All kinds of questions arise from it: questions of identity, of belonging, of home. Since I've moved out of the South, though, I've been learning to use that tension and explore those questions in my writing. I now live in Providence, Rhode Island where, among other things, I publish and edit the poetry journal, Frugal Chariot.

ON THE OTHER SIDE OF THE WAR: A STORY

I. The Way We Came To America

The way we came to America was this: my father, who was in the Army, made an overseas call to his mom and dad in West Virginia.

"Listen," he said, "I've decided to adopt this poor little Vietnamese baby and bring her to America. What do you think?"

Now, both Grandma and Grandpa were true hillbillies in their lineage, habits, and mental faculties—which means they were as broke, as stubborn, and as sharp as folks can be. Not that my father's story required much genius to be seen right through. A twenty-four-year-old enlisted man wanting to bring home some mysterious oriental infant? They hadn't brought him up *that* good.

"It's all right, Skip," they told him. "You can get married, if you love her, and bring 'em both. Bring 'em both on home."

II. No One Had Expected

No one had expected anything like that to happen, least of all the people it happened to.

My father had been quite prepared to meet and marry a sweet girl with a name like Layuna or Ginny Lee. A girl who hailed from one of the good neighboring towns of Beckley or Rainelle. A girl with a daddy, like his, who liked to work on cars, who'd every once in a while hit the booze and start cursing about black lung. There'd been no Nguyen Ngoc Huong from Saigon in *his* crystal ball.

And my mother never dreamed she'd live in an aluminum house on wheels, or see shaved ice swirling down from the sky. Her kitchen window looked out onto a pasture of cows, who stood utterly still with the weather piling up around their legs. It was a difficult thing for her to understand.

So while my father was out climbing telephone poles for Ma

Bell, my mother was in the trailer with me, crying and crying for the cows who had not a plank against the cold.

III. Things Got Mixed Up

Things got mixed up sometimes between them. Though it was my father's unshakable belief that Common Sense prevailed in all circumstances, he seemed to forget that Common Sense is commonly rendered senseless whenever it crosses a few time zones.

For example, my mother would constantly confuse "hamburger" with "pancake," presumably because both were round, flat, and fried in a pan. So my father, after asking for his favorite breakfast, would soon smell the juicy aroma of sizzling ground beef coming from the kitchen. Other times, he'd find a stack of well-buttered flapjacks, along with a cold bottle of Coca-Cola, waiting for him at the dinner table.

One morning, before my father left for work, he asked my mother to make corn bread and pinto beans for supper. The result of this request was that my mother spent the remainder of the day peeling, one by one, an entire pound of pinto beans. How could she have known any better?

When my father returned home that night, he found her with ten sore fingers and a pot full of mush. He didn't know whether to laugh or cry, but he kissed her because there was nothing he could say.

IV. The Photograph

The photograph, circa 1965, is somewhat unusual. In the background there is a row of neat, nearly identical frame houses. The street in front of the houses is spacious and clean, as wholesome and as decent as sunshine.

Up a little closer, there is a car. It's a two-tone Chevy with curvaceous fenders, gleaming as though it's just been washed and waxed by hand. The weather looks like Sunday.

In the foreground, not unexpectedly, a woman with a small child. The woman is a wife because she wears a gold ring. She is also a mother because of the way she holds her child.

The woman has a slim, dainty figure. Her smile is wide and

loose, as though she is close to laughter. Maybe her husband, who is taking her picture, is telling a joke or making a silly face. It seems quite natural that the photographer is the husband. Who else would it be?

But something in the photograph seems not quite right. Strangers often tilt their heads when looking at it, as if it is uncomfortable to view straight up and down. Possibly, it's the incomparable blackness of the woman's hair, the way it seems forced into a wave it can barely hold. Or maybe it has something to do with the baby's eyes which, though blue, are shaped exactly like the woman's: round at the center, narrow at the corners, and heavy-lidded.

What are eyes like that doing among frame houses and a shiny Chevrolet? It seems a reasonable thing to ask.

V. When I Started School

When I started school there were numerous forms to be filled out. Some of the questions were so simple, I could have answered them myself.

The task belonged to my mother, though. She handled most of the questions with ease, and I liked to watch the way she filled all those boxes and blanks with her pretty handwriting.

There was one question, however, that gave my mother a lot of trouble. Even though it was multiple choice, none of the answers seemed to fit. She decided to ask my father what to do.

He didn't have an answer right away, and for some reason that made him angry. The problem was, I was supposed to be in a race, but he couldn't figure out which one.

Finally, he told my mother to put an "H" in that blank. "For *human* race," he said.

I didn't understand what that meant, back then. But it sounded like a good race to me.

Gish Jen

Here's the most telling thing I could tell you about myself: My name's not Gish. Actually, it's Lillian, a name I now like but hated every minute of my growing up. I associated with it the type of librarian who wears orange support hose—you know, the kind who blinks more than she talks—and so, in high school, when some new friends nicknamed me Gish, after Lillian Gish (whom I had never heard of at the time, though I didn't say so), I was, as we used to say, ecstatic. It was part of this whole arty thing. I think we were sophomores then, but it could be we were only sophomoric—a friend whose last name was Housman became A.E. at the same time—you get the picture. While A.E. went back to plain Maddy soon enough, though, I proved less sensible. That summer I went away; I found myself sitting in a circle of strangers; and when my turn came to introduce myself, I impulsively identified myself as 'Gish Jen' (so nonchalantly I had to repeat myself twice) as though everyone called me Gish and not two or three people, when they were in a silly mood.

The rest of the story you may guess.

Is this embarrassing? I only admit to it at all, to be honest, because academics now say it is not only okay to have taken a name for oneself, but that such self-naming can represent a critical step in the process of self-invention. I should be proud, in other words. Such imaginative force! Such derring-do!

My mother, though, sees it differently. 'Whatever you call yourself, your name is still Lil,' she tells me—and isn't that true too? My mother says a lot of things that are hard to argue with. Like once I claimed, 'Ma, you have no idea who I am. Absolutely no idea. You're clueless.' And she answered, 'Of course I know who you are. You're my daughter.'

How to debate? As I recall, I blinked and shut up.

THE WHITE UMBRELLA

When I was twelve, my mother went to work without telling me or my little sister.

"Not that we need the second income." The lilt of her accent drifted from the kitchen up to the top of the stairs, where Mona and I were listening.

"No," said my father, in a barely audible voice. "Not like the Lee family."

The Lees were the only other Chinese family in town. I remembered how sorry my parents had felt for Mrs. Lee when she started waitressing downtown the year before; and so when my mother began coming home late, I didn't say anything, and tried to keep Mona from saying anything either.

"But why shouldn't I?" she argued. "Lots of people's mothers work."

"Those are American people," I said.

"So what do you think we are? I can do the pledge of allegiance with my eyes closed."

Nevertheless, she tried to be discreet; and if my mother wasn't home by 5:30, we would start cooking by ourselves, to make sure dinner would be on time. Mona would wash the vegetables and put on the rice; I would chop.

For weeks we wondered what kind of work she was doing. I imagined that she was selling perfume, testing dessert recipes for the local newspaper. Or maybe she was working for the florist. Now that she had learned to drive, she might be delivering boxes of roses to people.

"I don't think so," said Mona as we walked to our piano lesson after school. "She would've hit something by now."

A gust of wind littered the street with leaves.

"Maybe we better hurry up," she went on, looking at the sky. "It's going to pour."

"But we're too early." Her lesson didn't begin until 4:00, mine until 4:30, so we usually tried to walk as slowly as we could. "And anyway, those aren't the kind of clouds that rain. Those are cumulus clouds."

We arrived out of breath and wet.

"Oh, you poor, poor dears," said old Miss Crosman. "Why don't you call me the next time it's like this out? If your mother won't drive you, I can come pick you up."

"No, that's okay," I answered. Mona wrung her hair out on Miss Crosman's rug. "We just couldn't get the roof of our car to close, is all. We took it to the beach last summer and got sand in the mechanism." I pronounced this last word carefully, as if the credibility of my lie depended on its middle syllable. "It's never been the same." I thought for a second. "It's a convertible."

"Well then make yourselves at home." She exchanged looks with Eugenie Roberts, whose lesson we were interrupting. Eugenie smiled good-naturedly. "The towels are in the closet across from the bathroom."

Huddling at the end of Miss Crosman's nine-foot leatherette couch, Mona and I watched Eugenie play. She was a grade ahead of me and, according to school rumor, had a boyfriend in high school. I believed it. Aside from her ballooning breasts—which threatened to collide with the keyboard as she played—she had auburn hair, blue eyes, and, I noted with a particular pang, a pure white folding umbrella.

"I can't see," whispered Mona.

"So clean your glasses."

"My glasses *are* clean. You're in the way."

I looked at her. "They look dirty to me."

That's because *your* glasses are dirty."

Eugenia came bouncing to the end of her piece.

"Oh! Just stupendous!" Miss Crosman hugged her, then looked up as Eugenie's mother walked in. "Stupendous!" she said again. "Oh! Mrs. Roberts! Your daughter has a gift, a real gift. It's an honor to teach her."

Mrs. Roberts, radiant with pride, swept her daughter out of the room as if she were royalty, born to the piano bench. Watching the way Eugenie carried herself, I sat up, and concentrated so hard on sucking in my stomach that I did not realize until the Robertses were gone that Eugenie had left her umbrella. As Mona began to play, I jumped up and ran to the window, meaning to call to them—only to see their brake lights flash then fade at the stop sign at the corner. As if to allow them passage, the rain had let up; a quivering sun lit their way.

The umbrella glowed like a scepter on the blue carpet while Mona, slumping over the keyboard, managed to eke out a fair rendition of a catfight. At the end of the piece, Miss Crosman asked her to stand up.

"Stay right there," she said, then came back a minute later with a towel to cover the bench. "You must be cold," she continued. "Shall I call your mother and have her bring over some dry clothes?"

"No," answered Mona. "She won't come because she . . ."

"She's too busy," I broke in from the back of the room.

"I see." Miss Crosman sighed and shook her head a little. "Your glasses are filthy, honey," she said to Mona. "Shall I clean them for you?"

Sisterly embarrassment seized me. Why hadn't Mona wiped her lenses when I told her to? As she resumed abuse of the piano, I stared at the umbrella. I wanted to open it, twirl it around by its slender silver handle; I wanted to dangle it from my wrist on the way to school the way the other girls did. I wondered what Miss Crosman would say if I offered to bring it to Eugenie at school tomorrow. She would be impressed with my consideration for others; Eugenie would be pleased to have it back; and I would have possession of the umbrella for an entire night. I looked at it again, toying with the idea of asking for one for Christmas. I knew, however, how my mother would react.

"Things," she would say. "What's the matter with a raincoat? All you want is things, just like an American."

Sitting down for my lesson, I was careful to keep the towel under me and sit up straight.

"I'll bet you can't see a thing either," said Miss Crosman, reaching for my glasses. "And you can relax, you poor dear." She touched my chest, in an area where she never would have touched Eugenie Roberts. "This isn't a boot camp."

When Miss Crosman finally allowed me to start playing I played extra well, as well as I possibly could. See, I told her with my fingers. You don't have to feel sorry for me.

"That was wonderful," said Miss Crosman. "Oh! Just wonderful."

An entire constellation rose in my heart.

"And guess what," I announced proudly. "I have a surprise for you."

Then I played a second piece for her, a much more difficult one that she had not assigned.

"Oh! That was stupendous," she said without hugging me. "Stupendous! You are a genius, young lady. If your mother had started you younger, you'd be playing like Eugenie Roberts by now!"

I looked at the keyboard, wishing that I had still a third, even more difficult piece to play for her. I wanted to tell her that I was the school spelling bee champion, that I wasn't ticklish, that I could do karate.

"My mother is a concert pianist," I said.

She looked at me for a long moment, then finally, without saying anything, hugged me. I didn't say anything about bringing the umbrella to Eugenie at school.

The steps were dry when Mona and I sat down to wait for my mother.

"Do you want to wait inside?" Miss Crosman looked anxiously at the sky.

"No," I said. "Our mother will be here any minute."

"In a while," said Mona.

"Any minute," I said again, even though my mother had been at least twenty minutes late every week since she started working.

According to the church clock across the street we had been waiting twenty-five minutes when Miss Crosman came out again.

"Shall I give you ladies a ride home?"

"No," I said. "Our mother is coming any minute."

"Shall I at least give her a call and remind her you're here? Maybe she forgot about you."

"I don't think she *forgot*," said Mona.

"Shall I give her a call anyway? Just to be safe?"

"I bet she already left," I said. "How could she forget about us?"

Miss Crosman went in to call.

"There's no answer," she said, coming back out.

"See, she's on her way," I said.

"Are you sure you wouldn't like to come in?"

"No," said Mona.

"Yes," I said. I pointed at my sister. "She meant yes too. She meant no, she wouldn't like to go in."

Miss Crosman looked at her watch. "It's 5:30 now, ladies. My pot roast will be coming out in fifteen minutes. Maybe you'd like to come in and have some then?"

"My mother's almost here," I said. "She's on her way."

We watched and watched the street. I tried to imagine what my mother was doing; I tried to imagine her writing messages in the sky, even though I knew she was afraid of planes. I watched as the branches of Miss Crosman's big willow tree started to sway; they had all been trimmed to exactly the same height off the ground, so that they looked beautiful, like hair in the wind.

It started to rain.

"Miss Crosman is coming out again," said Mona.

"Don't let her talk you into going inside," I whispered.

"Why not?"

"Because that would mean Mom isn't really coming any minute."

But she isn't," said Mona. "She's *working*."

"Shhh! Miss Crosman is going to hear you."

"She's working! She's working! She's working!"

I put my hand over her mouth, but she licked it, and so I was wiping my hand on my wet dress when the front door opened.

"We're getting even *wetter*," said Mona right away. "Wetter and wetter."

"Shall we all go in?" Miss Crosman pulled Mona to her feet. "Before you young ladies catch pneumonia? You've been out here an hour already."

"We're *freezing*." Mona looked up at Miss Crosman. "Do you have any hot chocolate? We're going to catch *pneumonia*."

"I'm not going in," I said. "My mother's coming any minute."

"Come on," said Mona. "Use your *noggin*."

"Any minute."

"Come on, Mona," Miss Crosman opened the door. "Shall we get you inside first?"

"See you in the hospital," said Mona as she went in. "See you in the hospital with *pneumonia*."

I stared out into the empty street. The rain was pricking me all over; I was cold; I wanted to go inside. I wanted to be able to let myself go inside. If Miss Crosman came out again, I decided, I would go in.

She came out with a blanket and the white umbrella.

I could not believe that I was actually holding the umbrella, opening it. It sprang up by itself as if it were alive, as if that were what it wanted to do—as if it belonged in my hands, above my head. I stared up at the network of silver spokes, then spun the umbrella around and around and around. It was so clean and white that it seemed to glow, to illuminate everything around it.

"It's beautiful," I said.

Miss Crosman sat down next to me, on one end of the blanket. I moved the umbrella over so that it covered that too. I could feel the rain on my left shoulder and shivered. She put her arm around me.

"You poor, poor dear."

I knew that I was in store for another bolt of sympathy, and braced myself by staring up into the umbrella.

"You know, I very much wanted to have children when I was younger," she continued.

"You did?"

She stared at me a minute. Her face looked dry and crusty, like day-old frosting.

"I did. But then I never got married."

I twirled the umbrella around again.

"This is the most beautiful umbrella I have ever seen," I said. "Ever, in my whole life."

"Do you have an umbrella?"

"No. But my mother's going to get me one just like this for Christmas."

"Is she? I tell you what. You don't have to wait until Christmas. You can have this one."

"But this one belongs to Eugenie Roberts," I protested. "I have to give it back to her tomorrow in school."

"Who told you it belongs to Eugenie? It's not Eugenie's. It's mine. And now I'm giving it to you, so it's yours."

"It is?"

She hugged me tighter. "That's right. It's all yours."

"It's mine?" I didn't know what to say. "Mine?" Suddenly I was jumping up and down in the rain. "It's beautiful! Oh! It's beautiful!" I laughed.

Miss Crosman laughed too, even though she was getting all wet.

"Thank you, Miss Crosman. Thank you very much. Thanks a zillion. It's beautiful. It's *stupendous!*"

"You're quite welcome," she said.

"Thank you," I said again, but that didn't seem like enough. Suddenly I knew just what she wanted to hear. "I wish you were my mother."

Right away I felt bad.

"You shouldn't say that," she said, but her face was opening into a huge smile as the lights of my mother's car cautiously turned the corner. I quickly collapsed the umbrella and put it up my skirt, holding onto it from the outside, through the material.

"Mona!" I shouted into the house. "Mona! Hurry up! Mom's here! I told you she was coming!"

Then I ran away from Miss Crosman, down to the curb. Mona came tearing up to my side as my mother neared the house. We both backed up a few feet, so that in case she went onto the curb, she wouldn't run us over.

"But why didn't you go inside with Mona?" my mother asked on the way home. She had taken off her own coat to put over me, and had the heat on high.

"She wasn't using her noggin," said Mona, next to me in the back seat.

"I should call next time," said my mother. "I just don't like to say where I am."

That was when she finally told us that she was working as a check-out clerk in the A&P. She was supposed to be on the day shift, but the other employees were unreliable, and her boss had promised her a promotion if she would stay until the evening shift filled in.

For a moment no one said anything. Even Mona seemed to find the revelation disappointing.

"A promotion already!" she said, finally.

I listened to the windshield wipers.

"You're so quiet." My mother looked at me in the rear view mirror. "What's the matter?"

"I wish you would quit," I said after a moment.

She signed. "The Chinese have a saying: one beam cannot hold the roof up."

"But Eugenie Roberts's father supports their family."

She signed once more. "Eugenie Roberts's father is Eugenie Roberts's father," she said.

As we entered the downtown area, Mona started leaning hard against me every time the car turned right, trying to push me over. Remembering what I had said to Miss Crosman, I tried to maneuver the umbrella under my leg so she wouldn't feel it.

"What's under your skirt?" Mona wanted to know as we came to a traffic light. My mother, watching us in the rear view mirror again, rolled slowly to a stop.

"What's the matter?" she asked.

"There's something under her skirt?" said Mona, pulling at me. "Under her skirt?"

Meanwhile, a man crossing the street started to yell at us. "Who do you think you are, lady?" he said. "You're blocking the whole damn crosswalk."

We all froze. Other people walking by stopped to watch.

"Didn't you hear me?" he went on, starting to thump on the hood with his fist. "Don't you speak English?"

My mother began to back up, but the car behind us honked. Luckily, the light turned green right after that. She sighed in relief.

"What were you saying, Mona?" she asked.

We wouldn't have hit the car behind us that hard if he hadn't been moving too, but as it was our car bucked violently, throwing us all first back and then forward.

"Uh oh," said Mona when we stopped. "*Another* accident."

I was relieved to have attention diverted from the umbrella. Then I noticed my mother's head, tilted back onto the seat. Her eyes were closed.

"Mom!" I screamed. "Mom! Wake up!"

She opened her eyes. "Please don't yell," she said. "Enough people are going to yell already."

"I thought you were dead," I said, starting to cry. "I thought you were dead."

She turned around, looked at me intently, then put her hand to my forehead.

"Sick," she confirmed. "Some kind of sick is giving you crazy ideas."

As the man from the car behind us started tapping on the window, I moved the umbrella away from my leg. Then Mona and my mother were getting out of the car. I got out after them; and while everyone else was inspecting the damage we'd done, I threw the umbrella down a sewer.

Cecilia Manguerra Brainard

I was born and raised in the Philippines, where heavy Western influence made me believe I was Americanized. After immigrating to the U.S. as a UCLA graduate student, I quickly discovered how very Filipino I was. Two decades and several visits to the Philippines later made me realize that I have been transformed into another creature altogether—a Filipino American.

When I first started writing I had difficulty finding my writing voice. The dominant Eurocentric point of view in literature, history, art, and so on, caused this; and I had to scrutinize myself, my past, as well as Philippine history and culture to define who I am and consequently to find my writing voice. While my book Woman With Horns and Other Stories (New Day Publishers, 1988) draws from my Filipino experience, my essays tend to explore my Filipino American experience.

I live in Santa Monica with my husband, a former Philippine Peace Corps Volunteer, and our three sons. I have just completed a novel, and am working on another one. Recently I was awarded a 1988-89 California Arts Council Artists Fellowship.

THE BLUE-GREEN CHIFFON DRESS

Summer vacation started off badly with my favorite guard dog getting killed. I was heading for the hammock with my *Lady Chatterley's Lover* tucked under my arm, and a plateful of green mangoes and a Coke in my hands when Sultan walked up to me, stiff and hostile. His eyes were giant marbles. I called him and he bared his teeth, growling a little. His mouth was foaming. I ran, sounding an alarm, and the next thing I knew one of the men shot him. I saw him writhing, blood gushing to the cracked brown earth. There was something other than blood that oozed out of his gut. I touched him; he was warm and became very still.

Sultan had been a sickly puppy. The servants had talked about drowning him but I took him under my care. He used to race to the gate when I arrived from school, and he'd jump up and lick my face. His death left me nauseous and sad.

To make me feel better, Mama took me to her couturier, who was famous in Ubec for his expensive high fashion clothes. We caught him peering out of his shop at the American soldiers walking by.

"That one looks like James Bond," he said, pinching my arm enthusiastically. "Oy, love those bushy eyebrows," he cooed with a roll of his eyes.

Eventually he got around to me, scrutinized me, and said I had grown. He sketched a few dress designs and he and Mama discussed the drawings, material, and cost while I roamed his shop.

I was studying his ready-made dresses, frowning at the price tags, when a blue-green chiffon dress caught my gaze. The color was stunning, bringing to mind the deepest part of the sea. The soft billowy cloth was draped across the bosom making a deep V-neckline. The skirt was generously gathered and flowed in the same draped effect.

I showed the dress to Mama who said it was too sophisticated

From Woman With Horns and Other Stories, *New Day Publishers*, 1988.

for a teenager. The couturier prodded me to try on the dress.

"Go ahead, Gemma," he insisted, and to my mother in an admonishing tone, "This is 1965, we must keep up with the times."

Before entering the fitting room, I glanced at him gratefully, our eyes locking briefly.

The bodice was loose so I stuffed Kleenex to fill it out. It was an enchanting dress and even my mother begrudgingly agreed. The couturier gushed over the blue-green hue.

"It makes your skin glow," he said. "Put your hair up in a French twist. We'll have to take in the tucks at the bust. And please wear a good padded bra," he added.

My cousin Yolanda and I went through the definitions of kissing, French kissing, petting, and intercourse again. Our favorite pastime was locking ourselves in the bedroom, slapping on makeup, and discussing sex.

"I still don't know exactly how *it* enters the woman's part," I said.

"*Idiota*, it just goes in," she replied in exasperation. She had this superior attitude since Tristan danced slow drag with her and became aroused—she said.

When our eyelashes were curved and stiff with mascara, we decided to iron our hair. We had read that it made your hair straighter and shinier. I spread my hair out on the board, warning her not to singe it. She lightly ran the iron over my hair, then I did hers. After, we swished our hair around our shoulders to see a difference.

"Manolete smiled at me in church yesterday," I announced. "He's so sexy, I think I'll make him Number Two."

We proceeded to work on our crush-lists, shuffling the names of the boys in order of their appeal. I demoted Mandy to Number Ten because he had gone out with Mercedes.

"They were necking. Why else do people park in Magellan Hills?" Yolanda said. "No big loss, Mandy has no imagination."

She added that her Number One was Ruy who claimed to have had an out-of-body experience. "At least Ruy has imagination," she insisted. "Who's your Number one?" she asked.

I told her it was Jose Marie, a senior engineering student—5'11", lean, intelligent, much older at twenty-one. I fancied myself IN LOVE with him and got sweaty palms when he danced with me.

During the summer, Ubec was pleasant. It was not as humid as Manila because the cool sea breeze blew through the ancient acacia and flame trees. There was so much color at that time of year: the sparkling blue sea; the brilliant clear sky; lush hibiscus, begonias and fuchsias; and bountiful fruit—yellow-green custard apples, luscious red mangosteens, succulent pink tambis.

The days flowed with little care. In the evenings we attended parties or watched stocky Basque players hit the balls at the Jai-a-lai. Sometimes we went to the Sand Trap Club to dance to Ama-pola's music. There were movies, swimming parties, and afternoon gossip sessions. And there was smoke-filled Eddie's Log Cabin, owned by an expatriate New Yorker, where we had greasy American-style hamburgers.

Our routine was disrupted when one of the local girls, Elena, suddenly left for Hongkong. In minutes, stories about her mysterious departure flew all over Ubec and continued flying for weeks. Her family insisted she needed extensive allergy tests. Gossip mentioned an illegal abortion and the American captain she had been dating.

Ubec's matrons immediately stepped up their campaign against the American soldiers from nearby Mactan Air Force Base. From their mahjong tables, they lectured: "*Madre mia*, stay away from those soldiers, you'll catch Vietnam Rose. They're trouble. Look what happened to Elena."

I had already heard World War Two stories about American G.I.'s spreading V.D., getting girls pregnant, ruining lives forever. We knew a girl who stood 5'9"—a giant to our eyes—with fair hair and skin. She stood out like an aberration beside the rest of us with our small frames, black hair, and brown skin. "A G.I. baby," she was called behind her back.

"Stay away from those soldiers," the matrons scolded as they shuffled the ivory pieces.

We, good girls, stayed away.

We watched—from a distance—the dazed, short-cropped strangers wandering around our city. We made up stories: that one was a CIA-agent; that brunet was on R & R; the slight one with a nervous laugh was flying to Vietnam the next day on a bombing mission. We read about Diem, napalm, deforestation, and body counts. We saw photos of Buddhist monks burning in fierce self-immolation. We drove by the Base, saw the runway, tower, barracks, and the numerous planes. Several times a day, we listened to those planes flying overhead. We were scandalized by the shanties, claiming to be bars and massage parlors, that mushroomed all over the place. We clucked our tongues at the girls in tight colorful clothes who hung around with the soldiers.

We watched—from a distance.

Eventually we tired of talking about Elena's disgrace. I resumed my crush-list, with Jose Marie maintaining his Number One place. I was glad he was invited to my cousin's End-of-Summer party. For days I fretted about the affair. I dieted, painted my nails pink, dyed my hair Jet Black with some cheap dye called Bigen that I later heard made some women blind.

On the night of the party, I stared at my blue-green dress as if it were some talisman. It would transform me into an enchantress, a goddess, and Jose Marie would be smitten and ask me to go steady with him. I kissed the back of my hand, imagining his lips on mine.

I tugged at my padded bra and put on the dress. I applied another layer of mascara and reddened my cheeks and lips. Then I slipped on my gold heels and studied myself in the mirror. I smiled, pleased with myself. Ordinarily I appeared average-looking with a pleasant round face—no bones to speak of, no strong facial characteristics that made people say: Oh, what pretty eyes, or, what a lovely mouth. Normally, I was just-average. But that night, I actually looked beautiful. I was glad I had saved the dress all summer, for the right moment, for that night.

The party was slow. The band, called "The Magnificent Seven," was off-key and the boys stayed in the patio drinking San Miguels, Rum Cokes, and a beer-gin-Coke concoction dubbed

Virgin Coke. The girls were huddled in the living room—which served as the dance floor—gossiping about Carla and the two American soldiers with her.

"I didn't want to invite her but her mother and mine are second cousins," Yolanda explained.

"Papa's going to whip me when he hears about this," whined Dolores, whom we called Turtle Face.

"They're just sitting outside, not doing anything," I ventured.

"You'll end up like Elena, Gemma," Turtle Face said. She stared at me. "So, that's your new dress by the famous Mario. By the way, where's Jose Marie?"

"He'll be here," I answered smugly, as I fussed with the folds of my skirt.

"I heard he and Mercedes are parked up in Magellan Hills. That Mercedes can probably find her way to those hills blind." Dolores' turtle mouth twisted into a little smile.

In my mind, Jose Marie plummeted from Number One to about Number Twenty. I felt angry and humiliated, and I consoled myself by thinking he would surely go to hell for necking with that cheap Mercedes.

I was forcing a smile, trying to save face, when someone asked me to dance. The band was terrible, no one was dancing, and someone was asking me to make a spectacle of myself. I glared up and caught a flash of red hair and a wide grin on an oval face. An American soldier.

The girls stared at us with unhinged mouths. I didn't know what to do so I got up to dance slow drag with the stranger. I thought I heard giggling in the room.

The American said something but the music was too loud. His mouth moved up and down, then he looked at me quizzically. I tapped my right ear and shrugged my shoulders. He tried once more and I heard, ". . . nice dress." Aside from Yolanda, he was the only person who had said my dress was nice. I smiled and he grinned wider. When the music ended, he walked me to my seat and left.

"What did the *Americano* say, Gemma? How'd it feel dancing with him?" Dolores asked.

I felt my chest constrict and I shouted, "Do I have to wash my hands so I don't catch anything deadly?" I waved my hands in front of her like a magician. "You are very provincial, do you realize that? Pro-vin-cial!" Then I left.

Outside I took a couple of deep breaths. I walked around the patio, past the boys who were getting drunk, until I found the American with another soldier and Carla.

Carla was wearing red with black net stockings. She worked as a secretary at the Base. We tagged her "fast" because she sported hickeys on her neck and dated American soldiers. It was rumoured that she went "all the way." That night her date was Marcus, a good-looking Mexican-American. Peter, who had danced with me, was his friend.

When I joined them, Carla was showing Marcus how to do butterfly kisses. She shoved her face close to Marcus' cheek and batted her eyelashes rapidly. The two boys laughed and I laughed tentatively. They were drinking Virgin Cokes and I started drinking. I was sixteen, Jose Marie and Mercedes were necking, and I could drink if I wanted to. The iced sweet drink flowed down my throat.

I was feeling like a ripe mango when Carla started telling jokes.

"There was this bar called Sally's Legs," she related between giggles, "and one afternoon, a cop stopped a bum outside the bar. 'What are you doing here?' the cop asked. 'Waiting for Sally's Legs to open so I can have a drink.'"

They laughed while I tried to figure out the joke. Carla whispered an explanation in my ear and I laughed hysterically.

"Sally's legs! I get it — Sally's legs!"

"You're drunk," Carla said.

"Am I? Am I? I've never been drunk before," I said, still laughing.

But soon I felt depraved. I was drunk, sitting there with American soldiers, laughing at dirty stories. I was truly lost. Trying to look dignified, I sat up, pulled my skirt over my knees, and folded my hands together. I studied the white wrought iron chairs that we sat on, the jasmine vine covered with sweet-smelling flowers that climbed the trellis.

I watched the two soldiers whose arms and legs flopped all over the place. They were nice-looking, with strong bodies and boyish

68

ways. I was surprised to realize that they were only a few years older than I. Still with milk on their lips, my mother would have said. They were talking now, their voices sounding like distant rain.

Peter said, "I'm tired. I just want to go home. First day in 'Nam I see these huge bundles stacked up near the plane and I lean against them. I'm smoking a cigarette like nothing's wrong, then later I find out those were dead bodies."

"Jeez!" exclaimed Marcus.

"No kidding, Marcus. Dead bodies."

"Peter, you've gotta be cool, man, or else you're not gonna make it," Marcus said. "You're feeling shitty 'cause you're going back tomorrow. Gotta be cool, man. Be like the NBC guy standing in front of a pile of dead gooks, saying, 'This is Walter Bullshit reporting from Da Nang.'" He held an imaginary microphone in front of his mouth, as if he had actually seen this happen.

"It's the waiting," Peter said. "It's draining. Like we're on a sweep last month and we're being real careful. You know somebody's going to get it and we watch our step carefully. Sweep and sweep, and you're waiting. You're so tight, then Boom! This poor guy beside me loses his leg. Just like that."

I became sad listening to them and my mind latched on to the image of Sultan's body on that dry earth. They could die too, I thought, on some brown earth someplace, far away from their homes.

"For me it's the food, man. Boy, do I miss Mama's carnitas and tamales. I'm sick of that shit they feed us." Marcus ran his tongue around his lips. "One more month, man, and I am through. I'm going home! I'm gonna stuff myself with enchiladas, rellenos, and I'm gonna cruise down Colorado Boulevard and just have a good time, you know."

"One more month, that's great, Marcus," Peter said.

"How much longer do you have to stay in Vietnam?" I asked Peter, when Carla and Marcus went dancing.

"Six months."

He became quiet and I was feeling uneasy because we were alone. But he sighed and sat back to look at the sky. "Back home," he said, "the Big Dipper's over there." He waved his hand vaguely in the air.

I tilted my head and located the Big Dipper, wondering how the constellations could move when one was in another place. A multitude of stars shimmered in the sky; the moon was a mere crescent. A soft breeze was redolent with jasmine, gardenias, and dama de noches.

Peter took a deep breath and said very softly, "That feels good." He paused then spoke in a distant voice. "It's real funny, but sometimes, in the middle of nowhere, I'll think of my baseball cards. When I was a kid, I collected baseball cards — Willie Mays, Mickey Mantle, Ted Williams — I had them all. But I don't remember what happened to them. My mind starts going through the entire house. I'll search my room, my sister's, my parents' room, even the garage. I rummage through all the desks, drawers, and cabinets. It's crazy. I've even written my Mom to ask about those cards."

He sighed, then he turned to me and said, "That's a real pretty dress."

"My friend doesn't like it very much."

"Maybe your friend's jealous because you're pretty."

I laughed remembering Turtle Face. He grinned and ran his hand through his hair. I had never before seen hair as red as the mangosteen fruit. My apprehension left me and I watched the stars with him. He liked the night and things of the night. These made him feel safe, he explained, in a way that implied he didn't feel safe too often. When we saw a falling star, he gave a quick low whistle. "Now I can make a wish," he said.

As he was pointing out Orion's Belt, he put his arm around my shoulders, his fingers brushing my nape. My heart pounded against my ribs but I didn't move or say anything. He was so close and I could smell him — a strange musky scent. He was quiet for a while then with his other hand, he turned my head toward him and he kissed me. His mouth was warm and yearning. There was a sadness to his kiss. It made me think of Sultan and how warm he had felt before he became still.

When Carla and Marcus returned, Peter kept his arm around me, but the spell was broken, the magic moment lost.

70

The next day, I listened to the American planes blasting overhead. Was Peter in one of them? I wondered. Would I ever see him again? I looked at my blue-green chiffon dress lying on a chair—it was magical after all.

Another plane zoomed overhead, making the windows rattle, leaving my soul with strange reverberations. I thought summer vacation was over. School would start. The rains would come.

Tahira Naqvi

Originally from Pakistan, Tahira Naqvi now lives in Bridgewater, Connecticut with her husband and three sons. She received an M.A. in psychology from Punjab University in 1969, and in 1984, completed an M.S. in education from Western Connecticut University where she currently teaches English.

"My husband and I arrived in the United States in 1971 with our two-month-old son and a resolve to return to Pakistan as soon as my husband had taken his Boards in Internal Medicine. After the Boards came a job, then private practice, and the resolve to return became a dream.

"But we have experienced a phenomenon which is unique to our group; as time passed we became more and more Pakistani. Away from home, we developed bonds with home that were so tangible they could not be ignored. Before long Pakistani culture, values, mores, the total way of life there, jelled to become the core of the life we were living in this country, and around this core has grown our American experience. The duality of this existence creates an enriching sense of accomplishment on the one hand, and unending internal conflicts, tensions, anxiety, and dilemmas that are at once comic and disturbing on the other. And for me, as a writer, this duality has been a blessing: it has provided me with the impetus for my writing. And when I write, I'm whole again.

"I am also an active translator of Urdu fiction. In translation I have found a connection to my culture that placates and excites at the same time, something so essential I'm drawn to it like a child to a treasure toy. Perhaps that is because I am a translation myself, an ongoing work in progress."

BRAVE WE ARE

"Mom, Ami," he asks, the little boy Kasim who is my son, who has near-black eyes and whose buck teeth give him a Bugs Bunny-look when his mouth is open, as it is now, in query, "what does hybrid mean?"

"Hybrid?" I'm watching the water in the pot very closely; the tiny bubbles on it quivering restlessly indicate it's about to come to boil. Poised over the pot, clutching a batch of straw-colored Prince spaghetti, is my hand, suspended, warm from the steam and waiting for the moment when the bubbles will suddenly and turbulently come to life.

I'm not fussy about brands, especially where spaghetti is concerned (it's all pasta, after all), but I wish there was one which would fit snugly into my largest pot; the strands bend uncomfortably, contort, embroiling themselves in something of a struggle within the confines of the pot once they've been dropped into the boiling water. Some day, of course, I must get a pot large enough to accommodate all possible lengths.

"Yeah, hybrid. Do you know what it means?"

I am compelled to tear my gaze away from the water. Kasim's face looks darker now than it did when he left for school this morning. Perhaps running up the steep driveway with the March wind flapping against his lean frame has forced the blood to rush to his face. Flushed, his face reminds me he is still only a child, 'only nine—just a baby,' as my mother often says when I scold him in her presence, arguing with him as if he were a man behaving childishly.

A new spelling word? Such a difficult word for a fourth-grader. "Are you studying plants?"

"No. But can you tell me what it means?" Impatient, so impatient, so like the water in the pot that now hisses and tumbles, asking for immediate attention. He slides against the kitchen counter and hums, his fingers beating an indecipherable rhythm on the formica, his eyes raised above mine, below mine, behind me, to the window outside which white, lavender and gray have mingled to become an untidy brown. He reaches for the cookie jar and I throw in the spaghetti.

"Well, that's a hard word. Let's see." Helplessly I watch him as he breaks a Stella Doro biscuit in his mouth and crumbs disperse, in a steady fall-out, over the counter, the kitchen tile, some getting caught in his blue-and-green striped sweater, like flies in a spider's web. "It's a sort of mixture, a combination of two different kinds of things." I know immediately 'things' is susceptible to misinterpretation; I rack my brain for a good example. If I don't hurry he's going to move away with the notion that his mother doesn't know what hybrid means.

"You mean if we mix orange juice with lemonade, it's going to become hybrid juice?" The idea has proven ticklish; he smiles, crumbs from the biscuit dangling on the sides of his face—they don't bother him as much as they bother me. I rub a hand around his lips just as he leans toward the cookie jar again; another biscuit is withdrawn. I turn down the heat under the spaghetti to medium and start chopping onions.

Today I'm making spaghetti the way my mother makes it in Lahore, like *pulao*, the way I used to make it soon after I got married; that was about the only thing I could cook then, so I took pains to prepare it to perfection. There, we call it noodles (although it's unmistakably spaghetti), and there's no tomato sauce or meatballs in or anywhere near it, no cheese either; and no one there has heard of romano or mozzarella. The idea of cheese with our recipe would surprise the people in Lahore; even the most adventurous among them would grimace.

"Well that too." And why not? My eyes smart from the sharpness of the onions; I should have washed them before chopping. "The word is used when you mix two different kinds of plants or animals, it's called cross-breeding." This gets harder and harder. I know his knowledge of 'breeding' is limited and 'cross' isn't going to help matters any.

"What's cross-whatyumaycallit?"

An example. An example that will put a seal on hybrid forever. 'My mother told me,' he should be able to claim.

Tears from the onions I have been chopping roll down my cheeks and I sniffle. The onions are for the ground lamb which

74

will be cooked with vegetables, fresh garlic, coriander, cumin, a touch of turmeric and lots of fresh ginger root. I'll combine this mixture with the boiled spaghetti and my husband and I alone will eat what I make; my sons like spaghetti the way it should be, the way it is.

Setting the knife down on the chopping board, I tear out a sheet from the roll of kitchen towels on my right and rub my eyes and nose with it. The kitchen window, which I now face as I do innumerable times during the day, is like a magic picture, ever-changing, but faithfully reflecting the movement of time and seasons. It can elevate or, when the tones on its canvas are achromatous, it heralds monotony, dullness. Right now, the sun is visible again and the white of the snow is distinguishable from the lavender of the bare, thin stalky birches, unhealthy because we haven't tended them well; sharply the sun cuts shadows on the clean, uncluttered snow.

Why does snow always remind me of the Lahore summer? Incongruent, disparate, the two seasons have so little in common. March is spring, grass flushed with verdurous largesse, roses that bloom carelessly with what seems to be unaffected, spontaneous ease, like a child's quick laugh, skies so clear, giving a new meaning to the word blue, the air you breathe carrying a coolness which is not transferable to words and can only be felt, like passion. Why do I turn to my cleaning lady, Eileen, and say, "Eileen, do you know what it's like this morning in Lahore? It's lovely, just lovely; springtime." She turns from the pot she is scrubbing in the kitchen sink, the one in which I burnt chicken the night before because I was watching M.A.S.H. with the boys and forgot all about it, and looks at me incredulously, (as if she didn't already know, hadn't already heard it from me a hundred times): "No kidding. Really?"

An example, yes. "Now take an apple. A farmer may cross-breed a McIntosh with a Golden Yellow and get something which is a little bit like both. That'll be a hybrid apple. Get it?"

"You mean the apple's going to have a new name, like McIntosh Yellow?"

"Yes." I return to the onions, making a mental note to turn to the spaghetti next, which, langurously swelled now, will have to be drained soon.

"But what about animals? You said there's cross-something in animals too."

"Yes there is. A cow from one family can be bred with a steer from another family, and they'll end up with a calf that's like both of them." I wash my hands and he skips on the floor, dance-like steps, his arms akimbo.

"But man's an animal too, right? Do people cross-breed?"

He's humming again. I know what it is now: "Suzie Q/ Suzie Q/ I love you/ I love you/ O Suzie Q!" It's from a song on his older brother's tape, a catchy tune, sort of sticks with you so you can't stop humming it. The boys were amused when I expressed interest in the song; what do I know about music, their kind of music? I tried to bribe my oldest son once, nearly three years ago, to practice an Urdu gazal by Ghalib and, egged on by the hundred dollars I was offering him (a bribe really, rather than a reward), he did start, mastered two lines from the first stanza ("It was not fated that I should meet my beloved/ Life would have merely prolonged my waiting"), and then, unable to sustain his interest (despite the twenty-five-dollar-a-stanza rate), he abandoned the project. "The words are too difficult to follow," he said, "the music's easy, but I can't keep up with the lyrics." And I would've given him the money too; actually I had decided I would give him all of it after the second stanza.

"Does that mean Mary is hybrid?" Kasim continues, without waiting for my answer.

I turn the heat under the spaghetti to low—so what if it's a bit overdone. The yellow-white strands jump at each other in frantic embraces, hurried as if there's no time to be lost.

"Mary? What are you talking about?" I know exactly what he's talking about, his vagueness passes through the sieve in my head and comes out a clarity, I fill in the blanks, uncannily, never ceasing to be surprised at how this process works.

"You know, Mary Ahmed, Dr. Ahmed's daughter, she's in my class?"

Yes, I know Mary well. Her full name is Marium. Her father, Anwar Ahmed, and my husband went to the same medical college in Pakistan, and they were also together at Grasslands Hospital in New York during their internship years. His wife, Helen, is English, a few years older than I, very tall, very pale, once a nurse, now dividing her time between weekly meetings of the Bridgetown Historical Society and sessions of the Friends of Bridgetown Library. We're good friends, Helen and I, and at least once a month we meet for lunch at a restaurant in neighboring Newtown, or Woodbury. She'll tell me how difficult Anwar is sometimes, how inflexible on certain matters ("He just won't agree to meet Richard's girlfriend," she'll say), and although I know why his son's girlfriend is getting the cold shoulder from Anwar, I'll shake my head and affirm that inflexibility, offering my own husband's as an example; together to do what all women do most successfully: spend a great deal of time talking about men.

Helen is attractive, and her eyes are so blue they seem transparent. Mary is their youngest child, the older two children boys, and I remember when Mary was born, Anwar said, "We're going to call her Marium, it's a name familiar to everyone." Familiar and convenient (he meant, but didn't want to upset Helen), since it's tri-religious. That doesn't sound right, but if we can say bisexual, we can say tri-religious too. Why not? After all, Islam, Christianity and Judaism all profess a claim to this name. Before the child was quite one, 'Marium' was shortened to 'Mary.'

Kasim is sitting at the breakfast table now, some of his earlier energy dissipated. A small piece of Stella Doro lies before him forlornly on the table and he fusses with it slowly, obviously unwilling to consume the biscuit now, content only to play with it. "You know, her mother's English, her father's Pakistani like us, and she's got dark skin and blue eyes."

"Yes she does have blue eyes, doesn't she?" I grapple with something to blunt the sharpness of his next statement which I anticipate and know I cannot repel.

"Well, she's hybrid too, isn't she?"

Brave we are, we who answer sententiously questions that spill forth artlessly from the mouth of nine-year-old purists, questions that can neither be waivered nor dismissed with flippant ambiguity. Vigilant and ever alert, we must be ready with our answers.

"Technically speaking, she is. Wait. I mean, you could say she is.

But we don't use this word for people." It does have a poetic ring to it. "Honey, don't say anything like this to her, okay?"

"Why? Is it a swear?"

"No! Of course it isn't. It's just a word not used for people, that's all. Understand?"

"But what do you call them then? Mary's like the McIntosh Yellow, isn't she? Isn't she? Her name's Mary Ahmed, isn't it?"

"Yes, sweetheart, it is. But there's nothing wrong with that name; a name's a name, that's all." Kasim looked contemplative. I know he doesn't quite believe what I have just said. He's telling himself, *Her mother's English, her father's Pakistani, and she has dark skin like mine, blue eyes like her mother's, so she's hybrid—Mom doesn't know.*

"She's a person, Kas, not lemonade or orange juice. Anyway, you didn't tell me where you heard the word. Is it on your spelling list for this week?"

"No, no. Mrs. Davis was reading to us something about plants in the *Weekly Reader*. It's not homework." He shrugs, abandons the Stella Dora and, humming, leaves the kitchen.

"Get to homework now," I call after him, wondering if there's an equivalent of 'hybrid' in Urdu, a whole word, not one or two strung together in a phrase to mean the same thing. Offhand I cannot think of one.

Without meaning to I throw some oregano into the boiling spaghetti. I shouldn't have; how's oregano going to taste with coriander and cumin? Well, no matter—it's too late now.

After I have drained the spaghetti I will take some out for the meat mixture, saving the rest for my children. Then I'll add to our portion (my husband's and mine), the lamb and vegetable mixture and turn everything over ever so gently, making sure that the spaghetti isn't squelched: the strands must remain smooth, elusive, and separate.

Tina Koyama

Tina Koyama, a third-generation Japanese American, is a Seattle native. She received her B.A. and M.A. in English from the University of Washington.

Her work has appeared in The Forbidden Stitch, Breaking Silence: An Anthology of Asian American Poets, The Seattle Review, Willow Springs Magazine, Cotton Boll/Atlanta Review, Intro 13, Intro 14, The Arts, Washington *and other periodicals and anthologies.*

She once folded 1,000 cranes as part of Ploughshares' Million Cranes peace project for the 40th anniversary of the bombing of Hiroshima. She recently completed folding another 1,000 cranes that will decorate her wedding as she marries the man with the "soft grey voice" in October 1989.

FAMILY DINNER

"Thank you for the turkey. Thanks for our health too, and we hope next year will be a good one." Seated before us at the head of the table, hands folded, my father fidgets like a child.

Startled, I glance at him through the side of my eye, then stare at my plate. For the benefit of the man I've brought to Thanksgiving dinner, my father has said grace for the first time in his life. For the moment, we let neither the 20-pound turkey in the table's center nor the wet-earth fragrance of matsutake divert our attention. Our faces, our hands, even steam from the rice are suspended. I am annoyed, embarrassed and moved by his awkward sincerity.

Suddenly the moment cracks open like an egg, and all arms are in motion: my mother fluffing the rice, my father pouring champagne, the candied yams, broccoli, soy sauce, rolls, corn, stuffing, matsutake gravy and butter criss-crossing from hand to hand.

My mother uncoils the cord on the electric knife and prepares to assign carving duty. Some years she announces that it's "American style" for the man of the house to have the honor and presents the knife to my father. Once she challenged my sister to try it because a woman should learn to do it too. And sometimes she does the task herself, efficiently separating the dark meat from the light on the platter, all the while apologizing that she should someday learn the correct way to carve.

Tonight she turns to the man beside me, her eyes neither asking for help nor bestowing an honor. She offers Greg the knife as she might fresh towels or a cup of coffee. In her shy English, she tells him how to work the switch on the electric knife.

What does she know of this blue-eyed man, a foot taller than herself, cheerfully slicing white meat, except what her last unmarried child tells her with flushed animation one moment, self-conscious lack of detail the next? What do I know of him except his soft grey voice, the passion with which he launches a balloon from the doorstep or touches the back of my neck?

Dinner is early enough tonight that Lake Washington still mimics the sky's ink-blue.

"Let's have a toast!" my father shouts. [Everyone clinks someone else's glass.] The only glass I can't reach is my father's, but he doesn't notice.

Or at least we both pretend not to. With my father, it's easy to pretend something doesn't matter, to let my mother be the buffer between the words we don't say. We argue freely and loudly about who should be president or the morality of killing animals for sport. But how often has my mother been the one to say he's proud of my poems even when he doesn't read them all the way through? Does it startle him to see me as a woman? Or am I still the child who screams for him to kill a spider on the wall?

Done with the polite nonsense of champagne, my father pours V.O. for the Men—himself and my sister's husband—and offers some to Greg. He accepts, passing my father's first test. In my father's home, this sturdy brick house where I grew up, a real man drinks hard liquor, doesn't help with dishes and plays pool in the basement to scratchy recordings of Japanese music.

This could be a long night.

"I betcha never had this stuff, huh, Greg?" my father says with his mouth full, passing him a plate of raw squid and a pair of chopsticks. The smooth white flesh shines like glass.

Greg crooks an eyebrow, says, "I'll try anything." As the V.O. pours and my father's laugh grows louder, he occasionally lets slip words in Japanese to him. For the first time I notice how much my parents' two languages interchange from listener to listener, word to word. How easily I've always understood both languages, answered in one, sometimes listened to neither.

My parents, my sister, her husband—they all try hard to be normal. So do I.

I poke around inside the turkey for the wishbone and, finding it, offer one end to Greg. I start to give him a flirtatious look when I feel the weight of my family's scrutiny. "I have a wish for both of you," my mother says with quiet mystery. Does he notice my wince? Like saplings too green and wet to burn, the oily bone tears apart rather than breaks.

On the sundeck, bonsai trees paint dark silhouettes against the sky.

*

In September I sat by a fireplace in Minnesota as Greg's father told childhood stories. The state park cabin smelled of cedar and burning birch. His sister worked a needlepoint of geese in flight; his mother and aunt paged through magazines. We all settled into the deep worn furniture, the warmth, the contentment that follows a big dinner and a day of hiking among Norway pines so old they wear scars from more than one forest fire.

"Dad, tell about when you made firecrackers for the Fourth of July." Like a child, Greg made requests. "What about the time your dog heard wild noises outside?"

Outside, a single loon call rose from Lake Itasca, pure and clear in the night. We all held our breath, but no others followed.

In the circle of his family, even as I felt warmth pass from the logs to hands, from words to words, I shifted back and forth inside myself, now lover and guest, now stranger and intruder. Simultaneously I looked in from a window and looked out from one. The way orange deepens to red and red to purple at dusk, what I know and love of him joined a spectrum of White Castles and trains and Minnesota farms, a past I have no part of, opened to me.

Wanting to hold his hand but feeling too self-conscious, wanting to give them all something in return, I started folding origami cranes. "If I fold the necks short, like this," I told them, "they become loons."

If I fold one thousand cranes I get one wish, I thought. Nine hundred ninety-five to go.

As we walked back to our cabin, the sky was full of more stars than I've ever seen. The flashlight picked out two startled animal eyes in the darkness. I never felt so small. So whole.

*

My sister and I clear the dishes, the turkey now missing two legs, most of its breast and all of its dignity. The pieces of the broken wishbone lie between two plates. My mother runs the dishwasher and scrapes turkey skin, bits of rice and half a dinner roll into the dog's dish. A floor below, three billiard cues crack against the balls. I expect the usual bad recordings to vibrate the floor, but the music we hear surprises me. My father owns two tapes that are not Japanese: Crystal Gayle and Neil Diamond. Tonight Crystal's the lucky one.

I sneak downstairs. A little self-conscious, Greg takes billiard instructions from my father, who belches with glee. Full of turkey, whiskey and happiness, my father closes his cataractal eye, aims the cue stick. He misses and groans in mock agony.

It's Greg's turn. I watch his long fingers around the pool cue, the angle of his body leaning over the table. I imagine how his hands will feel tonight, his palms on my face, my back. In candle darkness, his eyes will look more grey than blue, at once tender and whimsical, grey as the horizon behind Lake Washington. Our skins will be bubbles, membranes so thin they collide without breaking, neither liquid nor solid nor gas, the spheres of our souls joined by one surface, nothing between them but heartbeat.

"Don't it make my brown eyes blue," croons Crystal. Making another tally-mark by his name, my father snickers, "Aw, whatsamatter, can't you beat a half-blind man?" He winks his good eye at Greg. The man his youngest daughter brought home smiles at me as I slip back upstairs.

*

Two shopping bags strain at the handles from the weight of sliced turkey wrapped in foil, jars of soup, pumpkin pie, cottage cheese cartons of candied yams and stuffing—one bag for each of us. My mother checks the jar lids once more as Greg and I pull on our jackets, say good-night, good-night. She makes sure I haven't forgotten my gloves. We all feel the sting of November air through the opened door.

When I lived here, she watched me walk out this door with boys-almost-men, then men, each a tiny hope as much for herself as for me. She'd sent us off with good-bye, good-bye, have a good time, drive carefully, what time will you be home—all wrapped in the package of her wave as she stood in the driveway, her face full of anticipation and anxiety.

Tonight she reminds the man I love now to heat the turkey broth with noodles, grasps his hand with both of hers and shyly thanks him for joining us.

As I pull away from the curb, I watch her in the rearview mirror, her hand waving high above her head.

The freeway to his house is dotted with headlights, cars full of people full of food. We both heave sighs, mine more of relief than contentment. The C-shaped moon tries to hide behind parting clouds. Streetlights throw white lines into Lake Union. I want to sigh again, but something still bumps against my heart. "What was it you wished for?" I ask him.

"Huh?"

"The wishbone. What did you wish for?"

Stars blink. The sky, the water, the freeway—wherever I look spots of light move in the darkness. "It doesn't matter," he says, squeezing my shoulder playfully. "It's probably the same wish."

Sara J. Lau

I was born and raised in Northern California. I wrote Long Way Home *in this mother's voice because she was the only one who could tell the story. I often ask myself why my mother's immigrant past has such a hold on my thoughts. It shouldn't. After all, my mother never talks about her life in China; only present time matters. I suppose her very silence draws me to wonder. I am always reminded that this is not her country and will never be. Yet when I was growing up, I didn't really consider the pain of assimilation, though it was always right in front of me, in my parents' alienation from American culture, in my own ignorance of their traditions.*

I write because I too am unsettled, by contradictions that I cannot leave unchallenged. When Gloria Anzaldúa says "How hard it is for us (as women of color) to think we can choose to become writers, much less feel and believe that we can," I recall that I did think, feel and believe that I could (which may attest to my naivete more than anything else). I need to believe that my writing is necessary, that I have the power to speak not only for myself, but for those who do not speak for themselves. My mother's eloquence does not translate in English; it has only the power to move me and those who know my mother's story; she would view her life as unexamined by herself, and thus unarticulable in her own voice. (I think differently.) That's my challenge as a writer, to bring her stories—and what must then become our stories—to light."

(The quote from Anzaldúa is from This Bridge Called My Back.)

LONG WAY HOME

My daughter Julie wasn't in school today.

—This must be a mistake, I say to the lady at the desk. Julie Chow, C-H-O-W? She's in grade nine. She never misses school.

—No mistake, there's only one, she says, not looking down at her list. Was she expecting you? No, how could she, I surprise myself by coming. The drive here, my only thought is how happy she'll be to see me. My Julie can miss one day of school, I'd say. We can spend the day together. Instead she's gone.

—You check again, I say. She goes to the back room. I sit. Julie's my baby, a good kid. Not like my other two. Jeffrey, the oldest, changed his major five times. Still at school, doesn't know what he wants to become. Not like Darlene, the middle one, trouble-maker. She quit school and moved out of the house two weeks ago. Living across town with her lazy-bum friend Thao. Today she's flying to New York, then maybe all the way to China. Going back, she calls it. The last fight we had, she said, I want to go back to China. I said, how you go back to some place you never been? But she didn't listen. Julie's the only one who listens anymore.

I look at the magazines on the side table, *Parent, Family Circle, Good Housekeeping*. Americans need magazines to tell them how to take care of their kids and clean house. Now that it's just Julie and my husband at home, the house never gets dirty. Julie helps, she cooks and cleans. The night Darlene left, it was just me and Julie home, making dinner. Her father worked late as usual. Darlene been back a week, on vacation from school. All week she been quiet, not talking back. At first I thought she was sick. Then I found her ironing and folding a load of clothes I washed, not just picking out her own. Julie said, Darlene really wants to help you with the housework. I watched Darlene wearing clothes I bought her, things she never wore before: that night, a pink blouse, matching pant-suit. This from a girl who dressed like a bum on the street. She's not sick, I said to myself, she just wants something. The longer I thought, the more it distracted me. Worse than when she talked back, I thought. Talking back's just words, questions she yells at me so she can answer them herself. Easy game to figure. But what to do when she's tricky, sneaks around, acts like she's changed? All week I wondered, what's she want? To disrupt the household, lead Julie, who don't know any better, to follow her? I could hear them whisper each night in the room they shared. I laid in my bed and let them talk. I thought, my Julie will tell me what she says in the morning. Meantime, I burned incense to fill the air with something familiar, ward off the bad luck of Darlene's secrets. I prayed to the Goddess, keep Darlene out of trouble till she's back in school. I made sure Julie stayed close to me. I thought that would be enough.

We were eating dinner when Darlene walked in with her news.

—I need to talk to you, she said.

—Eating's not the time for talking, I said. You let your sister digest her food. For a second, the old Darlene flashed up, talk-back angry, words ready to fly. But Julie interrupted.

—I'm almost done, she said. Can't you just let her say what she wants, Mom? For a moment the only sound was Julie's chopsticks clicking.

—So talk, I said. I got up to clear the dishes. Darlene had nothing to say until Julie nodded at her. Then she started.

—I'm not used to explaining myself, she said. I get that from you, I think. But let me try. She folded her hands, bent her head down like she was praying, American-style. Then she told me how she wasn't learning anything at school, waste of her time, my money, how she wanted to leave, to go travel. Leaning forward, she unlocked her hands to mark out the places she saw, the distances she felt she could cross. Then she looked straight at me and said "China," like it was a home she could go back to. She had learned Mandarin at school, knew a little Cantonese from home. She began talking faster, it seemed she'd been thinking a long time about leaving. Julie kept nodding, like she would never get tired of hearing her sister talk.

—You quit school? You want to leave? was all I could say.

—Not yet, but eventually, she said. Then in a rush: Don't you see, I'm going back to find myself, understand who I am. I'm going back to find *you*, our family, the village you grew up in. All the things you didn't want to talk about, she said. She turned to Julie, you understand, don't you?

I watched her talk to her sister. She thought all she had to do was say "China" and I'd send her off with oranges and blessings. I dropped the plate I was rinsing in the soapy water.

—You want to find me, you find me here, I said. You want to find yourself? You go find a job instead, you go find a husband. Don't talk to me about China.

That made both of them sit up. Then Darlene turned to Julie and said, I knew this was going to happen, didn't I tell you?

—Don't you talk to Julie neither. You so backwards. All those years at school and you don't learn nothing—

Darlene jumped out of her chair, still saying, I knew this was going to happen, I knew it. I pushed Julie behind me.

—You want to go so bad? I said. You go. Go, Johnny, go. You talk big, but no action.

She was already half-way to the door. Julie tried to go after her, but I held her arm.

—Ungrateful, no respect, I said to Darlene, your father and me worked so hard for your future. You think anybody there looks out for you like we do?

She slammed the door. Julie seemed shocked, she shook her head.

—She shouldn't have left like that. She just shouldn't have left.

Julie understood. She and I, we always thought the same. Darlene was wrong. Children supposed to respect elders. Who takes care of the parents when they get old? But Julie still looked upset. Maybe I kicked Darlene out, but she was all set to go, I thought. She's the one who wanted to leave so bad she didn't care who she left behind.

—See how far she goes, I said. I bet you she comes back tomorrow.

I said this for Julie not to feel so sad. For myself, I don't need that troublemaker. She did come back the next day, but only to pack. Julie was at school. That was two weeks ago. She hasn't been back since.

What's taking so long to find Julie? I think. All day, in my head, I see pictures of Julie at school. They keep me company when I clean house, take care of my business. The drive here, I imagine her next to me, so full of the surprise of my coming to get her, she can't think of anything else. She touches me, looks back to see if this is real, to see if we're moving. She waves good-bye to the school and settles down by me. We can go anywhere, I say. This is our day. She feels what I feel.

I can't wait anymore. I walk around the counter to look for the lady. Just then she comes back with Julie's folder.

— Behind the desk, she says. She shoos me back with the folder.

— Where's Julie? I say.

— According to our records, Mrs. Chow, your daughter's missed school the past four days.

I shake my head. This can't be.

— Julie's not that kind of girl. She likes school. She tells me all the time. You must have made a mistake.

The lady pushes the folder at me.

— We haven't made the mistake. Your daughter hasn't been to school all week. You, of all people, ought to know. It's your signature on each of these excuses.

She spreads them out on her desk. She's right, my name is on every note. The stories are different, but the handwriting is all the same.

* * *

I drive for twenty-five minutes looking for Julie. Then I remember, each day she comes home from where she goes. In my kitchen, I switch the light on to check the notes. *Julie is feeling unwell this morning. . . . Please excuse Julie, today is her grandfather's funeral. . . . Julie is taking a trip to visit a sick relative. . . .* I line up my copies to match the writing on birthday cards, Happy Mother's Day letters from Julie. No mistake. I switch the light off to save energy, then sit where I can see the door. The quiet makes this room seem smaller and darker. I feel the quiet press on me, growing heavier as I wait. Nothing to reflect off the dark cabinets. I'm always hustling in the kitchen, no time to sit like now, I get used to the noises. Dinner time, the whole family at the table. When they were younger, Jeffrey and Darlene sometime raced to see who finished dinner fastest, because I told them, eat first, then talk. Then while we still ate, they'd tell riddles and jokes, try to trick

90

me into talking. How long ago was that? I wonder. Other times, mostly new year's, I'd set places at the table for the ancestors, moon cakes and tea, extra chairs sitting empty for them. One of my kids, must be Darlene—she asks such questions—said, they come all the way from China? And that's all you give them. I told her, they don't come to eat but to see if we remembered to set a place for them. Their visit means prosperity, I said. I think how we're not so regular about holidays anymore. My husband says he's tired, it's high time the kids took care of these responsibilities. My husband just don't care to keep touch with old ways. It's hard to keep up when you're so far away.

Sitting in the kitchen, I wonder, when was the last time they all eat here, my kids? Few years back, I remember each time one of them left home to live at school, how hard it was to get through meal-times. Darlene used to sit across the table from me. No way I could miss not seeing her there. After a time, though, it was like they were never here in the first place. Not so much that I don't miss them, I just get so used to the feeling of missing all the time, I forget what it's like to have. I read the notes again and think of the Julie who wrote these stories.

Thirty-seven years I been in this country, since I was fifteen. When I first came, I stayed with my sister and her husband. The rest of the family lived in Canada. I tell my mother I miss hearing her voice in the mornings. I worked after school, saving money for a visit. She says, Start your own family, you don't need us. When I tried to remember what my mother sound like, that's what I hear. I give my sister the money to put in the bank. No more use to save. Next time I see my mother, I visit with my husband, Jeffrey and Darlene not babies anymore. When I asked her, she didn't remember saying this, but she agreed, that's how the country is. Not like before, in China, where grandparents, parents, kids lived in the same house. There everyday they leave a place for the ancestors, those still living and those passed away. Here, nothing to do but get used to this place. No looking at what's past. It just makes you wander after ghosts, looking for something that isn't there anymore. Look ahead, she said. So I did.

How come then, I want to ask, Julie tells me lies to get out of school? How come Darlene don't care to come home? How come she – now my Julie too – want to throw away the future we give them? I want to say to my mother: I never told them any different story than the one you told me.

I hear a key in the door. Julie steps in, head bent like she's tired, carrying her school bag. It seems just like she's coming back from a long day at school. I sit for a moment, thinking she has. She walks into the kitchen before she sees me, smile on her face, not sad at all. That surprises me, lifts the weight then drops it to press again.

– How was school today? I ask.

– Mom, I didn't see you. She hugs me, still smiling. She's thin, but strong, not leaning on me at all. I take her hand before she backs off.

– What did you do in school today? I ask. She pulls away to sit in the chair across from mine. Tilts her head back, thinking.

– I learned about geography, she says, then glances away. Very interesting to see how far places are.

I don't answer. She goes on chattering about distances, playing with her braids. I watch her mouth move as she tells her story, not listening to what she says. All morning I worried, and here she comes home with these stories. Always a quick talker, I used to be so proud of her, mouth so clever.

– So you had a good day at school? I say.

– Yes, I did, she says, nodding.

I close my eyes. I wish for the silence again, these lies weigh too heavy.

– Mom, are you okay? she asks. She's leaning forward, afraid now. I have her attention. You look kind of tired.

This is the Julie I know, looking at me in the eye, the only one who asks me how I feel. The same Julie who tells me about classes she was never in.

– It's nothing, I say. She comes around to my side.

– I have some news for you. Maybe this'll cheer you up, she says, smiling, and I watch her. I don't know what to think. Today my English teacher said I had the best paper in class, in all of her classes. She read it out loud and said, tell your mother she should be very proud of you.

Another lie, I think. More stories. I stare at her, hard. Just like Darlene, saying one thing, doing another. I think of how I came to school to cheer her up, how I worried all morning for nothing. And all the time, she was cutting school, not sad about her sister leaving. She doesn't even remember, it seems.

—Aren't you happy, Mom? she says, kneeling.

—Today your sister's going away.

—I know, she says and nods. Is that what's making you so sad? Don't worry, she's going to be alright. Besides, we don't need her. You said that.

Lying again. Why's she so happy coming home, when I thought she was the one who missed Darlene?

—I thought you might be sad about your sister, I say. I visited you at school. You weren't there. Gone all week, they said—

—Let me explain—She looks down. Just like Darlene, trying to get away, I think. Then it hits me.

—You been seeing Darlene, right? Okay, if you want to see her, you can see her all the time. You go with her.

* * *

I pull Julie by the ear to the car. Mom, mom she keeps saying over and over. I'm so heat up I press the gas too much and choke the engine.

—Don't you 'mom' me. You get yourself a new mom.

—I just told you what you wanted to hear, she says.

—Put your seat-belt on. Zip your mouth. Talk is cheap, action counts.

I concentrate on driving. She still doesn't know what's going on. But I see the whole picture. It's no good to tell her not to go after Darlene. I could talk till my mouth is dry. Cow climb a tree before anyone listens to what I say. So I don't say nothing.

Darlene's staying with Thao, she's Vietnamese, came over with her mother during the war. Dropped out of high school, now she runs around with white boys. No future, those people. I parked down the street last week and saw Darlene on the front step with some of them, just sitting in the sun. Doing nothing, the whole afternoon. Is that what Julie wants? I think. I look at her, corner of my eye, she's looking down at her lap. She could have been there that afternoon with those people. I step on the gas, take the short cut. I park across the street, cross the yard pulling Julie along. All the curtains are shut. Looks like nobody's home, but I know better. Darlene told me Thao's mom speaks no English, never goes out. I'm not going till I see Darlene, tell her all the things I've saved up the past two weeks. If she leaves, never comes back, I'll be left to carry them. Why you try to take my Julie away? I want to say. Why you want to go so far, never come home again? What you think to find?

I ring the doorbell, lean on it. Nobody answers. I bang on the door.

—You come out of there. I know you're still here. You hear me.

—Mother, Julie says.

I rattle the doorknob. She tugs my sleeve.

—I don't want to go anywhere, I just wanted to see her. Don't you miss her? You don't want her to go without—

—Too late, I say and pull my arm away. When you go, you take your sister with you, I yell. I don't miss nobody, I say to myself.

Not going to miss someone who might not come back. That's what I'll say when she opens the door.

Someone on the other side unlocks the door, opens it just enough to look out. It's Thao, not Darlene. But I can hear someone moving behind her.

—Tell Darlene I want to talk to her.

—I can't—she says, shaking her head. She left for the airport two hours ago. She's gone.

She tries to shut the door, but I push on it.

—I have to see her, I say.

—I told you already she's gone, she says, almost in a whisper. Her plane's leaving in half-an-hour. Now go away. Please, leave us alone.

Julie's pulling on me to go. I hear whispering behind the door. Thao turns her head. I push hard on the door, it opens, and I see Thao's mom in night-clothes and stained slippers. She scolds us in Vietnamese, eyes dart from me to Thao, then all round the room, like she hears someone calling her. All the while tears roll down her face.

Thao steps in front of her, turns her back to me.

—Go, get out of here.

Julie leads me down the steps. I lean on her. Crazy woman, I think, nobody listens. I feel the weight then, all the things I never said to Darlene, now no chance.

In the car, Julie waits for me to start the engine. Where do we go now, I wonder.

—Mom, I'm not going to leave you. I promise, she says, staring straight ahead. I know what she sees: Thao, her arm around her mother. Remembering too when she said goodbye to Darlene. Julie lies, she doesn't know it, but she will leave me.

She reaches out and squeezes my hand.

—Where are we going now, she asks. Home?

—Not yet, I say. I think, I don't want to walk through those dark rooms yet.

—If you want, Julie says slowly. I know the name of the plane Darlene's taking. I just want to see her. Maybe we can make it if we hurry.

I nod, and we start out. Julie still believes we have enough time. It seems almost like we intended all along to see her off. Maybe I did. On the highway, I turn to look at Julie. What did Darlene ever do for you, I think, that I couldn't?

—What did you do when you went to see her? I ask.

Julie waits so long, I think she hasn't heard me.

—Nothing special—nothing different—

I press the pedal down, until we're racing along the highway. It's too late to catch her plane. But I drive on. I shift my eyes from the road to the sky. She can't speak Cantonese, I think, how's she going to know what's our village? Who can tell her where we lived, point to the house that's not there anymore? Gone long time, any family. If she finds them, do they remember us, those who left? We didn't look back, no reason for them to look for us now. No one waits to take her in, no place sits at the table for her.

Julie squeezes my hand, points out the window.

—Look, a sign: Airport, 1/2 mile. She leans forward, still hoping.

I hold my breath, watch the planes lift into the air.

Ibarionex R. Perello

Wen-Wen C. Wang

I'm twenty-two years old, and this is my first publication outside of the San Francisco Bay Area. I spent the past four years at laboratory benches and library cubicles, surrounded by petri dishes, spectrophotometers and six-point-two-pound books. I co-wrote my first major volume seven years ago—a totally unstructured three hundred page screenplay—and I've been writing for fun ever since.

I graduated in 1989 from the University of California at Berkeley with a bachelor's degree in microbiology & immunology and a minor in English. I will spend the coming year teaching English at Beijing University in the People's Republic of China.

Besides plating bacteria and scribbling on paper, I enjoy swimming in the rain; napping in sunshine; and spending lots of time with my family, friends and my dog Rocho.

96

BACON AND COFFEE

With a sigh I begin. "Went out the front door, took a few steps, found a piece of chicken skin to mend my leather pants."

"Go on, go on," my grandmother urges, "you're doing just fine."

"If it *is* chicken skin, I'll mend my leather pants," I say, sighing again, "if it *isn't* chicken skin, I don't have to mend my pants."

"Not bad, not bad," she approves, nodding her head slowly, deeply. "Your Chinese isn't as bad as I thought. Let's try another one."

Every time my grandmother visits, she makes me translate something, just to test me out and keep me on my toes. The next one is too hard, way too fast. Another tongue twister, something about cold tofu. I just smile and shake my head, turning back to my cooking. Gramma seats herself behind me at the kitchen table, silently sipping her coffee.

It's too quiet. Just the snapping and popping of bacon in hot grease. *She's* too quiet. I don't even have to turn around; I know what she's doing. She's staring at me, staring at my hair, thinking, "gee, isn't it red for a Chinese girl." The bacon doesn't need to be flipped, but I flip it anyway.

"Two healthy parents with black hair," she begins, "and the girl gets red hair." She's thinking "gee, she doesn't look like my granddaughter, does she. Orangutans have red hair; Chinese have black hair." I reach across the counter and turn the radio up. Otis Redding sings about sitting on the dock of a bay.

My mom floats in from the bathroom and sits at the kitchen table, twirling a long black curl around her finger. Then she gets up, walks over and turns the volume down. I say, "Mom, I like this song," and I turn the volume back up. Now my grandmother gets up, walks over and turns the radio off.

"Let's talk," she suggests, "we're not talking. Why do we bother getting together if we're not going to talk?" I invited them here for a reason, but I don't feel like talking about it yet. So I tell them this is my apartment, this is my radio, I can turn the volume up if I want to. I turn the radio back on, wondering why I'm acting this way. I can hear my grandmother thinking "gee, what an insolent brat." She turns the radio off. I turn it on. She turns it off. I turn it on. I look at my mom. She has no lips. Just a thin horizontal line between her nose and her chin. This only happens when she's mad. Still glaring at me, she yanks the cord out of the wall, wraps it around the radio and carries it off to the bedroom, her translucent white gown floating behind her.

Gramma sits down at the table and tucks the paper napkin under her chin. She's got tiny eyes, so she thinks I don't notice, but I can see her eyes scanning the apartment. I wonder if the world looks any smaller to someone with such tiny eyes.

She's checking out my furniture. I know she doesn't like it. Furniture should be wood. Real wood. Dark wood carved by hand and coated with wax. I have a second-hand couch, cream with a print of giant pastel insects. I know she doesn't like it.

Today she's wearing a thick goldish-brown robe. Like the color your apple turns if you take a bite and let it sit too long. It looks silky. I hate the touch of cold silk in the mornings. No one in their right mind would put a bamboo pattern like that on real silk. It probably isn't silk. Polyester. It's probably polyester satin. I hate the touch of polyester.

"Put your robe on," she says, suddenly aware that I'm staring at her. "There's a draft in here." I look down at my fuschia tee-shirt, extra extra large. There's a poem on the front, written by Peter in black ink when we first started going out. Roses are red, violets are blue, You think that I'm sexy, I'm glad that you do.

"Put on a robe," she repeats.

"I'm not cold," I say, still looking at my shirt.

"You don't have to troop around the house naked. No one here's going to look at you."

"I'm not cold," I say a little louder.

"Ai-ya. If you're sick during finals and get straight C's . . ."

"I'm not cold." We've never had a meal without arguing about something. If I tell them now, we're going to fight about it. If I wait and tell them later, they'll wonder why I waited, and we'll end up fighting about it anyway.

I slap the pancakes and bacon onto three plates and bring them over to the table. I notice my grandmother poking at the bacon as

I pour the coffee. "Nice plates," Gramma says, fingering the dime store specials. She likes the color. Chinese think that red means prosperity or something. It's the only color the store had left.

Mom sits down and starts straightening the silverware, making the fork and the knife and the spoon all perfectly parallel. Gramma doesn't like using more than one utensil per meal. "Chopsticks are best," she would say between mouthfuls. "Get stranded in the woods, find a couple twigs, and an Asian can still eat with dignity." But if you're stranded in the woods, there won't be anyone around to notice.

I sit down and begin to eat, wrapping two slices of wet bacon in a pancake and eating it with my fingers. I don't have to look up. I know they're both staring at me. Normally my mom might say something, but this is my apartment. My grandmother opens her mouth, sticking her tongue out just a little, just beyond the edge of her teeth, placing a square inch of bacon on her tongue. Now her tongue retracts back into her mouth with the square of bacon on top. It seems like such a complicated way to eat. I take another bite of my bacon sandwich and watch as she repeats the process, this time her brows wrinkled and her eyes staring at the ceiling. She looks perplexed.

"What is this?" she asks, a little piece of bacon flying out of her mouth and landing somewhere in my plate.

"It's bacon," I say, looking for the trajectory among my pancakes.

"This is not bacon. What is it?"

"It's bacon!" I repeat, raising my voice. Gramma looks at her plate, shaking her head. She cuts a pancake in half. I turn to my mother. "Mom, what does this taste like to you?"

"I'm pretty sure it's bacon," my mom admits dabbing bacon grease and vermillion lipstick from the corner of her mouth. Gramma picks up a slice with her fingers, waving it at me as she talks.

"This is not bacon. It doesn't look like bacon, it doesn't taste like bacon, it's not bacon."

"Okay," I confess, "it's got some soybeans in it."

"Then it's not bacon." She smiles wryly. "Bacon comes from the rear end of a pig. Soy beans come from a plant. Why do you call it bacon if it's not bacon?"

I take another bite and stare out the window at the people walking two stories below. There's a man down there, and a boy. I can barely hear the man yelling, the boy's dog barking back. Wouldn't it be funny if a pancake fell out of the sky and hit one of them. My grandmother hates me. She hates me because I'm a girl with red hair. If I were a girl with black hair, she might like me a little more. If I were a boy with no hair, she'd love me. That's the way these Chinese traditionalists are.

"One of these days I'll fry you a couple strips of real bacon," Gramma offers, "nice and dry, extra thick."

"They don't sell that extra thick stuff anymore," my mom explains. I have no idea what they're talking about. This stuff looks pretty thick to me.

"Sure they do," my grandmother replies, pushing her finger into a pancake, waiting for the dough to spring back.

"No they don't, Ma. I've been to the store, I checked. They don't sell that anymore, that extra thick stuff."

"Well, if you go to the butcher shop, they do."

"Ma, no one goes to butcher shops anymore."

"I do."

"Well that's you. Everyone's been going to grocery stores for the past hundred years, except you."

"Well maybe that's why my bacon tastes better than theirs. Or yours," she says, smiling at me.

I chew my bacon, thinking this really does taste pretty bad. My mom chews hers, making little sounds and pretending that it tastes good. Gramma just pushes the food around and around on her plate.

"Well," my grandmother admits, "the coffee is pretty good."

"The coffee is wonderful," my mom agrees.

"I knew you'd like it. It's my favorite. Best in town."

I should have made rice porridge, I think to myself. Everyone likes rice porridge. Rice porridge the way it was meant to be served, in porcelain bowls with little salty gross things on the side, like tiny fish with silver eyeballs and brown salty-sweet crunchy fungus. They tell me it's a vegetable; I think it's a fungus. But every time I see my grandmother, I try extra hard to be anti-traditional. I don't know why.

"If you feed this to your kids and tell them it's bacon," she starts up again, "they're going to think that this is bacon. And pretty soon the whole world will stop eating bacon because it tastes so bad."

"Ma," my mom pleads, "don't get so upset. We'll call it something else if you want." She says this just to shut my grandmother up; I can tell. She used to talk to me like that when I was a kid.

"That's not the point," Gramma continues, shaking her head. "Behind my back, you'll be calling it bacon." She sighs. "You may not be interested now, but when I'm long gone, you'll wonder how bacon tastes the way God intended it to be. And generations hereafter will be doomed to *this*," she mutters, picking up a slice and dropping it onto her plate.

"Try a pancake. The pancakes aren't bad," I suggest.

"What pancakes?" she asks.

"These," I say, pointing to the pancakes on her plate.

"I saw you put these in the toaster. I thought it was bread."

"They're toaster pancakes," I explain, "they come in a box, frozen, and you heat them up in the toaster."

"Never heard of such a thing," she grumbles.

"Jesus Christ, Ma," my mom signs, "if it's that bad, don't eat it."

"That's not my point either." Gramma fills her mouth with coffee and takes a long contemplative look out the window. My mom plays with a chip in her nail polish. I spread a warm pancake with super-chunky peanut butter and apricot-pineapple jam. Sitting across the table, I can smell both of them: my mom's perfumed talc and my grandmother's mothballs. Gramma always smells like mothballs. I told her once that she shouldn't use mothballs so much because they're carcinogenic. What a waste of tax dollars, she had said. Moths don't deserve to live. Who cares if they get cancer. The room is silent; I take a gulp of coffee; my grandmother giggles.

"What?" my mom asks Gramma.

"Oh, nothing. We all picked up our coffee mugs and drank at the same time." We fall silent again. I can hear the coffee being swallowed, the refrigerator humming in the corner, the water rushing through the pipes in the ceiling, rushing to the showers downstairs.

"I'm engaged to Peter," I blurt.

"What?!?" my mom gasps, her eyes opened wide, wider than I've ever seen them before.

"Where's the ring? I see no ring," Gramma complains.

"I don't have one yet. It's a verbal agreement."

"Oh, God," my mother mumbles, closing her eyes. Gramma just shakes her head. "What about your kids?" my mom asks, her eyes still closed. "It's not fair to the kids."

"Why not?" I ask, pretending not to understand her. "We'll have two."

"Honey," my mom pleads, then pauses before continuing. "He doesn't treat you right. There's no ring. You're so young. What if you get divorced?"

"She'll end up like you," my grandmother retorts, "and the two of you divorcees can keep each other company."

"If I get divorced, I'll find someone new," I explain, "simple."

"No, no, nooo!" my mom yells. "It'll be too late. Women get one shot at these things. Why Peter?"

"Mom," I say, "people get divorced every day. What do you think happens to all these people?"

"The men remarry, and the women stay single."

"Oh, Mom! For Christ's sake!"

"There's a shortage of men, and women are in a crisis. It's hard enough for American women, and you think you can just run out there and take your pick?"

"I *am* an American woman."

"I tell you, you only get one chance. I know."

"What makes you think I can't stay married?" I ask, my legs getting tight.

"Why Peter?"

"Why not Peter?" I ask, looking up and seeing her face turning red, her lips vanishing into the familiar horizontal line.

"He's an American mutt! Your kids! Think about your . . ."

"Hey!" I yell, "We're getting married. That's it. Who I marry is my own fucking . . ."

By the look on my mom's face, I know I'd better stop. I look down and fidget with my napkin as my mother stands up and starts grabbing the dishes from the table, letting the silverware fall clanking to the floor, throwing the uneaten pieces of bacon onto my plate. She drops the plates noisily into the sink and heads for the bathroom.

"She's right, you know," Gramma begins softly, "he doesn't treat you very well." The bathroom door slams.

"Gramma," I say, "you've seen him twice. How do you know how he treats me?"

"I know these things. I'm seventy years old."

"No. You know nothing about it."

"Let me finish," she commands.

"I should have told you over the phone."

"We've been here at your apartment for two days, and he hasn't even called. If he loved you so much, he would be here now. And where's the ring? There's no ring. How can he propose without a ring? If you demand anything from a man, demand respect. No ring. No flowers. No letters. He has no respect. How can you marry a man like that?"

"You should listen to your mother."

"She'll get over it. When we have kids, we'll dye their hair before she visits."

"That's not my point," Gramma says.

"That *is* your point," I return.

"You can color your hair whenever you want, but husbands aren't so easy to change," Gramma says, sounding like she just jumped out of a fortune cookie. "You have to change them when they're young and soft."

"I should've sent a telegram."

"A man in a new relationship is like soft clay in water. You can change him at first, but when he gets used to you, he won't budge."

"I shouldn't have opened my mouth until after the honeymoon."

"You've been seeing Peter for three years, and he's still not treating you right. It's too late for him. He won't change." Mom comes out of the bathroom, calmer now, and quiet. With my fork I draw smiley faces in the hardened grease on my plate. Gramma continues. "Tell him to treat you better now, and he'll say 'hey. You're not the same woman I used to know.' And all your differences will be your fault. But if you start out with someone new, and he doesn't treat you right, you can say, 'hey. Where'd you get your manners?' And all your differences will be his fault."

"With all your manipulations," my mom remarks, "you sent Dad to an early grave."

"If you had listened to any of my advice, you wouldn't have gotten divorced. At least we stayed married," Gramma retorts.

"At least *my* husband is still alive."

"*Ex*-husband."

"*Deceased* husband." No one speaks, but I can see my grandmother's face turning red, her hands trembling.

"It doesn't bother me that you never took my advice," my grandmother says slowly, restrained. "But don't stop me from giving advice to my granddaughter, and don't you ever talk to me like that again."

"I appreciate your concern," I tell my grandmother sincerely, watching my mother get up and start washing the dishes. "But Grampa and Dad were from Beijing. Peter's an American boy. There isn't that much to change about him."

"No!" she yells. "You're wrong! When two people live together, they have to change."

"Ma," my mother breaks in, "don't pretend you know so much. When I was growing up, all I saw was you and Dad fighting and then *you* giving in."

"That's the trick," Gramma smiles, turning toward my mother. "When he thinks he's won, he's more open to suggestion. And eventually he does what you want him to do, but it's *his* choice, and he thinks it's *his* idea to change. Two people have to learn to complement each other."

"Like one living and one dead," my mom mumbles.

"So every time we disagree, I have to give in so he can think he's won?" I ask, irritated. "Is that the only way to have a happy marriage? To give in and protect my husband's stupid ego and . . ."

"That's not my point. You missed the whole point. Why do I bother talking if you don't listen?"

"Because you like to talk," my mom says simply.

"I have fifty years more experience than you, and you think I have nothing to offer. So you're no better off than I ever was, or your mom or anyone else."

"Things have changed," I try to explain.

"Some things," my grandmother explains, her fingers tightening around the coffee cup, "*some* things. But some things can never change because you young people think you know everything! My mom approaches from behind, patting Gramma on the back, trying to calm her down. She pushes my mom away, frustrated. "You won't understand until it's your turn in my shoes, and it'll be too late! TOO LATE!" Wincing, Gramma grabs the flesh above her heart, and my mom's face freezes. Then taking three shallow breaths, Gramma shakes her head and stares out the window. The room falls silent. I can hear my grandmother breathing, my mom tapping her fingernails rapidly on her knee. I take a gulp of lukewarm coffee.

"Ha-ha," I laugh, suddenly realizing how fake I sound.

"What?" my mom asks.

"We all picked up our coffee mugs and drank at the same time." I look at my grandmother for a response. She didn't hear me. She just stares out the window.

"Young and stupid," she mutters, "both of you."

Fae Myenne Ng

Her short fiction has been published in Harper's, The P.E.N. Syndicated Fiction Project, The American Voice, The City Lights Review *and anthologized in* Calyx *and* The Pushcart Prize XII: Best of The Small Presses. *Her collection of stories received an Honorable Mention in the 1989 PEN Nelson Algren Fiction Award.*

A RED SWEATER

I chose red for my sister. Fierce, dark red. Made in Hong Kong. Hand Wash Only because it's got that skin of fuzz. She'll look happy. That's good. Everything's perfect, for a minute. That seems enough.

Red. For Good Luck. Of course. This fire-red sweater is swollen with good cheer. Wear it, I will tell her. You'll look lucky.

We're a family of three girls. By Chinese standards, that's not lucky. "Too bad," outsiders whisper, ". . . nothing but daughters. A failed family."

First, Middle, and End girl. Our order of birth marked us. That came to tell more than our given names.

My eldest sister, Lisa, lives at home. She quit San Francisco State, one semester short of a psychology degree. One day she said, "Forget about it, I'm tired." She's working full time at Pacific Bell now. Nine hundred a month with benefits. Mah and Deh think it's a great deal. They tell everybody, "Yes, our Number One makes good pay, but that's not even counting the discount. If we call Hong Kong, China even, there's forty percent off!" As if anyone in their part of China had a telephone.

Number Two, the in-between, jumped off the 'M' floor three years ago. Not true! What happened? Why? Too sad! All we say about that is, "It was her choice."

We sent Mah to Hong Kong. When she left Hong Kong thirty years ago, she was the envy of all: "Lucky girl! You'll never have to work." To marry a sojourner was to have a future. Thirty years in the land of gold and good fortune, and then she returned to tell the story: three daughters, one dead, one unmarried, another who-cares-where, the thirty years in sweatshops, and the prince of the Golden Mountain turned into a toad. I'm glad I didn't have to go with her. I felt her shame and regret. To return, seeking solace and comfort, instead of offering banquets and stories of the good life.

I'm the youngest. I started flying with American Airlines the year Mah returned to Hong Kong, so I got her a good discount. She thought I was good for something then. But when she returned, I was pregnant.

"Get an abortion," she said. "Drop the baby," she screamed.

"No."

"Then get married."

"No. I don't want to."

I was going to get an abortion all along. I just didn't like the way they talked about the whole thing. They made me feel like dirt, that I was a disgrace. Now I can see how I used it as an opportunity. Sometimes I wonder if there wasn't another way. Everything about those years was so steamy and angry. There didn't seem to be any answers.

"I have no eyes for you," Mah said.

"Don't call us," Deh said.

They wouldn't talk to me. They ranted idioms to each other for days. The apartment was filled with images and curses I couldn't perceive. I got the general idea: I was a rotten, no-good, dead thing. I would die in a gutter without rice in my belly. My spirit—if I had one—wouldn't be fed. I wouldn't see good days in this life or the next.

My parents always had a special way of saying things.

Now I'm based in Honolulu. When our middle sister jumped, she kind of closed the world. The family just sort of fell apart. I left. Now, I try to make up for it, but the folks still won't see me, but I try to keep in touch with them through Lisa. Flying cuts up your life, hits hardest during the holidays. I'm always sensitive then. I feel like I'm missing something, that people are doing something really important while I'm up in the sky, flying through time zones.

So I like to see Lisa around the beginning of the year. January, New Year's, and February, New Year's again, double luckiness with our birthdays in between. With so much going on, there's always something to talk about.

"You pick the place this year," I tell her.

"Around here?"

"No," I say. 'Around here' means the food is good and the living hard. You eat a steaming rice plate, and then you feel like rushing home to sew garments or assemble radio parts or something. We eat together only once a year, so I feel we should splurge. Besides, at the Chinatown places, you have nothing to talk about except the bare issues. In American restaurants, the atmosphere helps you along. I want nice light and and a view and handsome waiters.

"Let's go somewhere with a view," I say.

We decide to go to FOLLOWING SEA, a new place on the Pier 39 track. We're early, the restaurant isn't crowded. It's been clear all day, so I think the sunset will be nice. I ask for a window table. I turn to talk to my sister, but she's already talking to a waiter. He's got that dark island tone that she likes. He's looking her up and down. My sister does not blink at it. She holds his look and orders two Johnny Walkers. I pick up a fork, turn it around in my hand. I seldom use chopsticks now. At home, I eat my rice in a plate, with a fork. The only chopsticks I own, I wear in my hair. For a moment, I feel strange sitting here at this unfamiliar table. I don't know this tablecloth, this linen, these candles. Everything seems foreign. It feels like we should be different people. But each time I look up, she's the same. I know this person. She's my sister. We sat together with chopsticks, mismatched bowls, braids, and braces, across the formica tabletop.

"I like three pronged forks," I say, pressing my thumb against the sharp points.

My sister rolls her eyes. She lights a cigarette.

I ask for one.

I finally say, "So, what's new?"

"Not much." Her voice is sullen. She doesn't look at me. Once a year, I come in, asking questions. She's got the answers, but she hates them. For me, I think she's got the peace of heart, knowing that she's done her share for Mah and Deh. She thinks I have the peace, not caring. Her life is full of questions, too, but I have no answers.

I look around the restaurant. The sunset is not spectacular and we don't comment on it. The waiters are lighting candles. Ours is bringing the drinks. He stops very close to my sister, seems to breathe her in. She raises her face toward him. "Ready?" he asks. My sister orders for us. The waiter struts off.

"Tight ass," I say.

"The best," she says.

My scotch tastes good. It reminds me of Deh. Johnny Walker or Seagrams 7, that's what they served at Chinese banquets. Nine courses and a bottle. No ice. We learned to drink it Chinese style, in teacups. Deh drank from his rice bowl, sipping it like hot soup. By the end of the meal, he took it like cool tea, in bold mouthfuls. We sat watching, our teacups of scotch in our laps, his three giggly girls.

Relaxed, I'm thinking there's a connection. Johnny Walker then and Johnny Walker now. I ask for another cigarette and this one I enjoy. Now my Johnny Walker pops with ice. I twirl the glass to make the ice tinkle.

We clink glasses. Three times for good luck. She giggles. I feel better.

"Nice sweater," I say.

"Michael Owyang," she says. She laughs. The light from the candle makes her eyes shimmer. She's got Mah's eyes. Eyes that make you want to talk. Lisa is reed-thin and tall. She's got a body that clothes look good on. My sister slips something on and it wraps her like skin. Fabric has pulse on her.

"Happy birthday, soon," I say.

"Thanks, and to yours too, just as soon."

"Here's to Johnny Walker in shark's fin soup," I say.

"And squab dinners."

"I LOVE LUCY," I say.

We laugh. It makes us feel like children again. We remember how to be sisters.

I raise my glass, "To I LOVE LUCY, squab dinners, and brown bags."

"To bones," she says.

"Bones," I repeat. This is a funny that gets sad, and knowing it, I keep laughing. I am surprised how much memory there is in one word. Pigeons. Only recently did I learn they're called squab. Our word for them was pigeon—on a plate or flying over Portsmouth Square. A good meal at 40 cents a bird. In line by dawn, we waited at the butcher's listening for the slow, churning motor of the trucks. We watched the live fish flushing out of the tanks into the garbage pails. We smelled the honey-brushed cha sui bows baking. When the white laundry truck turned onto Wentworth, there was a puffing trail of feathers following it. A stench filled the alley. The crowd squeezed in around the truck. Old ladies reached into the crates, squeezing and tugging for the plumpest pigeons.

My sister and I picked the white ones, those with the most expressive eyes. Dove birds, we called them. We fed them leftover rice in water, and as long as they stayed plump, they were our pets, our baby dove birds. And then one day we'd come home from school and find them cooked. They were a special, nutritious treat. Mah let us fill our bowls high with little pigeon parts: legs, breasts, and wings, and take them out to the front room to watch I LOVE LUCY. We took brown bags for the bones. We balanced our bowls on our laps and laughed at Lucy. We leaned forward, our chopsticks crossed in mid-air, and called out, "Mah! Mah! Come watch! Watch Lucy cry!"

But she always sat alone in the kitchen sucking out the sweetness of the lesser parts: necks, backs, and the head. "Bones are sweeter than you know," she always said. She came out to check the bags. "Clean bones." She shook the bags. "No waste," she said.

Our dinners come with a warning. "Plate's hot. Don't touch." My sister orders a carafe of house white. "Enjoy," he says, smiling at my sister. She doesn't look up.

I can't remember how to say scallops in Chinese. I ask my sister, she doesn't know either. The food isn't great. Or maybe we just don't have the taste buds in us to go crazy over it. Sometimes I get very hungry for Chinese flavors: black beans, garlic and ginger, shrimp paste and sesame oil. These are tastes we grew up with, still dream about. Crave. Run around town after. Duck liver sausage, beancurd, jook, salted fish, and fried dace with black beans. Western flavors don't stand out, the surroundings do. Three pronged forks. Pink tablecloths. Fresh flowers. Cute waiters. An odd difference.

"Maybe we should have gone to Sun Hung Heung. At least the vegetables are real," I say.

"Hung toh-yee-foo-won-tun!" she says.

"Yeah, yum!" I say.

I remember Deh teaching us how to pick bak choy, his favorite vegetable. "Stick your fingernail into the stem. Juicy and firm, good. Limp and tough, no good." The three of us followed Deh, punching our thumbnails into every stem of bak-choy we saw.

"Deh still eating bak-choy?"

"Breakfast, lunch and dinner." My sister throws her head back, and laughs. It is Deh's motion. She recites in a mimic tone. "Your Deh, all he needs is a good hot bowl of rice and a plate full of greens. A good monk."

There was always bak-choy. Even though it was nonstop for Mah—rushing to the sweatshop in the morning, out to shop on break, and then home to cook by evening—she did this for him. A plate of bak-choy, steaming with the taste of ginger and garlic. He said she made good rice. Timed full-fire until the first boil, medium until the grains formed a crust along the sides of the pot, and then low-flamed to let the rice steam. Firm, that's how Deh liked his rice.

The waiter brings the wine, asks if everything is alright.

"Everything," my sister says.

There's something else about this meeting. I can hear it in the edge of her voice. She doesn't say anything and I don't ask. Her lips make a contorting line; her face looks sour. She lets out a breath. It sounds like she's been holding it in too long.

"Another fight. The bank line," she says. "He waited four times in the bank line. Mah ran around outside shopping. He was doing her a favor. She was doing him a favor. Mah wouldn't stop yelling. 'Get out and go die! Useless Thing! Stinking Corpse!'"

I know he answered. His voice must have had that fortune teller's tone to it. You listened because you knew it was a warning.

He always threatened to disappear, jump off the Golden Gate. His thousand-year-old threat. I've heard it all before. "I will go. Even when dead, I won't be far enough away. Curse the good will that blinded me into taking you as wife!"

112

I give Lisa some of my scallops. "Eat," I tell her.

She keeps talking. "Of course, you know how Mah thinks, that nobody should complain because she's been the one working all these years."

I nod. I start eating, hoping she'll follow.

One bite and she's talking again. "You know what shopping with Mah is like, either you stand outside with the bags like a servant, or inside like a marker, holding a place in line. You know how she gets into being frugal—saving time because it's the one free thing in her life. Well, they're at the bank and she had him hold her place in line while she runs up and down Stockton doing her quick shopping maneuvers. So he's in line, and it's his turn, but she's not back. So he has to start all over at the back again. Then it's his turn but she's still not back. When she finally comes in, she's got bags in both hands, and he's going through the line for the fourth time. Of course she doesn't say sorry or anything."

I interrupt. "How do you know all this?" I tell myself not to come back next year. I tell myself to apply for another transfer, to the East Coast.

"She told me. Word for word." Lisa spears the scallop, puts it in her mouth. I know it's cold by now. "Word for word," she repeats. She cuts a piece of chicken. "Try," she says.

I think about how we're sisters. We eat slowly, chewing carefully, like old people. A way to make things last, to fool the stomach.

Mah and Deh both worked too hard; it's as if their marriage was a marriage of toil—of toiling together. The idea is that the next generation can marry for love.

In the old country, matches were made, strangers were wedded, and that was fate. Those days, sojourners like Deh were considered princes. To become the wife to such a man was to be saved from the war-torn villages.

Saved to work. After dinner, with the rice still in between her teeth, Mah sat down at her Singer. When we pulled out the wallbed, she was still there, sewing. The street noises stopped long before she did. The hot lamp made all the stitches blur together. And in the mornings, long before any of us awoke, she was already there, sewing again.

His work was hard, too. He ran a laundry on Polk Street. He

sailed with the American President Lines. Things started to look up when he owned the take-out place in Vallejo, and then his partner ran off. So he went to Alaska and worked the canneries.

She was good to him, too. We remember. How else would we have known him all those years he worked in Guam, in the Fiji Islands, in Alaska? Mah always gave him majestic welcomes home. It was her excitement that made us remember him.

I look around. The restaurant is full. The waiters move quickly.

I know Deh. His words are ugly. I've heard him. I've listened. And I've always wished for the street noises, as if in the traffic of sound, I believe I can escape. I know the hard color of his eyes and the tightness in his jaw. I can almost hear his teeth grind. I know this. Years of it.

Their lives weren't easy. So is their discontent without reason?

What about the first one? You didn't even think to come to the hospital. The first one, I say! Son or daughter, dead or alive, you didn't even come!

What about living or dying? Which did you want for me that time you pushed me back to work before my back brace was off?

Money! Money!! Money to eat with, to buy clothes with, to pass this life with!

Don't start that again! Everything I make at that dead place I hand . . .

How come . . .
What about . . .
So . . .

It was obvious. The stories themselves meant little. It was how hot and furious they could become.

Is there no end to it? What makes their ugliness so alive, so thick and impossible to let go of?

"I don't want to think about it anymore." The way she says it surprises me. This time I listen. I imagine what it would be like to take her place. It will be my turn one day.

114

"Ron," she says, wiggling her fingers above the candle. "A fun thing."

The opal flickers above the flame. I tell her that I want to get her something special for her birthday, ". . . next trip I get abroad." She looks up at me, smiles.

For a minute, my sister seems happy. But she won't be able to hold onto it. She grabs at things out of despair, out of fear. Gifts grow old for her. Emotions never ripen, they sour. Everything slips away from her. Nothing sustains her. Her beauty has made her fragile.

We should have eaten in Chinatown. We could have gone for coffee in North Beach, then for jook at Sam Wo's.

"No work, it's been like that for months, just odd jobs," she says.

I'm thinking, it's not like I haven't done my share. I was a kid once, I did things because I felt I should. I helped fill out forms at the Chinatown employment agencies. I went with him to the Seaman's Union. I waited too, listening and hoping for those calls: "Busboy! Presser! Prep Man!" His bags were packed, he was always ready to go. "On standby," he said.

Every week. All the same. Quitting and looking to start all over again. In the end, it was like never having gone anywhere. It was like the bank line, waiting for nothing.

How many times did my sister and I have to hold them apart? The flat ting! sound as the blade slapped onto the linoleum floors, the wooden handle of the knife slamming into the corner. Was it she or I who screamed, repeating all their ugliest words? Who shook them? Who made them stop?

The waiter comes to take the plates. He stands by my sister for a moment. I raise my glass to the waiter.

"You two Chinese?" he asks.

"No," I say, finishing off my wine. I roll my eyes. I wish I had another Johnny Walker. Suddenly I don't care.

"We're two sisters," I say. I laugh. I ask for the check, leave a good tip. I see him slip my sister a box of matches.

Outside, the air is cool and brisk. My sister links her arm into mine. We walk up Bay onto Chestnut. We pass Galileo High School and then turn down Van Ness to head toward the pier. The bay is black. The foghorns sound far away. We walk the whole length of the pier without talking.

The water is white where it slaps against the wooden stakes. For a long time Lisa's wanted out. She can stay at that point of endurance forever. Desire that becomes old feels too good, it's seductive. I know how hard it is to go.

The heart never travels. You have to be heartless. My sister holds that heart, too close and for too long. This is her weakness, and I like to think, used to be mine. Lisa endures too much.

We're lucky, not like the bondmaids growing up in service, or the new-born daughters whose mouths were stuffed with ashes. Courtesans with the three-inch foot, beardless, soft-shouldered eunuchs and the frightened child-brides, they're all stories to us. We're the lucky generation. Our parents forced themselves to live through the humiliation in this country so that we could have it better. We know so little of the old country. We repeat the names of Grandmothers and Uncles, but they will always be strangers to us. Family exists only because somebody has a story, and knowing the story connects us to a history. To us, the deformed man is oddly compelling, the forgotten man is a good story. A beautiful woman suffers.

I want her beauty to buy her out.

The sweater cost two weeks pay. Like the 40-cent birds that are now a delicacy, this is a special treat. The money doesn't mean anything. It is, if anything, time. Time is what I would like to give her.

A red sweater. 100% angora. The skin of fuzz will be a fierce rouge on her naked breasts.

Red. Lucky. Wear it. Find that man. The new one. Wrap yourself around him. Feel the pulsing between you. Fuck him and think about it. 100%. Hand Wash Only. Worn Once.

Franco Salmoiraghi

Susan Nunes

Susan Nunes was born and raised in Hilo, Hawaii, and now lives in Honolulu. She grew up in two worlds, those of her Japanese mother and Portuguese father, and much of her fiction is about piecing together the scattered impressions of a divided yet doubly rich family. Her stories of Hilo were collected in A Small Obligation and Other Stories, *and her work has appeared in such journals and anthologies as* Hawaii Review, Passages To The Dream Shore, *and the* Best Of Bamboo Ridge. *She is the author of two children's books,* Coyote Dreams *and* Tiddalick, *both published by Macmillan.*

118

A MOVING DAY

Across the street, the bulldozer roars to life. Distracted, my mother looks up from the pile of linen that she has been sorting. She is seventy, tiny and fragile, the flesh burned off her shrinking frame. Her hair is grey now—she has never dyed it—and she wears it cut no-nonsense short with the nape shaved. She still has a beautiful neck, in another life, perfect for kimono. She has taken a liking to jeans, cotton smocks, baggy sweaters, and running shoes. When I was a child she wouldn't leave the house without nylons.

Her hands, large-jointed with arthritis, return with a vengance to the pile of linen. I have always been wary of her energy. Now she is making two stacks, the larger one for us, the smaller for her to keep. There is a finality in the way she places things in the larger pile, as if to say that's *it*. For her, it's all over, all over but this last accounting. She does not look forward to what is coming. Strangers. Schedules. The regulated activities of those considered too old to regulate themselves. But at least, at the *very* least, she'll not be a burden. She sorts through the possessions of a lifetime, she and her three daughters. It's time she passed most of this on. Dreams are lumber. She can't *wait* to be rid of them.

My two sisters and I present a contrast. There is nothing purposeful or systematic about the way we move. In fact, we don't know where we're going. We know there is a message in all this activity, but we don't know what it is. Still, we search for it in the odd carton, between layers of tissue paper and silk. We open drawers, peer into the recesses of cupboards, rummage through the depths of closets. We lift, untuck, unwrap, and set aside. The message is there, we know. But what is it? Perhaps if we knew, then we wouldn't have to puzzle out our mother's righteous determination to shed the past.

There is a photograph of my mother taken on the porch of my grandparents' house when she was in her twenties. She is wearing a floral print dress with a square, lace-edged collar and a graceful skirt that shows off her slim body. Her shoulder length hair has been permed. It is dark and thick and worn parted on the side to fall over her right cheek. She is very fair; "one pound powder," her friends called her. She is smiling almost reluctantly, as if she meant to appear serious but the photographer has said something amusing. One arm rests lightly on the railing, the other, which is at her side, holds a handkerchief. They were her special pleasures, handkerchiefs of hand-embroidered linen as fine as ricepaper. Most were gifts (she used to say that when she was a girl, people gave one another little things — a handkerchief, a pincushion, pencils, hair ribbons), and she washed and starched them by hand, ironed them, taking care with the rolled hems, and stored them in a silk bag from Japan.

There is something expectant in her stance, as if she were waiting for something to happen. She says, your father took this photograph in 1940, before we were married. She lowers her voice confidentially and adds, now he cannot remember taking it. My father sits on the balcony, an open book on his lap, peacefully smoking his pipe. The bulldozer tears into the foundations of the Kitamura house.

What about this? My youngest sister has found a fishing boat carved of tortoise shell.

Hold it in your hand and look at it. Every plank on the hull is visible. Run your fingers along the sides, you can feel the joints. The two masts, about six inches high, are from the darkest part of the shell. I broke one of the sails many years ago. The remaining one is quite remarkable, so thin that the light comes through it in places. It is ribbed to give the effect of cloth pushed gently by the wind.

My mother reaches for a sheet of tissue paper and takes the boat from my sister. She says, it was a gift from Mr. Oizumi. He bought it from an artisan in Kamakura.

Stories cling to the thing, haunt it like unrestful spirits. They are part of the object. They have been there since we were children. In 1932, Mr. Oizumi visits Japan. He crosses the Pacific by steamer, and when he arrives he is hosted by relatives eager to hear of his good fortune. But Mr. Oizumi soon tires of their questions. He wants to see what has become of the country. It will be arranged, he is told. Mr Oizumi is a meticulous man. Maps are his passion. A trail of neat X's marks the steps of his journey. On his map of China, he notes each military outpost in Manchuria and appends a brief description of what he sees. Notes invade the margins, march over the blank spaces. The characters are written in a beautiful hand, precise, disciplined, orderly. Eventually, their trail leads to the back of the map. After Pearl Harbor, however, Mr. Oizumi is forced to burn his entire collection. The U.S. Army has decreed that enemy aliens caught with seditious material will be arrested. He does it secretly in the shed behind his home, his wife standing guard. They scatter the ashes in the garden among the pumpkin vines.

My grandfather's library does not escape the flames either. After the Army requisitions the Japanese school for wartime headquarters, they give my mother's parents twenty-four hours to vacate the premises, including the boarding house where they lived with about twenty students from the plantation camps outside Hilo. There is no time to save the books. Her father decides to nail wooden planks over the shelves that line the classrooms. After the Army moves in, they rip open the planks, confiscate the books, and store them in the basement of the post office. Later, the authorities burn everything. Histories, children's stories, primers, biographies, language texts, everything, even a set of Encyclopaedia Brittanica. My grandfather is shipped to Oahu and imprisoned on Sand Island. A few months later, he is released after three prominent Caucasians vouch for his character. It is a humiliation he doesn't speak of, ever.

All of this was part of the boat. After I broke the sail, she gathered the pieces and said, I'm not sure we can fix this. It was not a toy. Why can't you leave my things alone?

For years the broken boat sat on our bookshelf, a reminder of the brutality of the next generation.

Now she wants to give everything away. We have to beg her to keep things. Dishes from Japan, lacquerware, photographs, embroidery, letters. She says, I have no room. You take them, here, *take* them. Take them or I'll get rid of them.

They're piled around her, they fill storage chests, they fall out of open drawers and cupboards. She wants only to keep a few things—her books, some photographs, three carved wooden figures from Korea that belonged to her father, a few of her mother's dishes, perhaps one futon.

My sister holds a porcelain teapot by its bamboo handle. Four white cranes edged in black and gold fly around it. She asks, Mama, can't you hang on to this? If you keep it, I can borrow it later.

My mother shakes her head. She is adamant. And what would I do with it? I don't want any of this. Really.

My sister turns to me. She sighs. The situation is hopeless. You take it, she says. It'll only get broken at my place. The kids.

It had begun slowly, this shedding of the past, a plate here, a dish there, a handkerchief, a doily, a teacup, a few photographs, one of Grandfather's block prints. Nothing big. But then the odd gesture became a pattern; it got so we never left the house empty-handed. At first we were amused. After all, when we were children she had to fend us off her things. Threaten. We were always *at* them. She had made each one so ripe with memories that we found them impossible to resist. We snuck them outside, showed them to our friends, told and retold the stories. They bear the scars of all this handling, even her most personal possessions. A chip here, a crack there. Casualties. Like the music box her brother brought home from Italy after the war. It played a Brahms lullaby. First we broke the spring, then we lost the winding key, and for years it sat mutely on her dresser.

She would say again and again, it's impossible to keep anything nice with you children. And we'd retreat, wounded, for a while. The problem with children is they can wipe out your history. It's a miracle that anything survives this onslaught.

There's a photograph of my mother standing on the pier in Honolulu in 1932, the year she left Hawaii to attend the University of California. She's loaded to the ears with leis. She's wearing a fedora pulled smartly to the side. She's not smiling. Of my mother's two years there, my grandmother recalled that she received good grades and never wore kimono again. My second cousin, with whom my mother stayed when she first arrived, said she was surprisingly sophisticated—she liked hats. My mother said that she was homesick. Her favorite class was biology and she entertained thoughts of becoming a scientist. Her father, however, wanted her to become a teacher, and his wishes prevailed, even though he would not have forced them upon her. She was a dutiful daughter.

During her second year, she lived near campus with a mathematics professor and his wife. In exchange for room and board she cleaned house, ironed, and helped prepare meals. One of the things that survives from this period is a black composition book entitled, *Recipes of California*. As a child, I read it like a book of mysteries for clues to a life both alien and familiar. Some entries she had copied by hand; others she cut out of magazines and pasted on the page, sometimes with a picture or drawing. The margins contained her cryptic comments: "Saturday bridge club," "From Mary G. Do not give away," underlined, "chopped suet by hand, wretched task, bed at 2 a.m., exhausted." I remember looking up "artichoke" in the dictionary and asking Mr. Okinaga, the vegetable vendor, if he had any edible thistles. I never ate one until I was twenty.

That book holds part of the answer to why our family rituals didn't fit the norm of either our relatives or the larger community in which we grew up. At home, we ate in fear of the glass of spilled milk, the stray elbow on the table, the boarding house reach. At my grandparents', we slurped our chasuke. We wore tailored dresses, white cotton pinafores, and Buster Brown shoes with white socks; however, what we longed for were the lacy dresses in the National Dollar Store that the Puerto Rican girls wore to church on Sunday. For six years, I marched to Japanese language school after my regular classes; however, we only spoke English at home. We talked too loudly and all at once, which mortified my mother, but she was always complaining about Japanese indirectness. I know that she smarted under a system in which the older son is the center of the familial universe, but at thirteen I had a fit of jealous rage over her fawning attention to our only male cousin.

My sister has found a photograph of my mother, a round faced and serious twelve or thirteen, dressed in kimono and seated, on her knees, on the tatami floor. She is playing the koto. According to my mother, girls were expected to learn this difficult stringed instrument because it was thought to teach discipline. Of course, everything Japanese was a lesson in discipline—flower arranging, caligraphy, judo, brush painting, embroidery, everything. One summer my sister and I had to take ikebana, the art of flower arrangement, at Grandfather's school. The course was taught by Mrs. Oshima, a diminutive, softspoken, terrifying woman, and my supplies were provided by my grandmother, whose tastes ran to the oversized. I remember little of that class and its principles. What I remember most clearly is having to walk home carrying one of our creations, which, more often than not, towered above our heads.

How do we choose among what we experience, what we are taught, what we run into by chance, or what is forced upon us? What is the principle of selection? My sisters and I are not bound by any of our mother's obligations, nor do we follow the rituals that seemed so important. My sister once asked, do you realize that when she's gone that's *it*? She was talking about how to make sushi, but it was a profound question nonetheless.

I remember, after we moved to Honolulu and my mother stopped teaching and began working long hours in administration, she was less vigilant about the many little things that once consumed her attention. While we didn't slide into savagery, we economized in more ways than one. She would often say, there's simply no time anymore to do things right.

I didn't understand then why she looked so sad, but somehow I knew the comment applied to us.

So how do I put her wish, whatever it was, into perspective? It is hidden in layers of silk, sheathed in the folds of an old kimono that no one knows how to wear any more. I don't understand why we carry out this fruitless search. Whatever it is we are looking for, we're not going to find it. My sister tries to lift a box filled with record albums, old seventy-eights, gives up, and sets it down again. My mother says, there are people who collect these things. Imagine.

Right, just imagine.

I think about my mother bathing me and singing, "The snow is snowing, the wind is blowing, but I will weather the storm." And I think of her story of a country boy carried by the Tengu on a fantastic flight over the cities of Japan, but who chooses in the end to return to the unchanging world of his village. So much for questions which have no answers, why we look among objects for meanings which have somehow escaped us in the growing up and growing old.

However, my mother is a determined woman. She will take nothing with her if she can help it. It is all ours. And on the balcony my father knocks the ashes of his pipe into a porcelain ashtray, and the bulldozer is finally silent.

Amy Tan

I was born in Oakland, California, in 1952, two and a half years after my parents immigrated to the United States. My parents believed strongly in education and good English skills as the stepping stones to success in America. I was led to believe from the age six that I would grow up to be a neurosurgeon by trade and a concert pianist by hobby.

When I was 15, I spent a year at the hospital watching my older brother and then my father die of brain cancer. It was a year of prayers, faith healers, and miracle remedies. After they both died, my mother listened to her friends' advice to take my younger brother and me far away from our "diseased house." We took a boat to the Netherlands, and then, using a handbook of English-speaking schools, we eventually stopped in Montreux, Switzerland, because we were able to find an affordable, furnished apartment—a modern 100-year-old chalet set amidst 14th-century houses. I completed high school there, an outsider among the children of ambassadors, tycoons and princes.

I worked in a pizza parlor and got scholarships to put myself through seven years of college. Along the way, I met my husband, Lou, at age 18. We married four years later when I was finishing my master's and starting a doctoral program at U.C. Berkeley.

Like many American-born Chinese, I've had some difficulties reconciling which parts of me are Chinese and which are American. In October, 1987, I went to China with my husband and mother. It was just as my mother said: As soon as my feet touched China, I became Chinese. In Beijing and Shanghai I met my half-sisters for the first time—the daughters my mother had to leave behind when she came to the United States in 1949. I met my uncle, a high-ranking communist official, who believes in duty and country first and who once renounced his mother, my grandmother, because she had capitulated to the evils of a corrupt society; she became a number-three concubine and then committed suicide at age 39. All of this has somehow found its way into my fiction, which has now become The Joy Luck Club.

LINDO JONG
DOUBLE FACE

from *The Joy Luck Club*

My daughter wanted to go to China for her second honey-moon, but now she is afraid.

"What if I blend in so well they think I'm one of them?" Waverly asked me. "What if they don't let me come back to the United States?"

"When you go to China," I told her, "you don't even need to open your mouth. They already know you are an outsider."

"What are you talking about?" she asked. My daughter likes to speak back. She likes to question what I say.

"Aii-ya," I said. "Even if you put on their clothes, even if you take off your makeup and hide your fancy jewelry, they know. They know just watching the way you walk, the way you carry your face. They know you do not belong."

My daughter did not look pleased when I told her this, that she didn't look Chinese. She had a sour American look on her face. Oh, maybe ten years ago, she would have clapped her hands—hurray!—as if this were good news. But now she wants to be Chinese, it is so fashionable. And I know it is too late. All those years I tried to teach her! She followed my Chinese ways only until she learned how to walk out the door by herself and go to school. So now the only Chinese words she can say are *shsh, houche, chr fan,* and *gwan deng shweijyau.* How can she talk to people in China with these words? Pee-pee, choo-choo train, eat, close light sleep. How can she think she can blend in? Only her skin and her hair are Chinese. Inside—she is all American-made.

It's my fault she is this way. I wanted my children to have the best combination: American circumstances and Chinese charac-ter. How could I know these two things do not mix?

I taught her how American circumstances work. If you are born poor here, it's no lasting shame. You are first in line for a scholar-ship. If the roof crashes on your head, no need to cry over this bad luck. You can sue anybody, make the landlord fix it. You do not have to sit like a Buddha under a tree letting pigeons drop their dirty business on your head. You can buy an umbrella. Or go inside a Catholic church. In America, nobody says you have to keep the circumstances somebody else gives you.

She learned these things, but I couldn't teach her about Chinese character. How to obey parents and listen to your mother's mind. How not to show your own thoughts, to put your feelings behind your face so you can take advantage of hidden opportunities. Why easy things are not worth pursuing. How to know your own worth and polish it, never flashing it around like a cheap ring. Why Chinese thinking is best.

No, this kind of thinking didn't stick to her. She was too busy chewing gum, blowing bubbles bigger than her cheeks. Only that kind of thinking stuck.

"Finish your coffee," I told her yesterday. "Don't throw your blessings away."

"Don't be so old-fashioned, Ma," she told me, finishing her coffee down the sink. "I'm my own person."

And I think, How can she be her own person? When did I give her up?

My daughter is getting married a second time. So she asked me to go to her beauty parlor, her famous Mr. Rory. I know her meaning. She is ashamed of my looks. What will her husband's parents and his important lawyer friends think of this backward old Chinese woman?

"Auntie An-mei can cut me," I say.

"Rory is famous," says my daughter, as if she had no ears. "He does fabulous work."

So I sit in Mr. Rory's chair. He pumps me up and down until I am the right height. Then my daughter criticizes me as if I were not there. "See how it's flat on one side," she accuses my head. "She needs a cut and a perm. And this purple tint in her hair, she's been doing it at home. She's never had anything professionally done."

She is looking at Mr. Rory in the mirror. He is looking at me in the mirror. I have seen this professional look before. Americans

128

don't really look at one another when talking. They talk to their reflections. They look at others or themselves only when they think nobody is watching. So they never see how they really look. They see themselves smiling without their mouth open, or turned to the side where they cannot see their faults.

"How does she want it?" asked Mr. Rory. He thinks I do not understand English. He is floating his fingers through my hair. He is showing how his magic can make my hair thicker and longer.

"Ma, how do you want it?" Why does my daughter think she is translating English for me? Before I can even speak, she explains my thoughts: "She wants a soft wave. We probably shouldn't cut it too short. Otherwise it'll be too tight for the wedding. She doesn't want it to look kinky or weird."

And now she says to me in a loud voice, as if I had lost my hearing, "Isn't that right, Ma? Not too tight?"

I smile. I use my American face. That's the face Americans think is Chinese, the one they cannot understand. But inside I am becoming ashamed. I am ashamed she is ashamed. Because she is my daughter and I am proud of her, and I am her mother but she is not proud of me.

Mr. Rory pats my hair more. He looks at me. He looks at my daughter. Then he says something to my daughter that really displeases her: "It's uncanny how much you two look alike!"

I smile, this time with my Chinese face. But my daughter's eyes and her smile become very narrow, the way a cat pulls itself small just before it bites. Now Mr. Rory goes away so we can think about this. I hear him snap his fingers, "Wash! Mrs. Jong is next!"

So my daughter and I are alone in this crowded beauty parlor. She is frowning at herself in the mirror. She sees me looking at her.

"The same cheeks," she says. She points to mine and then pokes her cheeks. She sucks them outside in to look like a starved person. She puts her face next to mine, side by side, and we look at each other in the mirror.

"You can see your character in your face," I say to my daughter without thinking, "You can see your future."

"What do you mean?" she says.

And now I have to fight back my feelings. These two faces, I think, so much the same! The same happiness, the same sadness, the same good fortune, the same faults.

I am seeing myself and my mother, back in China, when I was a young girl.

My mother—your grandmother—once told me my fortune, how my character could lead to good and bad circumstances. She was sitting at her table with the big mirror. I was standing behind her, my chin resting on her shoulder. The next day was the start of the new year. I would be ten years by my Chinese age, so it was an important birthday for me. For this reason maybe she did not criticize me too much. She was looking at my face.

She touched my ear. "You are lucky," she said. "You have my ears, a big thick lobe, lots of meat at the bottom, full of blessings. Some people are born so poor. Their ears are so thin, so close to their head, they can never hear luck calling to them. You have the right ears, but you must listen to your opportunities."

She ran her thin finger down my nose. "You have my nose. The hole is not too big, so your money will not be running out. The nose is straight and smooth, a good sign. A girl with a crooked nose is bound for misfortune. She is always following the wrong things, the wrong people, the worst luck."

She tapped my chin and then hers. "Not too short, not too long. Our longevity will be adequate, not cut off too soon, not so long we become a burden."

She pushed my hair away from my forehead. "We are the same," concluded my mother. "Perhaps your forehead is wider, so you will be even more clever. And your hair is thick, the hairline is low on your forehead. This means you will have some hardships in your early life. This happened to me. But look at my hairline now. High! Such a blessing for my old age. Later you will learn to worry and lose your hair, too."

She took my chin in her hand. She turned my face toward her, eyes facing eyes. She moved my face to one side, then the other. "The eyes are honest, eager," she said. "They follow me and show respect. They do not look down in shame. They do not resist and turn the opposite way. You will be a good wife, mother, and daughter-in-law."

130

When my mother told me these things, I was still so young. And even though she said we looked the same, I wanted to look more the same. If her eye went up and looked surprised, I wanted my eye to do the same. If her mouth fell down and was unhappy, I too wanted to feel unhappy.

I was so much like my mother. This was before our circumstances separated us: a flood that caused my family to leave me behind, my first marriage to a family that did not want me, a war from all sides, and later, an ocean that took me to a new country. She did not see how my face changed over the years. How my mouth began to droop. How I began to worry but still did not lose my hair. How my eyes began to follow the American way. She did not see that I twisted my nose bouncing forward on a crowded bus in San Francisco. Your father and I, we were on our way to church to give many thanks to God for all our blessings, but I had to subtract some for my nose.

*

It's hard to keep your Chinese face in America. At the beginning, before I even arrived, I had to hide my true self. I paid an American-raised Chinese girl in Peking to show me how.

"In America," she said, "you cannot say you want to live there forever. If you are Chinese, you must say you admire their schools, their ways of thinking. You must say you want to be a scholar and come back to teach Chinese people what you have learned."

"What should I say I want to learn?" I asked. "If they ask me questions, if I cannot answer . . ."

"Religion, you must say you want to study religion," said this smart girl. "Americans all have different ideas about religion, so there are no right and wrong answers. Say to them, I'm going for God's sake, and they will respect you."

For another sum of money, this girl gave me a form filled out with English words. I had to copy these words over and over again as if they were English words formed from my own head. Next to the word NAME, I wrote *Lindo Sun*. Next to the word BIRTHDATE, I wrote *May 11, 1918*, which this girl insisted was the same as three months after the Chinese lunar new year. Next to the word

BIRTHPLACE, I put down *Taiyuan, China*. And next to the word OCCUPATION, I wrote *student of theology*.

I gave the girl even more money for a list of addresses in San Francisco, people with big connections. And finally, this girl gave me, free of charge, instructions for changing my circumstances. "First," she said, "you must find a husband. An American citizen is best."

She saw my surprise and quickly added, "Chinese! Of course, he must be Chinese. 'Citizen' does not mean Caucasian. But if he is not a citizen, you should immediately do number two. See here, you should have a baby. Boy or girl, it doesn't matter in the United States. Neither will take care of you in your old age, isn't that true?" And we both laughed.

"Be careful, though," she said. "The authorities there will ask if you have children now or if you are thinking of having some. You must say no. You should look sincere and say you are not married, you are religious, you know it is wrong to have a baby."

I must have looked puzzled, because she explained further: "Look here now, how can an unborn baby know what it is not supposed to do? And once it has arrived, it is an American citizen and can do anything it wants. It can ask its mother to stay. Isn't that true?"

But that is not the reason I was puzzled. I wondered why she said I should look sincere. How could I look any other way when telling the truth?

See how truthful my face still looks. Why didn't I give this look to you? Why do you always tell your friends that I arrived in the United States on a slow boat from China? This is not true. I was not that poor. I took a plane. I had saved the money my first husband's family gave me when they sent me away. And I had saved money from my twelve years' work as a telephone operator. But it is true I did not take the fastest plane. The plane took three weeks. It stopped everywhere: Hong Kong, Vietnam, the Philippines, Hawaii. So by the time I arrived, I did not look sincerely glad to be here.

Why do you always tell people that I met your father in the Cathay House, that I broke open a fortune cookie and it said I would marry a dark, handsome stranger, and that when I looked

132

up, there he was, the waiter, your father. Why do you make this joke? This is not sincere. This was not true! Your father was not a waiter, I never ate in that restaurant. The Cathay House had a sign that said "Chinese Food," so only Americans went there before it was torn down. Now it is a McDonald's restaurant with a big Chinese sign that says *mai dong lou*—"wheat," "east," "building." All nonsense. Why are you attracted only to Chinese nonsense? You must understand my real circumstances, how I arrived, how I married, how I lost my Chinese face, why you are the way you are.

When I arrived, nobody asked me questions. The authorities looked at my papers and stamped me in. I decided to go first to a San Francisco address given to me by this girl in Peking. The bus put me down on a wide street with cable cars. This was California Street. I walked up this hill and then I saw a tall building. This was Old St. Mary's. Under the church sign, in handwritten Chinese characters, someone had added: "A Chinese Ceremony to Save Ghosts from Spiritual Unrest 7 A.M. and 8:30 A.M." I memorized this information in case the authorities asked me where I worshipped my religion. And then I saw another sign across the street. It was painted on the outside of a short building: "Save Today for Tomorrow, at Bank of America." And I thought to myself, This is where American people worship. See, even then I was not so dumb! Today that church is the same size, but where that short bank used to be, now there is a tall building, fifty stories high, where you and your husband-to-be work and look down on everybody.

My daughter laughed when I said this. Her mother can make a good joke.

So I kept walking up this hill. I saw two pagodas, one on each side of the street, as though they were the entrance to a great Buddha temple. But when I looked carefully, I saw the pagoda was really just a building topped with stacks of tile roofs, no walls, nothing else under its head. I was surprised how they tried to make everything look like an old imperial city or an emperor's tomb. But if you looked on either side of these pretend-pagodas, you could see the streets became narrow and crowded, dark, and dirty. I thought to myself, Why did they choose only the worst

Chinese parts for the inside? Why didn't they build gardens and ponds instead? Oh, here and there was the look of a famous ancient cave or a Chinese opera. But inside it was always the same cheap stuff.

So by the time I found the address the girl in Peking gave me, I knew not to expect too much. The address was a large green building, so noisy, children running up and down the outside stairs and hallways. Inside number 402, I found an old woman who told me right away she had wasted her time waiting for me all week. She quickly wrote down some addresses and gave them to me, keeping her hand out after I took the paper. So I gave her an American dollar and she looked at it and said, "*Syaujye*"—Miss— "we are in America now. Even a beggar can starve on this dollar." So I gave her another dollar and she said, "Aii, you think it is so easy getting this information?" So I gave her another and she closed her hand and her mouth.

With the addresses this old woman gave me, I found a cheap apartment on Washington Street. It was like all the other places, sitting on top of a little store. And through the three-dollar list, I found a terrible job paying me seventy-five cents an hour. Oh, I tried to get a job as a salesgirl, but you had to know English for that. I tried for another job as a Chinese hostess, but they also wanted me to rub my hands up and down foreign men, and I knew right away this was as bad as fourth-class prostitutes in China! So I rubbed that address out with black ink. And some of the other jobs required you to have a special relationship. They were jobs held by families from Canton and Toishan and the Four Districts, southern people who had come many years ago to make their fortune and were still holding onto them with the hands of their great-grandchildren.

So my mother was right about my hardships. This job in the cookie factory was one of the worst. Big black machines worked all day and night pouring little pancakes onto moving round griddles. The other women and I sat on high stools, and as the little pancakes went by, we had to grab them off the hot griddle just as they turned golden. We would put a strip of paper in the center, then fold the cookie in half and bend its arms back just as it turned hard. If you grabbed the pancake too soon, you would

134

burn your fingers on the hot, wet dough. But if you grabbed too late, the cookie would harden before you could even complete the first bend. And then you had to throw these mistakes in a barrel, which counted against you because the owner could sell those only as scraps.

After the first day, I suffered ten red fingers. This was not a job for a stupid person. You had to learn fast or your fingers would turn into fried sausages. So the next day only my eyes burned, from never taking them off the pancakes. And the day after that, my arms ached from holding them out ready to catch the pancakes at just the right moment. But by the end of my first week, it became mindless work and I could relax enough to notice who else was working on each side of me. One was an older woman who never smiled and spoke to herself in Cantonese when she was angry. She talked like a crazy person. On my other side was a woman around my age. Her barrel contained very few mistakes. But I suspected she ate them. She was quite plump.

"Eh, *Syaujye*," she called to me over the loud noise of the machines. I was grateful to hear her voice, to discover we both spoke Mandarin, although her dialect was coarse-sounding. "Did you ever think you would be so powerful you could determine someone else's fortune?" she asked.

I didn't understand what she meant. So she picked up one of the strips of paper and read it aloud, first in English: "Do not fight and air your dirty laundry in public. To the victor go the soils." Then she translated in Chinese: "You shouldn't fight and do your laundry at the same time. If you win, your clothes will get dirty."

I still did not know what she meant. So she picked up another one and read in English: "Money is the root of all evil. Look around you and dig deep." And then in Chinese: "Money is a bad influence. You become restless and rob graves."

"What is this nonsense?" I asked her, putting the strips of paper in my pocket, thinking I should study these classical American sayings.

"They are fortunes," she explained. "American people think Chinese people write these sayings."

"But we never say such things!" I said. "These things don't make sense. These are not fortunes, they are bad instructions."

"No Miss," she said, laughing, "it is our bad fortune to be here making these and somebody else's bad fortune to pay to get them."

So this is how I met An-mei Hsu. Yes, yes, Auntie An-mei, now so old-fashioned. An-mei and I still laugh over those bad fortunes and how they later become quite useful in helping me catch a husband.

"Eh, Lindo," An-mei said to me one day at our workplace. "Come to my church this Sunday. My husband has a friend who is looking for a good Chinese wife. He is not a citizen, but I'm sure he knows how to make one." So that is how I first heard about Tin Jong, your father. It was not like my first marriage, where everything was arranged. I had a choice. I could choose to marry your father, or I could choose not to marry him and go back to China.

I knew something was not right when I saw him: He was Cantonese! How could An-mei think I could marry such a person? But she just said: "We are not in China anymore. You don't have to marry the village boy. Here everybody is now from the same village even if they come from different parts of China." See how changed Auntie An-mei is from those old days.

So we were shy at first, your father and I, neither of us able to speak to each other in our Chinese dialects. We went to English class together, speaking to each other in those new words and sometimes taking out a piece of paper to write a Chinese character to show what we meant. At least we had that, a piece of paper to hold us together. But it's hard to tell someone's marriage intentions when you can't say things aloud. All those little signs—the teasing, the bossy, scolding words—that's how you know if it is serious. But we could talk only in the manner of our English teacher. I see cat. I see rat. I see hat.

But I saw soon enough how much your father liked me. He would pretend he was in a Chinese play to show me what he meant. He ran back and forth, jumped up and down, pulling his fingers through his hair, so I knew—*mangjile!*—what a busy, exciting place this Pacific Telephone was, this place where he worked. You didn't know this about your father—that he could be such a good actor? You didn't know your father had so much hair?

136

Oh, I found out later his job was not the way he described it. It was not so good. Even today, now that I can speak Cantonese to your father, I always ask him why he doesn't find a better situation. But he acts as if he were in those old days, when he couldn't understand anything I said.

Sometimes I wonder why I wanted to catch a marriage with your father. I think An-mei put the thought in my mind. She said, "In the movies, boys and girls are always passing notes in class. That's how they fall into trouble. You need to start trouble to get this man to realize his intentions. Otherwise, you will be an old lady before it comes to his mind."

That evening An-mei and I went to work and searched through strips of fortune cookie papers, trying to find the right instructions to give your father. An-mei read them aloud, putting aside ones that might work: "Diamonds are a girl's best friend. Don't ever settle for a pal." "If such thoughts are in your head, it's time to be wed." "Confucius say a woman is worth a thousand words. Tell your wife she's used up her total."

We laughed over those. But I knew the right one when I read it. It said: "A house is not home when a spouse is not at home." I did not laugh. I wrapped up this saying in a pancake, bending the cookie with all my heart.

After school the next afternoon, I put my hand in my purse and then made a look, as if a mouse had bitten my hand. "What's this?" I cried. Then I pulled out the cookie and handed it to your father. "Eh! So many cookies, just to see them makes me sick. You take this cookie."

I knew even then he had a nature that did not waste anything. He opened the cookie and he crunched it in his mouth, and then read the piece of paper.

"What does it say?" I asked. I tried to act as if it did not matter. And when he still did not speak, I said, "Translate, please."

We were walking in Portsmouth Square and already the fog had blown in and I was very cold in my thin coat. So I hoped your father would hurry and ask me to marry him. But instead, he kept his serious look and said, "I don't know this word 'spouse.' Tonight I will look in my dictionary. Then I can tell you the meaning tomorrow."

The next day he asked me in English, "Lindo, can you spouse me?" And I laughed at him and said he used that word incorrectly. So he came back and made a Confucius joke, that if the words were wrong, then his intentions must also be wrong. We scolded and joked with each other all day long like this, and that is how we decided to get married.

One month later we had a ceremony in the First Chinese Baptist Church, where we met. And nine months later your father and I had our proof of citizenship, a baby boy, your big brother Winston. I named him Winston because I liked the meaning of those two words "wins ton." I wanted to raise a son who would win many things, praise, money, a good life. Back then, I thought to myself, At last I have everything I wanted. I was so happy, I didn't see we were poor. I saw only what we had. How did I know Winston would die later in a car accident? So young! Only sixteen!

Two years after Winston was born, I had your other brother, Vincent. I named him Vincent, which sounds like "win cent," the sound of making money, because I was beginning to think we did not have enough. And then I bumped my nose riding on the bus. Soon after that you were born.

I don't know what caused me to change. Maybe it was my crooked nose that damaged my thinking. Maybe it was seeing you as a baby, how you looked so much like me, and this made me dissatisfied with my life. I wanted everything for you to be better. I wanted you to have the best circumstances, the best character. I didn't want you to regret anything. And that's why I named you Waverly. It was the name of the street we lived on. And I wanted you to think, This is where I belong. But I also knew if I named you after this street, soon you would grow up, leave this place, and take a piece of me with you.

Mr. Rory is brushing my hair. Everything is soft. Everything is black.

"You look great, Ma," says my daughter. "Everyone at the wedding will think you're my sister."

I look at my face in the beauty parlor mirror. I see my reflection. I cannot see my faults, but I know they are there. I gave my

138

daughter these faults. The same eyes, the same cheeks, the same chin. Her character, it came from my circumstances. I look at my daughter and now it is the first time I have seen it.

"Ai-ya! What happened to your nose?"

She looks in the mirror. She sees nothing wrong. "What do you mean? Nothing happened," she says. "It's just the same nose."

"But how did you get it crooked?" I ask. One side of her nose is bending lower, dragging her cheek with it.

"What do you mean?" she asks. "It's your nose. You gave me this nose."

"How can that be? It's drooping. You must get plastic surgery and correct it."

But my daughter has no ears for my words. She puts her smiling face to my worried one. "Don't be silly. Our nose isn't so bad," she says. "It makes us look devious." She looks pleased.

"What is this word, 'devious,'" I ask.

"It means we're looking one way, while following another. We're for one side and also the other. We mean what we say, but our intentions are different."

"People can see this in our face?"

My daughter laughs. "Well, not everything that we're thinking. They just know we're two-faced."

"This is good?"

I think about our two faces. I think about my intentions. Which one is American? Which one is Chinese? Which one is better? If you show one, you must always sacrifice the other.

It is like what happened when I went back to China last year, after I had not been there for almost forty years. I had taken off my fancy jewelry. I did not wear loud colors. I spoke their language. I used their local money. But still, they knew. They knew my face was not one hundred percent Chinese. They still charged me high foreign prices.

So now I think, What did I lose? What did I get back in return? I will ask my daughter what she thinks.

Deborah Fass

I was born and raised in California, the granddaughter of Eastern Euro-pean Jewish immigrants. I am primarily a poet and have had work published in anthologies and magazines including New Directions *and* Poetry: San Francisco. *As an undergraduate I studied Creative Writing at San Francisco State University and the University of New Mexico, and received a B.A. from the Poetics Program at New College of California. In 1984 I received a Japanese Monbusho Research Fellowship and came to Japan to study Japanese literature. I have an M.A. in English (Teaching English as a Second/Foreign Language) and have taught E.S.L. in California and Japan. I'm currently living in Kyoto, with my husband, who is a Japanese musician.*

THE JAPANESE MOUNTAINS

Afternoon comes to San Francisco in a foggy haze that could pass for gray dawn. Through the service porch window, open just enough for the cat to squeeze through, Laurel can see the whole block of backyards forming an ever-changing patchwork. She surveys the familiar textures. Her favorite patch is the garden next door, which she can barely see. Over the fence, she can make out a little pond, and sometimes irises. There are two bamboo trees whose small, slender leaves spill into her own backyard, blocking her view. She doesn't wish she could see the whole pond. She enjoys the sense of yearning it creates—just seeing a fraction of the pond—though sometimes she wishes she could see more of the irises.

Laurel scans the backyards but doesn't see Carlos, the family cat. She hears footsteps above her, in the service porch upstairs, and hears the timer of a dryer buzzing. She smiles, waiting for her own washing machine to finish its cycle. She feels a sense of community with the woman in the upstairs flat; two women doing laundry this early Saturday afternoon, scanning the backyards for the family cats, happy to spot one. As the dryer upstairs rumbles to a start, Laurel's washer stops, and she unloads the wet, clean clothes.

Laurel's dryer harmonizes with the one upstairs as she peers through the window, this time finding Carlos sitting on a fence. She is happy to see his little Siamese face, half hidden by the bamboo. She is always surprised at how small he looks outside.

In the kitchen, Kaz, her husband, is yawning and stretching. "Good morning," she greets him in Japanese. Since they met and were married in Japan, it seems appropriate that they continue to speak Japanese though they have been living in the States for almost two years. But Americans around them object. "Speak to him in American," they demand. Laurel thinks that just because they're now living in California they shouldn't have to speak a language that is new and uncomfortable for one of them. Her Japanese is in no way native-like, but it's a hobby and she's grateful for the opportunity to practice. She also realizes that her husband didn't come to the U.S. to study English, as she'd gone to Japan to study Japanese. So why should he be forced to speak English to her?

"Did you sleep well? Want some tea?" she asks, holding out a cup of hot green tea.

"I'm tired," he yawns, taking the tea. He was out until five o'clock in the morning, playing guitar with his Reggae band. He usually comes in around three, but this morning he was two hours late. Laurel had fallen asleep at about eleven, but had woken up at 2:30. She'd switched off the TV and switched on the reading lamp. I'll read until he gets home, she'd thought, but as four o'clock approached and his key hadn't yet made contact with the lock, she began to worry. She tried not to think about the daily news—the murders and accidents and all the other horrible possibilities. She read her novel, aware of every sound inside and outside the house. Carlos woke up and wanted to go out. He whined and scratched at the window. The rhythm of the leaky kitchen faucet became Kaz's footsteps on the sidewalk. She closed her eyes against the wee hours in this big city and imagined an old farmhouse in the mountains of southern Japan where she'd met Kaz. It was a friend's house, and its old wooden walls leaned uniformly to the right. She imagined May and wild wisteria blooming on the mountainsides. She could see them in the hills across the rice fields from the old farmhouse.

Laurel remembered her life there. In those mountains nature had the last word. The land whispered with flooding rains and grumbled with thunderstorms. In her house, water froze in the pipes in winter. Outside, all signs of life hid under the frost. In the spring, life exploded from every crevice. The mountains were freckled with purple and red and yellow. In the summer the air vibrated with life. Insects swarmed around the screen door and mated in midair. Laurel remembered walking between the flooded rice fields and seeing a dead firefly lighting up the dirt. She'd felt a kinship with the firefly. It was an unknowing player in nature's drama. In those mountains, survival stripped the superficial layers from daily life. She'd never felt more alive.

A fly landed on the bedroom wall and Carlos stalked it. He

made clicking sounds in his throat, trying to call the fly to him. Laurel's attention shifted to sounds in the street outside. As dawn began to highlight the window, she heard the familiar hum of Kaz's car, the engine stopping, and finally, the sound of his key. She relaxed. He was tired and apologetic. The singer had lost his car keys and Kaz had been helping him search for them. He smoked a joint and crawled into bed. Laurel continued reading her novel. Soon Kaz was sleeping. The room was growing brighter and brighter. Carlos whined at the sunlight. Laurel opened the service porch window and turned off the reading lamp. She snuggled up to Kaz's back and fell asleep.

Now Kaz is awake and drinking tea in the kitchen. Laurel is doing laundry and reading the paper. They make small talk: last night's gig, the height of the neighbor's pot plants.

What's missing, she wonders. Her husband is here, enjoying breakfast. Their washer and dryer are processing their clothes. But something, like an itch she can't locate, is annoying her. He has his music. It is his priority. Isn't there something she wants to do?

Maybe I should just have a baby, she thinks, I've got the washer and dryer. Her parents gave them to her as an anniversary gift. Her mother wants a grandchild. She isn't subtle. When they go shopping, she points to the baby shoes, saying, "Fill these!" Laurel just laughs. She also laughed at the birthday card her parents sent for her 30th birthday. It said, "As parents you've made us so proud. Now if you'd only make us grandparents." Under the message the card said, "Just kidding," but her mother had crossed that out and had written "Not kidding!" Laurel assured her parents they'd have a grandchild in the next few years. She wanted one anyway.

Maybe a baby would find and fill that empty place, she thinks as she folds the warm, bright clothes. She imagines a baby and sets the fantasy in the Japanese mountains. Maybe we should go back there, she thinks. At least there the isolation is physical. She can describe it: being the only foreigner around, on an island five thousand miles from home. But here, among her fellow country folk, the isolation is vast and intangible. It is constant, like a low-grade fever, and she cannot identify it. "Maybe a baby," she mumbles, but Kaz doesn't hear her. He's playing his guitar to the radio. Laurel picks up a stack of folded laundry and puts it away.

Amin Studio

Chitra Divakaruni

Chitra Divakaruni's work has appeared in many journals in the U.S. and India. In the U.S. these include . . . The Beloit Poetry Journal, Calyx, The Colorado Review, Primavera, and The Berkeley Poets Co-op Magazine. Her book of poems, Dark Like the River was published by the Writers Workshop, India, in 1984.

"Orginally from India, I came to U.C. Berkeley for my graduate studies in English, and I now live in the Bay Area where I teach English and Yoga at Diablo Valley College. My writing covers a wide variety of subjects, but much of it is about India, especially Indian women. I started writing seriously only about four years ago, after I left India. I think distance gave me a better perspective of things, of women caught in an oppressive social system, of conflicts between cultures and ways of life."

DOORS

It all started when Raj came to live with them.

Not that there hadn't been signs earlier. Asha's mother, for one, had warned of it right at the time of the wedding.

"It'll never work, I tell you. Here you are, living in the U.S. since you were twelve. And Deepak—he's straight out of India. Just because you took a few classes together at the University, and you liked how he talks, doesn't mean that you can live with him. What do you *really* know about how Indian men think? About what they expect from their women?"

"Now, Ma, don't start on that again. He's not like the others," Asha had protested. "And besides, I can adjust, too."

On the whole Asha had been right. She and Deepak had lived together happily enough for the last three years. In all matters, as their friends often commented envyingly, they were a well-adjusted couple. In all, that is, except the matter of doors.

Deepak liked to leave them open, and Asha like them closed.

Deepak had laughed about it at first, early in the marriage.

"Are the pots and pans from the kitchen going to come and watch us making love?" he would joke when she meticulously locked the bedroom door at night, although there were just the two of them in the house. Or, "Do you think I'm going to come in and attack you?" when she locked the bathroom door behind her with an audible click. He himself always bathed with the door open, song and stream pouring out of the bathroom with equal abandon.

But soon he realized that it was not a laughing matter with her. Asha would shut the study door before settling down with her dissertation. When in the garden, she would make sure the gate was securely fastened as she weeded. If there had been a door to the kitchen, she would have closed it as she cooked.

Deepak was puzzled by all this door-shutting. He himself had grown up in a large family, and although they had been affluent enough to possess three bedrooms—one for Father, one for Mother and his two sisters, and the third for the three boys—they had never observed boundaries. They had constantly spilled into each others' rooms, doors always left open for the chance remark or joke.

He asked Asha about it one day. She wasn't able to give him an answer.

"I don't know. It's not like I'm shutting you out or anything. I've just always done it this way. I know it's not what you're used to. Does it bother you?"

She seemed so troubled by it that Deepak, feeling a pang of guilt, emphatically denied any feelings of unease. And really, he didn't mind. People were different. And he was more than ready to accept the unique needs of this exotic creature—Indian and yet not Indian—who had by some mysterious chance become his wife.

So things went on smoothly—until Raj descended on them.

II

"Tomorrow!" Asha was distraught, although she tried to hide it in the face of Deepak's obvious delight. Her mind raced over lists of things to be done—the guest bedroom dusted, the sheets washed, a special welcome dinner cooked (that entailed a trip to the grocery), perhaps some flowers. . . . And her advisor was pressuring her for the second chapter of the dissertation, which wasn't going well.

"Yes, tomorrow! His plane comes in at ten-thirty at night." Deepak waved the aerogram excitedly. "Imagine, it's been five years since I've seen him! We used to be inseparable back home, although he was so much younger. He was always in and out of our house, laughing and joking and playing pranks. I know you'll just love him—everyone does! And see, he calls you bhaviji—sister-in-law—already!"

At the airport, Raj was a lanky whirlwind, rushing from the gate to throw his arms around Deepak, kissing him soundly on both cheeks, oblivious to American stares. Asha found his strong Bombay accent hard to follow as he breathlessly regaled them with news of India that had Deepak throwing back his head in loud laughter.

But the trouble really started after dinner.

"What a marvellous meal, Bhaviji! I can see why Deepak is getting a pot-belly!" Raj belched in appreciation as he pushed back his chair. "I know I'll sleep soundly tonight—my eyes are closing already. If you tell me where the bedclothes are, I'll bring them over and start making my bed while you're clearing the table."

"Thanks, Raj, but I made the bed already, upstairs in the guest room."

"The guest room? I'm not a guest, Bhavi! I'm going to be with you for quite a while. You'd better save the guest bedroom for real guests. About six square feet of space—right here between the dining table and the sofa—is all I need. See, I'll just move the chairs a bit."

Seeing the look on Asha's face, Deepak tried to intervene.

"Come on Raju—why not use the guest bed for tonight since it's made already? We can work out the long-term arrangements later."

"Aare yaar, you know I don't like all this formal treatment. Don't you remember what fun it was to spread a big sheet on the floor of the living room and spend the night, all us boys together, telling stories? Have you become Americanized, or what? Come along and help me carry the bedclothes down. . . ."

Asha stood frozen as his sing-song voice faded beyond the bend of the stairs; then she made her own way upstairs silently. When Deepak came to bed an hour later, she was waiting for him.

"What! Not asleep yet? Don't you have an early class to teach tomorrow?"

"You have to leave for work early, too."

"Well, as a matter of fact I was thinking of taking a day off tomorrow. You know—take Raju to San Francisco, maybe."

Asha tried to subdue the jealousy she felt.

"I really don't think you should be neglecting your work—but that's your own business." She tried to shake off the displeasure that colored her voice and speak reasonably. "What I do need to straighten out is this matter of sleeping downstairs. I need to use the dining area in the morning and I can't do it with him sleeping there." She shuddered silently as she pictured herself trying to enjoy her quiet morning tea with him sprawled on the floor nearby. "By the way, just what did he mean he's going to be here for a long time?"

"Well, he wants to stay here until he completes his Master's— maybe a year and a half—and I told him that was fine with us."

"You *what*? Isn't this my house, too? Don't I get a say in who stays here?"

"Fine, then. Go ahead and tell him that you don't want him to stay here. Go ahead, wake him up and tell him tonight." There was an edge to Deepak's voice that she hadn't heard before, and she suddenly realized, frightened, that they were having their first serious quarrel. Her mother's face, triumphant, rose in her mind.

"You know that's not what I want. I realize how much it means to you to have your old friend here, and I'll do my best to make him welcome. I'm just not used to having a long-term houseguest around, and it makes things harder when he insists on sleeping on the living room floor." Asha offered her most charming smile to her husband, desperately willing the stranger in his eyes—cold, defensive—to disappear.

It worked. He smiled back and pulled her to him, her own dear Deepak again, promising to get Raj to use the guest room, kissing the back of her neck in that delicious way that always sent shivers up her spine. And as she snuggled against him with a deep sigh of pleasure, curving her body spoonlike to fit his warm hardness, Asha promised herself to do her best to accept Raj.

III

It was harder than she had expected.

For the concept of doors did not exist in Raj's universe, and he ignored their physical reality—so solid and reassuring to Asha— whenever he could. He would burst into her closed study to tell her of the latest events at school, leaving the door ajar when he left. He would throw open the door to the garage, where she did the laundry, to offer help, usually just as she was folding her underwear. Even when she retreated to her little garden in search of privacy there was no escape. From the porch, he would solicitously give her advice on the drooping fuschias, while behind him the swinging screen door afforded free entry to hordes of insects.

Perhaps to set her an example, he left his own bedroom door wide open, so that the honest rumble of his snores assaulted Asha on her way to the bathroom every morning.

A couple of times she tried to explain to Deepak how she felt, but he responded with surprising testiness.

"What d'you mean he's driving you crazy? He's only trying to be friendly, poor chap. I should think you'd be able to open up a bit more to him. After all, we're the only family he has in this strange country."

What use was it to tell him that her own family had never intruded upon her like this? Instead, Asha took to locking herself up in the bedroom with her work in the evenings, while downstairs Deepak and Raj talked over the old days. Often, she fell asleep over her books and woke to the sound of Deepak's irritated knocks on the door.

"I just don't understand you nowadays!" he would exclaim with annoyance. "Why must you lock the bedroom door when you're reading? Isn't that being a bit paranoid? Maybe you should talk to someone about it."

Asha would turn away in silence, thinking, it can't be forever, he can't stay with us forever, I can put up with it until he leaves, and then everything will be as before.

And so things might have continued, had it not been for one fateful afternoon.

IV

It was the end of the semester, and Asha was lying on her bed, eyes closed. That morning her advisor had told her that her dissertation lacked originality and depth, and had suggested that she restructure the argument. His final comment kept resounding in her brain: "I don't know what's been wrong with you for the past few months—you've consistently produced second rate work; even your students have been complaining about you. Maybe you need a break—a semester away from school."

"Not from school—it's a semester away from home that I need," she whispered now as the door banged downstairs and Raj's eager voice floated up to her.

"Bhavi, Bhavi, where are you? Have I got great news for you!"

Asha put her pillow over her head, willing him away like the dull, throbbing headaches that came to her so often nowadays. But he was at the bedroom door, knocking.

"Open up, Bhavi! I have something to show you—I aced the Math final—I was the only one who did."

"Not now, Raj, please, I'm very tired."

"What's wrong? Do you have a headache? Wait a minute, I'll bring you some of my tigerbalm—excellent for headaches."

She heard his footsteps recede, then return.

"Thanks, Raj," she called out to forestall any more conversation. "Just leave it outside. I don't feel like getting up for it right now."

"Oh, you don't have to get up. I'll bring it in to you." And before she could refuse, Raj had opened the door—how could she have forgotten to lock it?—and had walked in.

Shocked, speechless, Asha watched Raj. He seemed to advance in slow motion across the suddenly enormous expanse of bedroom, holding a squat green bottle in his extended hand. His lips moved, but she could not hear him above the pounding in her skull. He had invaded her last sanctuary, her bedroom. He had violated her.

Through the red haze a piercing voice rose, screaming at him to get out, get out right now. A hand snatched the bottle and hurled it against the wall where it shattered and fell in emerald fragments. Dimly she recognized the voice, the hand. They were hers. And then she was alone in the sudden silence.

V

The bedroom was as neat and tranquil as ever when Deepak walked in; only a very keen eye would have noted the pale stain against the far wall.

"Are you O.K.? Raju mentioned something about you not being well." And then, as his glance fell on the packed suitcase, "What's going on?"

Very calm, she told him she was leaving. She felt a mild surprise when he swore softly and violently.

152

"You can't leave. You're my wife. This is your home. You belong here."

She looked at him a long moment, eyes expressionless.

"It's Raju, isn't it? You just can't stand him, can you? Well, I guess I'll have to do something about the poor chap."

She listened silently to his footsteps fading down the stairs, listened to the long low murmur of voices from the living room, listened to sounds of packing from the guestroom. She listened as Raj said his goodbyes, listened as the front door banged behind the men.

Much later she listened as Deepak told her that Raj would be staying in a hotel till he found a room on campus, listened as he stated that he would sleep in the guestroom tonight, listened to his awkward bedmaking efforts. She listened as a part of herself cried out to her to go to him, to apologize and offer to have Raj back, to fashion her curves to his warm hardness, to let his lips soothe her into sleep.

Then for the first time she lay down alone in the big bed and let the night cover her slowly, layer by cold layer. And when the door finally clicked shut, she did not know whether it was in the guestroom or deep inside her being.

Sussy Chako

Writing has always been and will probably always be a cross cultural experience for me. As a Chinese-Indonesian growing up and writing in English in British Hong Kong, I discovered very young how small the world is. In many of my stories and novels, I try to explore the East-West cross cultural dilemmas, comedies, intrigues, assumptions and stereotypes that I've known as a result of my particular circumstance. Writing is my way of recording, at times protesting and finally resolving the compromise of my creation into the universal human experience.

At present, I am working on a novel titled Wah Kiu (overseas Chinese). I have a BA in English from SUNY, Plattsburgh, and a MFA in fiction from the University of Massachusetts at Amherst. I've been writing fiction since I was eleven years old and am now thirty five.

I am married to an American of Greek descent, and have been in the United States for about eight years. I was born and raised in Hong Kong by immigrant parents who were Indonesian citizens of Chinese descent. I have traveled widely and lived in Asia Pacific, Europe and the U.S., and earn my living as a marketing communications management professional (at present in a major New York law firm).

THE FOURTH COPY OR
DANCING WITH SKELETONS
AND OTHER ROMANCES

Let's start with Once Upon A Time.

One Of Those Perfect Sun Days. A Novel by Grace Hsu. Return address: Public Publishing Co., Parsippany, N.J.

The manuscript arrives in the mail to her Manhattan apartment. Grace Hsu flips through the pages of her first and only finished creative writing effort from a college course ten years ago. No marks, no cover letter. Just coffee stains on the first page.

Edvard Munch's "melancholy adolescence"—the subject of her current reading—snickers in the background.

By late afternoon, Grace Hsu, thirty, successful Communications Consultant to the Architectural Profession, immigrant of two years to New York, is seeking consultation from her favorite cousin, the architect.

"But Andy, who sent it? No one, other than my parents and the university library, has a copy. It was a thesis. I never tried to publish it."

Andy Chiang, long accustomed to the crazy life of his Hong Kong cousin, says. "What about your professor?"

"He died a year after I graduated."

"So check out the publishing company," he says.

Three days later, she calls him again.

"If Public Publishing Co. exists, or ever existed, it's managed to escape the notice of the telephone company, the Chamber of Commerce, the local bookstores, newspapers, and magazines. In fact, it's a phantom as far as the entire town of Parsippany is concerned. On top of that, the library copy hasn't been moved, and my parents have nothing to do with this. *Gwai goo.*"

"What was that?"

"Ghost story, in Cantonese."

"Is that what your novel is?"

"What?"

"A ghost story."

"You know, I don't remember. Sort of, not exactly."

"So why don't you read it. It'll take your mind off all this."

"But Andy . . ."

"So what's it about?"

"What?"

"Your novel, silly."

"Oh, it was, I don't know, about 'sun days.' Perfection, I guess."

"A notion long laid to rest in your life, right? Hey, we've got a presentation brochure to finish."

She hears him chuckle as he hangs up.

*

The opening paragraph of her manuscript reads:

It was one of those perfect sun days. Trees were just the right green, sky the right blue. Roads clean after last night's typhoon. Lazy sun day, nothing to do. Harbour still quiet in the early morning light. Rare day for her city.

In this early morning, it was her city. No tangled traffic, nor blaring horns, nor screaming televisions. She was glad it was after the rains. None of that dog shit marred the beauty of her pavements. She loved walking in her city the way it was now. Pavements clean, the bowling alley still free from its habitual rumblings. Nothing open for business yet.

Grace marvels at this opening. Could five-million-people-in-less-than Manhattan-size Hong Kong once really have been her image for perfection?

The phone rings, and it's her sister Juliana in Paris. Part of Juliana's marketing research job involves making numerous international phone calls to never-to-be audited phone numbers. Juliana calls this and other trans-Atlantic calls her "executive perks," something she believes is more than owed to her after a Phd, MBA—both summa cum laude—and Parisian sexism when she job hunted.

Grace tells her the *gwai goo*.

Julianna says, "That was the story about your fear of dogs."

156

"Hey, you're right. I'd forgotten."

"How could you do that, forget I mean. After all, it's not as if you've written fifty novels."

"No, but . . ."

"You were going to become a writer."

Such accusation. Grace—tough enough to brazen divorce in Hong Kong, and then hightailing it back, alone, to the Land of Liberty—Grace has let her less tough, married-with-child-stuck-in-Paris Juliana down.

After the phone call Grace muses: a very long time since dogs were her adversary, or the Chinese custom of eating dog meat, or blood.

*

Her professor's voice infiltrates:

"The first time I saw you in class, a little Chinese girl, new in America, with your hair in pigtails, and you told me you wanted to write about a girl's fear of dogs. I didn't have much hope for your story. And then, this."

Grace awakens with a start. Three in the morning, glasses askew on her face, and the lights blazing in her living room. A fallen pillow and backache the only testimonials to her haphazard sleeping patterns.

The book on Munch lies open at a drypoint titled "Death and the Maiden, 1894." A naked young girl, her long black hair loose down her back, embraces a skeleton.

Round about the third draft, her professor had insisted, "But who's this 'Jimmy' in your story? You never make it quite clear."

She had hesitated before replying, "Jimmy's the nickname her school gave the Biology lab skeleton."

"Then say so," he had said.

And she remembers the immense feeling of relief that overcame her: it was all right for a virgin to make love to a skeleton! Most of all, it was all right that she could have imagined it, could have conceived of it within the framework of her secondary school life, and finally could articulate it here in the Land of Liberty.

She glances at the Munch. In any event, Munch thought it was all right too.

*

At the end of her novel, she is surprised to find a one page synopsis, of sorts, on the last page. It reads:

It was one of those perfect sun days, no more no less. The sun reflected that very perfection in the park below. But she knew that perfection would have to be marred by the imperfect happenings of the day. Somehow, she never could retain those perfect moments. For an instance, she completely understood the feelings of Anny in Sartre's *Nausea.*

If it were the wedding that bothered her, she showed no signs of it. The barkings in the distance drummed through her brain: one of these days, one of these perfect sun days . . .

He could not have been happier. He had waited for this day with an anxiety that spelled not months, but years. Not years of wanting her, but years of a longing, an unsatisfied craving that was finally to be sated. It had to happen one day, and as far as he was concerned, it would be today, his wedding day.

She raised the knife. It came down like a flash on the chopping block. The rawness of meat, the bloody mess that lay before her. Outside, the sun continued shining in the perfection of its day. Still time to retain perfection.

She hid the knife under her pillow. Another victim of the block, another one to the slaughter.

It was one of those perfect sun days, no more or less. The sun reflected that very perfection in her untouched self. Outside, the sirens screamed.

He had only wanted a wife.

The asylum at Castle Peak is quiet these days. There have been no outbursts lately. Just the occasional ones from the girl whose father sold dog meat.

*

Emerging from the West Fourth subway stop in the Village, she hears a man call. "Grace! Grace Hsu!"

A vaguely familiar figure hurries through the crowds.

"My God, it is you. You haven't changed, Grace, not a bit. You could still be eighteen!"

Who is he, this rather sticky, curly-haired man with a European accent? She smiles.

"You don't remember me?"

When it finally clicks that this is Vincent, that this is the college senior with whom she fell in love and to whom she surrendered that precious virginity, she wants to laugh.

They go for a drink. He tells her all about his marriage and children and divorce. And by the second drink, his voice is soft and warm and sentimental.

and all she can remember is that there was no blood, no pain, no feeling. just a horrible numbness, a sense of nothingness. that she had surrended nothing, gained nothing. that a whole American freshman year where students didn't study but worried about beer blasts and "scoring" was nothing, nothing, nothing she could ever explain to parents to her culture. and a year later, she wrote that story that novel about perfection and blood as if the blood of her fictional murder could bring life into the madness of reality.

and all she can remember is that in hong kong, chinese racist and sexist hong kong. everything submerged way down deep because there was no space in her life to say she was turned on by a boy who was eurasian and ugly and totally cerebral that even now after the orgasms her body responds to a cerebral stimulus before anything else.

and all she can remember is that she left something behind in that novel, her copy, the fourth copy because

*

Let's begin again. It is one of those perfect sun days. Grace Hsu sips her wine and smiles at the man to whom she gave up her virginity. Ten years ago. He is a stranger now, who talks of a life in America she never shared. All the time he speaks, her mind returns to the novel. She remembers the scene with the skeleton, when she finally called Jimmy the skeleton. Her protaganist, a Chinese girl in a Catholic school in Hong Kong, is engaged to a Eurasian boy who loves dogs. The boy desperately wants to make love to her, but insists that they wait because that would be proper. The protaganist expresses no feeling about her virginity.

But in her biology class, she is seduced by the skeleton, by the body that once was. The American nun who teaches biology to her Chinese charges is enthusiastic about her subject and gives the skeleton a name. One night, at midnight of course, she the protaganist goes to her school and keeps a rendevous with the skeleton. They dance, they embrace, they make love. She has her first orgasm.

She is sixteen.

The man whom she loved at eighteen, and to whom she gave up her virginity recalls her to the present tense.

"Will I see you again, Grace? I mean, this is such a coincidence, and surely, old friends should keep in touch? You really do look lovely."

This is not the way she remembers their original encounter ten years ago. Then, he called her the baby freshman, who was not nearly as glamorous as the buxom blondes he was accustomed to dating. She remembers thinking at the time that there was no such thing as a buxom blonde Chinese. Of course, there were so few Chinese at her upstate New York alma mater: perhaps fifty in all, of which five were female. But all that was normal, was reality, at the time.

So she says, "No, I don't think it would be a good idea. I'm seeing someone now."

"I understand," he says, smiling, friendly.

Does he suspect the lie, she wonders, as she watches him walk away.

*

But why did she have to kill him? Grace tosses this question around and around in her mind as she orders the events of her days. Telephone rings, messenger arrives, people people people in some form or another touching her life. And all the time, Grace wonders, why did she have to kill him?

For dramatic effect?

She remembers that this is how she explained the story to friends in college:

"With the murder, she destroys the ugly side of life. Then, she isn't afraid of dogs any longer. At the asylum, she's surrounded by dogs, and perfect sun days."

A friend had said, "Sounds too unreal."

And she had replied, "But who decides what reality is anyway?"

He dies, Grace thinks, because he is drunk. Yes, the lover cum husband is drunk on his wedding night, turning the first intercourse into a travesty. That's why he had to die. Narrative license, poetic convenience.

But

There, Grace thinks, is that voice again. Where's its coming from? Telephone rings. Have to make another call. The prints won't be ready till Friday?! Why not?

But, The husband was drunk only in the story. The husband doesn't die in the novel. The one page synopsis was for the story, before it became a novel. Remember?

She doesn't remember as she calls cousin Andy to explain that she'll be ready for his presentation on Monday.

The original brochure reads: "Architecture is both an art and a science. The architect must blend the structural integrity of design with the demands imposed by the space . . ."

How awful, Grace thinks, that such talented designers cannot begin to communicate with words. She compares the original brochure with her final copy and wonders why she finds words for architects easy to craft when she started with little or no knowledge of architecture.

Not the thing, but the perception of thing.

There is that voice again. Perhaps Andy's right, calling her his crazy Hong Kong cousin.

"You were going to be a writer, remember?"

Why is it Juliana remembers, but she doesn't?

*

because she hasn't wanted never wanted to face that yes she is crazy always has been crazy not crazy in the sickopsycho sense but crazy for keeping the lid on. that one day in the manuscript she let loose on the insanity of simultaneously-schizophrenically being chinese and catholic and western and hong kong and american and female and male and virgin and whore. and life and death. that one day in the manuscript she glimpsed if only just for a moment that her perception of thing was never is never would never be the thing as perceived by anyworld she lived in that she

*

Let's go back to reality.

For days, Grace cannot dismiss the image of the butcher block.

Her parents call.

"Are you making enough money?" Dad asks.

"When are you coming back to visit us?" Mum asks.

"I'm sorry I haven't written," Grace says.

"I read in Time magazine," Dad says, "that American statistics now show a growing number of single people households."

"When will you marry a rich man?" Mum repeats her lifelong serious-joke to all the girls.

"I don't know if I want to stay in America," Grace says.

"Make sure you get your citizenship first?" Mum insists.

"You don't plan to go back to Paris again, do you?" Dad begins. "Not more of that Bohemian life?"

"Maybe the novel makes her think she should be a writer again," Dad, the thwarted-as-a-violinist-father-breadwinner says to Mum.

"Grace, writing is very difficult. You're better doing your consulting work," Mum, the thwarted-in-her-medical-career-mother-wife says. "Remember, when you first came back from America, I told you you have to get a job first and when you settle down, then you can write?"

"Dad, Mum, better not spend too much money on this call. I'll say goodbye now."

"Okay, dear. *Kung Hei Fat Choy* for the Chinese New Year," her parents say together.

"*Kung Hei Fat Choy*," she replies.

After she hangs up, she wonders what her parents would say if they knew the legal, semi-legal, and almost-illegal means she used to live and work in Paris, and now in America.

Just before she immigrated to New York, Grace screamed for many days.

No one heard her screams.

The silent screams of normal neuroses. One interracial marriage. One divorce. A series of multinational lovers. One attempted rape by a former colleague. One abortion. One suicide attempt.

Just the typical adventures of the average self-proclaimed feminist of the latter part of the twentieth century. Everywoman wants "a relationship." No woman wants a "bad" relationship. In fact, it's generally accepted that "no relationship is better than a bad relationship."

As far as Grace is concerned, so much for relationships.

*

she is nowoman not everywoman but still woman. that she is experiencing not jet lag but race lag woman lag culture lag that is catching up to her at thirty. that she wrote "sun days" at eighteen and then attempted to live "sun days" between eighteen and thirty to find not Anny's nauseé but a dance with a skeleton the only ecstasy left to her.

the fourth copy has returned not as gwai goo not to haunt but to remind her of possibilities of options even though this is yet another option in a series of options must she really explore all try all is this what a romantic disposition is all about

*

Grace Hsu dances in the privacy of her Manhattan home with an invisible partner. "He" died many years ago in the middle of a manuscript.

Andy calls her all the time these days, wondering what has happened to his Hong Kong cousin. Grace has been difficult to reach, recalcitrant. She isn't the laughing, crazy, well adapted English-without-an-accent cousin anymore of whom he is so proud. Perhaps New York has gotten the better of her. The last time he spoke to her, she snapped his head off, saying he was an egocentric, sexist, American male who should know better since he's Chinese American. None of which makes much sense to him. At least, he doesn't think it should make much sense to him.

Andy consults his friend the psychiatrist and describes these symptoms of irrational behavior, all of which stem from, he is sure, the appearance of that manuscript.

Does she have a boyfriend? The friend asks.

Andy isn't sure. Grace doesn't tell anyone much about her love life, although he's sure she has one. She does occasionally mention dating.

Does she have friends?

Oh yes, Andy says, she has lots of friends and always has. She's the outgoing, friendly type.

Does she write poetry or fiction? Is she the temperamental artistic type?

Andy doesn't think she's temperamental at all, but thinks she does write a little on the side, but only a little.

Is there a history of mental instability, of imbalance? His friend inquires politely.

Andy doesn't know. Chinese people don't talk about these things, he says.

But, says his friend, this is America. Here we talk about these things.

Yes, says Andy, he knows.

*

In her Manhattan apartment, Grace dances with her invisible partner. The book lies open at the Munch drypoint.

In America, her professor had said, we talk about these things.

Yes, said Grace, she knew.
Yes, says Grace, she knows. That's why she returned.

Let's start with Once Upon a Time . . . .

Wakako Yamauchi

I was born in Westmoreland, California, a desert township near the Mexican border and I spent my early years in Imperial Valley where my father farmed. In 1942 we were all sent to Poston located in the Arizona desert, one of the 10 camps where Japanese and Japanese Americans were incarcerated during World War II.

After the war I moved to Los Angeles to study painting. I married there and off and on during marriage and motherhood, I wrote short stories of the Japanese in America. They often appeared in the Rafu Shimpo English Section until "And the Soul Shall Dance" found its way into Aiiieeeee: An Anthology Of Asian American Writers. Since then other stories were published in Asian American journals, college text books, women, minority and regional anthologies.

I think I write primarily because I want to preserve a time and place, a people, and maybe even a feeling that will never return. My stories are permeated with this landscape of longing.

166

AND THE SOUL SHALL DANCE

It's all right to talk about it now. Most of the principals are dead, except, of course, me and my younger brother, and possibly Kiyoko Oka, who might be near forty-five now, because, yes, I'm sure of it, she was fourteen then. I was nine, and my brother about four, so he hardly counts at all. Kiyoko's mother is dead, my father is dead, my mother is dead, and her father could not have lasted all these years with his tremendous appetite for alcohol and pickled chilies—those little yellow ones, so hot they could make your mouth hurt; he'd eat them like peanuts and tears would surge from his bulging thyroid eyes in great waves and stream down the dark coarse terrain of his face.

My father farmed then in the desert basin resolutely named Imperial Valley, in the township called Westmoreland; twenty acres of tomatoes, ten of summer squash, or vice versa, and the Okas lived maybe a mile, mile and a half, across an alkaline road, a stretch of greasewood, tumbleweed and white sand, to the south of us. We didn't hobnob much with them, because you see, they were a childless couple and we were a family: father, mother, daughter, and son, and we went to the Buddhist church on Sundays where my mother taught Japanese, and the Okas kept pretty much to themselves. I don't mean they were unfriendly; Mr. Oka would sometimes walk over (he rarely drove) on rainy days, all dripping wet, short and squat under a soggy newspaper, pretending to need a plow-blade or a file, and he would spend the afternoon in our kitchen drinking sake and eating chilies with my father. As he got progressively drunker, his large mouth would draw down and with the stream of tears, he looked like a kindly weeping bullfrog.

Not only were they childless, impractical in an area where large families were looked upon as labor potentials, but there was a certain strangeness about them. I became aware of it the summer our bathhouse burned down, and my father didn't get right down to building another, and a Japanese without a bathhouse . . . well, Mr. Oka offered us the use of his. So every night that summer we drove to the Okas for our bath, and we came in frequent contact with Mrs. Oka, and this is where I found the strangeness.

Mrs. Oka was small and spare. Her clothes hung on her like loose skin and when she walked, the skirt about her legs gave her a sort of webbed look. She was pretty in spite of the boniness and the dull calico and the barren look; I know now she couldn't have been over thirty. Her eyes were large and a little vacant, although once I saw them fill with tears; the time I insisted we take the old Victrola over and we played our Japanese records for her. Some of the songs were sad, and I imagined the nostalgia she felt, but my mother said the tears were probably from yawning or from the smoke of her cigarettes. I thought my mother resented her for not being more hospitable; indeed, never a cup of tea appeared before us, and between them the conversation of women was totally absent: the rise and fall of gentle voices, the arched eyebrows, the croon of polite surprise. But more than this, Mrs. Oka was *different*.

Obviously she was shy, but some nights she disappeared altogether. She would see us drive into her yard and then lurch from sight. She was gone all evening. Where could she have hidden in that two-roomed house—where in that silent desert? Some nights she would wait out our visit with enormous forbearance, quitely pushing wisps of stray hair behind her ears and waving gnats away from her great moist eyes, and some nights she moved about with nervous agitation, her khaki canvas shoes slapping loudly as she walked. And sometimes there appeared to be welts and bruises on her usually smooth brown face, and she would sit solemnly, hands on lap, eyes large and intent on us. My mother hurried us home then: "Hurry, Masako, no need to wash well; hurry."

You see, being so poky, I was always last to bathe. I think the Okas bathed after we left because my mother often reminded me to keep the water clean. The routine was to lather outside the tub (there were buckets and pans and a small wooden stool), rinse off the soil and soap, and then soak in the tub of hot hot water and contemplate. Rivulets of perspiration would run down the scalp.

When my mother pushed me like this, I dispensed with ritual, rushed a bar of soap around me and splashed about a pan of water. So hastily toweled, my wet skin trapped the clothes to me, impeding my already clumsy progress. Outside, my mother would be murmuring her many apologies and my father, I knew, would be carrying my brother, whose feet were already sandy. We would hurry home.

I thought Mrs. Oka might be insane and I asked my mother about it, but she shook her head and smiled with her mouth drawn down and said that Mrs. Oka loved her sake. This was unusual, yes, but there were other unusual women we knew. Mrs. Nagai was bought by her husband from a geisha house; Mrs. Tani was a militant Christian Scientist; Mrs. Abe, the midwife, was occult. My mother's statement explained much: sometimes Mrs. Oka was drunk and sometimes not. Her taste for liquor and cigarettes was a step into the realm of men; unusual for a Japanese wife, but at that time, in that place, and to me, Mrs. Oka loved her sake in the way my father loved his, in the way of Mr. Oka, the way I loved my candy. That her psychology may have demanded this anesthetic, that she lived with something unendurable, did not occur to me. Nor did I perceive the violence of emotions that the purple welts indicated—or the masochism that permitted her to display these wounds to us.

In spite of her masculine habits, Mrs. Oka was never less than a woman. She was no lady in the area of social amenities; but the feminine in her was innate and never left her. Even in her disgrace, she was a small broken sparrow, slightly floppy, too slowly enunciating her few words, too carefully rolling her Bull Durham, cocking her small head and moistening the ocher tissue. Her aberration was a protest of the life assigned her; it was obstinate, but unobserved, alas, unheeded. "Strange" was the only concession we granted her.

Toward the end of summer, my mother said we couldn't continue bathing at the Okas'; when winter set in we'd all catch our death from the commuting and she'd always felt dreadful about our imposition on Mrs. Oka. So my father took the corrugated tin sheets he'd found on the highway and had been saving for some other use and built up our bathhouse again. Mr. Oka came to help.

While they raised the quivering tin walls, Mr. Oka began to

talk. His voice was sharp and clear above the low thunder of the metal sheets.

He told my father he had been married in Japan previously to the present Mrs. Oka's older sister. He had a child by the marriage, Kiyoko, a girl. He had left the two to come to America intending to send for them soon, but shortly after his departure, his wife passed away from an obscure stomach ailment. At the time, the present Mrs. Oka was young and had foolishly become involved with a man of poor reputation. The family was anxious to part the lovers and conveniently arranged a marriage by proxy and sent him his dead wife's sister. Well that was all right, after all, they were kin, and it would be good for the child when she came to join them. But things didn't work out that way; year after year he postponed calling for his daughter, couldn't get the price of fare together, and the wife—ahhh, the wife, Mr. Oka's groan was lost in the rumble of his hammering.

He cleared his throat. The girl was now fourteen, he said, and begged to come to America to be with her own real family. Those relatives had forgotten the favor he'd done in accepting a slightly used bride, and now tormented his daughter for being forsaken. True, he'd not sent much money, but if they knew, if they only knew how it was here.

"Well," he sighed, "who could be blamed? It's only right she be with me anyway."

"That's right," my father said.

"Well, I sold the horse and some other things and managed to buy a third-class ticket on the Taiyo-Maru. Kiyoko will get here the first week of September." Mr. Oka glanced toward my father, but my father was peering into a bag of nails. "I'd be much obliged to you if your wife and little girl," he rolled his eyes toward me, "would take kindly to her. She'll be lonely."

Kiyoko-san came in September. I was surprised to see so very nearly a woman; short, robust, buxom: the female counterpart of her father; thyroid eyes and protruding teeth, straight black hair banded impudently into two bristly shucks, Cuban heels and white socks. Mr. Oka brought her proudly to us.

"Little Masako here," for the first time to my recollection, he touched me; he put his rough fat hand on the top of my head, "is very smart in school. She will help with your school work, Kiyoko,"he said.

I had so looked forward to Kiyoko-san's arrival. She would be my soul mate; in my mind I had conjured a girl of my own proportions: thin and tall, but with the refinement and beauty I didn't yet possess that would surely someday come to the fore. My disappointment was keen and apparent. Kiyoko-san stepped forward shyly, then retreated with a short bow and small giggle, her fingers pressed to her mouth.

My mother took her away. They talked for a long time—about Japan, about enrollment in American school, the clothes Kiyoko-san would need, and where to look for the best values. As I watched then, it occurred to me that I had been deceived: this was not a child, this was a woman. The smile pressed behind her fingers, the way of her nod, so brief, like my mother when father scolded her: the face was inscrutable, but something—maybe spirit—shrank visibly, like a piece of silk in water. I was disappointed; Kiyoko-san's soul was barricaded in her unenchanting appearance and the smile she fenced behind her fingers.

She started school from third grade, one below me, and as it turned out, she quickly passed me by. There wasn't much I could help her with except to drill her on pronunciation—the "L" and "R" sounds. Every morning walking to our rural school: land, leg, library, loan, lot; every afternoon returning home: ran, rabbit, rim, rinse, roll. That was the extent of our communication; friendly but uninteresting.

One particularly cold November night—the wind outside was icy; I was sitting on my bed, my brother's and mine, oiling the cracks in my chapped hands by lamplight—someone rapped urgently at our door. It was Kiyoko-san; she was hysterical, she wore no wrap, her teeth were chattering, and except for the thin straw zori, her feet were bare. My mother led her to the kitchen, started a pot of tea, and gestured to my brother and me to retire. I lay very still but because of my brother's restless tossing and my father's snoring, was unable to hear much. I was aware, though, that drunken and savage brawling had brought Kiyoko-san to us. Presently they came to the bedroom. I feigned sleep. My mother gave Kiyoko-san a gown and pushed me over to make room for her. My mother spoke firmly: "Tomorrow you will return to them; you must not leave them again. They are your people." I could almost feel Kiyoko-san's short nod.

All night long I lay cramped and still, afraid to intrude into her hulking back. Two or three times her icy feet jabbed into mine and quickly retreated. In the morning I found my mother's gown neatly folded on the spare pillow. Kiyoko-san's place in bed was cold.

She never came to weep at our house again but I know she cried: her eyes were often swollen and red. She stopped much of her giggling and routinely pressed her fingers to her mouth. Our daily pronunciation drill petered off from lack of interest. She walked silently with her shoulders hunched, grasping her books with both arms, and when I spoke to her in my halting Japanese, she absently corrected my prepositions.

Spring comes early in the Valley; in February the skies are clear though the air is still cold. By March, winds are vigorous and warm and wild flowers dot the desert floor, cockleburs are green and not yet tenacious, the sand is crusty underfoot, everywhere there is the smell of things growing and the first tomatoes are showing green and bald.

As the weather changed, Kiyoko-san became noticeably more cheerful. Mr. Oka who hated so to drive could often be seen steering his dusty old Ford over the road that passes our house, and Kiyoko-san sitting in front would sometimes wave gaily to us. Mrs. Oka was never with them. I thought of these trips as the westernizing of Kiyoko-san: with a permanent wave, her straight black hair became tangles of tiny frantic curls; between her textbooks she carried copies of *Modern Screen* and *Photoplay*, her clothes were gay with print and piping, and she bought a pair of brown suede shoes with alligator trim. I can see her now picking her way gingerly over the deceptive white peaks of alkaline crust.

At first my mother watched their coming and going with vicarious pleasure. "Probably off to a picture show; the stores are all closed at this hour," she might say. Later her eyes would get distant and she would muse, "They've left her home again; Mrs. Oka is alone again, the poor woman."

Now when Kiyoko-san passed by or came in with me on her

way home, my mother would ask about Mrs. Oka—how is she, how does she occupy herself these rainy days, or these windy or warm or cool days. Often the answers were polite: "Thank you, we are fine," but sometimes Kiyoko-san's upper lip would pull over her teeth, and her voice would become very soft and she would say. "Drink, always drinking and fighting." At those times my mother would invariably say, "Endure, soon you will be marrying and going away."

Once a young truck driver delivered crates at the Oka farm and he dropped back to our place to tell my father that Mrs. Oka had lurched behind his truck while he was backing up, and very nearly let him kill her. Only the daughter pulling her away saved her, he said. Thoroughly unnerved, he stopped by to rest himself and talk about it. Never, never, he said in wide-eyed wonder, had he seen a drunken Japanese woman. My father nodded gravely, "Yes, it's unusual," he said and drummed his knee with his fingers.

Evenings were longer now, and when my mother's migraines drove me from the house in unbearable self-pity, I would take walks in the desert. One night with the warm wind against me, the dune primrose and yellow poppies closed and fluttering, the greasewood swaying in languid orbit, I lay on the white sand beneath a shrub and tried to disappear.

A voice sweet and clear cut through the half-dark of the evening:

> Red lips press against a glass
> Drink the purple wine
>> And the soul shall dance

Mrs. Oka appeared to be gathering flowers. Bending, plucking, standing, searching, she added to a small bouquet she clasped. She held them away; looked at them slyly, lids lowered, demure, then in a sudden and sinuous movement, she broke into a stately dance. She stopped, gathered more flowers, and breathed deeply into them. Tossing her head, she laughed—softly, beautifully, from her dark throat. The picture of her imagined grandeur was lost to me, but the delusion that transformed the bouquet of tattered petals and sandy leaves, and the aloneness of a desert twilight into a fantasy that brought such joy and abandon made me stir with discomfort. The sound broke Mrs. Oka's dance. Her eyes grew large and her neck tense—like a cat on the prowl. She spied me in the bushes. A peculiar chill ran through me. Then abruptly and with childlike delight, she scattered the flowers around her and walked away singing:

Falling, falling, petals on a wind . . .

That was the last time I saw Mrs. Oka. She died before the spring harvest. It was pneumonia. I didn't attend the funeral, but my mother said it was sad. Mrs. Oka looked peaceful, and the minister expressed the irony of the long separation of Mother and Child and the short-lived reunion; hardly a year together, she said. We went to help Kiyoko-san address and stamp those black-bordered acknowledgements.

When harvest was over, Mr. Oka and Kiyoko-san moved out of the Valley. We never heard from them or saw them again and I suppose in a large city, Mr. Oka found some sort of work, perhaps a janitor or a dishwasher and Kiyoko-san grew up and found someone to marry.

Chris Felver

Jessica Hagedorn

Born and raised in the Philippines, Jessica Hagedorn is the author of Dangerous Music *(now in its third printing) and the award-winning* Pet Food & Tropical Apparitions, *both published by Momo's Press. The working title for her contemporary Philippine novel is* Dogeaters, *scheduled for publication by Pantheon in 1989.*

Poems, theater and performance pieces, essays and short fiction have been published in The Seattle Review, Conditions, Ikon, Rolling Stone, Heresies, Bridge, Washington Review Of The Arts, Rolling Stock, *and* Yardbird Reader, *among others.*

Plays and performance pieces have been presented most notably at Joseph Papp's Public Theater, New York City's Dance Theater Workshop, The Kitchen, Franklin Furnace, Basement Workshop, The New Museum, The Whitney Museum At Philip Morris, Art On The Beach, The Danspace Project, and nationwide at The Intersection (San Francisco), NEXUS (Atlanta), Woodland Pattern (Milwaukee), Real Art Ways (Connecticut), and The Walker Art Center (Minneapolis).

For ten years, Jessica Hagedorn was the leader and songwriter for the influential art rock band, The Gangster Choir. Her anthem "Tenement Lover" is part of John Giorno's anthology record, A Diamond Hidden In The Mouth Of A Corpse *(Giorno Poetry Systems label, 1986).*

THE BLOSSOMING OF BONGBONG

Antonio Gargazulio-Duarte, also fondly known as Bongbong to family and friends, had been in America for less than two years and was going mad. He didn't know it, of course, having left the country of his birth, the Philippines, for the very reason that his sanity was at stake. As he often told his friend, the painter Frisquito, "I can no longer tolerate contradiction. This country is full of contradiction. I have to leave before I go crazy."

His friend Frisquito would only laugh. His laugh was eerie because it was soundless. When he laughed, his body would shake — and his face, which was already grotesque, would distort — but no sound would emit from him.

People were afraid of Frisquito. They bought his paintings, but they stayed away from him. Especially when he was high. Frisquito loved to get high. He had taken acid more than fifty times, and he was only twenty-six years old. He had once lived in New York, where people were used to his grotesque face and ignored him. Frisquito had a face that resembled a retarded child: eyes slanted, huge forehead, droopy mouth, and pale, luminous skin. Bongbong once said to him, "You have skin like the surface of the moon." Frisquito's skull was also unusually large, which put people off, especially women. Frisquito soon learned to do without women or men. "My paintings are masturbatory," he once said to the wife of the president of the Philippines. She never blinked an eye, later buying three of his largest murals. She was often referred to as a "trend-setter."

Frisquito told Bongbong, "There's nothing wrong with being crazy. The thing to do is to get comfortable with it."

Not only had Frisquito taken acid more than fifty times, he had also taken peyote and cocaine and heroin at a rate that doctors

From Dangerous Music, Momo's Press
Reprinted by Permission of the Author

often said would normally kill a man. "But I'm like a bull," he would say, "nothing can really hurt me, except the creator of the universe."

At which point he would smile.

Bongbong finally left Manila on a plane for San Francisco. He was deathly afraid. He wore an olive green velvet jacket, and dark velvet pants, with a long scarf thrown casually around his scrawny neck. Frisquito saw him off to the airport. "You look like a faggot," he said to Bongbong, who was once named best-dressed young VIP in Manila. Bongbong felt ridiculously out of place and took two downers so he could sleep during the long ride to America. He arrived, constipated and haggard, and was met by his sister and brother-in-law, Carmen and Pochoy Guevara. "You look terrible," his sister said. She was embarrassed to be seen with him. Secretly she feared he was homosexual, especially since he was such good friends with Frisquito.

Bongbong had moved in with his sister and brother-in-law who lived in a plush apartment on Twin Peaks. His brother-in-law Pochoy, who had graduated as a computer programmer from Heald's Business College, worked for the Bank of America. His sister Carmen, who was rather beautiful in a bland, colorless kind of way, had enrolled in an Elizabeth Arden beauty course, and had hopes of being a fashion model.

"Or maybe I could go into merchandising," she would say in the afternoons when she wouldn't go to class. She would sit in her stainless-steel, carpeted electric kitchen. She drank cup after cup of instant Yuban coffee, and changed her nailpolish every three days.

"You should wear navy blue on your nails," Bongbong said to her one of those afternoons, when she was removing her polish with Cutex lemon-scented polish remover. "It would look wonderful with your sallow complexion." Sallow was a word Bongbong had learned from Frisquito.

"Sallow? What does that mean?" Carmen never knew if her brother was insulting or complimenting her.

"It means pale and unhealthy," Bongbong said, "Anyway, it's in style now. I've seen lots of girls wearing it."

He wrote Frisquito a letter:

Dear Frisquito,

Everyone is a liar. My sister is the biggest one of them all. I am a liar. I lie to myself every second of the day. I look in the mirror and I don't know what's there. My sister hates me. I hate her. She is inhuman. But then, she doesn't know how to be human. She thinks I'm inhuman. I am surrounded by androids. Do you know what that is? I'm glad I never took acid.

I wish I was a movie star.

Love,
Bongbong.

The apartment had two bedrooms. Pochoy had bought a leather couch and a Magnavox record player on credit. He owned the largest and most complete collection of Johnny Mathis records. At night Bongbong would lay awake and listen to their silent fucking in the next room and wonder if Carmen was enjoying herself. Sometimes they would fuck to "Misty."

Carmen didn't cook too often, and Pochoy had a gluttonous appetite. Since he didn't believe in men cooking, they would often order Chinese food or pizzas to be delivered. Once in a while Bongbong would try to fix a meal, but he was never talented in that direction. Frisquito had taught him how to cook two dishes: fried chicken & spaghetti.

Dear Frisquito,

I can't seem to find a job. I have no skills, and no college degree. Carmen thinks I should apply at Heald's Business College and go into computer programming. The idea makes me sick. I am twenty-six years old and no good at anything. Yesterday I considered getting a job as a busboy in a restaurant, but Carmen was horrified. She was certain everyone in Manila would hear about it, (which they will) and she swears she'll kill herself out of shame. Not a bad idea, but I am not a murderer. If I went back to Manila I could be a movie star.

Love,
Bongbong.

Bongbong stood in the middle of a Market street intersection slowly going mad. He imagined streetcars melting and running him over, grinding his flesh and bones into one hideous, bloody mess. He saw the scurrying Chinese women, no more than four feet tall, run amok and beat him to death with their shopping bags, which were filled to the brim with slippery, silver-scaled fish.

He watched a lot of television. His eyes became bloodshot. He began to read—anything from bestsellers to plays to political science to poetry. A lot of it he didn't quite understand, but the names and events fascinated him. He would often visit bookshops just to get out of the apartment. He chose books at random, sometimes for their titles or the color of their bookjackets. His favorite before he went crazy was *Vibration Cooking* by Verta Mae Grosvenor. He even tried out some of Verta Mae's recipes, when he was in better moods on the days when Carmen and Pochoy were away. He had found Verta Mae's book for seventy-five cents in a used-bookstore which he frequented.

"What is this?" Carmen asked, staring at the bookcover, which featured Verta Mae in her colorful African motif outfit.

"That, my dear, is a cookbook," Bongbong answered, snatching the book out of her hands, now decorated in Max Factor's "Regency Red."

On the bus going home there was a young girl sitting behind Bongbong wearing a Catholic school uniform and carrying several books in her pale, luminous arms. When the bus came to a stop she walked quietly to the front and before getting off she turned, very slowly and deliberately, and stared deeply into Bongbong's eyes. "You will get what you deserve," she said.

One time when Bongbong was feeling particularly lonely he went to a bar on Union street where young men and women stand around and drink weak Irish coffees. The bar was sometimes jokingly known as a "meat factory." The young men were usually executives, or trying to look like executives. They wore their hair slightly long, with rather tacky muttonchop whiskers and they all smoked dope. The women were usually chic or terribly hip. Either way they eyed each other coolly and all wore platform shoes.

180

A drink was sent to Bongbong from the other end of the bar by a twenty-eight-year-old sometime actress and boutique salesgirl named Charmaine. She was from Nicaragua and quite stunning, with frizzy brown hair and the biggest ass Bongbong had ever seen.

"What're you having?" she asked, grinning. Her lips were moist and glossy, and the fertile crescent was tattooed in miniature on her left cheek.

Bongbong, needless to say, was silent for a moment. Ladies like Charmaine were uncommon in Manila. "Gimlet," he murmured, embarrassed because he disliked the idea of being hustled.

Charmaine had a habit of tossing her head back, so that her frizzy curls bounced, as if she was always secretly dancing. "Awright," she said, turning to the bartender, "bring the gentleman a gimlet." She giggled, turning to look fully at Bongbong. "I'm Charmaine. Wha's your name?"

Bongbong blushed. "Antonio," he said, "but I go by my nickname." He dreaded her next question, but braced himself for it, feeling the familiar nausea rising within him. Once Frisquito had told him that witches and other types of human beings only had power over you if they knew your name. Since that time Bongbong always hesitated when anyone asked him for his name, especially women. "Women are more prone to occult powers than men," Frisquito warned. "It comes natural to them."

Charmaine was smiling now, "Oh yeah? Whatisit?"

"Bongbong."

The bartender handed him the gimlet, and Charmaine shrugged. "That's a funky name, man. You Chicano?"

Bongbong was offended. He wanted to say No, I'm Ethiopian, or Moroccan, or Nepalese, what the fuck do you care . . . Silently he drank his gimlet. Then he decided, the nausea subsiding, that Charmaine wasn't malicious, and left the bar with her shortly after.

Charmaine showed him the boutique where she worked, which was next door to the bar. Bongbong stared at the platform shoes in the display window as if he were seeing them for the first time. Their glittering colors and whimsical designs intrigued him. Charmaine watched his face curiously as he stood with his face pressed against the glass like a small child, then she took his arm and led him to her VW.

She lived in a large flat in the Fillmore district with another sometime actress and boutique salesgirl named Colelia. They had six cars, and the place smelled like a combination of catpiss and incense.

Colelia thought she was from Honey Patch, South Carolina, but she wasn't sure. "I'm mixed up," she said. Sometimes she thought she was a geechee. She was the only person Bongbong knew who had ever read *Vibration Cooking*. She had even met Verta Mae at a party in New York.

Bongbong spent the night in Charmaine's bed, but he couldn't bring himself to even touch her. She was amused, and asked him if he was gay. At first he didn't understand the term. English sometimes escaped him, and certain colloquialisms, like "gay," never made sense. He finally shook his head and mumbled no. Charmaine told him she didn't really mind. Then she asked him to go down on her.

Dear Frisquito:

I enrolled at Heald's College today so that Carmen would shut up. I plan on leaving the house every morning and pretending I'm going to school. That way no one will bother me.

I think I may come back to Manila soon, but somehow I feel I'm being trapped into staying here. I don't understand anything. Everyone is an artist, but I don't see them doing anything. Which is what I don't understand . . . but one good thing is I am becoming a good cook.

Enclosed is a copy of 'Vibration Cooking' by Verta Mae.

Love,
B.

Sometimes Bongbong would open the refrigerator door and oranges would fly out at him. He was fascinated by eggs, and would often say to his sister, "We're eating the sunset," or "We're eating embryos." Or he would frown and say, "I never did like chickens."

He began riding streetcars and buses from one end of the city to the other, often going into trances and reliving the nightmare of the streetcar melting and running him over. Always the Chinese women would appear, beating him to death with silver-scaled fish, or eggs.

Bongbong saw Charmaine almost every day for a month. His parents sent him an allowance, thinking he was in school. This allowance he spent lavishly on her. He bought her all the dazzling platform shoes her heart desired. He took her to fancy nightclubs so she could dance and wiggle her magnificent ass to his delight. She loved Sly Stone and Willie Colon, so he bought her all their records. They ate curry and spice cake every night of the week (sometimes alternating with yogurt pie and gumbo) and Charmaine put on ten pounds.

He never fucked her. Sometimes he went down on her, which she liked even better. She had replaced books and television in his life. He thought he was saved.

One afternoon while he was waiting for Charmaine in the bar where they had met, Bongbong had a vision. A young woman entered the bar, wearing a turban on her head made of torn rags. Her hair was braided and stood out from her scalp like branches on a young tree. Her skin was so black she was almost blue.

Around her extremely firm breasts she wore an old yellow crocheted doily, tied loosely. Her long black skirt was slit up the front all the way to her crotch, and underneath she wore torn black lace tights and shocking pink suede boots laced all the way up to her knees. She carried a small basket as a handbag, and she was smoking Eve cigarettes elegantly, as if she were a dowager empress.

She sat next to Bongbong and gazed at him coolly and deliberately. People in the bar turned their heads and stared at her, some of them laughing. She asked Bongbong for a match. He lit her cigarette. His hands were trembling. She smiled, and he saw some of her teeth were missing. After she smoked her cigarette, she left the bar.

Another day while Bongbong was walking in the Tenderloin, he had another vision. A young woman offered to fuck him for a mere twenty-five dollars. He hesitated, looking at her. She had shoulder-length, greasy blond hair. She had several teeth missing too, and what other teeth she had left were rotten. Her eyes, which were a dull brown, were heavily painted with midnight-blue mascara. She wore a short red skirt, a tight little sweater, and her black sheer tights had runs and snags all over them. Bongbong noticed that she had on expensive silver platform shoes that were sold in Charmaine's boutique.

He asked her name.

Her voice was as dull as her eyes. "Sandra," she replied.

He suddenly felt bold in her presence. "How old are you?"

"Nineteen. How old are you, honey?" She leered at him, then saw the blank look on his face and all the contempt washed out of her. He took her to a restaurant where they served watery hamburgers and watery coffee. He asked her if she had a pimp.

"Yup. And I been busted ten times. I been a hooker since I was thirteen, and my parents are more dead than alive. Anything else you wanna know?"

Her full name was Sandra Broussard. He told her she was beautiful. She laughed. She said her pimp would kill her if she ever left the business. She showed him her scars. "He cut my face once, with a razor," she said.

He felt useless. He went back to the apartment and Carmen was waiting for him. "We've decided you should move out of this place as soon as possible," she said. "I'm pregnant, and I want to redecorate your room for the baby. I'm going to paint your room pink."

He went into the bathroom and stared at the bottles of perfume near the sink, the underarm deodorant, the foot deodorant, the cinnamon-flavored mouthwash, and the vaginal spray. They used Colgate brand toothpaste. Dove soap. Zee toilet paper. A Snoopy poster hung behind the toilet. It filled him with despair.

Bongbong moved into Charmaine's flat shortly after. He brought his velvet suit and his books. Colelia reacted strangely at first. She had been Charmaine's lover for some time, and felt Bongbong would be an intrusion. But all he did was read his books and watch television. He slept on a mattress in the living room. He hardly even spoke to Charmaine anymore. Sometimes they would come home from work in the evenings and find Bongbong in the kitchen, preparing Verta Mae's "Kalalou Noisy

184

Le See" or her "Codfish with Green Sauce" for all of them. Colelia realized he wasn't a threat to her love life at all. Life became peaceful for her and Charmaine.

During the long afternoons when Colelia and Charmaine were gone and the cats were gone and the only thing Bongbong could sense was the smell of piss from the catbox, he would put on his velvet suit and take long walks in the Tenderloin, trying to find Sandra Broussard. He thought he saw her once, inside a bar, but when he went in he found it was a mistake. The woman turned out to be much older, and when she turned to smile at him, he noticed she wore the hand of Fatima on a silver chain around her neck.

When he really thought about it, in his more lucid moments, he realized he didn't even remember what she really looked like anymore. Dullness was all he could conjure of her presence. Her fatigue and resignation.

Charmaine, on the other hand, was bright, beautiful, and self-ish. She was queen of the house and most activity revolved around her. Colelia always came home from work with a gift for Charmaine, which they both referred to as "prizes." Sometimes they were valuable, like jade rings or amethyst stones for Char-maine's pierced nose, or silly—like an old Walt Disney cup with Donald Duck painted on it.

Bongbong found the two women charming and often said so when he was in a talkative mood. "You are full of charm and your lives will be full of success," he would say to them, as they sat in their antique Chinese robes, painting each other's faces.

"You sound like a fortune cookie," Charmaine would say, glaring at him.

He would be silent at her outbursts, which naturally made her more furious. "I wish you'd tell me how much you want me," she would demand, ignoring her female lover's presence in the room.

Sometimes Charmaine would watch Bongbong as he read his books, and she would get evil with him out of boredom. She was easily distracted and therefore easily bored, especially when she wasn't the center of attention. This was often the case when Colelia was at work and it was Charmaine's day off.

Bongbong said to her, "Once you were a witch but you misused your powers. Now you resent me because I remind you of those past days."

Charmaine circled Bongbong as he sat in the living room immersed in *Green Mansions* by W. H. Hudson. He had found the hardback novel for one dollar in another secondhand-bookshop called Memory Lane.

"I'm going to take my clothes off, Bongbong," Charmaine would tease. "What're you going to do about it?" Bongbong would look up at her, puzzled. Then she would put her hands on her enormous hips. "Men like me most of all because of my ass, Bongbong . . . but they can't really get next to me. Most of them have no style . . . but you have a sort of style—" By this time she had often removed her skirt. "I don't wear panties," she said, "so whenever I want, Colelia can feel me up." Bongbong tried to ignore her. He was getting skilled in self-hypnosis, and whenever external disturbances would occur, he would stare off into the distance and block them slowly from his mind.

The more skilled he became in his powers, the more furious Charmaine would get with him. One time she actually wrenched the book from his hands and threw it out the window. Then she lay on the couch in front of him and spread her legs. "You know what I've got, Bongbong? Uterina Furor . . . That's what my mother use to say . . . Nuns get it all the time. Like a fire in the womb."

To make her smile Bongbong would kiss her between her legs, and then Colelia would come home and pay more attention to Charmaine and Bongbong would cook more of Verta Mae's recipes, such as "Stuffed Heart Honky Style" (one of Charmaine's favorites) and everything would be all right.

Charmaine's destructive moods focused on Bongbong twice a month and got worse when the moon was full. "You're in a time of perennial menstruation," Bongbong told her solemnly after one of her fits.

One morning while they were having breakfast together, Colelia accused Charmaine of being in love with Bongbong. "Why, I don't know—" Colelia said. "He's so funny-looking and weird. You're just into such an ego trip you want what you can't have."

Charmaine giggled. "Forever analyzing me! Don't I love you enough?"

"It's not that."

"Well, then—why bring him up? You never understood him from the very beginning," Charmaine said. "Or why I even brought him here in the first place. I must confess—I don't quite know why I brought him home myself. Somehow, I knew he wasn't going to fuck me . . . I really didn't want a fuck though. It was more like I wanted him around to teach me something about myself . . . Something like that, anyway."

Colelia looked away. "That's vague enough."

"Are you really jealous of him?" Charmaine asked.

Colelia finally shook her head. "Not in that way . . . but maybe because I don't understand him, or the two of you together—I am jealous I guess because I feel left out of his mystique."

Charmaine embraced her, and the two of them wept.

Bongbong's visions and revelations were becoming more frequent. A Chinese woman with a blonde wig and a map of the world on her legs. A black man with three breasts. A cat turning doorknobs. A tortoise crawling out of a sewer on the sidewalk, and junkies making soup out of him. Frisquito assassinating the president of the Philippines who happened to be his wife in drag who happened to be a concert pianist's mother . . . The visions were endless, circular, and always moving.

Dear Frisquito:

Yesterday a friend of Charmaine's named Ra brought a record over by a man named John Coltrane. Ra tells me that Mr. Coltrane died not too long ago, I believe when we were just out of high school. Ra decided that I could keep the record, which is called 'Meditations', I believe it is the title of one of your paintings.

Every morning I plan on waking up to this man's music. It keeps my face from disintegrating. You once said your whole being had disintegrated long ago, and that you had the power to pick up the pieces from time to time, when it was necessary—such as the time you gave an exhibit of your works for the benefit of the First Lady. I think there may be some hope left for me.

Yesterday I cooked Verta Mae's 'Uptight Ragout' in your honor.
                                                              Love,
                                                                 B.

Bongbong now referred to himself as "B." He could not stand to speak in long sentences, and tried to live and speak as minimally as possible. Charmaine worried about him, especially when he would go on one of his rampages and cook delicious gumbo dinners for herself and Colelia, and not eat with them.

"But B," she protested, "I never see you eat anymore."

One time he said, "Maybe I eat a saxophone."

He loved the word saxophone.

His parents stopped sending money, since Carmen wrote them that he had never attended one day of school at Heald's Business College. His father wrote him and warned him never to set foot in the Philippines again, or he would have him executed for the crime of deception and subversion to one's parents, a new law put into practice in the current dictator's regime.

Bongbong decided to visit Carmen. She was almost six months pregnant, and very ugly. Her face had broken out in rashes and pimples, and her whole body was swollen. Her once shimmering black hair was now dry and brittle, and she had cut it short. Her nails were painted a pale pink, like the bedroom that had once been his. He stared at her for a long time as they sat in the kitchen in silence. She finally suggested that he see the baby's room.

She had decorated the room with more Snoopy posters, and mobiles with wooden angels hung from the ceiling. A pink baby bed stood in the center of the room, which was heavily scented with floral spray.

"It's awful," Bongbong said.

"Oh, you're always insulting everything!" his sister screamed, shoving him out the door. She shut the door behind her, as if guarding a sacred temple, and looked at him, shaking with rage. "You make everything evil. Are you on drugs? I think you're insane," she said. "Leave this house before I call the police." She hated him because he made her feel ashamed in his presence, but she couldn't understand why.

Frisquito, who never answered any of his letters, sent him a check for a considerable amount of money. A postcard later arrived with the note, "Don't Worry" scratched across it, and Frisquito's valuable signature below the message. Bongbong, who now wore his velvet suit everyday, went to a pawnshop and bought a soprano saxophone.

In the mornings he would study with Ra, who taught him circular breathing. He never did understand chords and scales, but he could hear what Ra was trying to teach him and he surprised everyone in the house with the eerie sounds he was making out of his new instrument. Charmaine told Colelia that she thought Bongbong was going to be all right, because Bongbong had at last found his "thing."

Which was wrong, because Bongbong's music only increased his natural visionary powers. He confessed to Ra that he could actually see the notes in the air, much like he could see the wind. Ra would study him and smile, not saying anything.

Bongbong would watch Charmaine at the kitchen table eating breakfast, and when she would look up at him, she would suddenly turn into his mother, with Minnie Mouse ears and long, exaggerated Minnie Mouse eyelashes, which glittered and threw off sparks when she blinked. This would frighten him sometimes, because he would forget who Charmaine was. As long as he could remember who everyone was, he would feel a surge of relief. But these moments were becoming more and more confusing, and it was getting harder and harder for him to remember everyone's names, including his own.

Colelia decided that Bongbong was a "paranoid schizophrenic" and that she and Charmaine should move out, for their own safety. "One of these days we'll come home from work an find all our kittykats with their throats slit," she said. She refused to eat any more of Bongbong's cooking, for fear he would poison her. "He doesn't like women basically. That's the root of his problem," she told Charmaine. "I mean, the guy doesn't even jack-off! How unnatural can he be? Remember Emil Kemper!"

"Remember Emil Kemper!" became the motto of the household. Emil Kemper was a young madman in Santa Cruz, California, who murdered his grandmother when he was something like thirteen years old, murdered his mother later on after he was released from the looney bin, cut her head off, and murdered about a million other female hitchhikers.

Charmaine sympathized with Bongbong, but she wasn't sure about him either. Only Ra vouched for his sanity. "Sure the cat is crazy," he said, "but he'll never hurt any of you."

Bongbong practiced the saxophone every day, and seemed to survive on a diet of water and air. Charmaine came home from the boutique one night and brought him two pairs of jeans and two T-shirts. One T-shirt had glittery blue and silver thread woven into it, and Bongbong saw the shirt become a cloud floating above his narrow bed. "Well," Charmaine said, trying to sound casual as she watched Bongbong drift off dreamily, "Aren't you going to try it on? Do you like it? I seriously think you should have your velvet suit drycleaned before it falls apart."

Bongbong touched the cloud. "Oh, how beautiful," he said.

He never wore the shirt. He hung it above his bed like a canopy, where he could study it at night. His ceiling became a galaxy. To appease Charmaine (he was very sensitive to her feelings, and loved her in his own way), he wore the other shirt and sent his velvet suit to the cleaners.

Frisquito sent him more money the next month, and Bongbong bought a telescope.

Dear Frisquito,

Do you know I am only five feet and two inches tall? Without my platform shoes, of course. Why do people like to look like cripples? Yesterday I saw a fat young woman wearing platform shoes that made her feet look like boats. Her dress was too short on her fat body and you could see her cellulite wobbling in her forest green pantyhose. Cellulite is the new fad in America. Some Frenchwoman discovered it and is urging everyone to feel for it in their skin. It's sort of like crepe-paper tissue that happens when you put on too much weight. I told the fat young woman she was beautiful, and she told me to fuck off. She was very angry, and I realized there are a lot of angry people around me. Except in the house I live in, which is why I've stayed so long.

The Coltrane record is warped from having been left in the sun. I am writing a song about it in my head.

> With my telescope I can see
> everyone, and they don't have to
> see me.
>
> Love,
B.

Bongbong often brought the telescope up to the roof of their building and watched the people on the streets below. Then at night he would watch the stars in the sky and try and figure out different constellations. Charmaine took him to the planetarium for his birthday, and they watched a show on Chinese astronomy called "The Emperor of the Heavens," narrated by a man called Alvin. Bongbong was moved to tears. "I love you," he told Charmaine as they laid back in their seats and watched the heavens.

But he had forgotten that she was Charmaine Lopez, and that she lived with him. He thought she was Sandra Broussard, or the blue lady with the rag turban on her head. When the show was over he asked her to marry him.

He didn't say another word until they reached the flat. He cooked Verta Mae's "Jamaican Curried Goat" for his birthday dinner and Colelia gave him a cake which had a sugarcoated model airplane on it. Bongbong removed the airplane and hung it next to the canopy above his bed.

After dinner he asked Charmaine if she would sleep with him. She didn't have the heart to refuse, and after kissing Colelia on the forehead, followed Bongbong into his room. The next morning Charmaine told Colelia they should both move out.

"Was he a freak? I mean, did he hurt you?" Colelia asked.

Charmaine shook her head. "No. But I don't want to live around him any more. It may be best if we left today."

They packed their clothes and rounded up their cats and left in Charmaine's VW, leaving Bongbong with a note on the kitchen table.

We will send for the rest of our things. Forgive us.

C & C.

Bongbong awoke from a beautiful dream in which he had learned how to fly. Everything in the dream had an airy quality. He floated and glided through the atmosphere, and went swimming in the clouds, which turned out to be his glittery blue sweater. Charmaine Lopez and her dancing girls did the rhumba in the heavens, which were guarded by smiling Chinese Deities. Alvin from the planetarium sang "Stardust" for him as he flew by. He was happy. He could play saxophone forever. Then he saw Frisquito flying far away, waving to him. He tried and tried, but he couldn't get any closer to him. Frisquito became smaller and smaller, then vanished, and when Bongbong opened his eyes, he found Charmaine gone.

He decided to stay in the flat, and left the other rooms just as they were. Even Ra stopped coming to visit, so Bongbong had to teach himself about the saxophone. There were brief moments when he found that the powers of levitation were within him, so while he would practice the saxophone he would also practice levitating.

Frisquito,

Just two things. The power of flight has been in me all along. All I needed was to want it bad enough.

Another is something someone once said to me. Never is forever, she said.

Love.

He didn't sign his name or his initial, because he had finally forgotten who he was.

192

Rosanna Yamagiwa Alfaro

Rosanna Yamagiwa Alfaro was brought up in the Midwest where there often wasn't another Asian American for miles around. Her subject matter has been half Asian, half generic. Behind Enemy Lines, *her play about the Japanese American internment camps, was produced by Peoples Theater in Cambridge in 1981 and by Pan Asian Repertory in New York in 1982.* Mishima *was produced by East West Players in Los Angeles and* Martha Mitchell *by Theater Center Philadelphia, both in 1988. She has published many short stories and poems in magazines including* Descant, Waves, The Harvard Advocate, The Capilano Review, *and* The Boston Globe Magazine.

PROFESSOR NAKASHIMA AND
TOMIKO THE CAT

Professor Nakashima held Tomiko under his arm and waved goodbye to the Sobels. Tomiko was a large Persian cat who had been with the Sobels all of her eighty-seven cat years. Whenever the Sobels went away on their summer and winter vacations she worked herself into such a state that she would moult until she was nearly bald. "Don't call us when it happens," said Amy. "Just keep her away from drafts and remember, it all grows back as soon as we return."

Amy was Japanese-American and obstinately cheery. She had been brought up in postwar Southern California like himself. They had, in fact, been childhood sweethearts, lost touch when they went their separate ways to college, then, inevitably it seemed, gotten back together when he and Amy's husband Tom discovered they were colleagues at Brandeis.

The snow was beginning to fall again when Professor Nakashima, Tomiko held tightly under his arm, retreated into the Sobel's house. The new flurries would freshly dust the piles of snow that had slowly accumulated over the past month. The only challenge to all that whiteness were the nests of dog shit, often still steaming on the edges of the shoveled paths, and the urine stains in the snow banks at every driveway. It was extraordinary, thought Professor Nakashima, the quantities of urine that must seep unnoticed into the ground during the summertime.

Once inside the Sobel's large house Professor Nakashima sat back on the great flowered sofa that Amy had spent an entire summer reupholstering. Tomiko drew blood as she sprang out of his arms. In one motion she displaced herself from armchair to bookcase to mantlepiece and began washing herself vigorously, anxious, no doubt, to rid herself of any trace of his human scent.

Professor Nakashima, out of work for 398 days, detested cats, which hadn't prevented him from leaving his small bachelor quarters to catsit in his ex-colleague's house for the Christmas vacation. Tom and Amy had stashed their two small children with the grandparents and were off to Puerto Rico for a month. Never mind that the university vacation was only three weeks long. Tom, to whom tenure and all other things came easily, had arranged it so he'd be away the entire month.

Even the heavens went out of their way to contribute to Tom's happiness, thought Professor Nakashima as he untied his shoes and sank back into the great sofa. The snow flurries had come down at just the right moment to heighten Tom's anticipation of escaping to warmer climes. Lying back, Professor Nakashima, who had put on a fair amount of weight since his enforced retirement, felt like a beached whale.

Later it seemed to him that he had spent most of his first three weeks there on the down-filled cushions of Amy's sofa. He simply found it very difficult to move. Even when he executed a slow turn from one side to the other he heard a thin whistle that seemed to be coming from his heart, as if it were letting out a little air. Spiritually, however, he moved more rapidly, going pleasantly from book to book, not from Tom's esoteric library, which reminded him too much of his own, but from Amy's Book-of-the-Month Club selections.

Since he had been denied tenure, Professor Nakashima had not opened a single book of far-eastern history. Of course, neither had many of his ex-colleagues, including Tom, a committee rat, who had taught the same courses for five years in a row and devoted his considerable talents entirely to administrative matters. There were even rumors afloat that Tom was the one who might most naturally take over the department once the present chairman retired.

For Professor Nakashima life made simpler demands — telephone messages to jot down, the cat to feed. Tomiko, perversely enough, had developed an attachment to him. She jumped on his lap and sat all over any book he happened to be reading. She wove back and forth ahead of him as he made his way to the kitchen, rubbing her cheeks on his stockinged feet. Since Amy, with her compulsive Japanese tidiness, had left the cans of catfood neatly stacked, all he had to do was alternate the tuna with the chicken liver. But Professor Nakashima soon discovered he hated the smell of cat food and couldn't bring himself to wash out Tomiko's bowl for over a week. At that point he gingerly threw the bowl into the garbage and thereafter Tomiko ate directly from the can.

Once in the kitchen there was also the matter of his own meals. The Sobels kept a well-stocked larder. Tom gave him the keys to the liquor cabinet and Amy said he was to help himself to anything he could find in the pantry. Though Professor Nakashima couldn't bring himself to touch a drop of Tom's liquor, he felt no compunctions about raiding the pantry. In the morning he poured milk into the miniature cereal boxes Amy bought for the children, thereby saving himself the bother of doing the breakfast dishes. He found pickled herring and sesame crackers for lunch, bottled chicken and truffles for dinner, and though he snacked continually he hardly made a dent in the pantry stores. How fortunate for Tom that Amy was so provident.

Whenever he felt a pang of guilt for poaching on the Sobel preserves he reminded himself that they, after all, owed him several meals of his own choosing. In the beginning Amy had invited him with other members of the history department for special Japanese meals she knew he would particularly enjoy. But lately, especially after the tenure decision, she tended to invite him alone on what he immediately recognized as the leftovers of some banquet they had had without him the night before. Not that they didn't enjoy his company. He still retained a special place in their household, much like a pet of long standing to whom one fed the best scraps under the table.

Within two weeks Professor Nakashima had poked through all the shelves, even finding the cookie jar where Amy stashed her jewels. Professor Nakashima ran the necklaces through his fingers, his long mandarin fingers that stayed thin and elegant in spite of his great weight. He could not remember Amy even wearing the simplest pin, but here was a wealth of gold and silver, emeralds and diamonds squirreled prudently away for a rainy day. He warmed a fat ruby brooch in his palm before letting it drop back into the cookie jar. Poor but honest, he thought, grimly calculating its worth in porterhouse steaks and smoked salmon.

Tom and his other Anglo-American friends cherished the illusion that Professor Nakashima had achieved his impressive girth on sake and sushi, when living on welfare as he did, he usually had to settle for beer and chips. Even when he was still receiving his assistant professor's wages he generally preferred Chinese to Japanese cuisine, finding it more varied and opulent, catering more to the palate than to the eye.

His appetites being what they were, Professor Nakashima took pains to weigh himself at the thinnest moment of every day—in the morning between urinating and having breakfast—and found he had lately been gaining weight at the rate of a pound a week. Having no full-length mirror in his bachelor's quarters, he had not fully appreciated the extent of his enormity. He knew he spilled over his belt, that he was a snug fit in Tom's leather Corbusier armchair, but turning sideways in front of the hall mirror was a revelation of such proportions that he instantly despaired of any diet or exercise.

And in the Sobel house, although he had yet to go out for groceries, he was growing, not shrinking. His shirts were all tight at the armpits. The few that used to hang straight now took the shape of his stomach. One day he tried on one of Tom's jackets and heard something rip at the shoulder. Then he discovered a wide denim smock of Amy's in the laundry bin and found it so much to his liking that he wore it an entire week both waking and sleeping.

In the bathroom the Sobels had a small magnifying mirror surrounded with lights and in it he discovered his first white hairs, not one but five all at once. As a child he had carefully pulled out a black hair and a white hair from his mother's head so he could examine them under a microscope. The black hair was thin, the white hair thick with a center that resembled the core of a carrot. His own white hairs, which he also pulled out, were stiff and curly. Professor Nakashima's sleek black hair had always been his sole point of vanity.

The time passed quickly or rather did not pass at all. He barely gave a thought to the snowy streets outside. At the end of the fourth week a postcard arrived from Amy complaining that Tom had decided to leave Puerto Rico a week early to attend a medieval history symposium in Ohio before flying home. The idea of leaving a tropical paradise early to return to wintry climes seemed absurd to Amy. Tom could travel without her. She would remain by herself in the sun.

Professor Nakashima derived a certain amount of satisfaction from the peevishness of Amy's note. Why she had married Tom in the first place had always been a source of mystery to him. He had naturally assumed that she would marry a Japanese-American like himself. He still averted his eyes whenever she addressed the tall bearded Tom with an endearment or when she stood, as she often did, with her arm around his waist. On the other hand, particularly lately, he found himself wondering what Tom could possibly see in Amy, built short and squat like a soup can. Poor Amy had never been thin but, like himself, had recently gained six hundred pounds. Unlike himself, she had Japanese-American stamped on her forehead, determined, tidy, sensible to a fault. She had probably sniffed out Tom's administrative potential from the beginning.

Amy's postcard also served as a reminder that he was not on his own turf, that the Sobels would be back in a week. That was all well and good, thought Professor Nakashima, since Tomiko was beginning to get on his nerves. It seemed he couldn't leave the room without her following at his heels. She was always with him, asleep on his lap, playing with his shoelaces, or even squatting on the toilet seat to watch him as he took his bath. The smell of cat was in the air and on his clothes. Also, as Amy had forewarned him, she was beginning to moult. Balls of cat hair would blow across the floor like tumbleweed. There was also the matter of the kitty litter. He had noticed after the second week that it had gotten permanently wet and lumpy, but overcome by an immense lethargy, he couldn't quite bring himself to change it.

Professor Nakashima suddenly decided that just as Amy felt the need for a vacation away from Tom, he owed it to himself to spend a few days away from Tom's namesake. Letting Tomiko out was impossible. She was one of those housecats that had never once set foot on the grass, accustomed all her life to the feel of wall-to-wall carpets. No wonder she was so neurotic and spent many of her waking hours on the window sill looking out longingly at the snow.

Fortunately the house was big enough for both of them. Professor Nakashima in one master stroke picked up his belongings from the guest bedroom and moved into the master bedroom with its own bathroom attached, complete with the only Japanese bath in Waltham. For his five day retreat he provided himself with a basket of supplies from Amy's pantry along with a large parcel of interesting tinned and bottled delicacies from Japan which had just arrived in a Christmas package from Amy's aunt and which he had absentmindedly opened.

For Tomiko he poured a large saucepan of milk and opened up five cans of cat food which he placed side by side on the floor. He even watered the plants, which Amy had thoughtfully gathered together on the kitchen table lest they fall victim to his benign neglect. Professor Nakashima watered them thoroughly, waiting until the water came out of the holes at the bottom of the flower pots. Then, having discharged all his responsibilities, he said goodbye to Tomiko and settled back on the crisp gingham spread of the Sobel's emperor size bed.

These were perhaps the most perfect days that Professor Nakashima ever spent in his adult life. Even Tomiko couldn't spoil his five day idyll though at first she sat outside his door for hours at a time, meowing pitifully, sticking her paw under the door and trying to pull it open. At night she would gallop up and down the hall like a horse, chasing some small object—a child's marble, perhaps, or a mouse.

But, generally speaking, Professor Nakashima settled back to enjoy his cans of eel and cuttlefish, his bottles of pickled tofu, mushrooms, ferns and leeks. New Year's Eve, he poured water into the large sunken tub just before midnight and splashed happily about, relishing the fact that his bath spanned two years. He was a great lover of the bath—in that one respect his Japanese genes seemed to assert themselves over his American environment. Or maybe it was because the bath was as close as he ever got these days to the sea. Even as a child he had been as graceful in the water as he was clumsy on land. Swimming, he displaced himself as effortlessly as the seals and walruses. Walking, he was out of his element.

The sunken bath, which was obviously also enjoyed by the Sobel children, had on its edge several small colorful bath toys

200

which he examined at his leisure. A small wind-up turtle that flapped its way across the tub and a toy pump were his favorites. They reminded him pleasantly of his own childhood when his mother, a large woman, took him into the bath with her and allowed him to dock his boats on her island tummy. His own stomach was now so large he had difficulty in viewing his private parts.

It was on his fifth night in the Sobel's room that Professor Nakashima received a midnight telephone call that effectively put an end to his holiday. It was Amy. She was sorry, she said, for waking him, but naturally she wanted to take advantage of the cheapest phone rates. "Of course, of course, how sensible," he said, adding pleasantly, "how Japanese."

The connection was bad. It seemed to him that her voice was coming from another planet. He slowly pieced together what it was she was saying, and trying to shake himself awake from the nightmare said, "You what?" and then, "For Christ's sake, Amy," because the woman he had known and in his own way adored ever since childhood, the woman with whom he had grown comfortably middle-aged and fat was now telling him she would be a week late because she was having as she put it, "a last ditch stab at happiness, freedom, love, whatever you want to call it" with, from all he could gather, a dermatologist attending a cosmetics colloquium in San Juan.

"Listen," she was saying, "You're the one person I can count on to square things with Tom. I'm not asking you to understand. I know we're the same age, but it's different for a woman. All these years I've been the typical housewife with nothing in my future except teenaged children, an empty nest, and menopause."

Professor Nakashima was stunned. He cut Amy short saying, "This must be costing you a small fortune." Never in his life had he come face to face with an act of such vulgarity, such wanton abandonment. How could Amy have gotten herself into such a mess? He had, for God's sake, been her devoted admirer for twenty years and never once thought of asking more.

And now that he had hung up on her, how was he to face Tom who like everyone else had taken Amy so much for granted as the fine dependable Japanese wife she used to be. Professor Nakashima was a sensitive man. He thought of the house, once tidy, now a pig's pen. He pictured himself in Amy's denim smock, welcoming the lord and master home, and Tom's sharp eyes instantly assessing the external damages. Well, even he was now in position to tell poor Tom a thing or two about putting the house in order.

Professor Nakashima slept fitfully. Each time he woke he had a tingling sensation in the scalp as if his hair were in the process of turning white or falling out. Early the next morning he opened the door and surveyed the disaster of the last five days.

The air was thick and sweet. In the kitchen all the cat food was gone but the milk was untouched and had curdled. Most likely Tomiko had eaten all the cat food in the first day and gone hungry for four. Also she had probably not had a drop to drink. The scatter rugs were askew in the hall. Cat hair was matted on all of the diningroom chairs. Still, he reflected, there was nothing he couldn't put back in order—he had a couple of days left before Tom returned. But then he saw the dark stains on Amy's flowered sofa. Looking more carefully, he discovered that Tomiko in her anger had defecated in the center of each down-filled cushion.

Sometime later he found the culprit under the radiator by the front door. She pretended not to recognize him but finally pulled herself out from her hiding place and sniffed at the crack under the door. She had shed a great deal in the last three days, giving her a thin patchy appearance.

"You've never been out in your life. What would an old cat like you do in all the snow?" he asked aloud, looking out through the leaded panes of the door. Outside there were flurries. Usually in Waltham the snow alternated with the slush, but this winter it never rained and never got above freezing. Nothing was washed away, all was accumulated.

Tomiko meowed pitifully. He felt sorry for her, the poor old cat who had never had a taste of freedom in all her eighty-seven years. Professor Nakashima realized he was perspiring. Perhaps one of the reasons Tomiko was moulting in winter was simply because the house was kept too hot. He felt his ankles tingle and knew that he would never be able to set things right before Tom came home. Summoning all his strength, he pushed open the door against the wind and watched as Tomiko, her long thin hair trailing behind her like a mandarin's beard, streaked out into the bright snow.

Arun Mukherjee

Arun Mukherjee, was born in Lahore in September 1946, eleven months before the partition of India. She considers her journey to Tikamgarh, a small town in Madhya Pradesh, India, as an eleven month old as her first immigration. She came to Canada in August '71, to do graduate work in English at the University of Toronto. She has taught at several Canadian universities and is the author of two books of criticism. She has published numerous articles and a book called The Gospel Of Wealth in the American Novel. *Her second book,* Toward an Aesthetic of Opposition: Essays on Culture, Literature and Cultural Imperialism *is in the press. She is now working on a book on Feminist Literary Theory and the Question of Race.*

Arun Makherjee's fiction explores North American life from the perspective of a multi-lingual, multi-cultural non-white immigrant woman (she speaks four languages and a Punjabi herself, is married to a Bengali).

VISITING PLACES

"Well, that's it folks! Our great trip to India," Jim said, as the last slide went off the screen. The small group of friends chipped in with words like wonderful, spectacular, romantic. "And, of course," Jim said, "as you saw for yourself, we could never have learned and enjoyed so much if it hadn't been for *Vineeta* here." Jim mispronounced my name in the typical Canadian fashion, putting the stress on the wrong place and retroflexing the "ta" ending.

Jenny and Roy and Janet all turned toward me now. Someone said, "Yes, it is just so-o different. Being with the families, eating what they eat, living the way they live."

Susan and Fred are always travelling somewhere. At least whenever I phone them, I find out about their latest bicycle trip to Scotland or their safari in Kenya or their backpacking in the canyons. They have a cottage somewhere and I have often fished for an invitation, unsuccessfully.

I keep telling my Canadian friends about my great curiosity to experience cottage-living, hoping some day someone will invite me. I heard Susan say to me, "We have never travelled in Asia but we hope to get to all those lovely places some day. Kathmandu, Sri Nagar, Agra, Jaipur. It would be marvellous if our plans coincided. Then we could have as much fun as Jim and Sara here."

"Wouldn't that be wonderful," I said in the spirit of the occasion. But I could feel my teeth gritting and my jaws beginning to hurt, something that happens to me when I am under stress. For I must admit, Jim and Sara had all the fun while I had all the dregs: the double anger of the whites and the natives had descended on me and made a wreck of me. So much so that I was hardly civil when I bid good bye to Jim and Sara at Palam airport in New Delhi. You see, I was awfully tired and depressed and one can hardly be civil under those circumstances. Even an Indian woman.

Fortunately, Jim and Sara seemed not to have noticed. And they had either forgotten those dreadful experiences in India or they hadn't really noticed what I had gone through. Anyway, their India was now a beautiful slide show: historical buildings, colourful clothes, wayside barbers, performing monkeys, even a snake charmer.

But the slide show inside my head at times begins to run automatically and brings back memories I so badly want to suppress.

There are so many things in my life I want to suppress. The contradictions of being a non-white Indian woman living in Canada, loving it and hating it, loving my white friends but hating them too. Just like my relationship with my parents, my in-laws, and with mother India herself.

I could start way way back, with my now shame-inducing desire of becoming a "foreign returned" Indian, like everybody else who mattered in Delhi U. But let me start with Jim and Sara. For starting the former way is much too painful and would require the narrating of a whole history of colonialism, something which George Woodcock would have no patience for and it would make him write a merciless review in *Canadian Literature*. So, let me just tell you about me with Jim and Sara.

Jim and Sara and I spent a couple of weeks together in India one winter. I was in Delhi researching Indian feminism for my thesis when I got their telegram. Yes, they were really coming, and that's when I began to get nervous. I was living with my brother, in his two rooms, one of which contained a portable gas burner and a cylinder.

"Are they coming *here?*" he asked. "Where will they *live?* They can't be expected to live like our Indian guests who crash in whether we want them or not."

Surely not. The rooms were awfully messy and small. Running water lasted hardly two hours in the morning. And there was, of course, no toilet paper.

"Maybe, I will go to the airport and bring them here, offer them some tea, and tell them they can live here if they can take it. Otherwise, they should go to a hotel." That was my way of opening a delicate negotiation with my brother to let them stay with us if they would.

I cleaned up as much as I could in the next couple of days, went to Connaught Place to buy some toilet paper and we were set.

When they arrived, they decided to stay with us even after

seeing the rooms. "We won't be here much anyway," Jim said, "So why waste money on hotels."

I should have seen them off two days later but foolishly accepted their invitation to travel with them. I pretended lack of funds at first, but when they offered to pay my expenses, how could I refuse!

They wanted to travel like Indians do, by train. So we went to Baroda House the next day to get our tickets. However, by the time Jim and Sara and I got there, it was already 11:30 and the booking clerks were busy. At one, they promptly closed their windows and told us to come back at two. That is when I began to see how different we, the Indians, were from them, the whites. For they were whites there, not Canadians. Such fine distinctions do not matter in India.

"We have lost a whole day just for buying train tickets," Sara cried. "We could be doing something exciting, but here we sit, waiting for him to open when he pleases and listening to him talk of his sons in America!"

True, the clerk had been garrulously chatting away. The atmosphere had been more of gossip than of work.

"Why can't they learn to be more efficient? That's why these countries don't make any progress."

I made a feeble protest about the inhumanity of too much efficiency. I malevolently suggested that Sara enjoy the beautiful gardens of Baroda House which were full of bird noises and extremely colourful bougainvellia at this time of the year. The sky was dark blue and there were a few white clouds merrily floating along. At such aesthetic moments, I become proudly patriotic.

But Sara was really upset and not the least bit interested in communing with nature. The last straw came when the clerk told us at two that Baroda House did not do second class reservations: the class Jim and Sara wanted to "experience."

I will spare you a detailed description of the explosion which followed: Sara, beside herself with anger, Jim trying to appear calm and in control but hardly succeeding, and I stubbornly refusing to criticize anything Indian. When our tempers cooled, we finally went to the right place, stood in a long line-up as second class travellers do in India and got our tickets.

But what happened on the train remains indelibly in my memory. The ticket collector had as usual sold an excess number of tickets in order to supplement his salary and, as a result, there was barely room enough for us to sit. The hard wooden bench, the mixed smells of sweat, smoke and food—typical of Indian railways by the way—were more than Jim could take. He screamed, fought, even got off the train to complain but to no avail. He wanted to stretch his limbs and didn't care what happened to the illegals. Sara and I got sent to the empty berths in the ladies' section and Sara even managed to fall asleep, but I kept thinking of Jim doing his *Tandava* dance in the aisles. Finally, the conductor made two of the rustic-looking illegals sit on the floor, and Jim could lie down, but only in the fetal position, as two other illegals refused to vacate their portion of the bench.

I could hear their entire conversation. "These *gora log*, you know, they have no strength. No Indian would have made such a fuss just for one night." "Absolutely. We say one should have space in one's heart. Then one can share even the little that one has."

"What do these white bastards think? *Han ji?* Are they still ruling us that we should be polite to them?"

And so it went, on and on, thankfully in Hindi. I was embarrassed but not entirely in disagreement.

The ambiguity of my position became clear to me when we checked in at a hotel in Amritsar the next day. While Jim and Sara went to their room to catch up on their sleep, I decided to stand in the corridor and look at the view. I was soon accosted by a type of Indian male I hate and fear from the bottom of my heart: the well-fed, government officer who exudes power from every pore and who drives hundreds of kilometers in a government jeep to see the latest movie in the big city; the type Shyam Benegal portrays so well in his movies, dining and wining with the contractors and womanizing at *their* expense. He hadn't even bothered to put on his *kurta*. "Haven't I seen you somewhere before?" he said, almost touching me.

This is a typical come-on Indian men learn from Hindi movies and I immediately said "no" while moving several steps back to keep my distance. "Are you sure? Weren't you at Agra Tourist Lodge last month with a party?"

Oh, my God. He thinks I am a call girl or something, I thought. Going around with foreigners.

I hurriedly made my retreat to my room and bolted it from the inside. Fortunately, our trip occurred long before Operation Blue Star. After Jim and Sara rested, we leisurely toured the Golden Temple, the narrow bazaars, and finally went to the house of the brother of a friend of theirs. He insisted we stay with them in their huge British bungalow, which we gladly did.

The man and his wife happened to be running a Christian missionary centre of some sort. Their children were home from Woodstock for the winter break and they talked of how Wood-stock students had the whole city of Mussoorie under their thumbs.

Our hosts talked to Jim and Sara about the stupidity of Hindus for building a shelter for old cows while human beings went starving on the street. However, an Indian woman is trained to be polite, obedient, accommodating, and I continued to smile.

Our next stop was Mussoorie. By now, Jim and Sara had decided to skip the experience of travelling second class. The first class was much more roomy and had thick "dunlopillo" cushions and the journey went uneventfully, except for the stench of sugar mills en route.

We took a deluxe bus from Dehra Dun to Mussoorie. While they had the address of a teacher in Woodstock, supplied by the friend's brother, I remembered that a classmate of mine was teaching in the Government College and decided to impose on his hospitality.

But to get to our destination we had to hire coolies to take our suitcases up the hill. It was a stiff climb and I was panting hard within five minutes. That's when Jim started: "You know, it is really cruel of us to burden this human being with our stuff. Their hearts get enlarged carrying so much weight and they have a very short life span." I protested, "But they are used to it, Jim," and immediately wished I could have bit my tongue, for we Indians use "used to" for practically everything. There was definitely a point to what Jim was saying. But my nationalistic pride wouldn't give up. "They've got to make a living, haven't they?" I said.

We parted company, only to meet in the market the next day.

Jim and Sara had obviously been bored by the Woodstock teacher and they followed me and my friend's family home.

"These whites," Lal was saying to me. "They have exploited us for centuries and now they come touring here, looking for the exotic India."

I tried to explain to Lal that Jim and Sara were not imperialists, just ordinary Canadians. But he wouldn't listen. "I don't care. They are all alike. They go back home with photographs of sunsets and minarets and publish a collection of poetry. I had a bunch of them teaching me a course on Canadian Literature this summer."

I didn't tell Lal that one of his teachers had indeed published a much-acclaimed volume of poems after his return from India, embellished with haunting photographs of minarets in sunset. I tried to keep on smiling and began to talk in English so that Jim and Sara could join in.

Jim and Sara needed travellers' cheques cashed and Lal obliged us by taking us to his bank. It was a beautiful walk. One could see way down in the valley. The air smelt of firs and deodars. I like the mountains in India.

But apparently Sara was not enjoying herself. She, or course, is not used to walking and was very tired. And by now I had come to realize that when she is tired she can be awfully difficult. I couldn't believe my ears when she said, "Why aren't we doing something exciting? Why can't we go mountain climbing?" "Because you don't have the right shoes," Jim said. But Sara was in a rotten mood. "I can't believe how awful it has all been. Why can't we do anything else except buy tickets and cash cheques? When are we really going to *see* the country?"

I could have killed her then, I was so angry. She was simply providing more ammunition to Lal's hatred. He winked at me triumphantly. I felt like crying, so I had to walk ahead of everybody to hide my tears. The beauty of the snow-capped Himalayas had been entirely ruined for me by Sara's whining.

At the bank, an unexpected disaster happened. Lal's friend insisted that we be served tea while the paperwork was being done, a typical Indian thing. Sara loves tea and she immediately agreed. However, when the tea came, it was Indian style. Leaves, milk, sugar, water, everything boiled together. Very strong and very sweet. I don't like it much either, but I often drink it out of politeness. Sara, however, had one sip and said, "It's awful." I wished I could disappear in the ground like Sita in the *Ramayana*. Lal's friend said, "I am sorry." He wanted to order a fresh supply but I told him not to because I knew his peon would only repeat the first attempt.

We decided to leave Mussoorie that night since Jim and Sara didn't want to spend any more time with the Woodstock teacher. We took the midnight bus leaving for Delhi. Lal was worried because a bus had been stopped en route a couple of weeks before and cash and jewelry seized from the passengers. I decided not to worry Jim and Sara about it. So they slept, or snoozed in their seats while I kept squirming all the way.

All three of us, by now, had our fill of "sightseeing" and decided to take it easy for the next day or two. Unluckily, it meant that Jim and Sara were home when little Kuttan came to sweep the rooms and do the dishes. "Don't tell me you have child labour in India," Jim said in a shocked voice. I was in a terribly embarrassing spot now, as a condoner, if not a direct employer, of child labour. As usual, Kuttan's blasted mother had sent her ten-year-old daughter, as though on purpose to embarrass me in front of my Canadian friends.

When we Indians, I mean comfortably off Indians, are in such spots, we say, "What about you!" and go on to talk about our having not yet recovered from the colonial legacy. But that sort of argument works only in the general sense, not when one is directly involved. Here I was, seeing our ten-year-old Kuttan wash our dishes in Delhi's awful December cold and going on as though everything was fine and dandy about the world. I mumbled something about Kuttan's mother forcing her to do it and left it at that. Talking about salad pickers in California and coffee pickers in Colombia would not have helped my floundering conscience. The fact that bothered me was how I had become so "used to" taking Kuttan's labour for granted.

Another embarrassing memory emerged at this moment. It was that of the wife of a visiting professor of American Literature in Delhi University. Our Chairman had asked me and the other girls in the class to go visit her at the university guest house. She had pointed to the construction workers outside her window, busily working at their tasks in the midday heat of the fierce April sun and said how pained she was by their misery. I had just hung my head in shame for not having felt it before.

And so it went on. The next few days were spent together touring the sights of Delhi. The only jarring elements were the beggars who missed no opportunity to harrass us. They would come and push their hands into our taxi while it waited at the traffic lights. I was dead set against giving alms and it only prolonged the embarrassing encounters. One shabby beggar with a child even tugged at my sleeve, which completely upset me so that I moved my arm with a big jerk which resulted in her child falling down. I felt so contrite that I handed her a *chavanni* which the beggar immediately used to buy ice cream for the screaming child.

One final embarrassment still awaited me. One day, my police-inspector uncle visited my brother's rooms and insisted, again in the typical Indian fashion, that I bring Jim and Sara to dinner at their place. Meanwhile, he left his chauffeur-driven car— purchased and maintained through corrupt money, I was sure— for my guests' pleasure. We were driven around in great style, but I burned all day because I had never been shown this preferential treatment by my uncle.

So what was embarrassing about that, you might ask. Nothing, I suppose. It is what happened at dinner that still rankles me. My brazen cousin who runs around chasing girls on a scooter, and is also rumoured to be involved in smuggling, asked Jim at the dinner table if he would consider selling his camera! "Jeans etc. I don't care about," he smirked. "They are really easy to get, but I really like your camera."

I wished for the umpteenth time, then, for mother earth to break open and welcome me in her lap as it had done for Sita. But no such luck. I heard Jim mumble that it was an old camera and that he was really attached to it. My cousin didn't seem to mind a bit. "Oh well. Suit yourself," is what he said, to my infinite surprise and proceeded to tell us how easy it was to buy imported goods in Delhi if you had the right kind of "dough."

It is torment enough to have such relatives but to expose them to the wide world! I shuddered at what Jim and Sara were going to think of me and my family and India from now on.

It was sheer luck that they were leaving the next day for the next leg of their Asia tour and my uncle regretted that he couldn't show them around, as his naughty niece hadn't told him about their visit. He regretted his inability to demonstrate to them the world-famous Indian hospitality and seemed to go on in that vein for a great length of time.

The next day, I bid Jim and Sara farewell at Palam, where we were driven in my uncle's car in the company of my cousin, dressed in his imported regalia.

I was a total wreck for about a week with exhaustion, depression, anger, frustration, shame and I don't know what else. I lost my temper fairly easily and screamed indiscriminately at my brother, at Kuttan, at the milkman, at the *subziewallah*, almost anybody who would allow me.

I even did something one day that put me through a terribly traumatic experience. Normally, you see, Indian women don't retaliate against people who feel their breasts and fall all over them in the crowded Delhi buses. But in this raw mood of mine, I just couldn't help knuckling a policeman who had been falling all over me as the crowd jostled in the bus. The bastard was sitting beside me on the ladies' seat while several women stood, too polite to ask him to get up. I, of course, pretended that the sharp turn had made me do it. But the policeman was much too smart. "You think you are very beautiful, woman, but I wouldn't waste a rupee to fuck you," he said. Lots of people heard him but nobody dared say anything.

I got off at the next stop and cried my fill. For the next several days I couldn't face the world, or myself. Then I sobered up and went back to my interrupted research on Indian feminism.

I didn't hear from Jim and Sara for a long time. When I came back to Canada and saw Sara at the Roberts Library, we picked up again. She was as bubbly as ever and immediately began to talk of what a wonderful time we'd had together.

Well, I am glad she and Jim remember nothing of what I do. Is it that they are good actors? Or is it that they must, for their own sakes, believe that they did have a wonderful time? Now they are off to Jamaica for Christmas. One of Jim's friends has a beautiful house near the beach in Kingston . . .

Anthony DeSoto

Hisaye Yamamoto

My old stories were dug up by young people searching for their roots — they have been categorized as examples of early Japanese literature. No one has been more surprised than I by this turn of events. I just wanted to 'be a writer' and wrote about what I knew, never expecting the stories would be reprinted (and reprinted). Now it appears that some of these pieces also fit into the feminist mold. Wowie!

WILSHIRE BUS

Wilshire Boulevard begins somewhere near the heart of downtown Los Angeles and, except for a few digressions scarcely worth mentioning, goes straight out to the edge of the Pacific Ocean. It is a wide boulevard and traffic on it is fairly fast. For the most part, it is bordered on either side with examples of the recent stark architecture which favors a great deal of glass. As the boulevard approaches the sea, however, the landscape becomes a bit more pastoral, so that the university and the soldiers' home there give the appearance of being huge country estates.

Esther Kuroiwa got to know this stretch of territory quite well while her husband Buro was in one of the hospitals at the soldiers' home. They had been married less than a year when his back, injured in the war, began troubling him again, and he was forced to take three months of treatments at Sawtelle before he was able to go back to work. During this time, Esther was permitted to visit him twice a week and she usually took the yellow bus out on Wednesdays because she did not know the first thing about driving and because her friends were not able to take her except on Sundays. She always enjoyed the long bus ride very much because her seat companions usually turned out to be amiable, and if they did not, she took vicarious pleasure in gazing out at the almost unmitigated elegance along the fabulous street.

It was on one of these Wednesday trips that Esther committed a grave sin of omission which caused her later to burst into tears and which caused her acute discomfort for a long time afterwards whenever something reminded her of it.

The man came on the bus quite early and Esther noticed him briefly as he entered because he said gaily to the driver, "You robber. All you guys do is take money from me every day, just for giving me a short lift!"

Handsome in a red-faced way, greying, medium of height, and dressed in a dark grey sport suit with a yellow-and-black flowered shirt, he said this in a nice, resonant, carrying voice which got the response of a scattering of titters from the bus. Esther, somewhat amused and classifying him as a somatotonic, promptly forgot about him. And since she was sitting alone in the first regular seat, facing the back of the driver and the two front benches facing each other, she returned to looking out the window.

At the next stop, a considerable mass of people piled on and the last two climbing up were an elderly Oriental man and his wife. Both were neatly and somberly clothed and the woman, who wore her hair in a bun and carried a bunch of yellow and dark red chrysanthemums, came to sit with Esther. Esther turned her head to smile a greeting (well, here we are, Orientals together on a bus), but the woman was watching, with some concern, her husband who was asking directions of the driver.

His faint English was inflected in such a way as to make Esther decide he was probably Chinese, and she noted that he had to repeat his question several times before the driver could answer it. Then he came to sit in the seat across the aisle from his wife. It was about then that a man's voice, which Esther recognized soon as belonging to the somatotonic, began a loud monologue in the seat just behind her. It was not really a monologue, since he seemed to be addressing his seat companion, but this person was not heard to give a single answer. The man's subject was a figure in the local sporting world who had a nice fortune invested in several of the shining buildings the bus was just passing.

"He's as tight-fisted as they make them, as tight-fisted as they come," the man said. "Why, he wouldn't give you the sweat of his . . ." He paused here to rephrase his metaphor, ". . . wouldn't give you the sweat off his palm!"

And he continued in this vein, discussing the private life of the famous man so frankly that Esther knew he must be quite drunk. But she listened with interest, wondering how much of this diatribe was true, because the public legend about the famous man was emphatic about his charity. Suddenly, the woman with the chrysanthemums jerked around to get a look at the speaker and Esther felt her giving him a quick but thorough examination before she turned back around.

"So you don't like it?" the man inquired, and it was a moment before Esther realized that he was now directing his attention to her seat neighbor.

218

"Well, if you don't like it," he continued, "why don't you get off this bus, why don't you go back where you came from? Why don't you go back to China?"

Then, his voice growing jovial, as though he were certain of the support of the bus in this at least, he embroidered on the theme with a new eloquence, "Why don't you go back to China, where you can be coolies working in your bare feet out in the rice fields? You can let your pigtails grow and grow in China. Alla samee, mama, no tickee no shirtee. Ha, pretty good, no tickee no shirtee!"

He chortled with delight and seemed to be looking around the bus for approval. Then some memory caused him to launch on a new idea "Or why don't you go back to Trinidad? They got Chinks running the whole she-bang in Trinidad. Every place you go in Trinidad . . ."

As he talked on, Esther, pretending to look out the window, felt the tenseness in the body of the woman beside her. The only movement from her was the trembling of the chrysanthemums with the motion of the bus. Without turning her head, Esther was also aware that a man, a mild-looking man with thinning hair and glasses, on one of the front benches was smiling at the woman and shaking his head mournfully in sympathy, but she doubted whether the woman saw.

Esther herself, while believing herself properly annoyed with the speaker and sorry for the old couple, felt quite detached. She found herself wondering whether the man meant her in his exclusion order or whether she was identifiably Japanese. Of course, he was not sober enough to be interested in such fine distinctions, but it did matter, she decided, because she was Japanese, not Chinese, and therefore in the present case immune. Then she was startled to realize that what she was actually doing was gloating over the fact that the drunken man had specified the Chinese as the unwanted.

Briefly, there bobbled on her memory the face of an elderly Oriental man whom she had once seen from a streetcar on her way home from work. (This was not long after she had returned to Los Angeles from the concentration camp in Arkansas and been lucky enough to get a clerical job with the Community

Chest.) The old man was on a concrete island at Seventh and Broadway, waiting for his streetcar. She had looked down on him benignly as a fellow Oriental, from her seat by the window, then been suddenly thrown for a loop by the legend on a large lapel button on his jacket. I AM KOREAN, said the button.

Heat suddenly rising to her throat, she had felt angry, then desolate and betrayed. True, reason had returned to ask whether she might not, under the circumstances, have worn such a button herself. She had heard rumors of I AM CHINESE buttons. So it was true then; why not I AM KOREAN buttons, too? Wryly, she wished for an I AM JAPANESE button, just to be able to call the man's attention to it, "Look at me!" But perhaps the man didn't even read English, perhaps he had been actually threatened, perhaps it was not his doing—his solicitous children perhaps had urged him to wear the badge.

Trying now to make up for her moral shabbiness, she turned towards the little woman and smiled at her across the chrysanthemums, shaking her head a little to get across her message (don't pay any attention to that stupid old drunk, he doesn't know what he's saying, let's take things like this in our stride). But the woman, in turn looking at her, presented a face so impassive yet cold, and eyes so expressionless yet hostile, that Esther's overture fell quite flat.

Okay, okay, if that's the way you feel about it, she thought to herself. Then the bus made another stop and she heard the man proclaim ringingly, "So clear out, all of you, and remember to take every last one of your slant-eyed pickaninnies with you!" This was his final advice as he stepped down from the middle door. The bus remained at the stop long enough for Esther to watch the man cross the street with a slightly exploring step. Then, as it started up again, the bespectacled man in front stood up to go and made a clumsy speech to the Chinese couple and possibly to Esther, "I want you to know," he said, "that we aren't all like that man. We don't all feel the way he does. We believe in an America that is a melting pot of all sorts of people. I'm originally Scotch and French myself." With that, he came over and shook the hand of the Chinese man.

"And you, young lady," he said to the girl behind Esther, "you deserve a Purple Heart or something for having to put up with that sitting beside you."

Then he, too, got off.

The rest of the ride was uneventful and Esther stared out the window with eyes that did not see. Getting off at last at the soldiers' home, she was aware of the Chinese couple getting off after her, but she avoided looking at them. Then, while she was walking towards Buro's hospital very quickly, there arose in her mind some words she had once read and let stick in her craw: *People say, do not regard what he says, now he is in liquor. Perhaps it is the only time he ought to be regarded.*

These words repeated themselves until her saving detachment was gone every bit and she was filled once again in her life with the infuriatingly helpless, insidiously sickening sensation of there being in the world nothing solid she could put her finger on, nothing solid she could come to grips with, nothing solid she could sink her teeth into, nothing solid.

When she reached Buro's room and caught sight of his welcoming face, she ran to his bed and broke into sobs that she could not control. Buro was amazed because it was hardly her first visit and she had never shown such weakness before, but solving the mystery handily, he patted her head, looked around smugly at his roommates, and asked tenderly, "What's the matter? You've been missing me a whole lot, huh?" And she, finally drying her eyes, sniffed and nodded and bravely smiled and answered him with the question, yes, weren't women silly?

(1950)

Linda Ty-Casper

I was born in Manila and received all my education there, except for the post graduate work. I am married to Leonard Casper, critic, professor, writer. We have two daughters. Gretchen has a doctorate in Political Science from Ann Arbor, and Tina enters college this year.

Asiaweek, for which I judged their annual literary contest last year, has asked me again to judge the short stories in 1988. In May of this year, I read from a work in progress (DreamEden, about the EDSA revolution of 1986) for the Friends of the Filipino People at the Harvard Divinity School. In June I presented a paper and read from my 1988 novel, A Small Party in a Garden at the Third International Feminist Book Fair in Montreal. The organizers had read my 1985 novel, Awaiting Trespass, which was adjudged to be one of the 5 best books in England and Ireland, written by women.

HILLS, SKY AND LONGING

She looks up at the larch and the redwoods growing in pairs out of dead stumps; at the reindeer moss caught between the gnarled branches of a live oak, then across the open sky where red-tailed hawks, miles apart but overlapped from where she stands, are clinging to the air, riding different currents; and for the first time she notices a dark spot in the sky. It appears wherever she looks above the hill of trees, some code signal perhaps, the kind that carries entire messages in short ciphers.

Puzzled, she turns about to face the break in the soft descent of the hills—higher but not steeper than she recalls the hills beyond Manila, slopes reaching toward the Pacific Ocean past Marikina on to Taytay—looks straight out to the same ocean coming at its opposite shore in wide arcs of surf made gentle by the distance, thirty-fifty miles away as the hawk flies or the peregrine falcon soars; faces the break where only after years has she finally located Peet's store where she buys coffee from Tanzania, the closest she can come to the dark taste of cafe barako from Batangas which her father used to drink.

Hostlike but more like cinder the longer she stares, the dark irregular shape appears in the horizon pushed up by the ocean. Against this sky but not against the grassruns on the hills ridged up to their crests with horizontal markings of the ocean's careful descent through the later buried ages—Eocene, Pliocene, Cambrian—to where it is now held by the shore at Half-Moon Bay. Where on the Philippine shoreline would she land if she could swim directly across, she wonders.

And climbs still higher on the hill as if she might be able to tell. Measuring ascent by counting steps, keeping her eyes away from the sky and also from the road where earthworms, crossing in the night, have become red gashes—the ends that are still alive inclining upward from the crushed parts already dried, reduced to needles on the asphalt—too close together and impossible to step between, impossible not to shudder.

Keeping her eyes on the Ray-O-Lite reflectors imbedded in the middle of the narrow road that bends with the hill, she climbs in a hurry, so that she has to breathe hard like someone in labor. It is not her intention to go up to the two rocks that form a throne from which to look down on the slope with its furry tumble of shrubs and grass whorled like the hide of cattle; but she climbs to those very rocks. From there she looks up at the sky again, starting from the edge of the slope, watching and climbing with the halting legs of newborn calves, until she reaches the part where the speck shows darkly, a fierce eye. There she fastens herself against the wind and the sun, waiting for the stain to disappear into the light, waiting the way ancients watched the sky, expecting the configuration of their altars to first appear in the heavens.

Suddenly she pulls out handfuls of wild wheat. Counting the steps back to the house, she keeps away thoughts of herself, thoughts swooping like peregrine falcons possessing the sky; wind emitting the sounds of continents blowing.

She skirts the plunge of the hill past red-winged blackbirds fat on the white fence, unscared of her passing; thinking with much longing, an almost mourning, words without song of mango trees whose flowering she has not seen these many years—twenty, measured like an infant's growing—mango trees as in her parents' yard with butterflies as large as her hands, throbbing outside their cocoons, drying darkly wet wings among the green fruits, the yellow flowers on acacias and narras released slowly by the sky.

And feels like a fugitive, someone with a different face, speech and dream, upon whom the cattle might come on the trail where they meditate with large eyes fixed on the distance.

The girls were frightened of the cattle when they were still young, holding on to her skirt, almost pulling her down the slopes—the wind comes around the hills with the roar of a storm at sea—while the cows walked among the poison oaks toward the trails where mountain cats guarded redwoods that had fallen upon each other during the logging years. They asked her: Why are trees only between the hills? Do the falcons see us? They tried to gather prickly poppies while the toad singing in the clasp of water paid them attention. She took them, buckled safely in the car, to the beaches; a different road each time or the same road differently, to stand on the waves and let the sea fumble between their legs, spraying their chins with laughter while the sun climbed inside their dresses.

Why did she not speak to them in her mother's songs or tell them of her father's porch, of their garden where the moon grew large, then small over the ginger plants with soft petals wet with fragrance? When did it start to matter?

The girls are no longer children. Edit will have none of her own to interrupt her painting, wants no children to whom to pass on the shape of her hands holding tight. Lara had that miscarriage which shocked her womb into closing.

She remembers the thought that coming upon the larch interrupted, but hurries away from it, reaches the house out of breath. Her pocketbook is in the front seat of the Volvo, the key in the ignition ready to go to town where she has a ten o'clock appointment with Dr. Carvers, homeopath; Rosalie's doctor. She mentioned she had ringing in her ears, not quite in those words, to Rosalie at their writing group. And Rosalie went with her the first time, to have her ears checked. Rosalie was born in Los Angeles, first generation of parents from Iloilo, but has no knowledge of Hiligaynon. On the phone Rosalie sounded American, no accent. Of course when you saw her, you knew . . .

Might as well go, she decides. She can always turn back, or drive until she runs out of gas or highway, out of life and its slow impartial ceasing. Life is change and loss one day; the next day, more change and loss; and ache. Like the ocean losing forever the slopes, on which it used to feast, to live oaks and madrone, to fences; while in the sky clouds repeat the slope of the hills, and birds with immature plumage resemble falcons.

She will see the doctor but not go to the writing group with another desperate poem, the pauses uncontrolled, as invisible as private ink. If she had courage her poems would recall the way rain pulled at the earth when she was a child, making the sky swell between the ricedikes.

Without seatbelt she takes each curve of the road downhill, knowing that if she pulls too hard right she will smash into the hill; too sharp left and she will hurtle down into redwoods almost as tall as the hills. Something makes her think of the hyacinths under the old acacia trees, small pink heads popping out after a rain among the roots of gardenias. How long does memory matter?

She can't drive slow against the pull of the earth and knows she'll reach the main road, Skyline Drive, with its stand of mailboxes, quicker than she wants to. Her heart would sooner turn around—the impulse to hide prevailing—back to the cattle ranged wider than the sky, their bodies pressed upon the hills like dark clouds.

Counting as if climbing up or down the hills, as if trying to fall asleep at night, she proceeds no further than the impulse, as another thought overtakes her. Lives are fables upon which to hang stories of waste and loss. She does not call the children because she might interrupt. In a poem she has not shown anyone—whatever made her write it!—she said only those who find love survive, only those who give love have hopes of the other world, the worlds existing inside each other here or in the final kingdom, held in the source of everything good that comes. Her idea of love is merged with the past, with sacrifice, premodern. Both girls call her by her first name, never learned to kiss her hand. She never taught them. It spoiled the significance of respect to have to teach it, she thought; or was too busy perhaps with John—Juanito back in the Philippines—on assignments that might take him to Tibet or Peru, Capo San Lucas or Nantucket where whales beach themselves in the hundreds for no human reason imaginable. He's now off to Mexico on the trail of the black monarchs that have left their nests in Anchorage to infest entire summer trees in the Yucatan with their wings throbbing life into their bodies.

She herself has no clues to whether she feels the earth flowering or closing for the winter, which brings not snow but rain to San Francisco; brings newts out of the ground and snakes with different bands across their bodies herringboned against predators; brings the wind moaning, slamming down toward the ocean; doors closing.

The slow drifting of her attention allows her to return to the thoughts that tempt her assent while the road veers and drops, climbs unaccompanied by her body. About to be married in the morning, Lara comes to her with a book, *Mr. B. T. Bear's Bow*

Ties. Read it to me; every word. Read every word: each word she read years and years ago with much love and resentment, weariness and, gain, love; years and years ago, buried ages.

Why did she not read Lara and Edit the rhymes she learned as a child, Leron Leron Sinta, Sitsiritsit alibangbang? She wants to remember them standing at the seawall over Manila Bay, as she stood as a child while on the waves outriggers held boats afloat and the sun burned behind the steamers. Why did she not choose memories for them when she could? Life the way it is and never . . . Whose memory mattered? What difference?

She reaches Dr. Cavers before she has decided to turn back or drive past. This time without Rosalie, she walks to the door as if merely entering a specialty shop with newly arrived woolen vests and silky blouses assembled by someone who imagined how the earth would appear to someone coming out of a winter cave.

Good morning. The nurse receptionist does not attempt to read her name from the computerized file filled with every medical fact about her. *The doctor will see you in a moment.* Their smiles meet, then return.

She has time to pick up a magazine or continue with her thoughts while pretending to read: Lara dropping by to show off her new Italian jacket, soft as butter, light as lambswool; Edit tricking her into a smile. *Mother sketch the cows if they intrigue you that much. Stare at the paper. The lines you need are all there. Make them appear with paint. Do with color what you will. We'll hang our works together. Or you can do quilts. Anything but poems . . .*

Dr. Cavers is standing outside his office. It's her turn. She gets up, heaving the straps of her pocketbook up on her shoulder as if it is full of weights under which she must struggle. Something worn in her speaks a greeting.

And how are the ears this morning? Still ringing?

No longer, she picks up the cadence of his speaking, surprised for she has forgotten about the ringing. *There's a speck . . .*

He smiles. *Yes.*

When I look up?

Does it hurt?

She shakes her head, cautioned by the leap in the question. She did not say the speck is in her eye.

Then why does it bother you? What do you think?

The sky cannot be injured, she answers.

He asks other questions, repeating the first visit, words probing fear inside the body. Rosalie says he's a real doctor. M.D. but decided to practice homeopathy to help bodies heal themselves. His questions help him decide what herb to use, herb maximized, distilled to a thousandth of its atom to make it potent. First, he must find the truth about her. It is no longer God alone who knows one's secret. He asks about her feelings. *Rejections? Headaches? Very bad headaches. Where in the head? Nothing relieves them? Do you have resentments? Sense of failure? When did you notice the speck? Any particular form? Fixed or changing? Do you see it with your eyes closed? Is it in your dreams? And your husband knows? Do you have the longings?*

Almost an hour passes during which her life remains under his scrutiny. She nods deeply to indicate yes; lightly to make the question pass. When I was a little girl, she catches herself from saying, but remains silent while Dr. Cavers talks to her as if she cannot understand long sentences, complete thoughts.

I know what to give. You take it right now. Only one thing. No mint. Interferes. And no coffee. Never those two.

The nurse comes in with a tiny heap of powder on a square of paper. Her manner is serious and also as if she is serving a meal in a restaurant.

No. No. Don't touch. Remember. Hands will destroy herb's potency. Here. Like before. The paper is folded. The powder is poured on her tongue. *No hands touching. Please. Never.*

It's gone, she says, swallowing.

Good. Another month, come back. Next time, will not be there. The speck.

Of course, she smiles. Not the sky. No. Sky will always be there. She repeats his halting speech in the thought she keeps from him.

Back on the road she carefully avoids the sky, avoids anything light enough to project a dark ember. At Peet's she stops for coffee, Coors, John Fifield Chablis. Careful choices. But on her way to the cashier she picks up bread crisps, cheeses, food neither John nor she eats, as if hunger is definitely coming with winter;

while she thinks of blue ricecakes, talangka and buro, ordinary feasts.

She slides down behind the wheel, the taste of laing on her tongue. Her mother insisted the gabi leaves be dried after they're cut fine, before they're cooked in freshly squeezed cream of grated coconut. She used to crush aspirin for the children, to stir into honey or ice cream. *Taste funny, sweetheart? All gone? No? Yes? All better now?* When she was a little girl it was cod liver oil they were made to swallow. The oil stained the cube of sugar which they chewed. A coin wrapped in a piece of paper was the reward for not throwing up . . .

At the mailbox, theirs in the middle of the stand, she looks for a postcard from John. She never went with him on his assignments. At first there were the girls, too young to enjoy the trip. Then, it was too much bother for the comfort of each other's bodies. That is what Dr. Cavers is waiting for her to admit, which might not be true.

She drives through redwoods, eight miles of second or third growth trees long ago planted by men who did not see them logged in their lifetime. She hurries but cannot drive faster than the pull of the earth will allow. The road curves and she forgets to anticipate it. The only winding road she remembers is the Zigzag to Baguio which rock slides endanger, along which small lakes formed by rocks soon turn the color of dead waters. She remembers the pine trees and leis of everlasting in the market. The girls never visited there. Soil and mantlerock and scrub. The flag flapping like flames.

Against the seat she eases her back. Pulling her elbows in, she shifts in time to avoid the one plunge on the way up that remains in the road after the reason for it has ended. Strangers can find their cars halfway out of the road in that spot, tires idling. Strangers whose faces and accents match. Puti.

Like a rattlesnake across the last hill the white fence runs through the grass, straightening out behind the house. She parks headon to the trash cans tied to the posts against raccoons. Large and fat like bear cubs, at night while she does the dishes, raccoons look into her kitchen window, letting her know she's the one trespassing.

She heads for the kitchen by way of the deck. Up nine steps she walks, both hands supporting the groceries. She is humming. The speck is far from her mind as she watches Tomcat asleep on the redwood table, gray head between large white paws, off by barely a whisker from the surface Poor Tomcat. Grown old, scared running by the stellar jays that drop like live bombers into his feedbowl, flaunting wicked tails of electric blue and forked crests of ebony. Poor dear Tomcat. Only part of the family still with her. Uncoordinated, he tumbles down the steps from chasing fieldmice which come in the rain. Tumbles Tom and Jerry style, right out of the cartoon.

Like a fieldmouse on tiptoe she steps quietly past the cat, light feathery steps that could blow away; pushes the screen aside, then the glass door, sets the groceries on the nearest counter.

Relieved of their weight she feels immediately taller and thinner, unaccountably younger, young enough to dash through life without allowing stares to bother her. She switches on the parchment lamp suspended in the dead center of the kitchen, fluffs her hair on the way to the refrigerator as if she might want to look pretty for someone coming through the vestibule any minute. *60 is not old*, Dr. Cavers told Rosalie. *Not all the time old.* She was twenty three when she and John emigrated, she carrying the plastic envelope that contained their medical records and x-rays. Honolulu was their port of entry.

Port of disappearance occurs to her and she tries to ignore it. Pushing up the banana magnet, the color of the slugs that feed on redwood roots, she pulls the door open, pours herself orange juice to replace the potassium her diuretic leeches out of her blood. An old postcard from John is still on the refrigerator. When he's home he likes to go to Half-Moon Bay for dinner, usually after a swim in the inlet at Pescadero. A night at the movie occasionally. A drink at La Honda Cafe, where the resident barfly is a fat poet who tames words the way he claims he tamed lions near San Gregorio.

A note is next to the postcard: 6 p.m. sharp. Meaning Edit will not wait to take her to the Gallerie Bleue. Edit has a painting there, by invitation. She paints horses and hills. All summer Edit worked on a hawk seen from the ground, floating. Nothing ethnic about it, nothing Filipino. Like John, the children laugh when people say, *Dima, Dimalanta? What kind of name is that?*

She takes down the brown macrame, switches it with the white on the size of a full length mirror, returns both to their original walls. Did anything make a difference, finally? She goes to the kitchen, heading for the deck when she finds herself saying: *Sigue. Tumingin ka. Huwag kang matakot.* It is in her mother's voice she urges herself.

Struggling against her own considerable cunning, she presses her face against the glass but, before she can look up at the sky, turns her back to face the room where she has switched on the lamp. She feels safe, until against the gaunt light she sees it again, somewhat different, darker even, fixed, but definitely there: a peregrine flying without wings.

*

Danielle Weil

Diana Davenport

Diana Davenport, who is half native Hawaiian, received her education at the University of Hawaii. The recipient of several fiction grants, she is the author of Wild Spenders (Macmillan 1984) *and two other novels. Her short fiction has appeared in* Hawaii Pacific Review, Womanspeak *(New Zealand),* Tok Isi *(Papua New Guinea),* DR/Politika Expres *(Yugoslavia),* Yellow Silk, *and* Ikon.

"It took me twenty years to find my voice, to begin to write about my Hawaiian heritage, and about the women of the North and South Pacific island nations, who are just beginning to emerge. This is what I shall be writing about for the rest of my life."

HOUSE OF SKIN
(Hawaii)

In one of the many periods of their marriage when Uncle Hiro was gone, Aunt Rachel kept a shark in her swimming pool. In the evenings, when jacarandas splashed the driveway, Kori-Kori, the old gardner, fed the shark. Afterwards, Rachel would sometimes swim in the pool beside that thing, in the crimson run-off of its feeding frenzy. The shark never bothered her; it hardly acknowledged her. Rachel said she could read its mind.

"We Hawaiians," she instructed me, "are *all* descendants of sharks."

On vacations from college in the mainland, I sat beside her pool in Honolulu, watching that long, gray thing blading along beside her in a daring and careful truce. The family said Rachel was the one I took after, not my mother. But watching her and the shark, I was not adequate to that kind of logic.

Our family was full-blooded Hawaiian on my grandmother's side, Hawaiian and Dutch on my grandfather's. Aunt Rosalind was the oldest daughter, Rachel the middle and my mother, Emmaline, the youngest. Grandfather True, who died full of rum in his sinuses, was never sure Rachel was his. After his death, Rosaline and my mother gave back most of the land our Dutch ancestors had appropriated from natives. With what little money he left, they built a school for orphans of the lepers kenneled away on a desolate peninsula of a neighboring island. As for Rachel, she gave nothing back. What she inherited, she said, she required.

At sixteen, she had eloped with Hiro, who was Japanese, ten years older, handsome and thuggish and moved like a thoroughbred. After their marriage, they stepped outside the family into another world, strolling the grounds of the Royal Hawaiian Hotel like tourists, dancing at the Halekulani like bored peacocks.

Rachel was twenty when I was born, and when I was two weeks old, she kidnapped me, and hid with me in the canefields until we were found. By then she knew she would never have her own children. Years later she told me why.

"I didn't want them inked up like Maoris," she said.

Her husband Hiro was a Yakuza, tattooed from his neck to his ankles. He wanted his children to be tattooed.

So Rachel had me instead.

When I was four, my parents took me away from Hawaii, and I entered the world a second time, blinking in the lights of the great cities of mainland America. My father was Caucasian, a haole, as the Hawaiians say, and wanted to live back east where he belonged and where, it turned out, my mother did not. I was twelve when she died and my father sent me home from the mainland to be raised by the family in Honolulu. Rachel took me in, and it was the terrible energy of the loss of my mother that bound us together for all time.

At first she was useless, in mourning for months, like a woman continually bludgeoned. Hiro took care of me, confusing me because he was handsome and sinister, yet something hummed beneath his threat, a gentleness. One day we sat on a sea-wall eating guavas with our hands.

"I was nine when *my* mother died," he said. "I could not stop crying. My father rowed me out beyond the reef and threw me in, and rowed away. I was a grown man by the time I reached shore."

He could have done anything with me then, a motherless home-less girl, open to whoredom, madness, oblivion. In the old ivory shop in the Royal Hawaiian, he bought a bracelet too heavy for my wrist, which I have long since grown into. In his open car we drove up Mt. Tantalus, listening to mynah birds mating in the jungle. We stood on the windy Pali and I cried with my face in my hands, asking what would become of me. Hiro put his arms around me, comforting me, and I saw the gun inside his jacket, like a rodent strapped somehow to his chest.

I remember my fascination. I remember forgetting my grief. "Do you kill people?" I asked.

He stepped back embarrassed, then looked out across the Pali. "There is no need to kill. One simply makes people too desperate to want to live."

"Will you kiss me?" I said.

He hugged me again; I felt the gun touch the side of my head.

234

Then he kissed me on the forehead like a father, because he was in his forties, and what he wanted was fatherhood.

"Do you love Aunt Rachel?" I asked.

"More than anything."

"If you *stop* loving her," I said, "I will marry you."

He doted on me in those months, and by the time Rachel came to her senses, I was in love with her husband, a feeling I never outgrew. Once, watching them embrace in the garden, I tried to split my twelve-year-old head open against a tree. Even after my first lover, seeing Rachel and Hiro together made me want to whimper and run on all fours.

Years later, she called me to her room. Rachel must have been near forty then, lying in a bed of robes and fans, looking operatic and perishable.

"I married him," she said, "because one night I saw him naked, and he looked so blue and evil, I thought if I stayed with him nothing could ever hurt me."

When he was ten years old, Hiro's father had sent him home to Japan to be educated. Instead he became a gangster. In Kyoto he studied Kendo, "the way of the sword," and adopted the philosophy of Bushido: the way of the warrior, prepared to die at any minute, which was the only way to live. He believed the true Samurai had the heart of a criminal.

When he was twenty-six and returned to Hawaii, his father saw the tattoos, and disowned him.

"The night before he left his father's house," Rachel said, "he stood bathing under a garden hose. That was when I first saw him. I looked over the wall, the moon was out and he looked like living mold." She smiled. "I let him take me right then, like two lizards in wet grass."

Hiro's business as Rachel described it, was the "water trade," which encompassed it all—liquor, prostitution, drugs—up and down the Asian coast from Malaysia to Hong Kong and Tokyo. He had set her up in a big house in Kahala, the Beverly Hills of Honolulu, and through the years she became something of a salonierre.

I would come home on college breaks and find artists and buffoons swaggering in her gardens on Sunday afternoons, orchids fluttering in their drinks, matching birds gyring overhead. Sometimes the carp in the pond surfaced, staring at the strangers, so that the strangers seemed to be a thought in some very cold-blooded mind. There were even gangsters there on Sunday afternoons. These were people Rachel hated, but they were part of Hiro's world, and so she competed with them in dangerous ways.

I used to fall asleep trying to picture him under the garden hose, making love to Rachel in the grass, his skin changing colors in the moonlight, volcanoes on his back smoking, flowers on his shoulders blooming as if from radiation. I could not imagine the front of him. Rachel said he was tattooed there, all of him. Everything.

One day I confronted him. "If you love Aunt Rachel, why do you always go away? Why do you spend so much time in Hong Kong?"

"Because," he said, "Hong Kong leaves me alone."

When he was with Rachel, it was like he was poured into her, like something swallowed by an animal drinking. Sometimes I wondered if he wore his gun to protect himself from her, from her beauty. She had an Oriental fineness of bone, but the rounded breasts and hips of a Hawaiian. Her hair was black, slick as tar, her lips full, and her eyes an odd green like spoiled bronze. Her father could have been anyone, Japanese, haole, a Swede—a diplomat or a sailor her mother encountered in a rebellious moment when my grandfather was deep in his rum. Hiro came and went for all the years of their marriage. Perhaps their love was so intense, his absence was how they kept from killing each other.

One night I stumbled over Rachel in a dim hallway of that large house. She rose like a spectre, holding out a photograph of Hiro and a young Oriental prostitute in a nightclub in Macao. Her arm was around his shoulder, and she was whispering in his ear. Things I had known, and never wanted to know.

"What did you expect?" I cried. "You knew what you married."

She slid to the floor again and sobbed, in a way I have never stopped hearing. I held her until she was limp, and when it was dawn I carried her to her room, hating Hiro for the way he pervaded that house.

"Why do you stay with him," I asked. "It's demeaning."

She squeezed my arm, pulling me close. "You're brave. You go everywhere. I've never left this island. I have to create my terrors."

After that, when he was gone too long she went through periods of squalor, insulting guests and the hangers-on, laughing at an Army General's regrettable taste in civilian clothes. She ran down a peacock in the driveway. And one night she killed the shark. Eight thousand miles away, I bolted up in the dark, holding my ribs. The young man lying beside me asked what was wrong.

"Metternich is dead. I know it."

" . . . Who is Metternich?" He asked.

"My aunt's shark. She shot him."

He was a medical student, a fraternity man, and Caucasian. He dressed, and leaving, turned to me from the doorway. "You island women are all the same. Voo-doo dollies."

I finally reached her by phone at 3 A.M. Pacific time.

"Please," she said, "Come home."

As the years passed we lived like acolytes, waiting for Hiro. He would return, stay a few weeks, and leave again. One night when I was thirty, he appeared on the grass in a white suit and tie and a black gangster's shirt, sleek as a cat, eyes narrow as seeds, so aristocratic in his bearing, I had to look away. He was sixty now, looking like a man of forty, his handsome face the color of lemon drops sucked to transparency, unmarked hands like slender yellow icicles, except for the missing digit of one hand, showing membership in the Yakuza. But the rest of him, I knew, was reptilian, forbidden.

By then I was married and divorced, and had known several men, but I still dreamed of Uncle Hiro, of peeling his clothes off expertly, as though skinning an animal, of finally seeing him naked.

One day I realized he had been home over a month. I found him feeding his carp in the pond, looking monkish and benign in a kimono and sandals. We moved with care along the stepping stones traversing the pond, and I realized he was going bald. I remembered his hair black and slick as a croupier, and now his skull shone through. Three carp surfaced, their scales brilliant in the sun, while Hiro explained how they were the bravest of fish, how the carp when caught, awaits the knife without flinching.

He knelt slowly, clearing the surface of the pond with chopsticks, delicately extracting a leaf, the feather of a bird, gestures serene as a lama. Through the years I had learned that he spoke mostly by implication. I had to look for the echo, not the sound; the shadow, not the light, but in this instance he spoke unequivocally.

"I have not been a good uncle. What you know of me is mythical."

"Why are you telling me this?" I asked.

He leaned back slowly. "Because it is time."

That night I sat up in a sweat, wondering if he were dying. I knew fully tattooed people like Hiro lived shorter lives because too little free skin was left to 'breathe.' He had begun the tattoos when he was sixteen and reached completion at twenty-six. I saw him, hour by hour, inch by inch, braving the insertion of black nara ink that turned blue when perforating live flesh, and the deadly Indian Red ink that glowed brown beneath the surface of the skin making a tattoo shine, and slowly poisoning the body.

I thought of a man with no childhood to speak of, and how the tattooist's needle was perhaps the first thing to pierce his unfeeling and unfelt existence. Perhaps the whores from Bangkok and Hong Kong and Macao meant nothing to Hiro. Perhaps his deepest love had been for his sensei, the tattooist, relentlessly penetrating him for ten years.

The chance gift of a good job took me to New York for a year, and in that time Hiro came home more and more often, yet Rachel said his health was perfect. And then one night it wasn't. She called to say he'd been shot in a gambling house in Shanghai and that they were flying him home. I called Honolulu every day for weeks, then every week for months. Rachel said Hiro's wound was healing slowly. Finally she said there was no more pain.

By the end of that year, desperately homesick, I left New York and took a plane pouring west against the sunset.

Rachel was heavier, and had stopped tinting her hair, but her beauty was still paradoxical and lush. Seeing me, she threw her arms out, and crossed the lawn at an odd, maniacal tilt, sweeping me in circles.

"Where is he," I cried, searching the grounds for Uncle Hiro, needing him to deepen the experience of coming home.

Almost ceremoniously, she led me across the lawn. There had been a greenhouse beyond the fish pond, and as Rachel drew me in that direction I saw the glass had been replaced by wood, so it now seemed a simple cottage set off by itself.

"Wait a few minutes, then knock," she said, and disappeared inside.

The sun was slipping, shooting boulevards into the sea. On the beach below, birds attacked each other instead of courting, and fish seemed to be swimming in lopsided circles. Finally, I knocked and, removing my shoes, entered a large room, dim, and smelling of cedar. Tatami mats covered the floor. The only furnishing was a low, black, lacquered table with a tea service, where Rachel knelt, virginal in a white kimono. Her hair was in the geisha style, and like a geisha girl, she bowed her head, seemingly shy.

I moved forward, enchanted, and knelt facing her, smelling jasmine tea. There was a window beside us, looking out on the ocean. There was no other entrance to the room. "But where is Uncle Hiro?"

She seemed to have fallen into a state of deep meditation, and I sat back confused. The sun shifted and light flooded the room. Suddenly the wall behind her resonated. A fierce red dragon was locked in mortal combat with a human warrior, both of them struggling under glass. What was mounted under the glass was large, life-size, and oddly shaped, remotely resembling a mounted deerskin.

The dragon seemed to gather strength each time the light shifted, so its eagle talons lengthened, its great scales glittered, and the goblin nose breathed flames. Above the head of the warrior, maple leaves fell, suggesting mortality. And lower, where the thing angled out in the shape of flattened thighs, blue carp with long eyelashes swam upstream trying to spawn.

Rachel lifted her head, her eyes fixed in a weird, exalted stare. "The bullet wound healed perfectly six months ago. But his breathing became difficult."

Sharp teeth clamped down on my brain, I was momentarily blinded. Then I rose unsteadily, and moved to the wall. The thing leapt out like a firmament, garish, blinding, but then up close, the elegance of fine calligraphy. I stared at the wonders of Hiro's skin, resplendently blue.

On each buttock, swords sliced through bursting red peonies, and yellow warrior lion-dogs barked at his shoulders. Thick green serpents encircled his arms, and around his calves Buddhist prayers curled diagonally. This childless man, who had had no childhood to speak of, had carried, tattooed on his belly, a perfectly-etched fat, laughing little boy, riding a whiskered catfish.

"After forty years," Rachel whispered, "I deserved to keep something of him, didn't I? *Didn't* I?"

Finally, she possessed Hiro completely, by possessing his armor against the world. I thought of a large, defenseless, skinned rabbit-like being roaming the afterlife, and leaned my head against the glass and screamed.

Mavis Hara

I am a san-sei, born in Hawaii. I began writing because the people associated with Bamboo Ridge Press encouraged me to 'write it down.' Tatsue is my mother's name and "An Offering of Rice" is a true story. In my mother's life, the family was the center of everything spiritual and material. The people in my mother's generation made daily offerings as part of the pattern of their lives; sometimes they made offerings of themselves as well.

AN OFFERING OF RICE

Tatsue wanted to stay downstairs and listen to the new Rudy Vallee song on her mother's radio, but Okasan was sick with asthma again and it was not easy for her to climb the stairs. Tatsue sighed as she uncovered the pot of freshly cooked rice and pressed the sticky grains into tiny brass dishes. The grains held together like a white moon. Okasan had taught her that rice offered to the ancestors and the gods should be smoothed and round, not triangular like the musubi humans ate because there were no corners in heaven. In Japan, they said everything in heaven was a circle.

Tatsue carried the offering dishes upstairs and put one in front of the Shinto shrine and the other in front of the larger Buddhist shrine. She lit three thin sticks of black sandalwood incense and planted the sticks upright in a bowl of grey ashes. Then she sat back on the silk cushion and whispered the name of Buddha, "Namu Amida Butsu."

Tatsue did not sit long. She left the rice at the altar until the incense burned away and added itself to the ashes in the bowl. While she was upstairs, she collected the family's laundry—a rice bag full from the room that her four brothers shared, another from the room she shared with her sister Kei, and the last from Otosan and Okasan's room. She carried all the bags down the stairs and left them next to the galvanized tin washtub beside the copper furo.

"Tatsue, hayaku yasai wo arainasai," Okasan called, and Tatsue hurried upstairs to collect the dishes of cooled rice from the altars, then back downstairs to the kitchen to help wash the vegetables for dinner. When she got there, the two youngest children, Masao and Kei were waiting.

"I like eat the mamai-san rice," Masao was saying.

Tatsue wished that for once she could eat the cold rice in the brass dishes but she gave Masao one of the servings and six-year-old Kei the other. The two children smiled happily as they chewed on their prizes. Okasan was already at the sink slitting the belly of the fat mullet she had bought from the fish peddler that afternoon. Tatsue avoided looking at the red intestines and the gills that sent blood swirling into the sink.

After dinner, Tatsue finished washing the dishes, then went back to the laundry room where Otosan had already heated the water in the copper furo. Behind her in the back room, she could hear someone crying. Someone was always crying. This time it was the little one, Masao. He was tired of following Kei around the house and wanted to accompany his older brothers out into the neighborhood. And he didn't want to wear Kei's old dresses anymore.

"I like pants." he cried. He was three now and knew the difference.

"Yakamashii!" Otosan shouted, and Masao sat down on the floor reduced to soft whimpering. He had felt the belt before.

Tatsue scooped hot water from the furo into one of the tin laundry tubs, then set the wooden washboard inside. She wanted some new clothes too. How she envied Nii-san, her older brother who worked at Fair Department Store. He always got to buy new things then acted so high nosed when he wore them.

She filled the second tub with cold rinse water and opened the rice bags and began to sort the clothes. She pulled out a sweat-streaked shirt. It was Yoshio's now. She remembered washing it when it had belonged to Nii-san. He and Otosan had not spoken to each other since the night Otosan had told him to leave school and go to work full time.

"Shikata ga nai. Can't help it. You have to work." Otosan had said.

"One more year until I finish!" Nii-san had argued. "One more year, I can work anyplace I like. I can make big money. Why you cannot wait one year and let me graduate?"

"Naze yuu koto kikan no?" Otosan yelled at him. "What kind of son are you? Men have to work." The old man had stood firm as iron. In the end, Nii-san did as he was told and handed over his paycheck every week. But he spent all the money Otosan gave back to him to buy all the latest styles.

"Hardhead. Big Face everytime," Tatsue whispered to herself. "Think he too good for us now."

Tatsue dunked and scrubbed. As she worked, she could hear her mother coughing in the back room. Okasan could never do all of this work by herself, and the boys would never set foot into the laundry to help. Woman's work, they called it. But beginning tomorrow, Tatsue would go to work too. This year she could work legally at the cannery without lying about her age.

The air outside was cool, the moon warm and silver through thin clouds. Tatsue finished hanging the wash and looked at the sky through her fingers. Her hands were thin and fragile-looking, and each oval nail contained the edge of a rising moon. Fred, the boy who walked her home every day from McKinley High School, said they were refined. She thought Fred was handsome. Otosan and Okasan didn't like him.

"His mouth is too big. His lips are too full. Your children will be ugly if you marry him." they said.

Tatsue looked down again at her hands and signed. She didn't know if they were refined, but she knew they were strong.

Tatsue went back into the house and climbed the stairs to her bedroom. She opened her drawer and looked at her apron and gloves and white cannery hairnet. She pulled a glove over her fingers. Tomorrow she would earn fifteen cents an hour as a packer. The man in the window of the payroll office would hand her a numbered pay envelope heavy with silver dollars every week. It would be like Otosan's and Nii-san's. Tatsue lay in bed and drifted to sleep. She dreamed of buying cotton so sheer it would wear out in a year. She dreamed of wearing dresses that would never have to be handed down.

At five the next morning, the air was damp and smelled cool and sweet. Tatsue made her bento lunch then hurried out of the house and met her friend Edith at the corner.

"Hey, you going work my table this year?" Edith asked as they fell into step together. "If the forelady like us, she keep us on long time. We can make plenty money."

They walked out of Desha Lane down King Street, toward Iwilei and the cannery. Other girls joined them. Girls from thirteen to eighteen years old, dressed in home-made dresses, and carrying lunch pails, rubber gloves, aprons, and hairnets in their hands. They laughed as they greeted one another. The clouds above the mountains of Nuuanu swirled like incense high into the limitless blue sky.

The air at the California Packers Cooperative cannery smelled like baked pineapple. It was so thick it clung to Tatsue's skin. The girls walked past the guards, through the iron gates, and into the noise of the mechanical landscape. They walked past the trains that brought the pineapple in from the country. Twelve-hour shifts were usual at this time, the peak of the season. Everyone worked from six to six with one break for lunch.

Tatsue and Edith went to the locker room and put on their caps and gloves and hairnets. They pinned the bango numbers to each other's shoulders.

Edith said, "Last year, I went get sick and my sister took my number and came work for me. The man from the payroll office came with the clipboard and check the numbers. They went pay me anyway. They no care. So long as somebody wear this number. Same thing to them."

The girls walked out into the clatter of the thousands of metal teeth that moved the conveyer belts. The pineapples moved through the cannery on the conveyor belts that joined one machine to another like tongues that stretched across the room. The pine went from the railroad cars to the Ginnaka machine, which chewed them out of most of their skins. The almost-naked pines then rode to the trimmers who would pick up the fruit in one hand and trim out the spots of rind, called eyes, with the sharp knives they held in the other. Tatsue was glad she was not a trimmer. Their hands ached from holding the heavy pineapples and their arms were marked with round sores caused by the pineapple juice dripping down their rubber gloves.

"Eh, packers! I remember you two from last year, come over hea to my table," the forelady with the loud voice called to them. They followed the pine down the conveyor belt that led from the trimmers to the slicing machines, where a large, smiling Portuguese woman was standing behind girls packing pineapples into cans.

"You going be first packer this year," the forelady said as she pulled Tatsue into place behind the girl who worked closest to the slicing machine. When the whistle blew, the night crew stopped and Tatsue and Edith stepped up to take their places. The mechanical teeth kept clattering and the pineapple flowed endlessly by.

The year before, the two girls had lied about their ages and come to work scared and silent. They had been afraid of the loud voices of the foreladies. They had been afraid of the machines. But Tatsue had made it. She was first packer this year.

"No dream, no talk, no take too much time!" The forelady scolded the new girls, but Tatsue and Edith were old-timers now.

Tatsue picked out the sweetest slices emerging from the slicer and packed them in the small cans in front of her. These were the premium pieces and would be sold for the most money. The girls farther down the line picked out the slices that went into cans that were larger and less costly. Broken slices would be fed into machines again and packed into cans to be sold as tidbits, and badly broken pieces would be thrown into mashing machines and pressed for juice.

Tatsue liked her new position. The pineapple slices came out of the machine clinging neatly together. The vibration of the belt shook them out of their neat arrangement so Tatsue edged closer to the slicing machine to catch the pineapple just as it emerged from the metal mouth. As she settled her body into the chattering mechanical rhythm, she thought of Fred and the wonderful dresses she could make with the money she earned this summer. She would hand Otosan her pay envelope and he would give her back silver dollars to save in her drawer so that she could buy material to make new dresses for school. Tatsue could see herself walking home with Fred in her new clothes. "You look like Olivia DeHavilland in that dress," he might tell her.

Maybe this year Otosan would let her go to the movies with Fred. She would lean close to him and he might kiss her, his full lips on hers in a kiss she had seen in the movies at the Waikiki theater. She dreamed and smiled.

Tatsue reached higher into the mouth of the machine for her next slices. Suddenly, she felt a stinging numbness in her hand. She looked at her glove. The fingertip was open like a mouth trying to scream. She saw the pink flesh around a circle of white bone, all that was left of the tip of her finger.

She bit her lips and pulled her mouth smooth and hard across her teeth so that she would not cry out. The blood-spattered pineapple slices moved down the conveyor belt, and somewhere down the row, Edith began screaming. The girls farther down the line saw the bloody slices and screamed too. As the foreladies gathered around Tatsue and swept her off to the dispensary, she heard the screaming spread. It echoed down the line from slices, to chunks, to crushed. She did not open her mouth.

At home, she slept. After three days, she cried silently when her mother changed the bandage. Okasan thought she was in pain and tried to give her some pills.

"No, I no like drink anything."

Otosan made the face he always made when Okasan told him to call the mid-wife, and went downstairs to his chair. Tatsue sank into bed and gathered the thick, soft, cotton futon around herself. Her tears sank into the quilt made of dresses she had worn as a small child.

A week after the accident, she came downstairs to sit at the kitchen table where Okasan was sewing. Otosan had been laid off from his carpenter's job at the Libby cannery. He sat in his chair reading his books and smoking the hand-rolled cigarettes he made each morning. Tatsue looked down at her bandaged hand. Now Nii-san was the only one in the household working.

Tatsue left the table and went into the laundry room. She did not see Otosan put down his cigarette and watch her carefully. She got a bucket and filled the two washtubs with water from the furo. It was hard working with one hand, but it was dark in the laundry room, and no one would see her eyes. There would be no new dresses. The outline of her bandaged finger blurred.

Tatsue put the wooden washboard in one tub and dropped two balls of bluing in the other. She opened the old rice bag containing the boys' dirty laundry and pulled out Nii-san's crisp new shirt. She pushed it into the water in the first tub, then laid it on the washboard and rubbed the brown bar of soap over it. She moved the shirt up and down over the wooden teeth of the washboard. As she tried to squeeze out the soap she heard someone speak.

"Tatsue."

She looked up, startled. Otosan was standing in the laundry room. She didn't know how long he had been watching her. She had never seen him in the laundry room before.

"Sonna koto sen demo ii, you don't have to do that," Otosan said softly. Then he took the shirt that she had been washing and twisted it in his carpenter's hands to ring it out. Tatsue watched in amazement as he dipped Nii-san's shirt into the blue rinse water. He was clumsy and did not rinse like a woman. He was inventing the motions as he went along. Tatsue realized he had never learned this; a Japanese man never washed clothes. The bluing in the water clung to his nails. Each of his nails was grooved so that it looked like the ribbed cotton of his undershirt. Tiny ribs ran vertically the length of each nail.

"I like that one, you always get that one!" They heard Masao and Kei from beyond the laundry room door and the asthmatic coughing that constantly filled the house.

Tatsue watched the yellow carpenter's calluses in Otosan's palms become grey and soft as he washed his eldest son's shirt in the soapy water. He didn't say anything, he didn't smile at her, he just continued washing and rinsing. Tatsue took the clothes he had finished and fed each piece into the hand-cranked wringer. Otosan watched until he was satisfied that the work was light enough for her do. Then he went back to washing. Tatsue could feel her tears drying, her mouth softening again, her lips rounding into a smile.

Otosan helped her in the laundry room the whole summer. She loved working silently next to him. He smelled like sawdust, cigarette smoke and soft grey ashes. They worked through June and July, until it was August, the week before school.

Twelve hands turned the lazy susan in the center of the table quickly past the vegetables from Okasan's kitchen garden to the shoyu cooked fish. The ball bearings Otosan had built into the table clattered. He handed Tatsue three silver dollars.

"That is all that's left. Shikata ga nakatta. We had to eat your finger." Otosan spoke gruffly, avoiding her eyes. The table stopped turning. Everyone stopped eating and stared at him with open mouths. Tatsue did not understand.

"CPC kara . . . the cannery paid me money for twelve weeks after your accident. They said 'workman's compensation.' I didn't tell you. I had to use the money to buy food for the whole family."

Tatsue's eyes stung. Mean old man! The cannery had been paying her the entire summer! She pressed her lips hard over her teeth. He had not been able to work, and Nii-san's money had not been enough! Otosan had taken her money and used it. Tatsue looked down at her healing finger. Its tip was gone and it was shorter than the rest. The new nail was growing in wrinkled with tiny ridges.

Then she remembered Otosan squatting beside her in the laundry room. All her life, she had been taught that a Japanese man does not do women's work. She could not help thinking of that as she remembered Otosan pushing Nii-san's shirts across the wooden ribs of the washboard, the soapy water eating away the hard calluses on his palms and cutting into the deep grooves in his fingernails. He was a practical man. He did not say anything. He did what was necessary. She stared at his fingers as they held out the last three silver dollars he had saved for her.

She looked at Nii-san in his stylish clothes. He was looking at her finger; his eyes softened, then began to glisten. She looked at the younger boys and her sister Kei in their hand-me-down clothes, at Masao in his new pants made of Otosan's old work-shirt, and at Okasan in her faded dress.

They were staring at her.

"Shi kata ga nai." It couldn't be helped. She began to mumble these words she had been taught. They were as familiar as the offerings she made every evening in a sweet cloud of incense to feed the hungry spirits gathering in the warmth around their family altar.

"Shi kata ga nai." She looked at them all sitting together in a circle around the kitchen table. And in her mouth, as she said those words, there was a satisfaction like the cold grains eaten from a small brass dish. It was a satisfaction which surprised her, and she felt nourished and warm as she swallowed. They were

250

smiling at her in the last orange light, the bottoms of the windows filled with the curved edge of the sun. She looked at their faces, and the warmth she felt was like a circle, a round ball, an offering of rice.

Wakako Yamauchi

MAYBE

When I am out of sorts, I often drive to the outer edge of the city to calm myself. I love the outskirts. It reminds me of the land as it must have looked before we covered the earth with cement. I find there a feeling of the prairie where I was born. Sometimes when I see an old house with peeling paint squatting on a mound of dry weeds, the setting sun bleaching its west wall, I think I hear the children that have played there, perhaps now as old as myself—if they have survived the depression, three wars, sickness, and heartbreak. At this point I remember where I am in the scheme of things, smaller than a grain of sand and as dispensable. It comforts me.

One day on such a drive, I found the factory just outside of town. Here narrow roads through low hills, and frame houses, shutters askew like unfocused eyes, along with rusting cars and oil drums, cling to the chain link fence that banks a structured city drain. The lots here are oddly shaped; city planners had exercised eminent domain and sliced the properties at their convenience, creating instant prosperity to the owners (providing rabbit skin coats and hand-tooled boots), maiming the lots for that brief prosperity (a tuft of fur caught in the chain links, a weathered boot lying with the flotsam in the weeds). A sign on the outer wall of the factory, HELP, succinct, desperate, still with a touch of humor, gave me courage to walk in. After all, I was no less in need, my alimony had dwindled to a trickle; after eight years, that's about par for course, my attorney said. Even after twenty-five years of marriage, he said. That's life. The owner himself, Chuck White, took me in like a lost member of a tribe. We're of the same generation.

I am embarrassed to tell you the name of the company; it's too presumptuous for the two stories of rotting wood and broken windows and air conditioners hanging off the walls. Those that still function, spin out tails of spidery dust in the tepid air. But that's only in the offices and not for the majority of us.

I will call it Zodiac Prints. When I joined them, they were printing signs of the zodiac on T-shirts and cloth posters. I was hired as a quality-control person. They put me at the end of a long conveyor belt that slowly passes through several silk screens, each a different color, and a drying process. I check the colors, the print, and the material for flaws, and I stack and bundle the finished product. They don't say Zodiac 'til I say they say Zodiac.

Although I was the last hired, I was sent to the end of the belt largely because of Chuck White. White people (no pun intended) do not observe the difference between native Japanese and Japanese-Americans. As I said, I was born in the Southern California desert, but people are often amazed that I can speak English and I guess Chuck White associates me with Japanese industry (Sony, Toyota, etc.), and just for walking in and asking for a job, I went to the back of the line which in this case is the top of the bottom. This inability of white America to differentiate has worked against thousands of us Japanese-Americans in 1942 when we were all put in concentration camps, blamed for Japan's attack on Pearl Harbor. Since then there have been other harrowing moments: the save-the-whale issue, the slaughter of dolphins, and always during trade treaties over Japanese exports—each movement sending waves of guilt by association. On the extreme, some of us have been clubbed to death by our super patriots and we have always been admonished to go back where we came from.

Anyway, back at the Zodiac, the story I hear is that Chuck White was having financial trouble and had taken steps toward declaring bankruptcy. He planned to drop out, wipe off the slate of debts, and start clean at another place under his wife's name— Zenobia. They say it isn't the first time Chuck did this, but the first with the new wife.

Preparations for the change had been made; a new site was selected, new business cards with Zenobia's name were printed and Zenobia was coming in daily to get a working knowledge of the business. Then suddenly the orders came pouring in and with it thousands of dollars. New people had to be hired. The factory started to hum again and the move was postponed. This is where I came in.

They say Zenobia, Colombian by birth, a ravishing overweight beauty at least twenty years Chuck White's junior (like my husband's new wife), changed from a quiet housewife to a formidable boss as easily as she would put on a coat, wearing all the executive qualities, the harassed eyes, the no-nonsense walk, the imperial forefinger, and also a touch of paternal benevolence—the sodas and tacos on the days that we worked overtime. Most of the workers are from Mexico, Nicaragua, and Costa Rica. The sales staff is white but they are not often at the factory.

Zenobia watches me when she thinks I'm not looking. I catch her reflection on the dirty glass panes and when I turn to face her, she flashes her perfect teeth. She doesn't like me. Maybe I remind her of someone. Maybe she's amazed that I can speak English. China, she calls me. Maybe she thinks I'm a communist.

Most of the time she's busy on the phone or is rushing off somewhere in her silver Mercedes. Probably to the bank. She wears Gloria Vanderbilt jeans and carries a Gucci bag and smells of expensive perfume. When Chuck White is out of town, she moves me from one floor to the other for unimportant reasons. Just to let me know how superfluous I am.

So it goes. I've had worse things happen to me and nothing about this job causes me to lose sleep. Almost nothing. There's a certain confidence in knowing you're over-qualified and Zenobia does not diminish me. Besides, I like the second floor; the project is more interesting. They tie-dye there. Twenty people bend over paint troughs, dipping and squeezing shirts, skirts, and other things and the items hang to dry on rows and rows of lines, dripping and making puddles of color on the worn floor.

There are three big German Shepherd dogs in the factory. During the worst of his days (I'm told), Chuck White had to sell his Bel Air house but Zenobia would not let him sell the dogs. So the dogs live in the ramshackle factory and they follow Umberto, who feeds and cleans up after them, everywhere he goes—roaming the floors (they're not permitted outside), up and down the stairs, stumbled on and cursed by the workers, in and out of rooms. When Umberto is not here, these monstrous animals lie disconsolately on the floor wherever their depression happens to drop them. Umberto calls them by name and rubs their monster heads and they thump their powerful tails and slosh him with saliva. He's patient and gentle. He's twenty-four and quite handsome.

Everyone here who is from the other Americas is between seventeen and twenty-five. They all speak Spanish, some a little English, and they generally work quietly, obeying Zenobia or Rachel (the floorlady) without question or comment. In the late afternoons and on pay days, Jesus (El Savior) begins to sing and an excitement prevails even though we groan and laugh at his comic straining for high notes. I am reminded of my own youth, after being released from camp, the period that I spent working in factories, looking over the boys, waiting for the end of day, looking forward to my pay check, mentally parceling out the money—to the lay-away at Lerner's, for rent, for food, for bus tokens. Fridays were just like these with another Jesus singing and cutting up, with everyone waiting for the factory whistle so we could go on with our real lives. I've come a full circle, back to a place that has remained unchanged in the changing times, in the age of the Pac Man and the computer. Maybe all displaced people go through a period of innocence before the desire to own, the ambition to be, propel us away from simple pleasures. The return is sweet with remembrance, along with a little sorrow—for the loss of innocence. But I'm older now and none of the senses are so acute and no pain so unbearable. And yet . . .

On a coffee break, I walk to the low hills for a breath of fresh air. Reynaldo and Anabella sit on top of the knoll on a scrap of plastic. Reynaldo is in charge of the keys to the factory and is married to Anabella. She doesn't speak much English so she always stays close to him, letting him transact the business of their lives. Faded pop cans lie in the dry grass.

"How romantic," I say to them.

"It is hot in the factory," Reynaldo says. Anabella whispers something.

"We are thinking about our son," Reynaldo says.

Why, Anabella looks no more than seventeen. I tell him this.

"She is twenty-one, same as me," Reynaldo says. "We are married already five years. Our son is in Mexico still. Today is his birthday."

Walking down the hill, I am filled with their longing. I stop to look back at them. Anabella waves.

Umberto is not conscientious about cleaning the factory. The women's bathroom is dotted with dog droppings. I complain and Umberto tells me not to use it.

"I cannot clean everything all the time and do the work also," he says. "The dogs, you know, they do it all the time. I cannot keep up. Go to the office toilet."

He tells me they pay him three dollars and thirty-five cents an hour—the minimum. He gets up at four to come to work; his bus fare is three dollars, and lunch from the catering truck almost always costs six dollars a day. He is so tired at the end of day, he cannot stay awake. He shakes his head. "I am still a young man," he says.

The reedy whistle of the catering truck rises above factory noises and a surge of people run to meet it. The chatter grows bright with food words: tortillas, polla, naranja. My high school Spanish is inadequate; I wish I knew what else is said. Umberto sits on the ground to eat, carefully placing the paper plate in the circle of his legs. I feel the sublime intimacy of the man and his food.

To get to the office bathroom, I must pass through Chuck White's office. He sits at a big desk looking over invoices in a pool of sunlight. The floor is carpeted, the walls are papered; the room is an oasis in the factory. He looks up briefly and smiles—almost an apology. "The other bathroom is filthy," I say. He nods and returns to his papers. No doubt he's heard of the fastidious Japanese.

Someone tried to bring some class to the bathroom and had

painted the walls a dark green and installed a pair of fancy faucets in the sink. An electric hotplate on a crate destroys the ambiance and there is a bottle of shampoo on the floor. The toilet here doesn't flush right either.

Umberto tells me that Reynaldo and Anabella live in the factory at night. I see no bed, no blankets, no clothes—only the hotplate and shampoo in the office bathroom. I think about the eerie loneliness of this huge factory at night, the three dogs groaning and snuffling and shuffling, the doors that hardly close, and Reynaldo and Anabella copulating on the production table with the smell of dogs and the spoiling vegetable dyes and the summer moon shining on their skin. And in the morning I see them putting away the evidence of their living: the underwear, the socks, the toothbrushes, combs, and towels.

But Umberto says Zenobia knows about this. She lets them stay because they have nowhere else to go. Umberto himself shares rent with six other people. "I have no room for them," he says.

In winter icy winds will blow through those broken windows and ill-fitting doors and the production table will be cold and hard, I tell Umberto.

"That's winter," he shrugs.

Reynaldo makes a sandwich from a loaf of Weber's bread and pressed meat. He spreads the bread with a thin swipe of mayonnaise and eats this with a gusto that can come only from hunger or habit. Anabella buys fried chicken, frijoles, and tortillas from the truck and shares these with Reynaldo. She eats slowly and sensually, careful not to lose a morsel from the chicken bones. She eats a sandwich too. I make fun; I point to her stomach and ask, "How many months?" She holds up four fingers.

I have a feeling Zenobia likes the sales staff as little as she does me. They bring her extravagant gifts and she puts on a dazzling smile and turns away, quickly dropping the smile as though she hopes her hypocrisy would be discovered. But on her birthday she invites them all to a party—everyone except me. I'd already contributed five dollars toward her gift and I had signed the birthday card.

258

She's happy all day, smiling and humming, but I pretend not to know what's up and try to look happy too. What do I care? If she has a conscience at all, she'll feel rotten when she sees my name on the card. I wish Rachel had let me do the shopping; I'd have fixed her good (I thought I'd given up feelings like that).

At the party they say Zenobia drinks too much and kisses all the young men. That's because she married an old man, Umberto says. Late in the evening she sniffs cocaine and turns up the music and wants to dance with all the guys. Chuck White serves the cake and goes to bed. Neighbors call to complain about the noise and everyone gets nervous thinking about police and raids and such things. These are always on the top of an undocumented alien's mind, Umberto says. Zenobia doesn't care; she married a white man and holds a green card. Umberto says everyone in the factory except the sales staff is undocumented. Reynaldo comes to sit with us.

"Are you illegal too?" I ask.

Reynaldo nods. "Everybody is. In this factory, in all the restaurants around here, all these places," he waves his hands. "These places, they would not stand without us." He pokes my arm and laughs. "Hey, you want to marry me? I'll give you one thousand dollars," he says.

"What will we do with Anabella?" I say.

"After the divorce, I will marry her," he says.

"But I have children older than you," I say.

He moves away and calls back, "One thousand dollars, Florence." Anabella smiles at me.

Andrea smiles at the bus stop with a plastic purse clasped to her breast. She is seventeen and the prettiest girl in the factory, but today she looks awful. It's before the lunch hour. "Is she sick?" I ask Umberto.

"Well, Chuck told her to go home,' he says.

The story is, Zenobia was so anxious to get an order off, she told Andrea to remove the bands before time and dry the shirts. Andrea did this, but she put the shirts in the tumble dryer and the wet dyes ran together and the whole order was ruined. Chuck White found the mess and fired Andrea. Even after he was told about Zenobia's instructions, he would not relent. "She should know better," he said and went to his office and closed the door.

Umberto taps his head. "She should know better," he says.

"Look how she holds her purse," I say.

"Well, she's sad," he says.

"Her mother will ask what happened and she'll have to say she lost her job."

"Rachel will find another for her," Umberto says.

"What will happen if she doesn't?" I ask.

"Then I will find for her," he says.

Reynaldo punches my arm every time he passes by, mocking me softly, "One thousand dollars, Florence." Sometimes he catches my eye from across the room and mouths, "One thousand dollars."

I call a young single friend to ask if she would marry Reynaldo. She is divorced and always in need of money but she tells me that immigration laws require a full three years of marriage before they will issue green cards. "That's longer than some real marriages last," my friend says. "One thousand dollars for three years is three hundred and thirty-three dollars a year," she says.

"And thirty-three cents," I add.

"I turned down ten thousand for the same service," she says. "And I could very well meet someone myself in three years. A real marriage, you know what I mean?"

I give Reynaldo the bad news. He looks hurt even though we only joke about it. I tell him my friend says three years is too long to be tied to a stranger.

"I just want a green card so I can bring my son here," he says. "My son was two years when we left him. He already forgot me, I think." Anabella turns her face away.

"I can't marry you, Reynaldo," I say.

"I know," he says. After a while he walks away.

I'm afraid I shall leave Zodiac soon. In the deceptive simplicity of the lives here, there is a quality I am unable to face. It's the underbelly of a smile. I know it well.

I remember our life in the Arizona camp—the first day our family entered that empty barrack room (our home for the next four years), my father squatted on the dusty floor, his head deep in his shoulders, and my mother unwrapped a roll of salami and sliced it for us. I wanted so much to cry, but my mother gripped my arm and gave me the meat. I turned to my father; he looked up and smiled. Two years later, the day I was to leave them and relocate to Chicago, my mother stood by the army truck that was to take us to the train in Parker. She had not wanted me to leave because my father was in the hospital with stomach ulcers. She did not touch me. The corners of her mouth wavered once, then turned up in a smile. And in the same tradition I smiled when he told me he was marrying a young woman from Japan. "That's good," I said.

It did not seem so brave or so sad then. Maybe living it is easier than remembering or watching someone else living it. My son is in Mexico still, ha-ha; he will soon forget me.

Late in the afternoon Reynaldo comes back to me and pokes my arm. "Thank you for telling your friend to marry me," he says.

"I'm sorry it didn't work out," I say. I ask him if he crossed the border at Tijuana. My sister lives in National City, just north of the border. I remember those immigration round-ups that show periodically on television nightly news: soft gray blurs running in the California twilight, crouching, routed out of bushes, herded into covered pick-up trucks, their faces impassive.

"We crossed the river in Texas," he says.

"You swam the Rio Grande at night?" I ask.

Reynaldo nods. "Anabella, you know, she does not swim so I . . ." he crooks his left arm to make a circle for Anabella's head and with his right arm he makes swimming strokes and looks at me and smiles.

Maybe it does not seem so brave or so sad to him. Maybe I should spare myself the pain.

Hisaye Yamamoto

THE HIGH-HEELED SHOES
A MEMOIR

In the middle of the morning, the telephone rings. I am the only one at home. I answer it. A man's voice says softly, "Hello, this is Tony."

I don't know anyone named Tony. Nobody else in the house has spoken of knowing any Tony. But the greeting is very warm. It implies, "There is a certain thing which you and I alone know." Evidently he has dialed a wrong number. I tell him so, "You must have the wrong number," and prepare to hang up as soon as I know that he understands.

But the man says this is just the number he wants. To prove it, he recites off the pseudonym by which this household, Garbo-like, goes in the directory, the address, and the phone number. It is a unique name and I know there is probably no such person in the world. I merely tell him a fragment of the truth, that there is no such person at the address, and I am ready to hang up again.

But the man stalls. If there is no such person available, it appears he is willing to talk to me, whoever I am. I am suddenly in a bad humor, suspecting a trap in which I shall be imprisoned uncomfortably by words, words, words, earnestly begging me to try some product or another, the like of which is unknown anywhere else in the world. It isn't that I don't appreciate the unrapturous life a salesman must often lead. And I like to buy things. If I had the money, I would buy a little from every salesman who comes along, after I had permitted him to run ably or ineptly (it doesn't really matter) through the words he has been coached to repeat. Then, not only in the pride of the new acquisition, but in the knowledge that he was temporarily encouraged, my own spirits would gently rise, lifted by the wings of the dove. At each week's end, surrounded knee-deep by my various purchases – the Fuller toothbrush, the receipt for the magazine subscription which will help a girl obtain a nine-week flying course which she eagerly, eagerly wants, the one dozen white eggs fresh from the farm and cheaper than you can get at the corner grocery, the first volume in the indispensable 12-volume Illustrated Encyclopaedia of Home Medicine, the drug sundries totalling at least two dollars which will help guarantee a youngish veteran a permanent job—I could sigh and beam. That would be nice. But I don't have the money, and this coming of ill temper is just as much directed at myself for not having it as it is at the man for probably intending to put me in a position where I shall have to make him a failure.

"And just what is it you want?" I ask impatiently.

The man tells me, as man to woman. In the stark phrasing of his urgent need, I see that the certain thing alluded to by the warmth of his voice is a secret not of the past, but, with my acquiescence, of the near future. I let the receiver take a plunge down onto the hook from approximately a one-foot height. Then, I go outside and pick some pansies for Margarita, as I had been intending to do just before the phone rang. Margarita is the seven-year-old girl next door. She has never known any mother or father, only *tias* and *tios* who share none of her blood. She has a face that looks as if it had been chiseled with utter care out of cream and pale pink marble. Her soft brown hair hangs in plaits as low as her waist. And these days, because the Catholic school is full and cannot take her, she wanders lonesomely about, with plenty of time for such amenities as dropping in to admire a neighbor's flowers. The pansies I pick for her, lemon yellow, deep purple, clear violet, mottled brown, were transplanted here last year by Wakako and Chester, a young couple we know who have a knack for getting things wholesale, and they are thriving like crazy this spring, sprawling untidily over their narrow bed and giving no end of blooms.

Later, there is a small, timid rat-tat-tat at the door. It's Margarita, bearing two calla lilies, a couple of clove pinks, and one tall amaryllis stalk with three brilliant brick-red flowers and a bud. She dashes off the porch, down the steps, and around the ivy-sprawled front fence before I can properly thank her. Oh, well. Taking the gift to the service porch, I throw out the wilting brown-edged callas she dashed over with last week, rinse out the blue potato glass, fill it with water, and stick in the new bouquet. But all the time the hands are occupied with these tokens of arrived spring and knowing Margarita, the mind recalls unlovely, furtive things.

When Mary lived with us, there was a time she left for work in the dark hours of the morning. On one of these mornings, about midway in her lonely walk past the cemetery to the P-car stop, a man came from behind and grabbed her, stopped her mouth with his hand, and, rather arbitrarily, gave her a choice between one kiss and rape. Terrified, she indicated what seemed to be the somewhat lesser requirement. He allowed her to go afterwards, warning her on no account to scream for help or look back, on penalty of death. When she arrived at her place of work, trembling and pale green, her office friends asked whether she was ill, and she told them of her encounter. They advised her to go to the police immediately.

She doubted whether that would help, since she had been unable to see the man. But, persuaded that a report, even incomplete, to the police was her duty to the rest of womankind, she reluctantly went to the nearest station with her story. She came back with the impression that the police had been much amused, that they had actually snickered as she left with their officially regretful shrug over her having given them nothing to go on. She told her boss and he called the police himself and evidently made his influence felt, for we had a caller that evening.

It was I who answered the knock. A policeman stepped in, and, without any preliminaries, asked, "Are you the girl that was raped?"

Making up with enough asperity for a sudden inexplicable lack of aplomb, I said, no, and no one had been raped, *yet*, and called Mary. She and the officer went out on the porch and talked in near whispers for a while. After he left, Mary identified him and his companion as the night patrol for our section of the city. He had promised that they would tell the dawn patrol to be hovering around about the time she left for work each morning. But Mary, nervously trying the dim walk a couple of more times, caught no sign of any kind of patrol. Thereafter, she and the rest of the women of the household took to traveling in style, by taxi, when they were called to go forth at odd hours. This not only dented our budgets, but made us considerably limit our unescorted evening gadding.

There were similar episodes, fortunately more fleeting. What stayed with me longer than Mary's because it was mine, was the high-heeled shoes. Walking one bright Saturday morning to work along the same stretch that Mary had walked, I noticed a dusty blue, middle-aged sedan parked just ahead. A pair of bare, not especially remarkable legs was crossed in the open doorway, as though the body to them were lying on the front seat, relaxing. I presumed that they were a woman's legs, belonging to the wife of some man who had business in the lumberyard just opposite, because they were wearing black high-heeled shoes. As I passed, I glanced at the waiting woman.

My presumption had been rash. It wasn't a woman, but a man, unclothed (except for *the high-heeled shoes, the high-heeled shoes*), and I saw that I was, with frantic gestures, being enjoined to linger awhile. Nothing in my life before had quite prepared me for this: some Freud, a smattering of Ellis, lots of Stekel, and fat Krafft-Ebing, in red covers, were on my bookshelves, granted; conversation had explored curiously, and the imagination conjured bizarre scenes at the drop of a casual word. But reading is reading, talking is talking, thinking is thinking, and living is different. Improvising hastily on behavior for the occasion, I chose to pretend as though my heart were repeating Pippa's song, and continued walking, possibly a little faster and a little straighter than I had been, up to the P-car stop. When I got to the print shop, the boss said, "You look rather put upon this morning." I mustered up a feeble smile and nodded, but I couldn't bring myself to speak of the high-heeled shoes. This was nothing so uncomplicated as pure rape, I knew, and the need of the moment was to go away by myself, far from everybody, and think about things for awhile. But there were galleys and page proofs waiting to be read, and I set to with a sort of dedicated vengeance, for I had recently been reprimanded for getting sloppy again. When the hectic morning of poring over small print was over and my elbows black, letting my thoughts go cautiously but wholly back to the time between leaving the house and boarding the P-car, I found there was not much to think about. I had seen what I had seen. I had, admit it now, been thrown for a sickening loop. That was all. But the incongruity of a naked man in black high-heeled shoes was something the mind could not entirely dismiss, and there were times afterwards when he, never seen again, contributed to a larger perplexity that stirred the lees around and around, before more immediate matters, claiming attention, allowed them to settle again.

There was a man in the theatre with groping hands. There was a man on the streetcar with insistent thighs. There was a man who grinned triumphantly and walked quickly away after he trailed one down a drizzly street at dusk and finally succeeded in his aim of thrusting an unexpected hand under one's raincoat.

I remembered them as I plucked the pansies, took them over to Margarita's house, came back home, answered the door, received the amaryllis, the callas, the pinks, and arranged them in the blue potato glass on top of the buffet. I remembered another man, Mohandas Gandhi, probably a stranger to this company, not only because I had been reading on him of late, but because he seemed to be the only unimpeachable authority who had ever been called on to give public advice in this connection. When someone had delicately asked Gandhi, "What is a woman to do when she is attacked by miscreants?," naming the alternatives of violent self-defense and immediate flight, he had replied, "For me, there can be no preparation for violence. All preparation must be for non-violence if courage of the highest type is to be developed. Violence can only be tolerated as being preferable always to cowardice. Therefore I would have no boats ready for flight. . . ." Then he had soared on to the nobler implications of non-violence, reproaching the world for its cowardice in arming itself with the atomic bomb.

I understood. When I first read these words, I had said, "Why, of course," smiling at the unnecessary alarms of some people. But I had read the words at a rarefied period, forgetting Mary, forgetting the high-heeled shoes. I decided now that the inspiration they gave to his probably feminine questioner was small potatoes. Of all the men suspected of sainthood, Gandhi, measured by his own testimony, should have been able to offer the most concrete comfort here. But he had evaded the issue. In place of the tangible example, vague words. Gandhi, in face of the ubiquitous womanly fear, was a failure. All he had really said was: don't even think about it. Then (I guessed), holding up his strong, bony brown hand, he had shaken his white-fuzzed, compactly-shaped head slowly back and forth and declined to hear the ifs and buts. The rest, as they say, was silence.

But could I have momentarily borrowed Gandhi's attitude to life and death, what would I have done as the man who called himself Tony rang my number? With enough straining, with maybe a resort to urgent, concentrated prayer, could I have found the gentle but effective words to make Tony see that there were more charming ways to spend a morning? I practiced this angle for awhile:

"I'm afraid you *do* have the wrong number." Soberly, hang up. Disconcerting enough, but rather negative.

"It's a nice day for the beach, sir. Why don't you go swimming? — might help you cool off a little." The voice with a compassionate smile. Too flippant.

"There are many lonely women in the world, and there are more acceptable ways to meet them than this. Have you tried joining a Lonely Hearts club? Don't you have any kind of hobby?" Condescending, as though I were forever above his need. Ambiguously worded, too, that last, fraught with the possibility of an abrupt answer.

"Listen, you know you aren't supposed to go around doing things like this. I think I know what made you do it, though, and I think a psychiatrist would help you quite a bit, if you'd cooperate." The enlightened woman's yap. Probably'd hang up on me.

Anyway, it was too late. And, after all, Gandhi was Gandhi, an old man, moreover dead, and I was I, a young woman, more or less alive. Since I was unable to hit on the proper pacifist approach, since, indeed, I doubted the efficacy of the pacifist approach in this crisis, should I, eschewing cowardice, have shouted bitter, indignant words to frighten Tony? Not that, either. Besides, I hadn't gauged his mood. He had spoken casually enough, but there had been an undertone of something. Restrained glee? Playfulness? Confidence? Desperation? I didn't know.

Then, to help protect my sisters, should I have turned toward the official avenues? Was it my responsibility to have responded with pretended warmth, invited him over, and had the police waiting with me when he arrived? Say I had sorrowfully pressed the matter, say Tony were consequently found guilty (of abusing his communication privileges, of course)—the omnipotent they (representing us) would have merely restricted his liberty for a while, in the name of punishment. What would he have done when he was let go, his debt to society as completely repaid as society, who had created his condition, could make him repay? Telephones in working order abound, with telephone books conveniently alongside him, containing any number of women's names, addresses, and numbers.

And what did Tony do when the sound of my receiver crashed painfully in his ear? Did he laugh and proceed to some other number? His vanity bruised, did he curse? Or perhaps he felt shame, thinking, "My God, what am I doing, what am I doing?" Whatever, whatever—I knew I had discovered yet another circle to put away with my collection of circles. I was back to what I had started with, the helpless, absolutely useless knowledge that the days and nights must surely be bleak for a man who knew the compulsion to thumb through the telephone directory for a woman's name, any woman's name; that this bleakness, multiplied infinite times (see almost any daily paper), was a great, dark sickness of the earth that no amount of pansies, pinks, or amaryllis, thriving joyously in what garden, however well-ordered and pointed to with pride, could ever begin to assuage.

The telephone rings. Startled, I go warily, wondering, whether it might not be Tony again, calling perhaps to avenge the blow to pride by anonymous invective, to raise self-esteem by letting it be known that he is a practical joker. I hold my breath after I say, "Hello?"

It is the familiar voice, slightly querulous but altogether precious, of my aunt Miné. She says I am not to plan anything for supper. She has made something special, ricecakes with Indian bean frosting, as well as pickled fish on vinegared rice. She has also been able to get some yellowtail, to slice and eat raw. All these things she and Uncle are bringing over this evening. Is about five o'clock too early?

It is possible she wonders at my enthusiastic appreciation, which is all right, but all out of proportion.

(1948)

Cecilia Manguerra Brainard

WAITING FOR PAPA'S RETURN

When Reverend Mother Superior tells Remedios her father has died, all she can think is how ugly the nun looks. Remedios stares at the mustache fringing the nun's upper lip; Reverend Mother Superior stares back with pale watery eyes.

"This morning, child. Heart attack," the nun says.

In the distance the three o'clock bell rings as if repeating the nun's words. It is an October Thursday, warm and humid. The sound stays with Remedios as the nun brings her to the chapel, "Let us pray so your father will go straight to heaven," she whispers. They kneel on the front pew and Remedios closes her eyes. The ringing that echoes in her head fades and she hears her father's voice loud and clear: I'll be back in two weeks.

She clings to those words, mulling them over. I'll-be-back-in-two-weeks. That means next week because Mama and Papa have already been gone for a week. She pictures her father with his oval face, his goldrimmed glasses, and his balding head. Leaning on his cane, he asked, "What do you want me to bring?"

"Mama says she'll buy me shoes, clothes, candies, and chocolates."

"But what do you want?" his gentle voice prodded.

"A walking doll and a tea set like Mildred's. Not the plastic tea set, I want the kind that breaks."

"All right," he replied, tousling her dark hair. "I'll scour all of Hongkong and I'll bring you your doll and tea set."

Those words her father said and he never lies. Remedios is confused: Reverend Mother Superior is the most important person in school and she doesn't lie either. She must have made a mistake. Papa and Mama will be back next week from their vacation.

Remedios thinks things over, trying to find a reason for this misunderstanding. Was it because she and Mildred giggled in church at the fat woman singing in a warbling voice? Mildred elbowed her in the ribs and they were bad, no doubt about it, snickering in the back row instead of paying attention to Father Ruiz's novena.

The chapel smells of melted wax, and when Remedios opens her eyes, she studies the bleeding Jesus nailed to the cross. "I'm sorry for having been bad," she prays over and over, until Reverend Mother Superior stands up and says, "Your aunt is picking you up, child."

They find Tiya Meding in the office. She is wearing a brown dress; her face is pale, her eyes, pink-rimmed. "Poor, poor child," she mumbles. In the car she looks at Remedios in a way that makes Remedios think her aunt is trying to discover something in her—and Remedios does not know what.

Feeling awkward, Remedios rolls down her window and watches the hawkers selling lottery tickets, boiled bananas, and soft drinks. Her aunt delicately blows her nose and sniffles.

"Look, there's the woman in black dancing in front of the church," Remedios points out.

"Crazy woman," Tiya Meding answers.

"Papa says she's pathetic."

"Pathetic, my foot. She's as loony as they come."

Remedios keeps quiet; pathetic is how her father describes the woman in black.

Her aunt's chauffeur—that is what Tiya Meding calls her driver—brings them to Vering the dressmaker. Remedios is surprised that she will have a dress sewn, and she nods approvingly at the design: puffed sleeves, boat neck, and shirred skirt.

"And pockets, two square pockets," Remedios says.

Vering sketches in the pockets.

"And I don't want this black cloth. Yellow organdy would be nicer."

The two women eye each other.

"But the dress has to be black," Tiya Meding insists.

"I don't like black. Papa says I look prettiest in yellow."

"The dress will be black, Remedios." Her aunt sets her jaw and Remedios knows there is no use arguing.

Before leaving the dressmaker's shop, Tiya Meding asks for pieces of black cloth the size of postage stamps, and she pins one on Remedios' blouse, right above her heart—a little bit of black cloth that flutters when the warm breeze blows.

At school she is the center of attraction, like the actress Gloria Romero or the one-eyed freak with the Chinese Acrobatic Troupe, stared at by everybody. When she picks up her schoolbag, the children glance curiously at her. The visitors streaming into Tiya Meding's house look at her, and when she and her aunt go to the funeral parlor and church "to make arrangements," people study her. Remedios feels as if her nose were growing from her forehead. Pairs of glassy eyes follow her around and she does not know what they want, how to escape them.

At her aunt's house, she tries to amuse herself by inspecting the numerous porcelain figures in the living room—pretty dainty women with ducks beside them, little angels kneeling down in prayer, but her aunt snaps: "Don't touch those. They're breakable." She goes to the piano and plays "Chopsticks," but her aunt lifts a reprimanding finger in the air. "The noise," she complains. Tiya Meding is on the phone and Remedios listens to her.

"Thank you," her aunt says. "Heart attack. Isn't that too bad? I warned my sister. An older man like that." Tiya Meding's diamond earrings dangle from her elongated ears and a huge diamond solitaire sparkles on her finger.

"Baubles," her father often says about Tiya Meding's jewelry. "She is a silly woman who likes baubles."

Remedios leaves the main house thinking to herself: Silly, silly woman. She goes to the dirty-kitchen and has a second lunch with the servants. Using her fingers, she makes a ball of rice and eats that with stewed fish. Later she helps the cook peel cassava and grate coconuts.

"Your father was a good man," the cook says. "He made my son the foreman at the road construction."

'Yes," Remedios replies, "I can't wait until he comes home."

After speaking, she wonders why she said those words at all. She understands what Reverend Mother Superior said, what all the commotion is about, yet deep in the very core of her, she *knows* her Papa will return.

The kitchen is sooty and smells of grease and bay leaves. The cook, standing next to the huge wood-burning stove, looks at her.

Remedios continues grating. She watches the curly slivers of white coconut meat fall into the basin. The kitchen smoke seems to engulf her and she feels warm. The pungent smell makes her temples throb. She begins to feel weak, just as she felt when her cousin told her she was adopted. He had lost in a game of checkers, and angrily, he told Remedios that her parents picked her up from a pile of trash, that she had been covered with fat flies. She did not cry; she crawled into bed to sleep off her tiredness. Her mother called the boy an idiotic pervert. Her father placed her on his knee.

"See this bump on my nose?" he asked.

"Yes."

"Don't you have a bump on your nose like mine?" His warm finger traveled down her nose over the slight protrusion.

She nodded.

"That means that you are my very own little girl. We didn't adopt you."

The darkness lifted, and the next time she saw her cousin she stuck her tongue out at him. But now the tiredness stays and she drags around until bedtime. It seems she has just tucked the mosquito net under the mattress when she falls asleep and has a dream.

It is Sunday, and she, Mama, and Papa are driving over bumpy, dusty roads to Talisay Beach. Remedios is happy because she enjoys clamming in the small inlet. But when they arrive, the sea is blood-red and smells foul. Remedios cries and her Papa asks why.

"Something terrible has happened," she says.

"It's all right," he answers. "I'm right beside you."

She dries her eyes and, noticing that the water has turned blue and the air clean once more, laughs and hugs her Papa.

"Don't cry. It makes me sad," her father says in her dream.

She wakes to Tiya Meding's voice telling her the plane is arriving in less than an hour. Trying to get excited, she bathes with her aunt's Maja soap and dabs Joy perfume behind her ears. Like a sleepwalker, she puts on her new black dress, white socks, and black patent shoes. Remedios ties yellow ribbons at the ends of her braids but Tiya Meding removes those. "Not for a year," she says.

Heavy-faced people wearing somber clothes crowd the airport. They stare at Remedios and she tries to figure out what they want from her. She laughs. "I can hardly wait to see them," she exclaims in a high thin voice. Pairs of eyes follow her, letting go only when the noisy plane arrives with a loud screech. The special cargo plane stops near the terminal, and some men open the side doors and struggle to bring a casket down. When Remedios spots her mother walking down the ramp, she runs shouting, "Ma!" The mourners around her pause. "Ma, where's my walking doll and tea set?" Her aunt tells her to be quiet. "She's just a child," someone says. "Just a child."

Her mother appears dreary in her black dress—Remedios really hates that color—and she weeps constantly. She will not talk, will not tell Remedios that everything will be fine.

A hollow feeling roots inside Remedios and sometimes she feels like the conch shell sitting on the writing desk. Other times it seems she is hanging on a thin thread, like the gray spider that swings back and forth from the ceiling. She feels odd, as if waiting for something to happen so all the staring will end, so the strangeness that has invaded her life will disappear.

The next day there is a Mass, then the men carry the coffin to the funeral car, so black and slick. When it starts raining, people scramble for umbrellas or newspapers and they mutter: Ah, a good sign, heaven is weeping. She, Mama, and Tiya Meding walk behind the funeral car to the old cemetery with gray crumbling crypts. Some women hold umbrellas over them to keep their heads dry. Remedios trudges along, splashing in puddles, watching the slum children playing in the rain.

At the cemetery, the men pick up the coffin, carry it to the family crypt, and open it. The priest sprinkles holy water inside. Her Mama, who emits wailing sounds and whose shoulders are shaking, bends over to kiss the man inside. Remedios has not looked but she knows that a man is in there. She has heard people talking: "Looks like he's sleeping, doesn't he? They sure did a good job."

Her Mama turns to her and Remedios walks toward the casket.

Tiptoeing, she peers in. The man's face is a waxy mask. He doesn't wear glasses and his tight little smile is a grimace. There is a smell like mothballs. Remedios feels faint. She wants to giggle, but stopping herself, she bends over and plants a kiss on the waxman's cool cheek.

The men close the coffin and slide it into the crypt with a grating sound. There is a dull thud when the marble slab covers the niche, and briefly Remedios feels a lurching inside her stomach. She closes her eyes and hears that voice loud and clear: I'll be back in two weeks. I'll bring you your doll and tea set.

When she opens her eyes and sees the mourners crying, for just a brief moment she understands that they want her to weep, that they have been waiting for her to cry. But soon she is thinking of dainty tea cups, the smooth feel of delicate china, the clinking sound as the cup hits the saucer. She is seeing her father smiling broadly as she hands him his cup, and they make a toast pretending to sip tea under the cool shade of the lush starapple trees.

Susan Landgraf

Sharon Hashimoto

Sharon Hashimoto was born in 1953 in Seattle, Washington. She received two B.A. degrees, in History and Journalism, and worked as a technical writer before returning to the University of Washington to pursue her fiction and poetry in the M.F.A. program eleven years later. A Teaching Assistant in the Asian American Studies Department, she is currently researching her family histories, in particular her grandmother's diaries and poetry.

Her poetry and short stories have appeared in Ironwood, The Stories We Hold Secret *(Greenfield Review Press),* Three Rivers Poetry Journal, Sou'Wester, *the* Seattle Review, The Nebraska Review, Gathering Ground *(Seal Press), and many others. In 1989, she was awarded a King County Individual Artist Grant to develop a collection of short stories as well as a Fellowship in Poetry from the National Endowment for the Arts.*

THE MUSHROOM MAN

Labor Day weekend.

And the air is rich with golden leaves that ride upon the wind. Dusty, sun-dried browns turn mushy, muddy wet black with hazy fog and misty rain. On cool clear nights the moon hangs low, glowing cheddar cheese yellow. And V-shaped flights of birds point arrows to the south.

Labor Day weekend, and the whispers begin.

Port Townsend. Shelton. Cascades.

Whispers that echo like wind through the trees, raining secrets that soak deep into the mind. Whispers that pour like rivers from overflowing mouths down Rainier Avenue and Jackson, Empire Way and Genesee. Whispers that speak of mushrooms.

"Last year, we only found about two dozen . . ."

". . . hope it rains . . . much too dry . . ."

"The Ogawas went last week . . ."

"Uwajimaya is selling them at five dollars a pound!"

Creamy, brown speckled caps with firm stems, smelling of pine and dark rich earth. Cooked in butter. Steamed in rice or soup. Frozen and hoarded like gold coins locked deep in icy safes. Sent by some to far away Hawaii, California, the East Coast—to be opened and relished by a black-haired, brown-eyed people. Found even in lean years, in ample abundance, by Osam.

"Osam? Tall, skinny . . . with horn rim glasses?"

"Didn't he work for the City?"

"You know, Toshio's middle son."

"He found how many?!" they would exclaim, their voices rising on the last note and lingering on the air with the tone of gentle wind chimes. "Where?" they would murmur, jealous of his riches, "Where does he go?"

And he would nod, smile and say nothing while passing out generous quantities to friends and families who knew better than to ask. Too many battles had been waged over "secret locations." Too many whispers and secrets had built walls between friends, made enemies among families.

Sure-footed Osam, whose journeying feet travelled far, past dull red mushrooms with shiny tops and fragile porcelain white mushrooms that dipped in the center. Keen eyes would spot treasure hidden beneath a mottled forest floor. And clever fingers would probe deep beneath tree roots to expose tender young buds.

Sam to some. Osam to others. Papa to me.

He was a centipede of tall long legs that walked swiftly down the rain-drenched streets of Seattle. Towering stilts that wandered deep into the woods, over decaying logs and padding softly over brown-green moss. Legs I used to hug tight and smile at the face that floated among the clouds above mine. Sweat and grass and the odor of trees and branches and the creek about him. That was Papa. Against the cool rubber of his boots, I would always smell mushrooms.

He was mountains and magic and memories—a mystery in the fine chain that bound me to him, and to Grandma and Grandpa. Sometimes he was sad and sometimes he was old, his eyes hungering for something distant, far-off. And watching him dreamily patch his worn faded boots, I would think questions at him, never daring to ask out loud. Where do the mountains begin, where do they end? Papa, do you know? How do you get there from here? Then feeling my eyes upon him, he would look up and push his glasses back up his narrow nose. His thin, even voice still tinged with smoky thoughts would remind me that homework must be done before bed.

A quiet man. A comfortable man. A quiet and comfortable house.

But some nights I would wake, snapped out of sleep like a rubber band. Listening to the house waiting, like the silence before a thunderstorm. Smothered and imprisoned between blankets and sheets, I would lie, feeling the tension run like electricity throughout the house. Then, just after midnight. Hushed, rough edged voices would claw the night. The edge of a broken glass it cut and made my dreams bleed into the dark.

Mama and Papa. Mostly Mama. Talking in broken Japanese. Whispers in bits of English.

". . . don't like you going by yourself. Why can't you take somebody with you?"

"Dare?"

"Davey . . .Sam . . . Big Joe . . ."

". . . hanashimasu . . ."

"Yes! My secre . . ."

"Shush! You'll wake the children!"

And the ricochetting emotions would bounce off the walls, always returning to me as I hid, buried in my bed, feeling the shadows hovering near. Then I would dream of dark clammy places that would yield to sweaty sheets and pillows thrown in fear upon the floor. Even morning sunlight and skies of robin egg blue would not chase away the autumn feelings in the air.

"Where does Papa go?" I once asked Mama as she packed a chicken-filled tupperware and a thermos into a sturdy cardboard box.

"Tomorrow? East to Mercer Island, all the way down I-90. To Easton, I think. To the Olympics, maybe, on Sunday. And back to work on Monday."

"Olympics. Easton." I murmured softly.

"What's that?"

I watched her carefully as she fitted paper plates and napkins beside the thermos. "Do we get to go?"

"Linda's going to Sally's birthday party tomorrow and you have a piano lesson."

"When do we get to go?"

And Mama stopped her quick, butterfly-like movements to stare at me. She frowned and her eyebrows were straight lines across her forehead. "When *we* get to go?" her quiet voice mocked mine. "When *he* asks."

She sat down heavily in the kitchen chair that wobbled because one leg had been bent, then sent me to the basement shelves for a can of olives. Anxious to escape her mood, I trampled half-running down the steps, jumping the fourth stair to the bottom.

"Please *walk* up the stairs," she shouted down to me.

"Yes Mama."

But I knew she was remembering . . .

Butter and heavily scented pine cut fresh that evening had run like bright streamers of heavenly aromas that lit up the house.

Papa had smiled and bubbled, a bright yellow balloon, as he carried in four boxes of freshly picked mushrooms.

"So many . . ." Mama had whispered, her voice filtered softly around, through and under the mountains of mushrooms. Quickly she had rolled up her sleeves, sorting the young buds from the wormy, blossomed mushrooms. I had watched her washing, cutting, dicing, cooking, freezing, streaming, preparing mushrooms in a thousand and one ways.

Puzzle pieces, I had thought to myself. Each gently gathered and somehow fitted into the quiet man leaning with one hip against the kitchen table. Part Mama. Part me and Linda, Grandma and Grandpa. Forests filled with pieces.

"Matsutake . . ." I had whispered. Mushroom man. Grown wild. Hidden in dark burrows beneath fallen trees. Dormant, but full of quiet secrets that touched me like the flying seasons. I had smiled up at Papa, not seeing the awful greyness creep into my father's face as his hands fluttered upwards to his chest before collapsing on the floor . . .

Winds blow chill on September days and the bright fall sun no longer warms my face and arms. The rain falls soft like chilly, early morning dreams and half-recalled memories that I try to forget. Falling leaves drift like Papa's rising voice, arguing with the doctor, with Mama, with strange voices that called to him from the past. That sometimes call to me.

Sometimes I sit in Papa's dusty room where he hung his compass and hip boots from a long nail pounded deep into the wall. The feet of his boots always swing when I enter searching for the light switch above the naval clock that used to keep perfect time. Sunlight has dulled the calendar painting of green grass in a green Japan with temples and women in kimonos. A picture of a very young Mama and Papa as a young man with old eyes is pinned to the wall. They stand before a row of dilapidated houses painted like neglected crops in a barren land. Mama says it was taken in Heart Mountain, that she remembers little of it. I look at her eyes in the picture and see how they have faded and dulled since then. Haunted eyes, I think to myself.

I remember Papa, bent but not broken, after his illness and the sudden quietness that filled the house. Of the smell of mushrooms that lingered for days. Of Mama's thin and worried face.

One Saturday morning I will always relive. Half-waking before the sun rose and listening for the birds that were no longer there, flown south to warm sunny lands. Wondering what had wakened me, I yawned and eased onto my side, heard the bed creak quietly beneath me. Mind drifting, I listened to the soft sounds of the early darkness. Distantly, I heard again the soft shuffle of boots on hardwood floors and the final sound of a door closing and came suddenly awake to awful loneliness.

I remember that evening and the phone ringing. Twice long, one short. Mama crying softly in her bed. Uncle Jinx and Aunt Fumi speaking softly to the neighbors:

"His heart. It was his heart."

". . . but where?"

"The south slope of Mount Rainier. Deep inside. Past the lumber roads and trails."

"She begged him not to go . . ."

". . . so stupid . . . so stubborn . . ."

"Greedy?"

"No."

"What then?"

"Maybe . . . I don't know . . ."

Labor Day weekend, and the whispers begin.

Shirley Geok-lin Lim

*Shirley Geok-lin Lim was born in the multi-racial, often colonized out-
post of Malacca, Malaysia. She received a Ph.D. in English and American
Literature from Brandeis University in 1973.* Her first book of poems, Crossing the Peninsula, *won the 1980 Commonwealth Poetry Prize. Her third and
most recent book of poetry is* Modern Secrets *(Dangaroo Press); she also has a
collection of short stories,* Another Country *(Times Books International,
1982), and is co-editor of* The Forbidden Stitch: An Asian American
Women's Anthology. *As a scholar, Lim attempts to uncover/recover Asian
American texts, to make visible the Asian sources of the Asian/American
equation. As a writer, she crosses and re-crosses east/west borders, looking for
the diaglogue/dialectic across cultures. She is currently working on a novel.*

A POT OF RICE

It was raining hard when she got back to the apartment. Stepping over the letters on the hallway floor, she headed for the bathroom and sat fully clothed on the toilet. A mouldy smell from the cold walls tickled her nose: she sneezed sharply and shivered under the green sweater, sodden as her hair. Between the subway stop and the apartment door was a good fifteen-minute walk and even running pell-mell she was soaked. She wrenched the matted wool over her head. The pink shirt beneath was wet also except, for some reason, around the bottoms. She tugged at the vinyl boots. They were too small to begin with and now the wet callouses stung, rubbed raw by the thudding sprint on cracked pavements.

Plump Steve Katz's face wobbled into view when she closed her eyes. Pinned to the grey sheet behind her lids, his pink adolescent head trembled prematurely bald. She wished she could like him more. He was one of the few students to show some curiosity about her, and if that large round body were expressive of feeling, she could almost believe he had a crush on her.

How her neck was aching!

The bus was half an hour late and the waiting passengers had backed up around the block. She stood all the way, mashed in the middle of the bus between two silky blond girls and a bulky woman in a nursing uniform who stared hard at her and leaned their bodies away distinctly because her clothes were already quite wet by the time the bus pulled in. That half an hour wait meant catching the Lex at Forty-second Street at 4:50 p.m. at the precise moment, it seemed to her, that thousands of offices, banks, stores, hospitals, schools, libraries, businesses, luncheonettes, and other containers of people burst their doors and leaked their smelly, twitching, tight-jawed, black-edged-under-fingernails contents into the avenues and underground tunnels. All the way home she had shrunk herself as small as a centre in a music box and now her body hurt.

Only the sad students liked her: the fat or short or stammering.

She didn't care to think of them as she rode the subway. These students like anyone who paused to smile. They stopped to smile themselves, perhaps because they had nothing better to do. Steve Katz, Bertha Willard. They hung around her after class, walked her to class from the office. Perhaps she never showed them she had anything to share except understanding that they all alike were missing.

A student like Robert Healey said nothing all the time. Yet he took up a whole corner of the classroom, his legs tightly encased in greasy blue dungarees sprawled wide and his handsome torso positioned boldly to face the open door. She didn't dare throw him a question, for it would have fallen on his thrust-out groin and twitched shamefully there. The papers he handed in always on time were dull. She wrote back, 'You can do much better work than this. C+.', but he didn't care and never came up to complain. He was like Susan Krammer, Jack O'Hagen, Donna D'Agostino–almost all the students in two sections of Introduction to Composition. They came to class on time and waited for the end of the hour before leaving–thank God for middle-class conformity–but their faces brooded above the open textbooks like those of hardened young criminals planning a jailbreak.

She felt exactly the same way. Finally stripped naked, Su Yu dried her damp arms and chest with a rough faded purple towel. To teach in Queens, to live in Brooklyn–she hadn't bargained for the jolting two-hour commute each way or for the dreary piles of compositions to be graded each week. It was like slogging through endless mud slides, the composted heaps of a city's garbage, while fluttering the girl-guide's bandana.

Robert Healey sprawled in a corner of her mind, relentlessly bored by her.

She slammed the refrigerator door. Already she knew she would serve rice for dinner. Mark would make a face. And she would make a curry, very spicy. The heat from the cloves and chilies and the white steam from the rice would warm her and spark the brown lonely kitchen with fiery scents.

Wrapped in the old navy-blue bathrobe she trudged old-womanish and barefoot across the kitchen from refrigerator to sink to stove. Through the window she saw the backyard still light in the early November evening. Large drops left over from the afternoon storm gathered on the drooping branches and fell steadily from the Ailunthus which thrust out of the glass-spangled earth to suck up half the open sky. Holding the pot full of rice and water she stopped to look. Light and sky. With a slight catch in her chest, she yearned for the white space not yet consumed by the tree or by the evening. Soon, she thought, the cold will lock up the yard again; the ground will freeze into a solid black sheet, and she will begin all over again to hate the landlady when the hot water runs out.

Her father had died last year. He had been dead for two weeks before she knew of it. Her brother wrote to tell her of what she could no longer help days after the funeral. Mark had been terrified by the crying jags which overtook her in the middle of sleep, but they gradually grew fewer, less uncontrolled. With her father's death there was no longer any reason to leave the city from whose harbour the Statue of Liberty seemed to gaze across the oceans to Singapore as if towards a giant Chinatown ghetto. Remaining in New York with Mark, she felt she was merely choosing to remain in open water, having left behind the narrow concrete island crowded with socialist housing developments.

Su Yu watched the water boil over the lid and the milky starch sizzle on the gas flame before she lowered the heat. Mark could not get rice to cook to the sticky texture she preferred because he did not allow the water to boil over. She could not eat the gritty grains he served. Their food habits made them strangers to each other while most Americans, she thought sadly, held hands over slices of toasted Wonder Bread.

When grandfather died, his massive mahogany coffin on the back of the estate truck was hidden by mounds of white and yellow frangipani. Houses almost three feet high with green and yellow translucent paper windows were massed on top of the truck. There were even paper and bamboo garages and paper cars—the latest in sporty convertibles—and skinny men in black suits and top hats: effigies burned at the grave site to keep grandfather company in the other world, together with mountains of gold and silver paper which the women, staying up the whole night in grandfather's house, giggling and gossiping, had shaped into bricks. Sons, daughters, grandchildren, uncles, aunts, cousins, second and third cousins, in-laws, employees, debtors, tenants, strangers also—half the town walked in the procession behind the truck which rolled slowly behind a trail of wailing trumpets, moaning oboes, banging cymbals, and rattling drums. Bare-chested gangsters leaped from the truck to herd away cyclists and rickshaws. Young men carried banners of bright-coloured cloth emblazoned with laments and old men pushed carts loaded with water pots for the family who stumbled in the heat behind the truck. Her black dress had just come from the dyer's and smelled sweetly of faded flowers. She wore grass sandals tied around her shoes and a hood of gunny sack. Everywhere women were crying and waving their arms helplessly.

What a splendid display of mourning that was, she thought, and felt tears of self-pity prick. This is the time of prayers for father, she remembered. Her mother would have the altar freshly dusted and a clean red paper cloth hung in the front. She would place bowls of rice and soy chicken and cups of tea and brandy before a large photograph of her husband. Was his appetite for good food and drink lost merely because his body had died? Su Yu stared at the pot of cooked rice. In its steam she saw her father's greedy smile appear like a sudden daydream.

Mark found the dining table set for worship when he got home after his late meeting. A blurred machine-made snapshot of Sue's father was propped before a candlestick which stood behind a cereal bowl filled with cooked rice and a plate holding a whole boiled chicken. The rice was ashy—was it from the candleflame or from the mould in the air? The chicken's boiled skin was discoloured, dotted with pink and black feather marks which showed garishly under the fluorescent light. Sue, wearing a red dress with gold barettes in her hair giggled when she saw his face. 'We mustn't eat until he has finished his meal,' she warned.

'What's all this?'

'I'm mourning the first year of my father's death. This is the ritual of ancestor worship.'

'Well, how do you know when your ancestor has finished eating? I'm hungry.'

'You throw two coins.' She held up two quarters.

'And then?'

'Oh, I forget! It's either two heads or two tails.'

'What will you do? You've forgotten! Does this mean I don't get to eat tonight?'

Su Yu smiled. 'I know my father, I'll know when he's finished eating.'

Mark went to the bedroom and turned on the television. He wasn't hungry any more, not for cold sticky rice anyway. And the chicken looked more like a dead thing than a meal, as if the essence of food had left and only the material stringy flesh remained. 'This is the first time,' he said loudly, hoping she would hear in the kitchen, 'you haven't served me first.'

1977

Bharati Mukherjee

Bharati Mukherjee is also the author of two novels, Wife *and* The Tiger's Daughter, *two works of nonfiction,* Days and Nights in Calcutta *and* The Sorrow and the Terror, *and an earlier collection of short stories,* Darkness, *which the* New York Times Book Review *named one of the best books of the year. Born and educated in Calcutta, she earned a Ph.D. at the University of Iowa, and has received grants from the National Endowment for the Arts and the Guggenheim Foundation for her fiction. She currently teaches creative writing at Columbia University and City University of New York. Stories from* The Middleman *have been selected for* Best American Short Stories 1987 *and* Editor's Choice.

THE MANAGEMENT OF GRIEF

A woman I don't know is boiling tea the Indian way in my kitchen. There are a lot of women I don't know in my kitchen, whispering, and moving tactfully. They open doors, rummage through the pantry, and try not to ask me where things are kept. They remind me of when my sons were small, on Mother's Day or when Vikram and I were tired, and they would make big, sloppy omelets. I would lie in bed pretending I didn't hear them.

Dr. Sharma, the treasurer of the Indo-Canada Society, pulls me into the hallway. He wants to know if I am worried about money. His wife, who has just come up from the basement with a tray of empty cups and glasses, scolds him. "Don't bother Mrs. Bhave with mundane details." She looks so monstrously pregnant her baby must be days overdue. I tell her she shouldn't be carrying heavy things. "Shaila," she says, smiling, "this is the fifth." Then she grabs a teenager by his shirttails. He slips his Walkman off his head. He has to be one of her four children, they have the same domed and dented foreheads. "What's the official word now?" she demands. The boy slips the headphones back on. "They're acting evasive, Ma. They're saying it could be an accident or a terrorist bomb."

All morning, the boys have been muttering, Sikh Bomb, Sikh Bomb. The men, not using the word, bow their heads in agreement. Mrs. Sharma touches her forehead at such a word. At least they've stopped talking about space debris and Russian lasers.

Two radios are going in the dining room. They are tuned to different stations. Someone must have brought the radios down from my boys' bedrooms. I haven't gone into their rooms since Kusum came running across the front lawn in her bathrobe. She looked so funny, I was laughing when I opened the door.

The big TV in the den is being whizzed through American networks and cable channels.

"Damn!" some man swears bitterly. "How can these preachers

From The Middleman and Other Stories, Grove Press, Inc.

carry on like nothing's happened?" I want to tell him we're not that important. You look at the audience, and at the preacher in his blue robe with his beautiful white hair, the potted palm trees under a blue sky, and you know they care about nothing.

The phone rings and rings. Dr. Sharma's taken charge. "We're with her," he keeps saying. "Yes, yes, the doctor has given calming pills. Yes, yes, pills are having necessary effect." I wonder if pills alone explain this calm. Not peace, just a deadening quiet. I was always controlled, but never repressed. Sound can reach me, but my body is tensed, ready to scream. I hear their voices all around me. I hear my boys and Vikram cry, "Mommy, Shaila!" and their screams insulate me, like headphones.

The woman boiling water tells her story again and again. "I got the news first. My cousin called from Halifax before six A.M., can you imagine? He'd gotten up for prayers and his son was studying for medical exams and he heard on a rock channel that something had happened to a plane. They said first it had disappeared from the radar, like a giant eraser just reached out. His father called me, so I said to him, what do you mean, 'something bad'? You mean a hijacking? And he said, *behn*, there is no confirmation of anything yet, but check with your neighbors because a lot of them must be on that plane. So I called poor Kusum straightaway. I knew Kusum's husband and daughter were booked to go yesterday."

Kusum lives across the street from me. She and Satish had moved in less than a month ago. They said they needed a bigger place. All these people, the Sharmas and friends from the Indo-Canada Society had been there for the housewarming. Satish and Kusum made homemade tandoori on their big gas grill and even the white neighbors piled their plates high with that luridly red, charred, juicy chicken. Their younger daughter had danced, and even our boys had broken away from the Stanley Cup telecast to put in a reluctant appearance. Everyone took pictures for their albums and for the community newspapers—another of our families had made it big in Toronto—and now I wonder how many of those happy faces are gone. "Why does God give us so much if all along He intends to take it away?" Kusum asks me.

I nod. We sit on carpeted stairs, holding hands like children. "I never once told him that I loved him," I say. I was too much the

294

well brought up woman. I was so well brought up I never felt comfortable calling my husband by his first name.

"It's all right," Kusum says. "He knew. My husband knew. They felt it. Modern young girls have to say it because what they feel is fake."

Kusum's daughter, Pam, runs in with an overnight case. Pam's in her McDonald's uniform. "Mummy! You have to get dressed!" Panic makes her cranky. "A reporter's on his way here."

"Why?"

"You want to talk to him in your bathrobe?" She starts to brush her mother's long hair. She's the daughter who's always in trouble. She dates Canadian boys and hangs out in the mall, shopping for tight sweaters. The younger one, the goody-goody one according to Pam, the one with a voice so sweet that when she sang *bhajans* for Ethiopian relief even a frugal man like my husband wrote out a hundred dollar check, *she* was on that plane. *She* was going to spend July and August with grandparents because Pam wouldn't go. Pam said she'd rather waitress at McDonald's. "If it's choice between Bombay and Wonderland, I'm picking Wonderland," she'd said.

"Leave me alone," Kusum yells. "You know what I want to do? If I didn't have to look after you now, I'd hang myself."

Pam's young face goes blotchy with pain. "Thanks," she says, "don't let me stop you."

"Hush," pregnant Mrs. Sharma scolds Pam. "Leave your mother alone. Mr. Sharma will tackle the reporters and fill out the forms. He'll say what has to be said."

Pam stands her ground. "You think I don't know what Mummy's thinking? *Why her?* that's what. That's sick! Mummy wishes my little sister were alive and I were dead."

Kusum's hand in mine is trembly hot. We continue to sit on the stairs.

She calls before she arrives, wondering if there's anything I need. Her name is Judith Templeton and she's an appointee of the provincial government. "Multiculturalism?" I ask, and she says, "partially," but that her mandate is bigger. "I've been told you knew many of the people on the flight," she says. "Perhaps if you'd agree to help us reach the others . . .?"

She gives me time at least to put on tea water and pick up the mess in the front room. I have a few *samosas* from Kusum's housewarming that I could fry up, but then I think, why prolong this visit?

Judith Templeton is much younger than she sounded. She wears a blue suit with a white blouse and a polka dot tie. Her blond hair is cut short, her only jewelry is pearl drop earrings. Her briefcase is new and expensive looking, a gleaming cordovan leather. She sits with it across her lap. When she looks out the front windows onto the street, her contact lenses seem to float in front of her light blue eyes.

"What sort of help do you want from me?" I ask. She has refused the tea, out of politeness, but I insist, along with some slightly stale biscuits.

"I have no experience," she admits. "That is, I have an MSW and I've worked in liaison with accident victims, but I mean I have no experience with a tragedy of this scale—"

"Who could?" I ask.

"—and with the complications of culture, language, and customs. Someone mentioned that Mrs. Bhave is a pillar—because you've taken it more calmly."

At this, perhaps, I frown, for she reaches forward, almost to take my hand. "I hope you understand my meaning, Mrs. Bhave. There are hundreds of people in Metro directly affected, like you, and some of them speak no English. There are some widows who've never handled money or gone on a bus, and there are old parents who still haven't eaten or gone outside their bedrooms. Some houses and apartments have been looted. Some wives are still hysterical. Some husbands are in shock and profound depression. We want to help, but our hands are tied in so many ways. We have to distribute money to some people, and there are legal documents—these things can be done. We have interpreters, but we don't always have the human touch, or maybe the right human touch. We don't want to make mistakes, Mrs. Bhave, and that's why we'd like to ask you to help us."

"More mistakes, you mean," I say.

"Police matters are not in my hands," she answers.

"Nothing I can do will make any difference," I say. "We must all grieve in our own way."

"But you are coping very well. All the people said, Mrs. Bhave is the strongest person of all. Perhaps if the others could see you, talk with you, it would help them."

"By the standards of the people you call hysterical, I am behaving very oddly and very badly, Miss Templeton." I want to say to her, *I wish I could scream, starve, walk into Lake Ontario, jump from a bridge.* "They would not see me as a model. I do not see myself as a model."

I am a freak. No one who has ever known me would think of me reacting this way. This terrible calm will not go away.

She asks me if she may call again, after I get back from a long trip that we all must make. "Of course," I say. "Feel free to call, anytime."

Four days later, I find Kusum squatting on a rock overlooking a bay in Ireland. It isn't a big rock, but it juts sharply out over water. This is as close as we'll ever get to them. June breezes balloon out her sari and unpin her knee-length hair. She has the bewildered look of a sea creature whom the tides have stranded.

It's been one hundred hours since Kusum came stumbling and screaming across my lawn. Waiting around the hospital, we've heard many stories. The police, the diplomats, they tell us things thinking that we're strong, that knowledge is helpful to the grieving, and maybe it is. Some, I know, prefer ignorance, or their own versions. The plane broke into two, they say. Unconsciousness was instantaneous. No one suffered. My boys must have just finished their breakfasts. They loved eating on planes, they loved the airline salt and pepper shakers. Half an hour more and they would have made it to Heathrow.

Kusum says that we can't escape our fate. She says that all those people—our husbands, boys, her girl with the nightingale voice, all those Hindus, Christians, Sikhs, Muslims, Parsis, and atheists on that plane—were fated to die together off this beautiful bay. She learned this from a swami in Toronto.

I have my Valium.

Six of us "relatives" – two widows and four widowers – choose to spend the day today by the waters instead of sitting in a hospital room and scanning photographs of the dead. That's what they call us now: relatives. I've looked through twenty-seven photos in two days. They're very kind to us, the Irish are very understanding. Sometimes understanding means freeing a tourist bus for this trip to the bay, so we can pretend to spy our loved ones through the glassiness of waves or in sun-speckled cloud shapes.

I could die here, too, and be content.

"What is that, out there?" She's standing and flapping her hands and for a moment I see a head shape bobbing in the waves. She's standing in the water, I, on the boulder. The tide is low, and a round, black, head-sized rock has just risen from the waves. She returns, her sari end dripping and ruined and her face is a twisted remnant of hope, the way mine was a hundred hours ago, still laughing but inwardly knowing that nothing but the ultimate tragedy could bring two women together at six o'clock on a Sunday morning. I watch her face sag into blankness.

"That water felt warm, Shaila," she says at length.

"You can't," I say. "We have to wait for our turn to come."

I haven't eaten in four days, haven't brushed my teeth.

"I know," she says. "I tell myself I have no right to grieve. They are in a better place than we are. My swami says I should be thrilled for them. My swami says depression is a sign of our selfishness."

Maybe I'm selfish. Selfishly I break away from Kusum and run, sandals slapping against stones, to the water's edge. What if my boys aren't lying pinned under the debris? What if they aren't stuck a mile below that innocent blue chop? What if, given the strong currents. . . .

Now I've ruined my sari, one of my best. Kusum has joined me, knee-deep in water that feels to me like a swimming pool. I could settle in the water, and my husband would take my hand and the boys would slap water in my face just to see me scream.

"Do you remember what good swimmers my boys were, Kusum?"

"I saw the medals," she says.

One of the widowers, Dr. Ranganathan from Montreal, walks

out to us, carrying his shoes in one hand. He's an electrical engineer. Someone at the hotel mentioned his work is famous around the world, something about the place where physics and electricity come together. He has lost a huge family, something indescribable. "With some luck," Dr. Ranganathan suggests to me, "a good swimmer could make it safely to some island. It is quite possible that there may be many, many microscopic islets scattered around."

"You're not just saying that?" I tell Dr. Ranganathan about Vinod, my elder son. Last year he took diving as well.

"It's a parent's duty to hope," he says. "It is foolish to rule out possibilities that have not been tested. I myself have not surrendered hope."

Kusum is sobbing once again. "Dear lady," he says, laying his free hand on her arm, and she calms down.

"Vinod is how old?" he asks me. He's very careful, as we all are. *Is*, not was.

"Fourteen. Yesterday he was fourteen. His father and uncle were going to take him down to the Taj and give him a big birthday party. I couldn't go with them because I couldn't get two weeks off from my stupid job in June." I process bills for a travel agent. June is a big travel month.

Dr. Ranganathan whips the pockets of his suit jacket inside out. Squashed roses, in darkening shades of pink, float on the water. He tore the roses off creepers in somebody's garden. He didn't ask anyone if he could pluck the roses, but now there's been an article about it in the local papers. When you see an Indian person, it says, please give him or her flowers.

"A strong youth of fourteen," he says, "can very likely pull to safety a younger one."

My sons, though four years apart, were very close. Vinod wouldn't let Mithun drown. *Electrical engineering*, I think, foolishly perhaps: this man knows important secrets of the universe, things closed to me. Relief spins me lightheaded. No wonder my boys' photographs haven't turned up in the gallery of photos of the recovered dead. "Such pretty roses," I say.

"My wife loved pink roses. Every Friday I had to bring a bunch home. I used to say, why? After twenty odd years of marriage you're still needing proof positive of my love?" He has identified his wife and three of his children. Then others from Montreal, the lucky ones, intact families with no survivors. He chuckles as he wades back to shore. Then he swings around to ask me a question. "Mrs. Bhave, you are wanting to throw in some roses for your loved ones? I have two big ones left."

But I have other things to float: Vinod's pocket calculator; a half-painted model B-52 for my Mithun. They'd want them on their island. And for my husband? For him I let fall into the calm, glassy waters a poem I wrote in the hospital yesterday. Finally he'll know my feelings for him.

"Don't tumble, the rocks are slippery," Dr. Ranganathan cautions. He holds out a hand for me to grab.

Then it's time to get back on the bus, time to rush back to our waiting posts on hospital benches.

Kusum is one of the lucky ones. The lucky ones flew here, identified in multiplicate their loved ones, then will fly to India with the bodies for proper ceremonies. Satish is one of the few males who surfaced. The photos of faces we saw on the walls in an office at Heathrow and here in the hospital are mostly of women. Women have more body fat, a nun said to me matter-of-factly. They float better.

Today I was stopped by a young sailor on the street. He had loaded bodies, he'd gone into the water when—he checks my face for signs of strength—when the sharks were first spotted. I don't blush, and he breaks down. "It's all right," I say. "Thank you." I had heard about the sharks from Dr. Ranganathan. In his orderly mind, science brings understanding, it holds no terror. It is the shark's duty. For every deer there is a hunter, for every fish a fisherman.

The Irish are not shy; they rush to me and give me hugs and some are crying. I cannot imagine reactions like that on the streets of Toronto. Just strangers, and I am touched. Some carry flowers with them and give them to any Indian they see.

After lunch, a policeman I have gotten to know quite well catches hold of me. He says he thinks he has a match for Vinod. I explain what a good swimmer Vinod is.

"You want me with you when you look at photos?" Dr. Ranganathan walks ahead of me into the picture gallery. In these matters, he is a scientist, and I am grateful. It is a new perspective. "They have performed miracles," he says. "We are indebted to them."

The first day or two the policemen showed us relatives only one picture at a time; now they're in a hurry, they're eager to lay out the possibles, and even the probables.

The face on the photo is of a boy much like Vinod; the same intelligent eyes, the same thick brows dipping into a V. But this boy's features, even his cheeks, are puffier, wider, mushier.

"No." My gaze is pulled by other pictures. There are five other boys who look like Vinod.

The nun assigned to console me rubs the first picture with a fingertip. "When they've been in the water for a while, love, they look a little heavier." The bones under the skin are broken, they said on the first day — try to adjust your memories. It's important.

"It's not him. I'm his mother. I'd know."

"I know this one!" Dr. Ranganathan cries out suddenly from the back of the gallery. "And this one!" I think he senses that I don't want to find my boys. "They are the Kutty brothers. They were also from Montreal." I don't mean to be crying. On the contrary, I am ecstatic. My suitcase in the hotel is packed heavy with dry clothes for my boys.

The policeman starts to cry. "I am so sorry, I am so sorry, ma'am. I really thought we had a match."

With the nun ahead of us and the policeman behind, we, the unlucky ones without our children's bodies, file out of the make-shift gallery.

From Ireland most of us go on to India. Kusum and I take the same direct flight to Bombay, so I can help her clear customs quickly. But we have to argue with a man in uniform. He has large boils on his face. The boils swell and glow with sweat as we argue with him. He wants Kusum to wait in line and he refuses to take authority because his boss is on a tea break. But Kusum won't let her cousin out of sight, and I shan't desert her though I know that my parents, elderly and diabetic, must be waiting in a stuffy car in a scorching lot.

"You bastard!" I scream at the man with the popping boils. Other passengers press closer. "You think we're smuggling contraband in those coffins!"

Once upon a time we were well brought up women; we were dutiful wives who kept our heads veiled, our voices shy and sweet.

In India, I become, once again, an only child of rich, ailing parents. Old friends of the family come to pay their respects. Some are Sikh, and inwardly, involuntarily, I cringe. My parents are progressive people; they do not blame communities for a few individuals.

In Canada it is a different story now.

"Stay longer," my mother pleads. "Canada is a cold place. Why would you want to be all by yourself?" I stay.

Three months pass. Then another.

"Vikram wouldn't have wanted you to give up things!" they protest. They call my husband by the name he was born with. In Toronto he'd changed to Vik so the men he worked with at his office would find his name as easy as Rod or Chris. "You know, the dead aren't cut off from us!"

My grandmother, the spoiled daughter of a rich *zamindar*, shaved her head with rusty razor blades when she was widowed at sixteen. My grandfather died of childhood diabetes when he was nineteen, and she saw herself as the harbinger of bad luck. My mother grew up without parents, raised indifferently by an uncle, while her true mother slept in a hut behind the main estate house and took her food with the servants. She grew up a rationalist. My parents abhor mindless mortification.

The zamindar's daughter kept stubborn faith in Vedic rituals; my parents rebelled. I am trapped between two modes of knowledge. At thirty-six, I am too old to start over and too young to give up. Like my husband's spirit, I flutter between worlds.

* * *

302

Courting aphasia, we travel. We travel with our phalanx of servants and poor relatives. To hill stations and to beach resorts. We play contract bridge in dusty gymkhana clubs. We ride stubby ponies up crumbly mountain trails. At tea dances, we let ourselves be twirled twice round the ballroom. We hit the holy spots we hadn't made time for before. In Varanasi, Kalighat, Rishikesh, Hardwar, astrologers and palmists seek me out and for a fee offer me cosmic consolations.

Already the widowers among us are being shown new bride candidates. They cannot resist the call of custom, the authority of their parents and older brothers. They must marry; it is the duty of a man to look after a wife. The new wives will be young widows with children, destitute but of good family. They will make loving wives, but the men will shun them. I've had calls from the men over crackling Indian telephone lines. "Save me," they say, these substantial, educated, successful men of forty. "My parents are arranging a marriage for me." In a month they will have buried one family and returned to Canada with a new bride and partial family.

I am comparatively lucky. No one here thinks of arranging a husband for an unlucky widow.

Then, on the third day of the sixth month into this odyssey, in an abandoned temple in a tiny Himalayan village, as I make my offering of flowers and sweetmeats to the god of a tribe of animists, my husband descends to me. He is squatting next to a scrawny *sadhu* in moth-eaten robes. Vikram wears the vanilla suit he wore the last time I hugged him. The *sadhu* tosses petals on a butter-fed flame, reciting Sanskrit mantras and sweeps his face of flies. My husband takes my hands in his.

You're beautiful, he starts. Then, *What are you doing here?*

Shall I stay? I ask. He only smiles, but already the image is fading. *You must finish alone what we started together.* No seaweed wreathes his mouth. He speaks too fast just as he used to when we were an envied family in our pink split-level. He is gone.

In the windowless altar room, smoky with joss sticks and clarified butter lamps, a sweaty hand gropes for my blouse. I do not shriek. The *sadhu* arranges his robe. The lamps hiss and sputter out.

When we come out of the temple, my mother says, "Did you feel something weird in there?"

My mother has no patience with ghosts, prophetic dreams, holy men, and cults.

"No," I lie. "Nothing."

But she knows that she's lost me. She knows that in days I shall be leaving.

Kusum's put her house up for sale. She wants to live in an ashram in Hardwar. Moving to Hardwar was her swami's idea. Her swami runs two ashrams, the one in Hardwar and another here in Toronto.

"Don't run away," I tell her.

"I'm not running away," she says. "I'm pursuing inner peace. You think you or that Ranganathan fellow are better off?"

Pam's left for California. She wants to do some modelling, she says. She says when she comes into her share of the insurance money she'll open a yoga-cum aerobics studio in Hollywood. She sends me postcards so naughty I daren't leave them on the coffee table. Her mother has withdrawn from her and the world.

The rest of us don't lose touch, that's the point. Talk is all we have, says Dr. Ranganathan, who has also resisted his relatives and returned to Montreal and to his job, alone. He says, whom better to talk with than other relatives? We've been melted down and recast as a new tribe.

He calls me twice a week from Montreal. Every Wednesday night and every Saturday afternoon. He is changing jobs, going to Ottawa. But Ottawa is over a hundred miles away, and he is forced to drive two hundred and twenty miles a day. He can't bring himself to sell his house. The house is a temple, he says; the king-sized bed in the master bedroom is a shrine. He sleeps on a folding cot. A devotee.

* * *

There are still some hysterical relatives. Judith Templeton's list of those needing help and those who've "accepted" is in nearly perfect balance. Acceptance means you speak of your family in the past tense and you make active plans for moving ahead with your life. There are courses at Seneca and Ryerson we could be taking. Her gleaming leather briefcase is full of college catalogues and lists of cultural societies that need our help. She has done impressive work, I tell her.

"In the textbooks on grief management," she replies—I am her confidante, I realize, one of the few whose grief has not sprung bizarre obsessions—"there are stages to pass through: rejection, depression, acceptance, reconstruction." She has compiled a chart and finds that six months after the tragedy, none of us still reject reality, but only a handful are reconstructing. "Depressed Acceptance" is the plateau we've reached. Remarriage is a major step in reconstruction (though she's a little surprised, even shocked, over *how* quickly some of the men have taken on new families). Selling one's house and changing jobs and cities is healthy.

How do I tell Judith Templeton that my family surrounds me, and that like creatures in epics, they've changed shapes? She sees me as calm and accepting but worries that I have no job, no career. My closest friends are worse off than I. I cannot tell her my days, even my nights, are thrilling.

She asks me to help with families she can't reach at all. An elderly couple in Agincourt whose sons were killed just weeks after they had brought their parents over from a village in Punjab. From their names, I know they are Sikh. Judith Templeton and a translator have visited them twice with offers of money for air fare to Ireland, with bank forms, power-of-attorney forms, but they have refused to sign, or to leave their tiny apartment. Their sons' money is frozen in the bank. Their sons' investment apartments have been trashed by tenants, the furnishings sold off. The parents fear that anything they sign or any money they receive will end the company's or the country's obligations to them. They fear they are selling their sons for two airline tickets to a place they've never seen.

The high-rise apartment is a tower of Indians and West Indians, with a sprinkling of Orientals. The nearest bus stop kiosk is lined with women in saris. Boys practice cricket in the parking lot. Inside the building, even I wince a bit from the ferocity of onion fumes, the distinctive and immediate Indianness of frying *ghee,* but Judith Templeton maintains a steady flow of information. These poor old people are in imminent danger of losing their place and all their services.

I say to her, "They are Sikh. They will not open up to a Hindu woman." And what I want to add is, as much as I try not to, I stiffen now at the sight of beards and turbans. I remember a time when we all trusted each other in this new country, it was only the new country we worried about.

The two rooms are dark and stuffy. The lights are off, and an oil lamp sputters on the coffee table. The bent old lady has let us in, and her husband is wrapping a white turban over his oiled, hip-length hair. She immediately goes to the kitchen, and I hear the most familiar sound of an Indian home, tap water hitting and filling a teapot.

They have not paid their utility bills, out of fear and the inability to write a check. The telephone is gone; electricity and gas and water are soon to follow. They have told Judith their sons will provide. They are good boys, and they have always earned and looked after their parents.

We converse a bit in Hindi. They do not ask about the crash and I wonder if I should bring it up. If they think I am here merely as a translator, then they may feel insulted. There are thousands of Punjabi-speakers, Sikhs, in Toronto to do a better job. And so I say to the old lady, "I too have lost my sons, and my husband, in the crash."

Her eyes immediately fill with tears. The man mutters a few words which sound like a blessing. "God provides and God takes away," he says.

I want to say, but only men destroy and give back nothing. "My boys and my husband are not coming back," I say. "We have to understand that."

Now the old woman responds. "But who is to say? Man alone does not decide these things." To this her husband adds his agreement.

Judith asks about the bank papers, the release forms. With a stroke of the pen, they will have a provincial trustee to pay their bill, invest their money, send them a monthly pension.

"Do you know this woman?" I ask them.

The man raises his hand from the table, turns it over and seems to regard each finger separately before he answers. "This young lady is always coming here, we make tea for her and she leaves papers for us to sign." His eyes scan a pile of papers in the corner of the room. "Soon we will be out of tea, then will she go away?"

The old lady adds, "I have asked my neighbors and no one else gets *angrezi* visitors. What have we done?"

"It's her job," I try to explain. "The government is worried. Soon you will have no place to stay, no lights, no gas, no water."

"Government will get its money. Tell her not to worry. We are honorable people."

I try to explain the government wishes to give money, not take. He raises his hand. "Let them take," he says. "We are accustomed to that. That is no problem."

"We are strong people," says the wife. "Tell her that."

"Who needs all this machinery?" demands the husband. "It is unhealthy, the bright lights, the cold air on a hot day, the cold food, the four gas rings. God will provide, not government."

"When our boys return," the mother says. Her husband sucks his teeth. "Enough talk," he says.

Judith breaks in. "Have you convinced them?" The snaps on her cordovan briefcase go off like firecrackers in that quiet apartment. She lays the sheaf of legal paper on the coffee table. "If they can't write their names, an X will do—I've told them that."

Now the old lady has shuffled to the kitchen and soon emerges with a pot of tea and two cups. "I think my bladder will go first on a job like this," Judith says to me, smiling. "If only there was some way of reaching them. Please thank her for the tea. Tell her she's very kind."

I nod in Judith's direction and tell them in Hindi, "She thanks you for the tea. She thinks you are being very hospitable but she doesn't have the slightest idea what it means."

I want to say, humour her. I want to say, my boys and my husband are with me too, more than ever. I look in the old man's eyes and I can read his stubborn, peasant's message: *I have protected this woman as best I can. She is the only person I have left. Give to me or take from me what you will, but I will not sign for it. I will not pretend that I accept.*

In the car, Judith says, "You see what I'm up against? I'm sure they're lovely people, but their stubbornness and ignorance are driving me crazy. They think signing a paper is signing their son's death warrants, don't they?"

I am looking out the window. I want to say, *In our culture, it is a parent's duty to hope.*

"Now Shaila, this next woman is a real mess. She cries day and night, and she refuses all medical help. We may have to—"

"—Let me out at the subway," I say.

"I beg your pardon?" I can feel those blue eyes staring at me.

It would not be like her to disobey. She merely disapproves, and slows at a corner to let me out. Her voice is plaintive. "Is there anything I said? Anything I did?"

I could answer her suddenly in a dozen ways, but I choose not to. "Shaila? Let's talk about it," I hear, then slam the door.

A wife and mother begins her new life in a new country, and that life is cut short. Yet her husband tells her: Complete what we have started. We, who stayed out of politics and came halfway around the world to avoid religious and political feuding have been the first in the New World to die from it. I no longer know what we started, nor how to complete it. I write letters to the editors of local papers and to members of Parliament. Now at least they admit it was a bomb. One MP answers back, with sympathy, but with a challenge. You want to make a difference? Work on a campaign. Work on mine. Politicize the Indian voter.

My husband's old lawyer helps me set up a trust. Vikram was a saver and a careful investor. He had saved the boys' boarding school and college fees. I sell the pink house at four times what we paid for it and take a small apartment downtown. I am looking for a charity to support.

We are deep in the Toronto winter, gray skies, icy pavements, I stay indoors, watching television. I have tried to assess my situation, how best to live my life, to complete what we began so many years ago. Kusum has written me from Hardwar that her life is now serene. She has seen Satish and has heard her daughter sing again. Kusum was on a pilgrimage, passing through a village when she heard a young girl's voice, singing one of her daughter's favor-

308

ite *bhajans*. She followed the music through the squalor of a Himalayan village, to a hut where a young girl, an exact replica of her daughter, was fanning coals under the kitchen fire. When she appeared, the girl cried out, "Ma!" and ran away. What did I think of that?

I think I can only envy her.

Pam didn't make it to California, but writes me from Vancouver. She works in a department store, giving make-up hints to Indian and Oriental girls. Dr. Ranganathan has given up his commute, given up his house and job, and accepted an academic position in Texas where no one knows his story and he has vowed not to tell it. He calls me now once a week.

I wait, I listen, and I pray, but Vikram has not returned to me. The voices and the shapes and the nights filled with visions ended abruptly several weeks ago.

I take it as a sign.

One rare, beautiful, sunny day last week, returning from a small errand on Yonge Street, I was walking through the park from the subway to my apartment. I live equidistant from the Ontario Houses of Parliament and the university of Toronto. The day was not cold, but something in the bare trees caught my attention. I looked up from the gravel, into the branches and the clear blue sky beyond. I thought I heard the rustling of larger forms, and I waited a moment for voices. Nothing.

"What?" I asked.

Then as I stood in the path looking north to Queen's Park and west to the university, I heard the voices of my family one last time. *Your time has come*, they said. Go, *be brave*.

I do not know where this voyage I have begun will end. I do not know which direction I will take. I dropped the package on a park bench and started walking.

Sylvia A. Watanabe

I was born in Hawaii and grew up listening to my father's stories. Even now when we go for walks he tells me the names of things — of plants, and birds, and trees. He tells me where to hunt guavas and when to go down to the beach to harvest seaweed. He has a reminiscence about every spot we pass. "This is the place where we went fishing the night before the tidal wave," he'll begin. Or, "This is the road where Happy Oshiro ran into the spirit of the dog girl on his way home from playing poker." My story, "Talking to the Dead," came out of these naming walks I take with my father.

In the last few years my fiction has appeared in literary journals and anthologies such as The Stories We Hold Secret *(Greenfield Review Press),* The Best of Bamboo Ridge *(Bamboo Ridge Press), and* Passages to the Dream Shore *(University of Hawaii Press). I have received a National Literary Award from the Japanese American Citizens League and a 1989 Creative Writing Fellowship in fiction from the National Endowment for the Arts.*

TALKING TO THE DEAD

We spoke of her in whispers as Aunty Talking to the Dead, the half-Hawaiian kahuna lady. But whenever there was a death in the village, she was the first to be sent for—the priest came second. For it was she who understood the wholeness of things—the significance of directions and colors. Prayers to appease the hungry ghosts. Elixirs for grief. Most times, she'd be out on her front porch, already waiting—her boy, Clinton, standing behind with her basket of spells—when the messenger arrived. People said she could smell a death from clear on the other side of the island, even as the dying person breathed his last. And if she fixed her eyes on you and named a day, you were already as good as six feet under.

I went to work as her apprentice when I was eighteen. That was in '48—the year Clinton graduated from mortician school on the G.I. Bill. It was the talk for weeks—how he returned to open the Paradise Mortuary in the very heart of the village and brought the scientific spirit of free enterprise to the doorstep of the hereafter. I remember the advertisements for the Grand Opening—promising to modernize the funeral trade with Lifelike Artistic Techniques and Stringent Standards of Sanitation. The old woman, who had waited out the war for her son's return, stoically took his defection in stride and began looking for someone else to help out with her business.

At the time, I didn't have many prospects—more schooling didn't interest me, and my mother's attempts at marrying me off inevitably failed when I stood to shake hands with a prospective bridegroom and ended up towering a foot above him. "It's bad enough she has the face of a horse," I heard one of them complain.

My mother dressed me in navy blue, on the theory that dark colors make everything look smaller; "Yuri, sit down," she'd hiss, tugging at my skirt as the decisive moment approached. I'd nod, sip my tea, smile through the introductions and boring small talk, till the time came for sealing the bargain with handshakes all around. Then nothing on earth could keep me from getting to my feet. The go-between finally suggested that I consider taking up a trade. "After all, marriage isn't for everyone," she said. My mother said that that was a fact which remained to be proved, but meanwhile, it wouldn't hurt if I took in sewing or learned to cut hair. I made up my mind to apprentice myself to Aunty Talking to the Dead.

The old woman's house was on the hill behind the village, in some woods, just off the road to Chicken Fight Camp. She lived in an old plantation worker's bungalow with peeling green and white paint and a large, well-tended garden out front—mostly of flowering bushes and strong-smelling herbs I didn't know the names of.

"Aren't you a big one," a gravelly voice behind me rasped.

I started, then turned. It was the first time I had ever seen the old woman up close.

"Hello . . . uh . . . Mrs. . . . . Mrs. . . . . Dead," I stammered.

She was little—way under five feet—and wrinkled, and everything about her seemed the same color—her skin, her lips, her dress—everything just a slightly different shade of the same brown-grey, except her hair, which was absolutely white, and her tiny eyes, which glinted like metal. For a minute, those eyes looked me up and down.

"Here," she said finally, thrusting an empty rice sack into my hands. "For collecting salt." And she started down the road to the beach.

In the next few months, we walked every inch of the hills and beaches around the village, and then some.

"This is *a'ali'i* to bring sleep—it must be dried in the shade on a hot day." Aunty was always three steps ahead, chanting, while I struggled behind, laden with strips of bark and leafy twigs, my head buzzing with names.

"This is *awa* for every kind of grief, and *uhaloa* with the deep roots—if you are like that, death cannot easily take you." Her voice came from the stones, the trees, and the earth.

"This is where you gather salt to preserve a corpse," I hear her

312

still. "This is where you cut to insert the salt," her words have marked the places on my body, one by one.

That whole first year, not a single day passed when I didn't think of quitting. I tried to figure out a way of moving back home without making it seem like I was admitting anything.

"You know what people are saying, don't you?" my mother said, lifting the lid of the bamboo steamer and setting a tray of freshly-steamed meat buns on the already-crowded table before me. It was one of the few visits home since my apprenticeship—though I'd never been more than a couple of miles away—and she had stayed up the whole night before, cooking. The kitchen table was near-overflowing—she'd prepared a canned ham with yellow sweet potatoes, wing beans with pork, sweet and sour mustard cabbage, fresh raw yellow-fin, pickled egg plant, and rice with red beans. I had not seen so much food since the night she tried to persuade her younger brother, my Uncle Mongoose, not to volunteer for the army. He went anyway, and on the last day of training, just before he was shipped to Italy, he shot himself in the head when he was cleaning his gun. "I always knew that boy would come to no good," was all Mama said when she heard the news.

"What do you mean you can't eat another bite," she fussed now. "Look at you, nothing but a bag of bones."

I allowed myself to be persuaded to another helping, though I'd lost my appetite.

The truth was, there didn't seem to be much of a future in my apprenticeship. In eleven and a half months, I had memorized most of the minor rituals of mourning and learned to identify a couple of dozen herbs and all their medicinal uses, but I had not seen—much less gotten to practice on—a single honest-to-goodness corpse.

"People live longer these days," Aunty claimed.

But I knew it was because everyone—even from villages across the bay—had begun taking their business to the Paradise Mortuary. The single event which established Clinton's monopoly once and for all was the untimely death of old Mrs. Pomadour, the plantation owner's mother-in-law, who choked on a fishbone during a fundraising luncheon of the Famine Relief Society. Clinton was chosen to be in charge of the funeral. He took to wearing three-piece suits—even during the humid Kona season—as a symbol of his new respectability, and was nominated as a Republican candidate to run for the village council.

"So, what are people saying, Mama," I asked, finally pushing my plate away.

This was the cue she had been waiting for. "They're saying that That Woman has gotten herself a new donkey . . ." She paused dramatically, holding my look with her eyes. The implication was clear.

I began remembering things about being in my mother's house. The navy blue dresses. The humiliating weekly tea ceremony lessons at the Buddhist Temple.

"Give up this foolishness," she wheedled. "Mrs. Koyama tells me the Barber Shop Lady is looking for help . . ."

"I think I'll stay right where I am," I said.

"My mother drew herself up. "Here, have another meat bun," she said, jabbing one through the center with her serving fork and lifting it onto my plate.

A few weeks later, Aunty and I were called just outside the village to perform a laying-out. It was early afternoon when Sheriff Kanoi came by to tell us that the body of Mustard Hayashi, the eldest of the Hayashi boys, had just been pulled from an irrigation ditch by a team of field workers. He had apparently fallen in the night before, stone drunk, on his way home from Hula Rose's Dance Emporium.

I began hurrying around, assembling Aunty's tools and bottles of potions, and checking that everything was in working order, but the old woman didn't turn a hair; she just sat calmly rocking back and forth and puffing on her skinny, long-stemmed pipe.

"Yuri, you stop that rattling around back there!" she snapped, then turned to the Sheriff. "My son Clinton could probably handle this. Why don't you ask him?"

"No, Aunty," Sheriff Kanoi replied. "This looks like a tough case that's going to need some real expertise."

"Mmmm. . ." The old woman stopped rocking. "It's true, it was a bad death," she mused.

"Very bad," the Sheriff agreed.

"The spirit is going to require some talking to. . . ."

"Besides, the family asked special for you," he said.

No doubt because they didn't have any other choice, I thought. That morning, I'd run into Chinky Malloy, the assistant mortician at the Paradise, so I happened to know that Clinton was at a mortician's conference in the city and wouldn't be back for several days. But I didn't say a word.

Mustard's remains had been laid out on a green formica table in the kitchen. It was the only room in the house with a door that faced north. Aunty claimed that you should always choose a north-facing room for a laying-out so the spirit could find its way home to the land of the dead without getting lost.

Mustard's mother was leaning over his corpse, wailing, and her husband stood behind her, looking white-faced, and absently patting her on the back. The tiny kitchen was jammed with sobbing, nose-blowing relatives and neighbors. The air was thick with the smells of grief—perspiration, ladies' cologne, last night's cooking, and the faintest whiff of putrefying flesh. Aunty gripped me by the wrist and pushed her way to the front. The air pressed closer and closer—like someone's hot, wet breath on my face. My head reeled, and the room broke apart into dancing dots of color. From far away I heard somebody say, "It's Aunty Talking to the Dead."

"Make room, make room," another voice called.

I looked down at Mustard, lying on the table in front of me—his eyes half-open in that swollen, purple face. The smell was much stronger close up, and there were flies everywhere.

"We're going to have to get rid of some of this bloat," Aunty said, thrusting a metal object into my hand.

People were leaving the room.

She went around to the other side of the table. "I'll start here," she said. "You work over there. Do just like I told you."

I nodded. This was the long-awaited moment. My moment. But it was already the beginning of the end. My knees buckled and everything went dark.

Aunty performed the laying-out alone and never mentioned the episode again. But it was the talk of the village for weeks—how Yuri Shimabukuro, assistant to Aunty Talking to the Dead, passed out under the Hayashi's kitchen table and had to be tended by the grief-stricken mother of the dead boy.

My mother took to catching the bus to the plantation store three villages away whenever she needed to stock up on necessaries. "You're my daughter—how could I *not* be on your side?" was the way she put it, but the air buzzed with her unspoken recriminations. And whenever I went into the village, I was aware of the sly laughter behind my back, and Chinky Malloy smirking at me from behind the shutters of the Paradise Mortuary.

"She's giving the business a bad name," Clinton said, carefully removing his jacket and draping it across the back of the rickety wooden chair. He dusted the seat, looked at his hand with distaste before wiping it off on his handkerchief, then drew up the legs of his trousers, and sat.

Aunty picked up her pipe from the smoking tray next to her rocker and filled the tiny brass bowl from a pouch of Bull Durham. "I'm glad you found time to drop by," she said. "You still going out with that skinny white girl?"

"You mean Marsha?" Clinton sounded defensive. "Sure, I see her sometimes. But I didn't come here to talk about that." He glanced over at where I was sitting on the sofa. "You think we could have some privacy?"

Aunty lit her pipe and puffed. "There's nobody here but us. . . . Oh, you mean Yuri. She's my right hand. Couldn't do without her."

"The Hayashis probably have their own opinion about that."

Aunty waved her hand in dismissal. "There's no pleasing some people. Yuri's just young; she'll learn." She reached over and patted me on the knee, then looked him straight in the face. "Like we all did."

Clinton turned red. "Damn it, Mama!" he sputtered, "You're making yourself a laughing stock!" His voice became soft, persuasive. "Look, you've worked hard all your life, but now, I've got my business—it'll be a while before I'm really on my feet—but you don't have to do this. . . ." He gestured around the room. "I'll help you out. You'll see. I'm only thinking about you. . . ."

316

"About the election to village council, you mean!" I burst out.

Aunty was unperturbed. "You thinking about going into politics, son?"

"Mama, wake up!" Clinton hollered, like he'd wanted to all along. "The old spirits have had it. We're part of progress now, and the world is going to roll right over us and keep on rolling, unless we get out there and grab our share."

His words rained down like stones, shattering the air around us.

For a long time after he left, Aunty sat in her rocking chair next to the window, rocking and smoking, without saying a word, just rocking and smoking, as the afternoon shadows flickered beneath the trees and turned to night.

Then, she began to sing—quietly, at first, but very sure. She sang the naming chants and the healing chants. She sang the stones, and trees, and stars back into their rightful places. Louder and louder she sang—making whole what had been broken.

Everything changed for me after Clinton's visit. I stopped going into the village and began spending all my time with Aunty Talking to the Dead. I followed her everywhere, carried her loads without complaint, memorized remedies and mixed potions till my head spun and I went near blind. I wanted to know what *she* knew; I wanted to make what had happened at the Hayashis' go away. Not just in other people's minds. Not just because I'd become a laughing stock, like Clinton said. But because I knew that I *had* to redeem myself for that one thing, or my moment— the single instant of glory for which I had lived my entire life— would be snatched beyond my reach forever.

Meanwhile, there were other layings-out. The kitemaker who hung himself. The crippled boy from Chicken Fight Camp. The Vagrant. The Blindman. The Blindman's dog.

"Do like I told you," Aunty would say before each one. Then, "Just give it time," when it was done.

But it was like living the same nightmare over and over—just one look at a body and I was done for. For twenty-five years, people in the village joked about my "indisposition." Last year, when my mother died, her funeral was held at the Paradise Mortuary. I stood outside on the cement walk for a long time, but never made it through the door. Little by little, I had given up hope that my moment would ever arrive.

Then, one week ago, Aunty caught a chill after spending all morning out in the rain, gathering *awa* from the garden. The chill developed into a fever, and for the first time since I'd known her, she took to her bed. I nursed her with the remedies she'd taught me—sweat baths; eucalyptus steam; tea made from *ko'oko'olau*—but the fever worsened. Her breathing became labored, and she grew weaker. My few hours of sleep were filled with bad dreams. She kept slipping and slipping away from me. In desperation, aware of my betrayal, I finally walked to a house up the road and telephoned for an ambulance.

"I'm sorry, Aunty," I kept saying, as the flashing red light swept across the porch. The attendants had her on a stretcher and were carrying her out the front door.

She reached up and grasped my arm, her grip still strong. "You'll do okay, Yuri," the old woman whispered hoarsely, and squeezed. "Clinton used to get so scared, he messed his pants." She chuckled, then began to cough. One of the attendants put an oxygen mask over her face. "Hush," he said. "There'll be plenty of time for talking later."

The day of Aunty's wake, workmen were repaving the front walk and had blocked off the main entrance to the Paradise Mortuary. They had dug up the old concrete tiles and carted them away. They'd left a mound of gravel on the grass, stacked some bags of concrete next to it, and covered them with black tarps. There was an empty wheelbarrow parked on the other side of the gravel mound. The entire front lawn was roped off and a sign put up which said, "Please use the back entrance. We are making improvements in Paradise. The Management."

My stomach was beginning to play tricks, and I was feeling a little dizzy. The old panic was mingled with an uneasiness which had not left me ever since I had decided to call the ambulance. I kept thinking maybe I shouldn't have called it since she had gone and died anyway. Or maybe I should have called it sooner. I

318

almost turned back, but I thought of what Aunty had told me about Clinton and pressed on. Numbly, I followed the two women in front of me through the garden along the side of the building, around to the back.

"So, old Aunty Talking to the Dead has finally passed on," one of them, whom I recognized as the Dancing School Teacher, said. She was with Pearlie Mukai, an old classmate of mine from high school. Pearlie had gone years ago to live in the city, but still returned to the village to visit her mother.

I was having difficulty seeing—it was getting dark, and my head was spinning so.

"How old do you suppose she was?" Pearlie asked.

"Gosh, even when we were kids it seemed like she was at least a hundred."

" 'The Undead,' my brother used to call her."

"When we misbehaved, my mother used to threaten to send us to Aunty Talking to the Dead. She'd be giving us the licking of our lives and hollering, 'This is gonna seem like nothing, then!' "

Aunty had been laid out in one of the rooms along the side of the house. The heavy, wine-colored drapes had been drawn across the windows, and all the wall lamps turned very low, so it was darker in the room than it had been outside.

Pearlie and the Dancing School Teacher moved off into the front row. I headed for the back.

There were about thirty of us at the wake, mostly from the old days—those who had grown up on stories about Aunty, or who remembered her from before the Paradise Mortuary.

People were getting up and filing past the casket. For a moment, I felt faint again, but I remembered about Clinton (how self-assured and prosperous he looked standing at the door, accepting condolences!), and I got into line. The Dancing School Teacher and Pearlie slipped in front of me.

I drew nearer and nearer to the casket. I hugged my sweater close. The room was air conditioned and smelled of floor disinfectant and roses. Soft music came from speakers mounted on the walls.

Now there were just four people ahead. Now three. I looked down on the floor, as the blackness welled up inside me.

Then Pearlie Mukai shrieked, "Her eyes!"

People behind me began to murmur.

"What . . . whose eyes?" The Dancing School Teacher demanded.

Pearlie pointed to the body in the casket.

The Dancing School Teacher peered down and cried, "My God, they're open!"

My heart turned to ice.

"What?" voices behind me were asking. "What about her eyes?"

"She said they're open," someone said.

"Aunty Talking to the Dead's Eyes Are Open," someone else said.

Now Clinton was hurrying over.

"That's because she's Not Dead," still another voice put in.

Clinton looked into the coffin, and his face turned white. He turned quickly around again, and waved to his assistants across the room.

"I've heard about cases like this," someone was saying. "It's because she's looking for someone."

"I've heard that too! The old woman is trying to tell us something."

I was the only one there who knew. Aunty was talking to *me*. I clasped my hands together, hard, but they wouldn't stop shaking.

People began leaving the line. Others pressed in, trying to get a better look at the body, but a couple of Clinton's assistants had stationed themselves in front of the coffin, preventing anyone from getting too close. They had shut the lid, and Chinky Malloy was directing people out of the room.

"I'd like to take this opportunity to thank you all for coming here this evening," Clinton was saying. "I hope you will join us at the reception down the hall. . . ."

While everyone was eating, I stole back into the parlor and quietly—ever so quietly—went up to the casket, lifted the lid, and looked in.

At first, I thought they had switched bodies on me and exchanged Aunty for some powdered and painted old grand-mother, all pink and white, in a pink dress, and clutching a white

320

rose to her chest. But the pennies had fallen from her eyes—and there they were. Open. Aunty's eyes staring up at me.

Then I knew. In that instant, I stopped trembling. This was *it*: My moment had arrived. Aunty Talking to the Dead had come awake to bear me witness.

I walked through the deserted front rooms of the mortuary and out the front door. It was night. I got the wheelbarrow, loaded it with one of the tarps covering the bags of cement, and wheeled it back to the room where Aunty was. It squeaked terribly, and I stopped often to make sure no one had heard me. From the back of the building came the clink of glassware and the buzz of voices. I had to work quickly—people would be leaving soon.

But this was the hardest part. Small as she was, it was very hard to lift her out of the coffin. She was horribly heavy, and unyielding as a bag of cement. It seemed like hours, but I finally got her out and wrapped her in the tarp. I loaded her in the tray of the wheelbarrow—most of her, anyway; there was nothing I could do about her feet sticking out the front end. Then, I wheeled her through the silent rooms of the mortuary, down the front lawn, across the village square, and up the road, home.

Now, in the dark, the old woman is singing.

I have washed her with my own hands and worked the salt into the hollows of her body. I have dressed her in white and laid her in flowers.

Aunty, here are the beads you like to wear. Your favorite cakes. A quilt to keep away the chill. Here is *noni* for the heart and *awa* for every kind of grief.

Down the road a dog howls, and the sound of hammering echoes through the still air. "Looks like a burying tomorrow," the sleepers murmur, turning in their warm beds.

I bind the sandals on her feet and put the torch to the pyre.

The sky turns to light. The smoke climbs. Her ashes scatter, filling the wind.

And she sings, she sings, she sings.